WITCHBLOOD
A KITSUNE CHRONICLES STORY

LISSA KASEY

WitchBlood : A Kitsune Chronicles Story
Copyright © 2018 Lissa Kasey
All rights reserved
Cover Art by Oliviaprodesign
Published by Lissa Kasey
http://www.lissakasey.com

Please Be Advised

This is a work of fiction. Names, characters, businesses, places, events and incidents are either the products of the author's imagination or used in a fictitious manner. Any resemblance to actual persons, living or dead, or actual events is purely coincidental.

This book is licensed to the original purchaser only. Duplication or distribution via any means is illegal and a violation of International Copyright Law, subject to criminal prosecution and upon conviction, fines, and/or imprisonment. This eBook cannot be legally loaned or given to others. No part of this book can be shared or reproduced without the express permission of the Author.

If you enjoyed this book, please post a review.

For Christy who gave me daily encouragement. My angel, Gabbie, who loves inspiring me by sleeping on my back while I write. And my other two babies, Gen and Mizu. Love you all.

PROLOGUE

I woke up dizzy, half-blind, and so nauseous I worried moving at all would make me hurl up an intestine or two. My chest ached, lungs feeling heavy. Something sounded liquid when I breathed, a nice accent to accompany the wheezing howl of a punctured lung.

The walls of my tiny home surrounded me with bright lights and silence. Living alone, and a healthy space away from civilization, had seemed like a good idea at the time. In the distance, the vague sounds of voices and music floated from the Volkov's home. The annual festival in full swing meant no one would hear me even if I could scream. Sensitive werewolf ears or not.

Robin's absence brought tears to my already blurred vision. He'd been limiting his visits because we'd argued one time too many about my choice of lovers. He'd been right. I choked back a sob of self-pity. No amount of wishing could change the past.

Dying alone had never crossed my mind before that moment. *Apa* often said I was young, and the young thought themselves invincible. I thought he was being overdramatic. Only it was true. If I had imagined for one second...

I swallowed back a mouthful of blood, not willing to let the memories of how I'd ended up here overwhelm me. I was dying. If I didn't do something, I would die, and *he* would win. Months of fighting for freedom, and a few weeks of living the dream had left me here. I hadn't expected his attack, should have adjusted my wards. I'd never thought he'd attempt such a vile act with the Volkov so near.

Was this another lesson? Was I once again being taught my place? Not a werewolf, so not worthy of protection? Perhaps this was to *toughen* me up. Could some of my wards have prevented all this pain? Probably. Why hadn't I thought ahead? Why had my brain refused to entertain the idea that he'd come after me? It wasn't like he hadn't before. This hadn't even been the second time.

I'd expected *Apa* to keep him away. Who wouldn't have faith in the Volkov, the king of werewolves, to protect them? He'd called me son my entire life and I thought of him as my father, *Apa*. Yet, maybe the words weren't enough. *He* was the Volkov's son by blood. Maybe that meant more. Or maybe I just hadn't been worth as much as I'd been led to believe.

Funny the things that seem to fall into place when you are dying. *Apa* never encouraged my independence. Although he'd given me access to the land and allowed me to make my own mistakes for years. He'd even supported my alchemy. Though I wondered now if that was only because it was useful to him. Maybe it hadn't been enough and now I was expendable.

How many times in my research had I read about forbidden spells? Alchemy in general was the exchange of one equal thing for another. The concept of life for life had intrigued many an alchemist in history. The equivalent exchange to create some kind immortality. Never were the stories about people dying from cancer and trying to save themselves or a loved one. No, they always turned dark. Making the alchemists out to be villains.

I'd barely begun to scratch the surface with my investigations into past works, but I'd read enough to know the basics. The horrors. Perhaps the history was biased. Survival could lead anyone to desperate measures. I was no exception. Maybe it didn't have to be the ultimate evil the books made it out to be. Life was everywhere, right? Humanity didn't have a patent on it. There was a lot of philosophy about the value of higher life forms. I'd never been so rigid. Growing up in a werewolf pack proved to anyone just how little life of any kind meant. Wolves died every day. Especially the Volkov's wolves.

A life for a life.

Ten feet from my doorstep I had a garden the size of a football field, filled with life. Would it be enough? My heart ached with the idea of the garden's destruction. I'd started it from a tiny plot and a handful of seeds when I'd been no more than ten years old. But I could start over as long as I didn't damage the earth too much.

What was my other choice? Take life from another person? Lie here and die?

I wasn't sure I could move at all. Blood pooled around me, staining the pale wood floor, and looking like a murder scene from a movie. If it weren't for the fact that all the lights were on, the blood might not have looked so fluorescent. Blood in general was more brown or dark red than anything as luminescent from the movies. I was losing blood fast. So I had to move.

My whole body trembled as I reached down to slide myself across the floor. My legs wobbled like jelly, unable to support my weight, and my arms shook with the effort of dragging myself to the door. I inched like a worm, pressing into the floor with what little strength I had to move forward. The soaking wetness of my blood made the floor slippery. I strained to reach for the door, which was only a few feet away. Grabbing at anything for leverage, I hauled my battered body across the small space. Blood continued to pool up into my throat, choking me, even as I sputtered and spit it out.

I refused to contemplate why I was nude, and ignored the other fluids and pain that stained my skin with violence. Bad memories wouldn't make me stronger. Fighting panic and rising death at the same time would not hasten my pace. Nor would it bolster my resolve to survive.

One eye went completely black like a switch had been flipped. I wasn't sure if it was my vision or just blood covering it. Either way, my depth perception shifted, disorienting me further. Reaching for the edge of the doorway, I fell out the open door and down the two steps to the ground.

For a few heartbeats I just rested there, assuring myself that I just needed a minute. Only I didn't really have a minute.

My head throbbed, and each breath bubbled with blood and hissed with air, a combination that just made me hurt even more. Why couldn't he have just killed me with one blow? Why hadn't I just died when he'd knocked me out? Or bled to death while unconscious? Why did I have to be awake for it? Was it some sort of cruel joke of the universe?

I swallowed more blood and spit out another mouthful, adding a horrible wet cough to the end. One more deep attempt for air, the tiny sips between the building fluid feeling like heavenly nectar, and I clawed at the earth to get a few feet further.

The garden was so close. The paving stones and fancy carved dirt path Oberon had laid two years' prior kept the grass at bay, and me from my target. I stretched toward the green, heart slowing with the effort.

My vision fogged further, the pinpricks of starlight vanishing into a shady darkness. I wasn't ready for this. Hadn't planned any of this. But I'd been cocky. The wolves always thought me cocky. Who was I to play their games? Who was I to tell them no? Or demand respect? Who was I to think anyone would protect me from my own bad decisions?

I blinked furiously into the darkness. Tears trailing down my cheeks, or maybe the warmth was just blood. I never thought my life would end this way. Alone. Lying in the dirt, staring up into a blackened sky. The feeling of abandonment raged within my heart. I'd fought for so long to be seen and heard, to prove myself worthy, only to die alone and unwanted.

My soul screamed into the silence, longing for something. Calling for something even if my voice couldn't release any sound. Surprisingly, it wasn't a sense of unfairness that I reached for, or even anger. It was a desperate plea of *not yet*. There was something out there, close, so close…

Something I needed in a way so visceral that my gut nearly leapt toward it. If I could have moved another inch I would have crawled toward it even if I'd been dragging organs and the last pieces of my battered body.

Please, I thought into the growing darkness I knew was death. I didn't know what I was asking for. Please don't let me die? Please let someone find me? Please let me die quickly?

My sluggish heart fought for each slowing beat. It echoed in my head, louder than I'd ever heard it before. I stared into the distance, vaguely able to make out some trees beyond the garden, and possibly the moon overhead in a giant crescent. A clear night to die. Might have even been beautiful if I could see the stars.

One of the trees moved. My whole body jerked involuntarily with fear. Was he returning? I accidentally sucked in a blood soaked breath, leaving me sputtering and choking.

The shape glowed with the slight edge of white. The moon's reflection perhaps? The scent of vanilla and man tickled my nose, faint beneath the metallic tang of blood. The shape dropped down beside me. Hands touched my face. Warmth spreading from his fingers into the very depths of my soul. His touch made me want like I'd never imagined wanting anything in my life.

I wanted to wrap myself around him, bathe in his essence, and beg him to never let me go. It didn't matter that I couldn't see his face and didn't know his name. My soul told me he was mine. It sang of promise, as his warmth trickled through the shattered walls of my personal wards.

What sort of magic was this? Was he fae?

He lifted my head and shoulders into his lap, his words a rush of noise around me without coherent sound. Or perhaps that was just my brain. The night itself was silent and unmoving. No wind, birds or bugs. A bad omen? Or permanent brain damage?

The form that held me, stroked my hair. His embrace felt like kindness, love, and sadness.

"Are you a spirit of dark or light?" I asked, not sure if sound actually left my lips.

His face nestled close to mine, little more than just a shadow in the darkness. His hand was warm on my cheek when he said, "I will be your light or dark. Your strength and pain. I offer you all of me. My soul to yours." Sweet words spoken with an unfamiliar voice. If I could have touched him then, I would have. I wanted to beg him to speak more, hold me tighter, and not leave me to die alone.

All I could think to say was, "Then kiss me and share your spirit."

Odd that the words seemed to choose themselves. I had no thoughts of kisses or spells before that moment as I was too far gone. But the second his lips touched mine, everything became liquid fire. His heat poured into me, soothing the wounds, pressing into places that hurt—a deep, raging, flame. We both gasped for breath as the power flowed between us. Healing me like nothing I'd ever imagined possible before.

I had a moment of terror when his hold on me went slack. A fine tremor ran through him, but I couldn't stop the flow of energy. Was I killing him? No! My heart screamed with the possibility of it. He couldn't die.

My lungs healed, and the throbbing behind my eyes faded. For a breath, my vision cleared enough that I could almost see him, make out pale eyes, and the outline of his lips. But I ripped myself out of his grasp, transforming as I did so. From human to fox in one breath to the next. He reached for me, the link still live between us.

His need echoed mine. The link between us carried the emotion to me in a wave of feeling. The way he reached for me made my heart ache to drop into his arms and beg for him to hold me.

Only the life I took from him was too much. His eyes drooped and his shoulders fell slack as he toppled backward.

I waited a few heartbeats in terror, watching for movement in his chest. Was I truly a monster? Had I destroyed someone so perfect for me? A moment passed into the next and finally I saw it. The small rise and fall of his chest. He was breathing. The link between us was fading, but I could still see it stretching between us. His energy flowing into me. Still healing.

The boisterous sound of voices moved toward us from the distance. I trembled, fear renewed. What if *he* found out he failed to kill me? Would he try again? This night hadn't been any sort of accident. I had to get away.

I took one last longing look at the man who'd saved my life, then turned to run away. Into the darkness of the forest I raced, leaving behind everything. My entire life had been in the camper, attached to a wolfpack who reviled me. Only now one small thing tugged at my heart, the mysterious stranger I'd left behind. The link between us thinned like over-stretched taffy. I thought it eventually would snap. But it just continued to stretch as I ran, connecting me forever to a man whose kiss I dreamt about nearly every night for the next year of my life.

CHAPTER 1

One year later.
Sometimes when on the run, all a man could hope for was a safe place to sleep and a bit of food. The delicious scent of freshly baked bread wafting through the air made me pull my dilapidated Volkswagen Beetle into the lot of a small bakery. Small bakeries were a good place to find day old bread for cheap and sometimes work for a few days. The place was busy, which made me hope the food was good, and even I, with my auburn hair, mixed heritage and magic blood, could easily get lost in the crowd.

All I needed was enough cash to refill the car and a bit of bread to stop the rumbling in my stomach. I could sleep in the car. Had been sleeping in the car for months, using motels to wash up when I had the cash, and gas station bathrooms when I didn't. Distance was all that was important, though really I could have crossed the ocean and still not been able to escape prying eyes.

Self-delusion. I was good at that.

The Sweet Tooth sat in a very classic looking brick building with wide windows painted in artful letters. The smell had drawn me from miles away. Pastry and sugar laden pictures on billboards, the promise of food filled with delight and pleasure, though temporary it may have been, lulled me off the highway to follow the signs to the tiny main street. I had high hopes of filling my empty stomach, and a few hours of under the table pay before jumping back on the road. Small places in the middle of nowhere like this often needed labor they didn't want to pay long term benefits for. Most of the time it was diners, but I'd done bakery service enough to know my way around a mixer. Had even been a short order cook for a few weeks in Chicago. When it came to food I was a Jack-of-all-Trades, and I liked eating it just fine too.

It wasn't until I stepped into the bakery, having to swerve around a group of customers leaving with arms full of baked goods, and others who waited in line at the counter, that I smelled more than just yeast and sugar.

Werewolf.

Fuck. My hunger took a nose dive as my anxiety rose. Dammit.

I didn't even know where I was. Some middle of nowhere town in Washington State. A commuter town I'd heard of at the last gas station. Was there a pack here? Small towns were sometimes good places for packs if there was a lot of room to run. Most stuck close to the state parks and I was further north than that, contemplating Canada. If I had a passport, I'd have already crossed the border. Might still do it on four paws rather than two legs if I really began to run out of real estate. Not that I was a fan of the cold, and going north only brought out the grumpy Texan in me.

I thought about stepping out before anyone noticed me, but the crowd shuffled toward the counter. Customers had come in behind me and were now blocking the door. It would have been odd if I left. Most people wouldn't have noticed, but I suspected the werewolf I'd smelled would notice. If not my skittish behavior, then he would have noticed my scent already.

Not that I was a werewolf. I wasn't a were-anything.

Witchborn. A tiny voice echoed in my head.

"Yeah, yeah," I grumbled to myself. Not like I could escape the truth. The factors of my birth were out my hands, much like the consequences of the past year. What I could control was the here and now. My stomach grumbled, reminding me it had been two days since I'd eaten last. I'd been running too hard to stop and hunt. Weeks I'd lived on nothing but occasional hunts and fast food. If I had to eat another mass produced burger for a buck, I'd puke.

You can always come home.

I ignored the voice. Wasn't sure if he was really speaking to me mind to mind or if it was just my imagination. *He* didn't need me and made that abundantly clear when he'd let his son chase me out of his pack. I didn't need him either. Or anyone, really. The past few months had proven that. On the run I'd met all sorts of beings. Fae, vampires, weres of all types, witches, goblins, ghosts, and more than a handful of spirits—not to be confused with ghosts since spirits had never been human. I'd survived them all. Often by the skin of my teeth and a lot of running. I was good at running. But tired. So incredibly tired. Then there was the sense of forever going in the wrong direction. A few weeks back I'd given in and just followed my senses thinking it would lead me back south. Only everything in me screamed north and west. But even chasing after that strange desire had become a burden. Running from one place to the next as some sort of *other* rushed me out of their territory. Was it too much to ask for a few days of rest before the next battle?

Come home.

No, I resolved, ignoring the memory of his voice. I didn't have a home anymore, no matter how much I longed for one.

Each time I thought of home, I remembered the kiss of a stranger that had saved me from near death, but feared the repercussions of survival. Easier to keep on the road.

I stepped up to the counter as my turn came, offering up as true of a smile as I could. The woman behind the glass display case of pastries smiled back. "How can I help you?"

"I'm wondering if you have any yesterday's bread for sale?" I leaned forward and whispered, "and perhaps a few hours of work for someone in need of gas money? I promise to leave by nightfall."

She wasn't pack, or at least didn't smell of wolf, though she may have been family to one for all I knew. But she just smiled. "Day old bread is there," she pointed to a shelf near the register. "We have pastries too, boxed up from yesterday. The second you'll have to speak to the manager about. I'll send him your way."

"Thank you," I told her sincerely and made my way to the bread. A whole loaf was two dollars. The loaf was also four times the size of supermarket bread. Two dollars was a lot, but I needed food. Something more than a squirrel or rabbit that I could eat on the go. I was tempted to get the cinnamon raisin bread instead of the plain, but knew the added sugar would only make me hungrier. The boxes of pastries, as delicious as they looked and smelled, were well out of my price range. I had ten dollars to my name, and would need a gallon or two of gas if I had to hightail it out of here.

A shadow passed over me as I looked over the bread. The smell of werewolf grew stronger. Not just werewolf, but an appealing musk of a dominant male wolf. If I closed my eyes and breathed in the scent for a while I might have been able to pick out a dozen nuances that made it enticing. Vanilla? Maybe a bit of cinnamon and cardamom? His scent drifted through my senses, awakening a memory of something vague yet familiar, ingrained deep within my brain. I could almost taste his kiss even before I'd seen his face. Strange. It had probably been too long since I'd had proper sleep.

"I'll give you half off," a male voice interrupted my day dreaming.

I glanced up, startled to see a tall, clean-cut man with dark blond hair and eyes a pale blue, like a bright sunny day. He wore an apron with a nametag that read 'Liam' and underneath written 'Manager.' His nostrils flared just a little. He'd obviously scented me. Knew I wasn't exactly human. The smile on his lips appeared genuine enough, but it was likely something he always wore to greet customers. The curve of those lips drew me in, the bottom plumper than the top. His face was just a slight bit more oval than round, and sprinkled through his dark blond hair were strands of platinum blond. Not in the way of artificial highlights, but almost as though they should have been peppered gray, only they were more a honey-wheat. If he'd had a bit of facial hair, I'd have been jelly in front of him. Not that there was anything wrong with his jaw or sculpted cheeks. I just thought a bit of facial scruff was sexy and made me think of hours in bed, letting that bit of hair tickle my skin.

He was handsome in the sort of way men had likely been fifty years ago, classically good-looking, though there was likely a mix of German and Russian maybe an offshoot of Italian with his mix of dark blond hair. He was movie star beautiful and appeared to be in his late twenties, but I wasn't fooled. My nose told me he was a werewolf, and werewolves lived until they killed each other or themselves. He could have been in his late twenties, or two thousand and still looked the same.

He wasn't a big man, though I knew from experience werewolves were good at hiding all their muscle under clothing. He was firm through the shoulders, not delicate or thin in anyway. Solid, without being intimidating. This man came across as normal, handsome, not scary. Which let me know he wasn't just a wolf, but an alpha.

Something about his presence whispered of longed for things like safety and home. It couldn't have been just him being an alpha. I'd met plenty of those and known to run right away. Usually my anxiety skyrocketed the second I found myself in the presence of another wolf, especially an alpha. A year on the run had taught me to fear everything. Except this man was beautiful, and while my heart raced, it was with desire not fear. A well of need pooled in my gut for little things, like the need to memorize his scent and bask in the pale blue gaze of his eyes. What would it be like if he held me? How would his lips taste? I was practically drooling on his shoes. Fuck.

My brain automatically shifted me into defense mode. *Apa* had often called me prickly for just this reason. My self-preservation habits amused him, which in turn annoyed me.

"Is that your way of telling me to get out of your territory? Offering me a discount on bread?" I squared my shoulders and stared up at him. He was probably a good half foot taller. I was used to being short. I'd stared scarier things in the face than him. If he expected the normal submission of a lesser wolf, he'd be mistaken. Meeting his eyes could be seen as a challenge, but it was unlikely he'd call me on it since I wasn't a wolf. Not unless he was a real asshole. Most alpha's were, but they were also good at restraint in public places.

The tiny smile on his lips curved up into an amused grin. Apparently I amused him too. He had dimples. The attraction hit me hard. Would he grow a little facial hair if I asked? Not enough to cover the dimples…

I sucked back a groan and reminded myself werewolves were bad news. No matter how pretty they were. I was a novelty to them. Exotic with my half Creole bloodlines, hair an odd brown with auburn highlights, eyes tilted and Asian. I was a mutt in all senses of the word. But different than most had ever met. The *witchborn* part only succeeded in tempting them like a moth to flame.

Werewolves and witches shouldn't mix. Not that I was really a witch any more than I was a werewolf. The magic was different, dangerous when mixed with other preters. Like oil and water. But I couldn't deny the blood that ran through my veins. It made me immune to most magics, including the werewolf bits that demanded obedience. Though there was a bit more to that than just my muddy blood.

"If I offer you a free sandwich, will you sit with me and tell me what brought you here?" Liam asked. "You look like you've come from adventure and could use a safe place to rest."

And wasn't that the truth. I didn't know where here was, but indulging just sounded like trouble since pretty wolf or not, I would not be staying. I'd learned the hard way that not moving just let danger catch up and new trouble find me.

Something in my gut said, *this is home*. But that wasn't right, so I shook it off. "Just the loaf if you don't mind, and I'll be on my way. I stopped for food."

Being near the weres was a bad idea. If only I could find a place on the planet that wasn't saturated in some sort of *other*. Weres were a gossipy bunch and would spread rumors of seeing me that would reach back to my *Apa* in no time. And Felix. The thought of him brought the anxiety cascading back in. My arms began to ache. Fuck, I needed to go.

"You asked Colleen for work," Liam said.

"She must have misheard. I'm just passing through."

"And what is your destination?"

Anywhere but here, I thought. "Canada," I told him then snagged a loaf and headed toward the counter. Now that I'd mentioned Canada I'd have to turn back and go the opposite way. Maybe down through Mexico. Though that was too close to home to be comfortable. I could have used a couple of hours of work and cash, but that had been before I knew an alpha managed the place. It didn't help that my body was screaming at me to throw myself at the man. Something about his scent made me think of rolling in his sweat and basking in his sex.

Instinct.

Stronger than I'd ever experienced before. I hated it, but still had yet to perfect ignoring it. He probably wasn't even interested in me. Most alphas were the hetero type. All else was taboo and to be hidden behind lies and secret encounters. I refused to be that lie anymore.

Liam followed me to the counter. He stepped behind the register and rang up the bread. I handed over my ten, the last of my money, and hoped a couple gallons of gas could get me somewhere quiet. He counted back my change, but instead of handing the bread back, he pulled out a large bag, stuffed a box of day old pastries in it, added the bread to the top and pushed it across the counter. He held the handle out for me.

I hesitated. Free stuff meant favors owed. It was never good to be *witchborn* and owe someone a favor. People tended to ask for stupid things like love potions and spells to bring back the dead, none of which I could do. My magic was a little more subtle than that.

"Take it," Liam said, jingling the bag. "If you find you need work, come back in the morning and I'll put you on the mixer. We start at five."

I gripped the cash to my chest and reached out for the bag. Our hands barely touched as I pulled the bag from him. It was enough. The familiar zing of werewolf coursed through me. It was a power, magic that my own recognized and rejoiced in. A sense of home that was a lie and a desire.

An addiction.

Not anymore. It wasn't mine. It would never be mine.

The wolf said nothing. Didn't even appear to feel the electricity from our touch, and maybe he didn't. I took the bag and backed out; grateful, hungry, tired, and terrified all at once. All I could see were his pretty blue eyes and wonder what they looked like when they bled to yellow as his wolf surfaced right before he claimed me.

Dangerous.

Oh yes, that was so dangerous. Because werewolves mated only to human women who would never know what they were. Old rules of dominant males, which was all to protect their fragile egos. Wolves lived lives of lies. I'd experienced that firsthand. And reminded myself again of the reason I was on the run as I backed out of the shop. The man looked away, focusing on someone else who needed help at the counter, but I felt his regard even as I darted out to my car and curled up inside like it could shield me from the shiver of fear coursing down my spine. What if he told someone he saw me? How long before Felix caught up?

Are you tired of running yet?

I was. But I wouldn't stop. Months. Almost a year had passed. I'd run through huge cities to try to get lost in the crowd, and endless miles of barren terrain only for something to always catch up with me. I should have been free. I shouldn't have still been heartbroken. He'd never promised anything. I'd known he'd marry a female again, have a family. He'd always been obsessed with family. He'd been cruel to ask me to stand by as he carried on with traditions that had nothing to do with me. He said I was *witchborn* and would never understand, though I'd been raised in the pack as one of them. He'd expected me to still be his lover. That alone told me he didn't know me at all.

I yanked the seatbelt into place. The car started, running on determination, and a bit of magic. My heart hurt at the thought of leaving, though I didn't know why. I backed out of the lot as hot tears filled my eyes. A lifetime as pack had not prepared me to live alone. Not emotionally. I could hunt and adapt with the best of the werewolves, but they were pack creatures, and my adoptive father had raised me to be the same. Unfair of him.

Come home.

But I wouldn't. They didn't want me there anyway. They looked at me and thought *small* and *weak* until I shoved their faces into the dirt. For years I'd fought my way to independence as anyone who thought I wasn't pack challenged me. Only to bask in Felix's protection for a while and lose it all. Stupid. I'd been so stupid.

I pointed the car back out onto the highway. Running. Always running. From what, I wasn't really sure I knew anymore. Myself maybe. Not that it mattered so long as I kept moving.

CHAPTER 2

It was, of course, my luck that the car would die in the middle of nowhere. I'd gotten about an hour outside the small town I'd last stopped in when the Beetle just puttered to a halt. There should have been gas in it, the gauge said it was at a quarter. Nothing else had seemed off.

Like most people, I opened the hood to look at the engine, but while I knew a little about cars, I couldn't even fathom where to begin. Listing off parts did not mean I knew how to fix something that was broken. Or even recognize what to fix. Usually my small bit of magic was enough to help. Something that shouldn't have been possible to most magic beings as they didn't like the products of humans. Iron and steel were not good conduits of magic for most. For me the object didn't matter much at all. I could just make things work. Most of the time. The Beetle, however, was not going anywhere.

I sighed, grabbed up the food I'd been carefully avoiding, and my things. Staying with the car would probably bring help eventually, or my adoptive father to scold me for running, and my Ex to drag me back.

Since I didn't want the latter, I planned to hike into the forest to find a place to bed down for a few hours. Food and rest, then I'd attempt to hitchhike. Made it halfway across the country that way. Being small helped. People didn't see me as a threat, even though I was male. With my long brown-auburn hair pulled up into a ponytail or a bun, tilted eyes, and willow-thin body, it made people think I was female at first. A tiny push of magic would make someone stop if they slowed. It was an innocuous spell. No real power to it, just a hint of suggestion like "help this one."

Tattoos wrapped my left arm in spells. Mostly protection, basic wards, and do-me-no-harm spells. Years of alchemy training and meditation with my adoptive father's local witch had taught me a few things. Mostly that I wasn't powerful enough to ever be a pack witch. Not that it had ever been a goal. Covering up the secrets of their existence, healing their wounded, and hiding their dead, had never appealed to me. I was better at mixing potions or adding a zip of magic to something baked than casting spells. For a while that had been enough.

As soon as I found a safe place and a good tattoo artist I had a few new spells to add. The last few weeks had been brutal, and I'd been unable to convince my brain that stopping for a minute wouldn't mean instant death.

I shook off the melancholy, needing food and sleep more than self-loathing. My stomach growled at me in frustration. The smell had been killing me. Each ingredient a mix of heaven in my nose. Werewolf attuned senses from a lifetime of living among them. I could smell the flour, yeast, eggs, and sugar, and practically salivated as I hauled the bag up with the rest of my things and made my way into the trees.

The car died far enough off the road, around a bend, that I didn't think many would see it. Plus it was that gross sort of olive green that could blend in with dry greens and knee-high weeds. I'd bought the car after working for a month in some mid-western town. It made a good place to sleep when it rained, but that's about all. Still, I'd miss it a little as it had become home in a small way.

If *Apa* really wanted me home, the car wouldn't stop a werewolf attack. It wouldn't even keep them from tracking me for long. But there would be nothing to stop him if he truly wanted me home. I suspected the only reason he hadn't come for me yet was because he understood how hurt I'd been.

Betrayed. Abandoned.

And dragging me back before his own pack was under control would just drive a deeper dagger into the chaos that was tearing them up. Without me around to stir up trouble, he would fix things, placate the old ones, and settle the new wolves. I'd done him a favor by running. In time he'd see it that way.

I walked through more wide, over-grown fields and minor hills than forest. There were trees, even some small copes of them, but nothing that would make me think this was wild, untamed land. Likely it was the edges of some farmer's property, too rocky to plant, or something. There was no sound of cars, people, or movement other than the occasional bird. I knew Washington had desert, had driven by quite a bit of it. This was sort of a mix between a desert and prairie land. Likely the soil was too filled with clay to plant. It wouldn't offer a lot of cover, but enough should anyone come searching.

I scented rabbits, a few deer, a coyote or two, no wolves, were or otherwise. Finding a small grouping of trees, I set up my tiny camp, the sleeping bag, the food, and a handful of minor wards to alert me if someone came my way. Only after that was done did I sit down and open the box of pastries. It smelled like heaven. I don't think I even tasted the first one. Just devoured it like the starving man I was.

The second, I ate slower, chewing and savoring the honey sweetened flavor of a tart of some kind. I ate two more, glutting myself before putting them aside and curling up in the sleeping bag. It didn't matter that the sun still shone somewhere above the trees. It was safer to sleep during the day and move at night. There were things that preferred the darkness, but as long as I kept going I'd be fine. In a few hours I'd go back and look at the car. Maybe with some rest and a clearer head, I could get it moving again. The manager from the bakery filled my mind as I began to nod off to sleep. His pretty eyes shining in the darkness. I could almost feel his lips on mine as though we'd met before. Though I was sure I'd have remembered that. He was a pleasant dream, and for now that was okay.

Burning heat seared through my left arm waking me out of a light sleep. I didn't move, listening instead to the approaching night and trying to identify the burn. The wards hadn't been triggered yet, but the magic scrawled into my flesh told me something was close and it meant me harm. The surrounding night sat in an unnatural stillness.

In the thicket there were enough trees and brush to hide me from most prying eyes. The sleeping bag I'd purchased was a dual-sided camouflage that blended well with almost any environment. The wards should have been mild enough to send curious eyes away. *Nothing to see here.* Usually it worked. Even on some of the more magical beings, unless they were searching for me in particular.

I kept my movements minimal, in case anyone was watching, and surveyed what little I could see from my spot among the weeds. The sun was setting in a fire-orange glow off to the west, barely visible through the trees. Nothing moved nearby. And that was the second indicator that something was really wrong. I couldn't hear anything but the wind. Not a single bird, squirrel or bug. Something dangerous was slinking through the trees and overgrown grass.

My first thought was that the alpha from the bakery had found my car and come looking for me. Though he hadn't seemed put out that I'd taken his offer of food and run, the continual ache in my arm said something angry lurked not far away. And that anger was directed at me or else my arm wouldn't have throbbed so.

If I hadn't worried it would sense my magic I'd have cast out senses through the ground to find out what it was, and which direction it was coming from. Had to be downwind since I couldn't smell anything unusual. No wolf, vampire, fae, or even the rare wendigo. Nothing but grass, dust, and leaves.

Slowly I crawled from the sleeping bag, rolling it up with practiced ease and tied it to the bottom of my backpack. My pack was already ready to go. I'd packed it before bed, even going so far as to bury the remaining food in the bottom of it to avoid attracting other wildlife. A year on the run and I had learned to be fast. I'd abandon it if I had to, though it would hurt. The little I'd acquired, a few changes of clothes, the pack itself, a good filtering water bottle, and the sleeping bag, were mine and mine alone. No one had given them to me. I hadn't stolen them, but if I had to leave it all, I would. My life was worth more than stuff.

The sky darkened overhead with approaching dusk. Lots of things hunted at night. I scanned the distance carefully, searching for movement. Nothing approached, but my arm still burned in silent warning. On my belly, I crawled to a brush line, near one of the trees for added cover. I'd have a better view if I climbed, but werewolves could climb just fine. Vampires could fly. And the fae would just rip the tree out from under me. It was unlikely that any fae or vampires would have tracked me this far. Though there was a Chicago area master vampire who'd acquired a taste for my blood who might still be following me. It had taken me two weeks to escape him mostly because he'd trapped my mind in a whirl of dreams of happier times. Maybe that was why I was still so raw. The emotional wound made fresh again by memories and vampire mind tricks. Fuck.

The wind shifted. The scent of werewolves filled my nose. Dammit. I knew I shouldn't have taken the free food. The bread had been plain, not easily tracked while stuffed away, but the sugar? A highly trained wolf could probably smell it from miles away.

There were few options. Run, which would attract the wolves and bring chase, forcing their beasts to hunt me even if that wasn't what they had come for. Hide, which was unlikely even with my strongest wards. Or surrender and possibly die. Not the greatest selection of choices.

I chose the first and ran toward the car, praying I'd get it to start. Determination could often give magic an added edge. Seconds later the sounds of snarls and huffs of a chase filled my ears. I ran until I could hear the claws ripping through the brush, snarls and snorts edging closer behind me. There was more than one. My sensitive nose differentiated at least three different scents, none of them familiar. I didn't stop to ask their names and looking back was only something people did in the movies right before they died. Instead I envisioned my legs and arms pumping hard enough to make me fly. I couldn't actually fly, but the visualization spell did increase my speed a little. The balance of weight and resistance was all the spell changed. Maybe it would be enough.

They should have been able to outrun me. I was human, mostly. On two legs I was slower than most weres, but had years practicing just what I was doing now. My adoptive father had always told me not to run as it only made an aggressive werewolf worse. When the other option was death, it wasn't much of an option. Rational thought told me that if they were sent by my adoptive father they didn't want me dead, probably just good and scared. If they weren't sent by him then I was just a trespasser and no one would miss me.

I reached the car in record speed, glad I'd left it unlocked. Not like there was anything in it to steal. I dove in through the passenger door, closing and locking it behind me and struggling out of the pack. The windows were up as I'd been unable to get them to work properly the entire time I'd owned the car. It was a small barrier, but all I really had. I flopped into the driver's seat and put the key in when metal screeched as one of the wolves landed on the roof hard enough to dent it.

Fuck.

It was a gray beast with endless fangs and claws that scraped at the windows. Werewolves were about twice the size of normal wolves. Bigger often than the human they'd been, and about a hundred times deadlier. Inside the car I'd drawn wards. Just minor protection spells to keep the glass from breaking and lend strength to the frame. It wouldn't hold for long.

The car didn't start. Didn't even sputter like it had any life left in it. I cursed it and kicked the dash. Now was not the time for it to ignore my magic.

One of the wolves jumped on the hood and lunged at the windshield with claws and fangs. Another scraped along the side of the car, producing the horrible high-pitched squeal of tearing iron. My wards would not stop them from tearing the car to pieces around me. The windshield began to splinter. Too much weight threw the whole car out of balance as the roof caved in, the sides were torn away and the windows smashed.

Choices. Life is filled with them. Some of them easy, like what to have for dinner. Others were a matter of life and death. Not really choices at all. I was out of choices. The car was coming apart around me. No one shifted to talk to me, so these wolves hadn't likely been sent by my adoptive father. Not unless he wanted me dead. And didn't the idea of that just burn like a knife to my guts? The only choice I had left was to abandon it all, change, and run.

As a human, I was slower than most werewolves even with my supply of spells. As a human, I was also limited in resources. My magic wasn't strong enough to hurt them so my spells focused on defense more than offense. I suspected that was the only reason I'd been allowed to live among the were for so long. For a time, I avoided changing because it seemed to attract the *others*. Like they could sense me pulling on whatever invisible magic that tied me to the universe. The only real power I had was my own change. Nothing so spectacular as a wolf. Not vicious or even all that predatory.

My alternate form was no match for a werewolf.

"My beautiful little fox," Felix had often said with a smile on his face. *"So wily and quick witted."* Only now did I realize how much he'd viewed me as a possession. Just a pretty toy to be set on a shelf.

I wasn't a toy. I was *witchborn*. Sometimes the only advantage I had from a change was that it startled others, gave me time to slip away, or even masked my scent. Often surprise and speed were all I really needed.

I wriggled out of my clothes as the windshield began to

crumple and the driver's side door squealed as it was ripped away. Weres took time to change, as long as a half an hour for some of the lesser wolves. The stronger wolves could shift in ten minutes or so. My change was seamless, a gift of magic born, not a curse of blood exchange.

One second I was human, the next I was fox. Small, slippery, and zipping between the legs of the wolf with the door under his fangs. Darting under his belly, I bolted, propelled by magic and fear. I crossed the road running, under, over and through, squeezing myself through openings that the wolves would never fit and zig-zagging to confuse whatever route they thought I'd take. They were behind me. I could hear them, but had to focus on my escape.

Run! My little fox brain didn't have all the same higher functioning I did as a human, but it was close. Panic, however, was still panic, and my fight or flight mode was stuck in all out flight. *Run, run, run,* I chanted to myself, not really paying attention to the path.

Even as a fox I was only barely faster than them. I wove through roads, brambles and trees, hoping to slow them down. One of them leapt, close enough to brush my tail, and I ran that much harder. It was a game to them now, I realized. Two off to my sides, herding me in for their alpha to catch. I wondered again if it was the alpha from the bakery. He'd seemed nice. Had pretty eyes and dimples. It was only fitting that he be a monster since I'd wanted him. A reminder of how bad I was at choosing men. A curse of my family maybe. My mother had the same hard luck. Falling in love with a man who died before he could know I'd ever been conceived. She'd always told me that love was something people wrote about in books. Lust was what happened in real life and got people in trouble. Once again I thought she might be right.

I ran out of road. There was a wall of some kind. Like the

sort built on the side of roadways, only there was no grade to it, it was just straight up and down as far as I could see. The two werewolves closed in from the sides, and the final one's claws crunched on gravel behind me. I hadn't even noticed we'd found a gravel road of some sort. A place for water runoff maybe. The place I was probably going to die.

Bracing myself with my back to the wall, I turned to face them, my fangs and claws no match for three werewolves, but I'd go down fighting. Better a fox than a human to be ripped apart and left for the crows. At least in this form I had fangs and claws too. The burning in my left arm intensified. More wolves? Fuck.

The large gray wolf growled at me, inching closer slowly. He must have been enjoying the scent of my fear. One of the other wolves boxing me in, took a swipe, which I dodged, but it caught the edge of my flank, opening a gash along my right hip. I yelped as pain flared. I expected them all to attack and end my run.

Only something flew overhead, landing with the force of a truck on top of the gray wolf. Another launched itself from the top of the wall into the wolf who'd injured me, tearing out its throat. The gray wolf battled a huge black wolf now. The two of them rolling, snarling, and tearing at each other. The third wolf came for me. I ducked and rolled beneath him, turning until my tiny claws were up to rake open his belly.

Hot blood poured over me, but the were just huffed and did a little skid-turn to raise a paw at me. I felt the hit before I really saw him move. Pain exploded through all of my senses. Stars, and swirls of color overflowed my vision as his claws connected with the side of my head. I was sure he punctured my skull, and I flew into the wall, body blossoming into pain. It was an explosion through my spine up into my brain. The world faded as I lay in a broken heap on the ground beside the wall, watching the black wolf fight the gray, and the second wolf, a pale brown one, launch itself at the wolf that had hit me.

This was it, I thought. So much for ever going home. Or finding a home. So much for the dreams of freedom. My heart pounded. I felt blood seeping from my head. There were tattoos on my left arm and right wrist that were supposed to help speed healing. It wouldn't be enough. Not if my spine was broken and my skull fractured. My body couldn't hold enough energy to heal bones and keep me from bleeding out at the same time. At least it would be fast, I had enough time to think as the darkness overrode my vision. I sank into the darkness, to the growls of the werewolves fighting, reminding me of home.

CHAPTER 3

"I plan to ask him when he wakes up."

"If he wakes up," someone was saying.

"He'll wake up. He's been in and out a couple times already," the first voice answered. His tone was soft, soothing and close. My whole body ached, it wasn't pleasant, but I didn't feel like I was dying. The pain also meant I wasn't actually dead. Which made me wonder where I was. Did the werewolves have me? If so, which ones?

It was sad that I immediately thought of begging them to call home for me. Not that I really had a home. Maybe *Apa* would take me back. Maybe he'd send help. Maybe he'd just put me out of his misery.

Inside my gut, almost for the first time in ages, something sat quietly and settled. Anxiety almost non-existent. I'd lived so long with the overwhelming pressure that its absence was remarkable. Had I truly felt this way before that night? Free of the endless fear? Usually not even sleep offered a full sanctuary. Maybe I wasn't dead, but dying, and that's why I felt no fear. I tried to open my eyes, but just didn't have the energy. Sleep lingered just out of reach, teetering me on the edge of the darkness again. I waited for it to pull me back down, only it didn't.

A warm hand touched my head as though feeling for a fever. "He's not running hot anymore. That's a good sign."

"His blood mixed with the wolf I killed."

I was with the wolves who'd attacked the ones chasing me. That, of course, didn't mean I was safe. "It's well known that he's immune." Werewolves were never born. They were made. Violence and death changed them much the same way vampires created their own. Most of the truly awful curses were blood related. I knew that from experience even if mine was from tainted blood at birth. Growing up in a wolf pack gave me plenty of opportunity to watch the *gift* become a curse.

"Witchborn usually are immune. For a good reason," the other snarled. "I say dump him back where he belongs. We don't need that kind of trouble here," the man sounded irate, moving back and forth, likely because he was pacing. "Felix has a reward out for him."

"Which Xander has already overridden. They almost went to war over it. Only no one will fight Xander. Not even Felix," the voice close to me said. "And if Felix comes my way, I'll just beat the shit out of him again."

"You're too cocky sometimes."

"It's not cocky when stating facts. The only reason Felix still lives is because Xander wishes it so."

Xander Volkov is my adoptive father and leader werewolves. Felix is his youngest son and my former lover. It was rare the two fought over anything. I was apparently the exception as they'd been fighting over me since I'd turned sixteen and caught Felix's ever roving eye.

"Let them sort it out. Dump him back in the Volkov's territory and be done with it."

"He is not a puppy to be dropped off on the side of the

road. If he wishes to leave once he's well, he can go. If he wants help returning to the Volkov, I will help. If he asks for sanctuary, that too, I will allow him."

"Even if it means bringing the wrath of the Volkov down on us? We are a small pack."

"A *growing* pack," the man closest to me said. "The Volkov put me in charge of the area. Gave me specific instructions. He's not going to come raging through because we've helped the *witchchild*."

"You're being unreasonable," the first man said.

There was a tiny bit of chill that charged the air. Anger from the man perched beside me. Restrained but unmistakable since it wafted through the room with tangible energy like tiny needles, just ready to strike.

"Forgive me, Alpha."

The silence lasted a moment longer before the man beside me said, "You can go. Call Dylan. Once he arrives he can replace you as guard. I think you're tired."

"Yes, sir." I heard a door open and close.

The man's hands were on me again, soft and soothing over my face and down my arms. My tattoos didn't react to him at all. No malice in him then. At least not for me. I sucked in a deep breath and tried again to open my eyes. There was a lamp in the corner as the only source of light, but even that hurt my eyes. I squinted back tears and rainbows. Had the wolf cracked my skull? It had felt that way at the time, only now it was just a mild throb. At least the anxiety didn't rear its ugly head.

"Sebastian Volkov, it's good to see you awake."

"Not dead?" I asked. The words came out in a half grumble as I blinked furiously to clear my vision. The light wasn't so bad, and the room was filled with shadows.

"No. Thankfully. Though our local witch suggests you rest a few days as your injuries were severe." The man who hovered over me finally solidified from a wobbly shadow into Liam, the manager from the bakery. An old memory leapt into my head of a night long ago, someone leaning over me in the dark as blood blotted out my vision, and then it was gone.

"Did you follow me?" I asked, trying to roll over only to realize I was naked in a bed, with only a thin blanket separating us. Fuck.

Not many knew of the number of tattoos I'd added in the past year for protection. I had hoped to keep that information from Xander and, most especially, Felix. Had that been why Liam was touching me? He was studying the spells? I'd need to start filling up my right arm soon with distraction and look-not-at-me spells. Though I really hated to lose full use of that one too.

"No. I didn't go looking for you until one of my wolves said they'd spotted your car on the side of the road. There is a lot of open land out here, and not much traffic. It was sheer luck that they spotted your car so soon."

"Friendly pack you have." I couldn't help but feel bitter about him sending wolves to follow me. How *lucky* was I to be found? Just another controlling alpha. I tugged the blanket up further. My hair felt crusty, likely from blood and I was still light-headed. In fact, my whole body ached as though I'd gone through a really intense workout with the trainer from hell. Running, right this second, wasn't an option. I'd have to heal, which left me vulnerable and in Liam's care. I really hated the idea that I'd have to stay for a few hours. Days was not possible. Especially now that Liam's pack knew about me.

"The wolves who attacked you were not mine. I was hoping you knew them. Two of them got away when we stopped to help you, or I would have followed them. I was more concerned about your injuries at the time. Though I do have a handful of wolves out searching for them. Your car is being towed to a local garage." It didn't sound like he was lying, but some alphas could do that, mask the truth by simply believing what they said.

"Can't afford to fix it anyway," I said. The Beetle had been reknitted together at a dozen shops across the country, and with more magic than most mundane folks would ever experience in their lifetime. The shredded heap the wolves had left was better off as scrap metal. Not even magic could put a car back together.

I tried to sit up, only to be hit with a wave of dizziness so bad I thought I was going to hurl. "Fuck." Nausea, vertigo, ear popping. A concussion. It wasn't the first time I'd had one of those.

Liam's arms wrapped around me and laid me back down. One hand cradled my neck as he adjusted the pillow beneath me. My vision swirled in colors. I couldn't go running with a concussion. It had been how the vampire ended up trapping me the last time. My stomach roiled with unease even as my vision began to clear to reveal Liam hovering uncomfortably close.

His fingers actually gripped my hand, pressing into a spot in my palm. The nausea faded. I'd have to remember that trick for the next time. Sadly, there would be a next time since someone was always beating me up. Felix said it was my mouth that got me in trouble, but I still thought picking on the smallest guy in the room just meant someone was compensating for something.

"You didn't recognize the wolves?" Liam asked again. "I had heard your nose is almost as good as most werewolves."

"No. I didn't recognize them," I clarified. He needed to stop touching me. It was turning me on. Hell, his touch made my skin sing. It was an odd feeling. Normally I didn't like people touching me. *Prickly.* Only for some reason his touch was comforting.

He traced the tattoos around my left wrist. My left arm was almost completely sleeved in ink. Some of the spells made it hurt too much to use, which was the reason I'd gone with my left rather than my right, since I was right-handed. The right had a few, but not the mesh of color of the left. The right one bore a handful of pale scars. Mostly from cuts for blood to seal a ward. They usually healed, but some I kept reopening because it was just easier to follow the line already there. His fingers traced a warm path over each and every one of them. If I'd been less injured, I'd likely be uncomfortably aroused.

"Tattoos don't stay for us. It heals," Liam said absently, his gaze focused on his fingers. I knew that. It was just something else that set me apart from the wolves. His touch found a spot that had been covered in an elaborate batch of woven bramble. A detailed protection and healing spell all in one. Beneath it had been a wolf. Sometimes the wolf still ached in my skin. The outline of it would redden and rise up in my flesh like an allergy. Usually only when Felix got near since it had been for him. A declaration he hadn't shared which is why I'd covered it. There had been no actual magic in the original tattoo, but sometimes things evolved that way.

I jerked my arm out of Liam's grasp. "Appreciate your help, Alpha," I told him neutrally. "I will be on my way as soon as I'm well enough."

Liam stared at me a moment, expression blank. There was something oddly familiar about him. He was powerful. Crazy powerful, unless I was mistaken, which was a rare occurrence. But he held it in check. He had no need to flex his power, or threaten those around him, because his presence was just that large. Only I hadn't noticed it in the bakery. Was he that good at hiding what he was? Or had I been distracted? He was the quiet scary. The smiling and kind face no one would suspect until it was too late.

Finally, he nodded as though making some sort of decision he didn't share. "Stay a few days. When you're well, we'll discuss this again."

"Nothing to discuss," I told him.

He gave me a look that probably cowed lesser wolves. But I'd lived my whole life in the shadow of the Volkov. There was no scarier wolf than the Volkov. I'd once glimpsed the monster inside him. Not his wolf. Not exactly. Something darker, more sinister. The tiny peek I'd had scared me half to death. I'd been twelve or there about, just beginning to explore alchemy. It had taken me weeks to stop avoiding him. And I only had because he looked so sad when he saw me duck away to escape being in his presence.

"I'll be doing you a favor if I leave sooner, rather than later," I told him. "Felix will know I'm here within hours."

"And he'll do what?" Liam wanted to know. "He has no claim to you. The Volkov has made that clear. Felix would need permission to enter my territory. Which he doesn't have."

I didn't think Liam was any match for Felix. Felix Volkov was a frightening man. Frightening, beautiful and ancient. I thought Felix around two or three hundred years old, but could never get an exact date from him. His current wife was his sixth, which was why he thought I shouldn't care. Who wouldn't want to be the lover of a man so rich and powerful, the son of the leader of werewolves? Who wouldn't want the money and protection of an ancient wolf most people feared? Me, apparently.

A grim smile curved the edges of Liam's lips. "You don't think I can protect you."

"I don't need anyone's protection." Only I was lying in bed with a concussion after being saved by a couple of werewolves from other werewolves. At least he was nice enough not to point out how terrible of a lie my statement was.

There was a knock on the door.

"Enter," Liam called over his shoulder.

A younger blond man entered. He looked early twenties. His hair fell over his shoulders in golden waves. He wore jeans and one of those striped button up shirts like people in the movies from Texas wore, and cowboy boots. He wasn't pretty, not like you'd expect with the long hair, but he wasn't ruggedly handsome either. He was more boy next door above average. His eyes were huge and brown to accompany the wide smile he wore.

"Boss, Carl has gone to bed for the night," the man said. He even had a thick Texan drawl. It made my heart ache for home, but I didn't recognize the man.

"Dylan," Liam acknowledged. "Dylan is my third. Carl, who left earlier, is my second. Dylan will be taking over guard duty for now. I will return to the scene of your attack and see if I can track the wolves." Liam tilted his head in my direction. "Do you think Felix sent them?"

"He doesn't have his own pack," I said. At least I didn't think Felix did. He was too volatile to ever have his own pack. While *Apa* had never actually said it in those words, he'd implied it on more than one occasion. "They didn't smell like Volkov wolves." But my adoptive father specialized in strays. He took in all manner of werewolves, saved them or killed them. It was just his way, and why he'd ended up with me.

"Hired?" Dylan said, more to Liam than me. "Seems like overkill and more than a little risky given the circumstances. Everyone knows not to touch the *witchborn*. Xander has always been really protective of his strays. And the stories about his fox child have made it all the way across the globe the last I heard."

"I'm not his," I told them. "He just got stuck with me." Did Dylan know the Volkov? Not many outside the Volkov pack called *Apa* anything other than the Volkov.

Liam just gave Dylan the barest of nods. He seemed reluctant to get up, but after a moment did. His hands fell away from my skin, taking with him his warmth. He stood, towering over me for a minute, shadows swallowing most of his face. He turned toward Dylan. "He needs rest."

I wish I could have placed his accent. It sounded old world, new American maybe. Not English. Or at least not quite. But I could have listened to him talk all day and analyzed the melodic staccato of his words. Living in the Volkov's pack had given me a lot of accents to store a mental database of global regions.

"I'm on it, Boss. I'll sit on him if I have to," Dylan joked. Something dark crossed Liam's face, and I could have sworn I caught a glint of yellow in his gaze. The wolf rising. Dylan must have seen it too, because he amended, "Figuratively, I mean. So he can rest."

Again Liam gave that small nod and stalked past Dylan out of the room. Dylan glanced once in my direction, before stepping out and closing the door. There was a click from the other side, telling me they'd locked me in. As if a simple lock had ever stopped me. I rolled over to get up, but the dizziness was too much and I just lay there panting for a minute. I buried my face in the pillow and closed my eyes. A little bit of sleep was okay. I'd be up and moving in a few hours no matter what Liam wanted. It would take an alpha greater than him to hold me. Even the Volkov hadn't been strong enough for that.

CHAPTER 4

The next time I woke it was to the smell of food. Real food. Not just bread and scraps, but eggs, bacon, toast, juice, and coffee. Fuck, I was so hungry. My backpack and clothes were spread out on a chair beside a dresser. The pack was torn, and the clothes were in a jumble. They hadn't been in the greatest of shape before the attack. I hoped I had something left to wear.

I was alone, and wherever the smell of food was coming from it was close but not in the room with me. Did they plan to torture me with the scent? I sighed and sat up slowly. My head ached, but it wasn't bad. No more dizziness. My hip hurt more. When I peeled back the blanket I realized I had stitches down my right side curving slightly around my stomach. Apparently the wolf had almost gutted me. Fuck.

It took a good five minutes and lots of struggling to get up without pulling too much on the stitches or falling over from the dizziness. But I stank and could smell a bathroom nearby. There was one door opposite the bed and I suspected that was the bathroom. I even had a vague memory of visiting it a time or two, but wasn't sure how I could have done that as injured as I was. There were no windows in the room, leading me to believe this was likely the safe room in the alpha's home.

Most alphas had large compound-like structures for homes. It was a place for the wolves to gather and feel safe. The bigger the compound, the bigger the pack. Safe rooms were created in the center of home to be easily guardable. It was a place for the injured to recover, or betrayers to be held, until the pack alpha could deal with them. I hoped I was considered the former. Not that there was much else the alpha could do to me. I felt like I'd already been run over by a truck.

I clutched the bed for support to keep myself from falling over, wishing the bathroom and my clothes weren't in opposite directions. I'd have grabbed my clothes and locked myself in the bathroom, but that meant five more steps I just wasn't ready for. How the hell was I going to get out of here while still feeling weak and helpless? Maybe Liam's witch was weak. She should have been able to heal most of the cut and the concussion with the help of my own magic. My own magic was just a simple binding spell to reknit my cells when they were strained or damaged so long as my body had the energy to expend. Seemed odd that the witch hadn't been able to provide more energy or strength to my own spell. I healed a little faster than most humans. Not as fast as wolves. There were other spells I could invoke, but they needed more energy than I could provide. And one spell I only used as a last resort because I was afraid of the damage it could do to others.

The door opened. I stood frozen, naked, too far from the bed to reach for the one thin blanket they'd given me, and not strong enough to dart to the bathroom. It was Liam. His eyes locked on me briefly, just the barest glance over my body before he stepped into the room and closed the door behind him. I took another hesitant step toward the bathroom.

"You could have called for help," he said.

"I don't need help to piss," I hissed at him. I might lie in the shower if I could make it that far. But I couldn't imagine how humiliating it would be to need help to pee. I reached the doorway and opened it to reveal a sizable bathroom. Of course the toilet was on the other side of it. Fuck.

Liam was suddenly behind me, arm wrapped around my waist, holding me up without any sign of strain. "Let me help you."

My face burned. It was another ten steps or so to the toilet.

He lifted me carefully, his arm a band of steel around my stomach. Before I could decide on a proper answer I stood in front of the toilet and he'd let go, turning his back to me as he started the shower. I sighed as the sudden sound of water covered my embarrassment. I flushed and hobbled toward the shower, steam already rising from it like a siren call. It had been months since I'd had a shower that hot, that deliciously soothing. It would probably hurt, since every inch of me ached, but I still wanted it.

Liam's arm around my waist stopped me and I made an undignified sound of protest. He had some sort of plastic that he pulled over my stitches, pressing down the edges until it was sealed, then he set me down in front of the shower. I stepped into the spray, not caring if I soaked the whole bathroom or had to have the stitches redone. The heat poured over me in a rain of heaven.

I stood with my back to the spray, letting the water massage away a million aches. The water turned pink as it flowed through my hair. Yeah, I had a feeling there was more than just a concussion. I reached up to touch my skull, fearing what I'd find there. Scars? More stitches maybe?

Suddenly Liam's arms were back around me, hand beneath mine. He was naked, his chest pressed to my back, his hips tilted away from mine.

The angry leviathan of anxiety reared its draconian head for the first time since waking up in Liam's safe room. I couldn't breathe. Terror roiled through me, shutting down my brain to nothing but physical sensation. The pain prickling from my arms wasn't a ward this time, just my body's reaction to the fear. My soul cowered in terror. Not yet. I wasn't ready yet. Not enough emotional or physical willpower to survive this again. I was too lost in the fear to try to reach for the desire I could feel tickling my senses.

"Hmm," he grumbled. "Just stay still. Let me help."

I'd experienced *help* before. That night a week after I'd told Felix I'd be leaving. He'd been furious. His *help* had left me broken and bleeding. I'd almost died and had to use a forbidden spell to heal just enough to escape. I wasn't strong enough to offer much of a fight this time, so I just stiffened in Liam's grasp, waiting for the attack.

It never came. Instead he gently washed my hair, fingers light as he massaged my scalp. "Breathe," he whispered. "You are safe. Focus on my fingers, the sound of my voice, the touch of the water on your skin. You are here in my den, safe and protected." He ran his fingers down my scalp, gentle, almost a petting motion, there was nothing violent or dangerous about it. "I'm going to count back from one hundred. Just listen to my voice. Ninety-nine…"

His words blurred as I fought to bury the panic in the soothing tone of his voice. I sucked in air when he told me to breathe and picked up the count with him somewhere around forty-three. By the time he reached one I was nearly putty in his hands. Relaxed into his touch.

He was pretty clinical about his care, washing me from head to toe and ignoring the tears I refused to admit were falling. Damn him for making me cave to the weakness. Damn him for making me crave safety.

I worked hard not to look at him, and not to examine how his skin was only a few shades lighter than mine. I would never be mistaken for a 'white' man. The brown of my skin was almost dark enough to put me on the danger side of the spectrum for any American-grown bigot. My momma had delicate features and had given me a lot of my own slight build. She told stories of her Japanese mother, gentle like a doll with porcelain skin, who'd fallen in love with her black-as-night father. We both had the Eastern tilt to our eyes. My own father was supposed to have been some cowboy she'd met in Texas and had a brief affair with. All I had of him were stories from my mother, heavily embellished as everything my mother said was. It was just something else that made me different.

I wondered how Liam saw me. Was I just the *witchchild*? A strange shifter? A mutt of mixed heritages and cultures? Maybe he just saw me as another of his flock to be protected. All the alpha's I'd met before him were more aloof. They took care of their wolves just fine, but most ruled more like kings. Packs were not democracies. An alpha would not accept a non-wolf like myself even if it was just the inconvenience of my healing. Most alpha's would have someone low on the food chain care for me if he worried about the Volkov's reaction. So Liam's proximity confused me.

As the anxiety faded, I tried to ignore the muscles in Liam's arms, the solid strength of his chest on my back, and the way his fingers felt on me. The contrast of our skins so alluring. I didn't know him. It could all be a game. An act. Maybe he was being nice until Felix could come and retrieve me, paying out a nice monetary reward for the return of his troublesome little fox. Still didn't explain his presence instead of another lesser wolf. An ache inside me burned with something unfamiliar and yet not. Longing. Not fear, desire. I wanted to turn around and bury my fingers in his hair, press my lips to his, and pretend I'd never met another man before him.

Foolish.

I'd never let myself be that weak again. Trust had brought me nothing but pain.

Liam shut off the water and grabbed up a towel. I reached for it. "I can take it from here," I told him trying to salvage some of my dignity. He wasn't aroused, though I'd worked hard to no more than glance at that part of him. It was more terror than curiosity. A year wasn't long enough. Liam was beautiful. A fine specimen of a man that any eye could admire. And perhaps I would have if I hadn't felt so vulnerable in that moment.

"You can barely stand. Just let me do this. I'll get you back to bed in a minute. Dylan is changing the bedding, and there will be food. You need to eat to heal."

"I'm not a wolf," I reminded him. Removing the smells of other wolves from the bed or forcing me to devour a dozen eggs wasn't going to cure or even soothe me. Though I really wished I had a den in which to hide and lick my wounds for a few days of safety. Liam's presence had given me a taste of that kind of safety I hadn't felt since I'd left my camper behind a year ago. All the wards and spells I'd placed on my camper had kept most everyone out. My biggest mistake was crafting the wards to recognize Felix and allow him in. I'd never do that again. Once I had a space of my own, it would be just mine, no exceptions. "You don't have to baby me like I'm some abandoned cub."

"Hmm," Liam said again, that non-committal sound, like he was humoring me. He dried me off, then himself before wrapping the towel around his waist. That was a little unfair. Most wolves weren't modest, and normally I wasn't either, but he was attractive and I was one big bruise. The huge mirror over the sink reflected just how bad I looked. My back was a patchwork of colors and not from tattoos. The entire left side of my face was swollen and angry purple. My hair looked dark brown when wet, but at least it didn't feel crusty anymore. It was just a tangled mess, and my scalp still hurt.

"You need a better witch," I grumbled at him as he carefully peeled the plastic off the stitches. My own spells should have healed most of the bruising unless my time was really off. "How long was I out?"

He put a clean towel around my waist, finally covering me. At least I wasn't hard. Just one big bruise. The towel irritated my stitches a little. "Three days, give or take a few hours."

How was that possible? Three days of sleep should have healed just about anything short of death for me. And three days was a lot of time to lose. There was no way that Felix hadn't caught up by now, not while I was among werewolves. Was he waiting until I let my guard down? Why hadn't he just taken me while I'd slept?

"That's not possible. I should have healed better than this, especially with the help of a decent healing witch."

"My witch was more focused on your head and spine than the bruises." He lifted me, this time in more of a bridal style carry, which I wanted to protest, but being lifted made my head swim and stomach lurch.

"Fuck," I muttered. I tucked my face into his shoulder to keep from throwing up. His skin was nice, deliciously hot, and smelling of soap and fresh skin. Why did I want to touch him so badly even when I felt like shit?

"The wolf cracked your spine in three places and punctured your skull. You lost a lot of blood. You were barely alive by the time we got you to her. My healer did fine. But even she is not a miracle worker. Some you'll have to heal on your own. Slower, yes, but safer."

"How am I still alive?" I asked, feeling small. All the aches and pains made sense now. The memory of blood seeping over my vision hadn't been just a dream. And the hot burn in my guts had been a near fatal stomach wound that their witch must have disinfected and healed as I felt no fog of septic blood running through my veins. My spine throbbed as though it had been rung out like a sponge and left to slowly flop back into shape. On my own, I'd have been dead. None of my spells were strong enough to heal that sort of damage. Not even my forbidden spell. I owed Liam and his witch a lot. What would they demand in return?

Back in the small room I'd been given, the bedding was changed to more than just a simple sheet, now it was a heap of pillows and soft looking comforters. There was a tray of food on the top of the dresser. My stomach churned. I was starving, but nauseous. Never a good combination.

"I suspect your resilience has a lot to do with your upbringing. The Volkov is not known to be an easy man, though his affection for his children is legendary." Liam set me carefully into the chair.

"I'm not really his," I reminded Liam.

"Does that mean he was less strict? Perhaps let you get away with more than the pack?"

I laughed lightly. "Hell no. I got a D on a math test once and he flipped. Made Oberon tutor me the whole semester." Oberon was *Apa*'s second. He ran the pack more than *Apa* did. Oberon was smart. If Oberon wanted to find you, he could hack into those new traffic cameras everywhere until he found you like some villain in a superhero movie. I'd been worried about him for a while. Had thought we were friends. But even Oberon wouldn't be able to defy the Volkov. Only there had been no sign of Oberon. I had also avoided modern technology like the plague.

"I heard Oberon invested your allowance." Liam pulled a small tray out from beside the dresser, popped it open to reveal a table of sort, and set the food on it. "Eat."

I stared at the plate. Heaping with eggs, bacon, sausage, and biscuits, it looked amazing. There was a separate plate filled with fresh berries, a glass of milk and a second of orange juice. I couldn't have eaten it all if I had been feeling well and starved two days. But I picked up the fork and willed my stomach to ease.

"He did," I told Liam about Oberon. "Turned my weekly five-dollar allowance into ten thousand before I turned sixteen." That money had been what I'd used to buy the camper and start my own little tea shop when I dropped out of school. I wondered if *Apa* had been angry with Oberon for helping me gain freedom. Oberon had become a little scarcer around then, but I'd also begun dating Felix at the same time.

Liam opened the top drawer of the dresser, pulling out clothes, sweats and a t-shirt. Standard werewolf one-size fits all clothes. He pulled them on, then opened the second drawer to find a brush and a comb. He glanced my way and appeared to notice I hadn't touched the food.

"Eat," Liam said again. This time there was some force behind his word. If I'd have been a wolf I'd have had to listen to his command. Even not being a wolf I felt the power thrum through me.

"Little nauseous," I said, offering the only excuse I had for the picking.

He stared at me for a minute with a frown, set the brush down and reached for my hand, again pressing some sort of nerve point that eased my stomach. I studied the placement of his fingers this time, and rubbed my hand when he let go. He picked up the brush again and went to work on my hair.

It was probably a snarled mess from the fight and two weeks without stopping much anywhere for more than a day or too.

"I should cut it," I said into my fork, shoveling the eggs into my mouth to enjoy the food before the nausea rose again. My hair would be easier to take care of if I cropped it short like most men.

"Don't," Liam said quietly, but again with that alpha force that tingled through my veins.

"I don't even know you," I told him. He didn't get to have a say on my hair. I let him help because I was too weak to do otherwise. But as soon as I was better I'd go. He couldn't keep me here. I couldn't stay here no matter how much I might want to.

"I'm Liam Ulrich, Alpha of the Northern Cascades pack."

"That's a pretty big area."

He shrugged.

I broke apart one of the biscuits, thrilled when I discovered a tiny bottle of fresh honey next to the juice. I slathered it on the biscuit and took a bite. It wasn't store bought. The biscuit or the honey. I knew homemade when I tasted it. Had spent years perfecting my own technique.

"I'm glad you like my cooking," Liam said. He efficiently detangled my hair and wove it into a simple braid.

I swallowed. "One of your pack didn't make this?" Normally alpha's didn't do mundane things like cooking, or cleaning. He was the manager of the bakery, which made sense since alpha's almost always owned a couple businesses in their territory. Packs were expensive to support. Often they owned a dozen businesses and employed pack to work in them. It was a win-win over all. The Volkov owned businesses all over the world. Oberon had grown the empire large enough that a lot of the Volkov wolves didn't have to work. The other wolves in the pack or a spouse managed the home for an alpha including cooking and cleaning. I'd always thought it was a sort of class separation, but it more likely had to do with time management, as alphas were always being called upon to help someone in the pack.

"I enjoy cooking," Liam said.

"I suppose you like showering with *witchborn*, too?" It was a taunt. Alpha's didn't do the lowly things in the pack. And I wasn't even pack. If he thought taking care of me was going to get him something, he was sorely mistaken. Prodding him was a bit like poking a bear with a stick. If he lashed out at least I could see beyond whatever game he was playing.

"I take care of all that are mine."

"I'm not yours," I said. "You are not my Alpha."

He was silent for a long minute, like he was debating what to say. "You're in my territory. That makes you mine until you heal and decide to move on," he said very matter of fact. Stupid alphas were always making demands and statements of power. He didn't get how much danger having me in his pack was.

"I shouldn't stay." Not even for another hour, but couldn't help that my voice sounded uncertain even to me.

"I don't think you'll be going anywhere soon." He finished the braid and put the brush away. "Eat. Then I'll help you back to bed."

"I can get back to bed on my own."

"Hmm."

I growled at him. He was so annoying.

He reached into a drawer and pulled out a T-shirt. He rolled up the shirt until he had the hole in the neck open wide and put it over my head. I had to put the fork down, and shoved my arms through the sleeves. The shirt was huge. I was sure it would fall past my hips if I stood up.

"No sweats. I sent Dylan out to find something for you to wear. None of my wolves are close to your size." Liam's eyes flicked to my mismatched, overly worn mass of clothes. "We washed those, but they are coming apart."

"They're fine," I protested. They were all I had. I already owed this man a lot for his help, the use of his witch, which I knew wasn't free, and protection while I was in his territory. Racking up a debt to him just meant more damage he could justify doing down the road. The fae were known to enslave anyone who owed them a debt. I'd seen an alpha do it a time or ten as well.

Liam squatted down to tug the shirt over my hips and steal away the towel. "Eat, then bed. That concussion isn't going to heal without rest. Your pupils are still huge. Can you see okay?"

"It's fine." Though my vision was a little blurry at the edges. I sighed, because he was right. And now that I knew about the stitches, I could feel them itchy and tight in my skin. I finished most of the eggs, the fruit, and all the juice. Was a little sad that I hadn't been brought coffee, but since I had a concussion that made sense as the caffeine could cause more damage as I was healing. It was the first time in almost a year I missed my collection of alchemy books. There had been a large mix of science and magic in those volumes. Probably something safe I could have used to speed my healing. I could take energy from the land, but hated to tax it that way when humanity was already such a parasite. But maybe there were other options I hadn't yet discovered. Not that I really had the time to sit around and read. Felix would come for me soon.

Liam took the tray away, and I hobbled toward the bed. He was back before I could get two steps closer to it, lifting me, and wordlessly setting me carefully on the bed. He shoved the blankets aside, pulling them over my legs, then smoothing them into place. "Rest. One of my wolves will be outside the door. Just call if you need something."

"Did you find the wolves?" I asked him before he could leave. "The ones that tried to kill me?" Were they sent by Felix? That thought instilled a fear in me I hadn't realized was still possible after all this time. Maybe they'd been hired by Hugo, the vampire from Chicago. Wolves sometimes worked for vampires or even fae if their alpha wasn't strong enough to provide for them. I'd met a lot of weak alpha's as I'd run across the country. Did *Apa* know just how many packs were struggling due to bad leadership? Being the most dominant did not mean being the smartest.

"No," Liam said after a quiet minute. "But we're still looking. Rest. You're safe here."

It wasn't a lie. I could tell if most anyone was lying. He believed what he said. If only I could believe it too.

CHAPTER 5

The sheets must have been spritzed with lavender, which was why I'd fallen asleep hard. When I'd lived in the Volkov pack I'd had a small camping trailer parked on the Volkov's land, surrounded with lavender, chamomile, and lemon balm. All things I'd planted and worked hard to maintain. In the cooler months I'd left the windows open so the scent would permeate the air with tranquility. It even worked on the wolves as the handful who trusted me enough to come to me for minor alchemy needs always seemed soothed by the scent.

At sixteen I'd barely survived the tension of living in the Volkov's home and was tired of the constant bickering his pack had over me. *Apa* had given me the little plot of land, expecting it to keep me distracted with my gardening and alchemy. I'd purchased the camper instead, and parked it on the land to live away from the trouble. He said nothing when I moved out. He'd been unhappy when a year later I'd decided to drop out of school and test for my GED. I was already making a modest living by then. I'd grown and sold my own tea and pastries for a few years. Creating blends of tea that *Apa* claimed could calm the most agitated wolf. Not that I'd ever gotten close to one of his rescues before he subdued them. I didn't have a death wish.

Apa would often stop by for tea, leave with packages of baked goods, and encourage me to continue my exploration of alchemy and herbalism. Many of the massive collection of books I had were given to me by him. Things found by a friend on a trip and sent to him or something he acquired while visiting another pack. I'd never thought it odd at the time that he just happened to find alchemy books in a world were science had become the rule to explain the unexplained. Only now, when I traveled from place to place, did I realize he must have sought out those books, because I found none anywhere. My library of books crammed into the tiny space of my home between the hundreds of tea canisters was something I missed every day.

I must have been dreaming of home because I awoke to the sound of light humming, thinking for a minute I was back in my camper bed, surrounded by lavender fields. *Apa* had sometimes done that. Escaped to my house, sitting and singing softly while I napped or worked on some concoction. My silence never seemed to bother him. Maybe my presence helped him like it did the other old wolves, soothing his beast.

The Volkov was old. Legend to be the oldest of all werewolves. There were no omegas in his pack other than me. The time he spent in my camper had become a hot button issue among his pack. They whispered about him being inaccessible and doting on a non-wolf. Shirking his responsibilities, I recalled overhearing once. None dared to say it to his face.

When *Apa* sang it was often sad old songs. Some in Russian, some in Swedish or Italian. I knew he spoke dozens of languages. Not all of the emotion could have been inflection of the languages. I didn't speak any of them to know if they were really sad songs, or if it was just something heavy in his heart. I'd been too afraid to ask.

In the dream, *Apa* sat on the edge of the couch which folded down into my bed. There wasn't really any place else to sit. Just the futon. I stood at the counter preparing tea. It was a lavender blend with hints of orange and mint, *Apa*'s favorite blend. He'd have run out soon after I left, though there was more in my camper.

"Only no one can get into your camper," *Apa* reminded me, though he didn't take a break in his song. "Had to tear up the ground just to get it to move."

The comment confused me. Why would my trailer need to move? The ward had been *Apa*'s suggestion when I moved out of his home. Protection against anyone who attacked his pack, or from the pack itself, though he'd never suggested as much.

"I would never have let the pack harm you," *Apa* protested.

Only he had. Felix.

I wasn't sure if the pain I felt from that reminder was his or mine. The singing went on and I continued to mix the tea, reciting the recipe from memory. It was a delicate balance. Too much orange would over power the lavender, and mint was such a strong herb that it had to be prepared just the right way. I felt *Apa* at my back. He'd sat there so often it should have been familiar. In a dream, the position shouldn't have bothered me at all, only it did. His presence made me uneasy, and I had to keep looking back at him, though he hadn't moved at all.

I could feel the sadness radiating from him, which made me more determined to finish the tea. I never seemed to have the right amount of ingredients.

That was how I knew it was a dream. Frustration. The

song a happy one, instead of *Apa's* woeful sadness. And the singing voice was female. Which was odd, as female werewolves were few.

I had to struggle to pull myself to consciousness. My brain clinging to the dream and sleep. My grogginess was likely due in part to the healing concussion, and part to the lavender. Odd how it smelled like the English lavender I'd grown. It was a common enough plant, rather than the rare red Spanish lavender I'd experimented with, but it was also the most potent. This didn't have the underlying scent of chemicals like most of the stuff mass produced for public consumption. If I didn't know better, I'd have said it came from my garden back home, which just added to the vivid dream.

I opened my eyes and there was a young girl sitting in the chair, which had been pulled up beside the bed. She was maybe fourteen or fifteen, with a dark batch of curls cropped short on her head and narrow, dark-rimmed, glasses framing her blue eyes. She wore jeans and a sweatshirt with a cat pictured on it. The shirt said "Cat's rule, Dog's drool." She sat with one foot tucked beneath her, the other swinging in the large chair, and played a game on her phone.

She looked my way and smiled. "Hello. Are you hungry? Dad said I was supposed to call for food if you're hungry." Dad? She didn't smell of werewolf. Not that a child as young as her would have survived the transition. And most wolves didn't tell their families what they were unless they were wolves themselves. I frowned at her trying to make sense of her presence.

"There are clothes for you there." She pointed to the nightstand beside the bed. A stack of clothes sat neatly folded. "But dad says you're supposed to eat first and he'll help you dress. He also said you're supposed to be careful of your stitches. He doesn't want you to break them."

"Who's dad?" I asked, pushing myself up, and careful to cover myself with the blankets as I was still only wearing the T-shirt.

She glanced at me. "Liam? Big, bad, alpha werewolf who is as beautiful as a movie star? My friends all talk about how handsome he is, so it's not just daddy worship. I know you've met him. He's been really growly about you. He gets that way when he takes a new wolf into his pack. Says it's an alpha thing. But he's growly about me too, all the time." She gave me a wide smile. "I'm Korissa."

Liam's daughter. Of course he was married. Probably had a half dozen kids. I knew he wasn't as young as he looked. I sighed, fantasy bubble bursting into shards of emotional glass. "I'm not a wolf."

"Nope. Me neither. But hey, we've all got troubles." Her smile was infectious. "I don't think I could be a werewolf. They're kind of assholes."

I agreed. "Your dad let you talk that way?"

She gave me a flash of teeth that I knew she'd learned from the wolves, like daring me to tell him. "As long as I keep my grades up, he mostly leaves me alone."

Mostly. I wondered what that mostly entailed. "I'm Sebastian," I gave her my name. Had Liam put her on guard because he knew I'd be less likely to bolt out of here when confronted with a child? Alphas were manipulative bastards, and I didn't think this one was any different.

"I am a little hungry," I acknowledged, planning to head into the bathroom when she got up.

She nodded and hopped out of the chair like her legs were springs. "Let me shout out for food."

I frowned at her, pulled the shirt down as far as I could, thinking her father probably wouldn't want a girl her age seeing a man naked, and slinked out of bed and into the bathroom. I closed the door behind me, irritated that it had no lock, but thankful I wasn't quite so dizzy. I even got to pee all by myself. I washed my hands and stared in the mirror. A lot of the bruising had faded, but half of my face was still splotched with gold, green, and purple blotches. I examined my scalp, having to lean over the counter to get close enough. I looked for anything that proved the wolf had nailed me with his claws, but there were no scars or even healing scratches, just bruises.

The door opened, and I froze, glancing in the mirror to see who was coming in. It wasn't Korissa, for which I was thankful because leaning over the counter caused the shirt to ride up a bit, probably giving an inappropriate view of my dangly bits from the back and maybe even a butt cheek. It was Liam. He had the stack of clothes in his hands, stepped into the bathroom and shut the door. He barely looked at me, just waited.

"I can dress myself."

"Hmm."

I wanted to smack him for that sound. It wasn't dismissive, but just one notch above a grunt of acknowledgment. "Not fair sending the kid. Her mom will be pissed you had her sitting next to a naked man's bed."

"You weren't naked, and her mother lives in southern Florida. Korissa sees her twice a year. They don't get along well as Elaine only cares for money, status, and the next boy toy she can manipulate. Korissa has been around werewolves her whole life. She's seen a naked man or two and doesn't care. I don't care as long as none of those men, werewolf or otherwise, disrespect her." He finally looked at me, eyes roving over me in a nonchalant, assessing way that I almost took for indifference, but his gaze lingered on my backside, which I knew was still covered but only barely.

I stepped away from the counter and tugged the shirt back down. "Can I get dressed?" I reached for the clothes. He gripped them tighter for a minute before finally stretching them out to me. "You're not as subtle as you think, you know," I told him. "You need to be careful around your wolves. Wolves hate us queers. You're just asking to be challenged." I was baiting him, almost begging him to attack, so I had a reason to run. It was stupid. There was no way I'd get by him, out of the bathroom, out of the locked room and out of whatever stronghold he'd created for his family and his wolves. Other wolves would linger around his house even if he hadn't been harboring a stranger. Likely, because I was there, half the pack would be on rounds to protect their territory and their alpha. But I needed justification to run. He'd been nice to me, which made me distrustful, and indebted to him all at once. Fucking Felix.

Instead of attacking, Liam looked amused. "Queers?" The word sounded odd coming from him. Like it wasn't something he ever said.

I took the stack of clothes from him, shuffled through them, thankful they'd brought me underwear and tugged them on while carefully keeping the T-shirt as low as possible. "Men who like men for fucking. Pansies? Faggots? Pillow biters? I'm sure you've heard of us. Where are you from anyway?" I was sort of getting the impression he wasn't American borne, but what did I know? People accused me of not being American all the time because my skin was brown. My mother was a beautiful, caramel skinned, black women from New Orleans. Like Korissa's mother apparently was, my mother also had little interest in raising a child. I don't know why she'd had me at all. She'd visited sometimes for holidays. Always bringing me small gifts that she liked more than anything I ever found useful. She made up stories sometimes about my father, or her family. I wasn't sure if any of it were true. But as a child I'd clung to those stories. Until I realized just how different from the wolves I really was.

"Pillow biters," Liam said, highly amused.

"I think that's English, but am not sure. I was never much for school. Got my GED instead of graduating. Never went to college." Just studied on my own.

"Yet your alchemy skills are whispered about across the globe," Liam said, shutting me up. People talked about me? My skills? Not just the unwanted *witchborn* the Volkov had been saddled with? "Don't put the pants on yet," he told me, stopping me as I dug out the pair of soft sweats he'd provided. "I want to look at your stitches."

"You have medical training?" I asked him. Again, unlikely. Most of them didn't really need medical help anyway as their hyperactive metabolism would heal just about anything shy of decapitation.

"A little," Liam said. "Mostly military and books as refreshers since." He crossed the room, then put the toilet lid down and waved his hand toward it. "Sit."

I narrowed my eyes at him, but did as asked. Part of the stitches were under the cloth I'd just pulled on, but not much. Who'd decided to get the stranger a pair of bikini briefs? Not the second, for sure, and not the daughter. Liam nudged me to turn my hip up toward him, his hand going so far as to cup my ass so he could view the stitches under the light of the bathroom mirror. I had to work to think about non-sexy things, like dying of a concussion, or waking to find little girls in my room, rather than having an incredibly attractive Alpha werewolf kneeling beside me and touching my ass.

His poking at the stitches hurt a little.

"I thought you said you had training?" I complained.

"They aren't ready to come out yet. At the bottom edge of the wound, the wolf's claw dug into your muscle. That part is healing slower than the rest. You shouldn't be walking around on it. There's no infection, which is good, just a tightness of the muscles. If you run on them now they will tear and reopen the entire wound. If you had a werewolf's metabolism you'd already be healed."

"Sorry, I'm not a werewolf." I felt like I'd been apologizing my whole life for not fitting in their exclusive little club.

"I meant that it needs more time to heal."

"You just want to keep me here. What are you waiting for? Is Felix on the way to pay you for keeping me in one place?"

He set me down, then leaned forward to tug the socks he'd brought onto my feet. "He knows you're here."

I stiffened and felt my heart begin to race in immediate terror. The leviathan perked up again, preparing to strike as the weight of anxiety began to settle into my chest. Liam threaded my feet through the bottom of the pants and tugged them up to my knees. He wrapped an arm around my waist and hauled me to my feet with almost no effort, then pulled up the pants. He had to smell my terror, feel me tremble. Hell, he could probably hear my heart racing.

In his arms, the panic attack didn't come. Rather it teetered on the edge, almost there, just not quite strong enough to take control.

"He won't enter my territory. You're safe here," he said quietly, not letting me go. His breath brushed my ear. I had an urge to throw myself into his arms and beg for his protection.

"I'm not safe anywhere." It had become the truth of my existence. The reason I ran. I thought that *Apa* would protect me. He was the strongest werewolf, maybe in the whole world. And yet he couldn't stop Felix. If the Volkov couldn't stop him, no one could.

"You don't believe I can protect you."

"I don't need anyone's protection." Couldn't trust anyone but me.

Liam sighed. "Felix has asked for entry into my territory. He says he wants to talk to you. Just talk. Do you want to speak to him? I can arrange a supervised meeting."

"No." Absolutely not. If I spoke to him, I might cave. I might forgive him and go back. There was no other horror in my head worse than returning to be the little fox hidden away and despised. *Raped and beaten for disobedience.*

Liam nodded, but didn't let me go. He was breathing heavily. Something had bothered him. But he was strong enough to be an unmovable wall against me. I couldn't tell if he was aroused or annoyed, though I'd probably have smelled his arousal. Finally, he let me go, and I almost whined when his body heat left me. He picked up the edges of the T-shirt I was wearing, and pulled it unceremoniously off over my head. I waited for him to give me the other shirt or attempt to dress me again, but he just stared again at my tattoos, and my bare chest.

"You're too thin," he said after a minute. "You need to eat. I can count all your ribs."

His words hit me like a fist in the gut. Of course he wouldn't want me. Once again I was basking in delusions. No one really wanted me. I wasn't beautiful or desirable. I was a possession. They just wanted to control me. I had to remember that.

"I should go," I said, snatching the clean shirt from him and scrambling into it. My back still ached but a lot of the bruising had eased. The sleep and food had recharged my own magic enough to help with the healing. Tomorrow, wherever I was, I'd be cutting the stitches out myself and back on the road. If I could spend some time in contact with the earth I could speed the healing, but first, I had to find a place safe enough to rest.

"Come eat. It's lunchtime," he said, finally stepping away and heading toward the bathroom door. He left the door open, and when I followed, I was surprised to see the bedroom door open, too. There was a dining room and kitchen connected as one giant room outside the small bedroom they'd given me. Korissa was cooking bacon. It smelled amazing. She had a heaping plate full of the crispy slices and was adding to the pile. There was also fresh baked bread, toasted with a bit of butter, bright red tomatoes, crisp lettuce, and a jar each of what appeared to be homemade mayonnaise and mustard. I practically salivated, but stayed behind Liam.

At the huge dining table sat Carl, Dylan, and at least a dozen other wolves I didn't know. All eyes were on me. "He doesn't look like much," one young-looking wolf said. "They whisper about him like he's some sort of demon, mystical and elusive, but I could take him."

Liam glanced in his direction and the wolf cowered. "Sorry, Alpha."

"Sebastian Volkov," Dylan said. "Welcome to the Northern Cascades pack. Don't mind Marlow. He's never been tactful. I'm sure you'll find your time with our pack enlightening, even if it isn't always restful."

"I'm not staying," I said. Liam put an empty plate in my hands, added four pieces of toasted bread to it and nudged me toward Korissa. I picked up the jar of mustard, sniffed it then set it down to scoop it onto the bread. I'd never been a mayonnaise fan. I added lettuce, tomato and a bit of bacon, not wanting to be a pig even though I already had two sandwiches on my plate. Liam added more bacon to my sandwiches until they were a heaping stack I would have to take apart to fit in my mouth.

"You're pushy," I grumbled at him as he added a handful of raw, sliced veggies to my plate.

Korissa laughed and nudged me. "I'm told that's a normal

thing for an Alpha, but I'm glad it's not just me he's pushy with."

I took my plate to the table, sitting as far away from the rest of the pack as I could. One of the female wolves got up and started to bring trays to the table, the bread, the bacon, and the fixings. It was odd that Liam had wanted me to eat first since I wasn't pack.

Korissa sat next to me. Her grin huge. "Bacon is the only thing I do well. Dad had already started, but I'm good at bacon." She snagged a couple slices of bread and began to build a sandwich almost twice the size of my own. "I can mix bread okay, and make cookies, but dad is the better chef."

I took a bite of my sandwich as everyone else filled their plates. Liam sat on the other side of me. The bread was fantastic. Sourdough. Crispy on the outside and heavenly soft on the inside. The bacon was salty and crunchy with none of those annoying undercooked bits that got too chewy. The mustard was a pop of fresh herbs. I couldn't help the little happy noises I made. How long had it been since I'd had something this good? Probably since before I left home.

Texas was hog country. Farms and wild hogs abound. We'd always had bacon, though I didn't often cook it myself. My *Apa* had liked to cook, but rarely did so. Not that I'd been allowed to come to his home on the rare occasion he cooked. It was easier for him to come to my home than me to his. His family hated me. Hated that he'd taken me in. I guess they thought he should have just killed the child who'd been left on his doorstep, never mind the fact that the child had only been a few months old and unable to stay in one shape for long. By six months old I could shift to a fox and back with breathless ease. There was no pain, not like wolves.

I didn't die to become what I was. Just born that way. A lot of wolves hated me for that fact alone. The food was a reminder of home, though the fixings were a sight better than they had been back then. The bread alone was worth moaning over.

"I'm glad you like my cooking," Liam said.

"Liam is an amazing cook," Dylan said. "We all take turns now, but everyone comes over when he cooks."

"So you're all here for the food, not me, right?" I asked, knowing the truth.

None of them would look at me or Liam. Liam ate his own sandwich as if he didn't care.

"It's different," one of the women said. There were two female werewolves at the table. A lot for a small pack like Liam's if this were all his wolves. "The whole pack feels different…"

"He's a witch. Not a wolf," Carl said.

"And yet my wolf is calm as a lamb while I sit two feet from a stranger," said an older male wolf with a well-trimmed white beard. He looked a little like a thirty-something, healthy Santa Claus. I got the feeling he was a dominant wolf. "They never said the *witchchild* was an omega. None of the stories. No one speaks of it."

I gripped my sandwich tighter. Most wolves thought omega meant weak. Submissive. Bottom of the pack. Only omegas weren't submissive at all. They were other. Neither dominant nor submissive. They could meet alpha eyes and disobey orders, but longed to please, serve, and care for others. Omegas also settled a pack. All the aggression inherent to werewolves escalated until fights ensued unless there was an omega to balance the pack. There were only a handful of omegas in the world. Only two were wolves, though I'd heard it was fairly common for an alpha to marry a human omega to help keep his pack in check.

I hadn't known what it meant at all for most of my years. Until *Apa* had told me the real reason he'd let me stay with Felix as long as he had. I kept Felix calm. The older the wolf, the more unsettled it became, the more violence it craved. The human half battled the wolf for control. I could understand as many lived centuries, learning to love family, children, and friends only to watch them all die weakened by the human side. It wasn't only a disease of the wolves. It happened to vampires, which made them such lethal, heartless bastards, and of course the fae who thought humans were little more than toys. Omegas could calm wolves, but I was pretty sure it didn't work on vampires or fae.

The Volkov was an old wolf. He'd had hundreds of children, with only a handful surviving the change, and even less still alive today. Female werewolves couldn't have kids. The change was too violent, but males mated just fine with humans. The Volkov had his share of wives and probably mistresses over the years.

I knew Felix was old. Not as old as the Volkov, but centuries past most wolves' expiration date. Felix never spoke of his past wives, though I'd heard from around the pack that there had been many. But he could recite the names of every child he'd ever lost. Dozens. I could see now how those had built up to bring the madness on him.

Only an insane wolf would attack an omega, and in the end, Felix had, more than once. Felix' sanity had been flipping for years. Xander Volkov had tried to save his son's life. It would have been noble if I had not been the one to suffer. It had been a dream in the beginning. Felix had doted on me, romanced me and taught me lust. For a while I truly believed he loved me, and I returned his love. We spent three years together before that first night when Felix had accused me of flirting with another wolf.

The wolf had come to my trailer for tea and something to help his human mate sleep as she was pregnant. There had been no flirting. Felix had simply smelled another wolf in my house, the home he insisted I keep separate from his own, and attacked me. He'd beaten me with his fists until I blacked out, and it was the beginning of the end. But Felix's unraveling was not my fault. I'd spent a year convincing myself it was not my fault.

Being an omega wasn't a magical cure-all for crazy. It wasn't even a real power. More a presence, like an alpha had presence. I couldn't command a person to be calm, though sometimes just being in the room with them would ease their nerves. An alpha could force their will on another. I could only suggest a change in thought. It wasn't enough to stop Felix, and maybe that was why I felt he was a little more than justified in the attack that had driven me to run. He'd needed my help and I'd failed him. A tiny voice inside my head whispered that I deserved what had happened.

"And no one will continue to speak of it," Liam said tightly.

"Other packs will try to take him from us. Maybe that's why the other wolves attacked him," Santa Claus said again. "Should have killed them all. Wolves who attack an omega are all mad. I couldn't imagine fighting through this calm to chase him down and bleed him. I haven't felt this calm since long before I was changed."

"Me neither," Dylan agreed. "Not in over two hundred years. And I'm across the room." He didn't look that old. He looked like an early twenty-something cowboy. But maybe that was just when he'd been changed. Most wolves stopped aging when they changed. Some of the powerful wolves could reverse aging, which was why the Volkov looked twenty-five when he was probably a thousand or something. If Dylan was over two hundred, how old did that make Liam?

I glared at Santa Claus and Dylan. Talking about me like I wasn't there. I wasn't weak. I didn't need protection. I wasn't just a tool to be used to control their wolves. "I'll be leaving soon," I told them. "There is no need to put your pack in danger." Maybe appealing to Liam's need to protect his pack would gain me easier freedom. I didn't want to be fighting my way out of his territory, and somehow I figured he'd be watching me closely, waiting for me to run. It made me mad. "I don't *belong* to anyone."

Liam nodded like he agreed, but he said, "I have offered you sanctuary. I ask nothing except that you heal, and that you tell me before you go."

I narrowed my eyes at him.

"If you decide to stay," he continued, like he couldn't feel my glare. "There is work for you. I have a number of businesses for you to choose from. And you don't have to stay in the pack house."

That comment brought an uproar of protest from the wolves.

"You can't let him just wander around the territory. It's asking to be attacked."

"He's safest at the pack house."

"It's better if he returns to the Volkov."

"An omega would help the pack grow, but only if he's near you, Alpha."

"Enough," Liam said, his voice quiet but firm and echoing with power over the room that silenced everyone. His eyes had gone yellow. They weren't truly different in color; it was more a fluorescent glow that said his wolf was just below the surface. He didn't seem to be having trouble holding his wolf back. More likely it was a display of his power since normal wolves couldn't change just one part of themselves at a time, and once triggered, most couldn't stop a change. "I am Alpha. Do any of you seek to challenge me?"

He was offering himself up over me? I shook my head. This was so stupid. All this wolf politics shit. I tried to get up but Liam put a firm hand on my knee, fingers close to my stitches, adding just enough pressure to hurt without damaging anything.

None of the wolves would meet Liam's eyes, and no one stepped up to challenge him. "As I was saying." He turned back to me, his hand loosening, but not leaving my leg. "There is no need for you to stay in the pack house, though you are welcome to, if you wish. The Volkov knows you're here and does not demand that you be removed from my territory. He was clear in stating that the *witchchild* is free to travel wherever he wishes un-accosted."

That shocked me. Since when had *Apa* made such a decree? And why? It was the equivalent of giving me diplomatic immunity no matter where I went. It sounded too good to be true.

"Our rules are much like other packs, respect is earned, but we support everyone within the pack," Liam said. "I take care of all my wolves."

I wanted to remind him again that I wasn't a wolf, but Korissa jumped in, "You'll have to take turns cooking too. The whole pack takes turns. Can you cook?"

"I'm more of a baker," I said, too distracted by all my thoughts to really realize what I was saying. "Made world famous scones, coffee cakes, and brownies." Then there was the tea. I'd run out of my own blend ages ago, and had been unable to find the right ingredients to make more.

The wolf vanished from Liam's eyes. He smiled and it was like someone had turned the sun on, his dimples in full force. "Excellent. I need a full time pastry chef."

"I'm not certified. No degrees or anything."

"Let me worry about that. If you're well enough I'll take you to the bakery tomorrow."

A job meant I'd be staying. I didn't want to stay. But I sort of did. I needed money. So maybe I'd stay a few days if Liam could keep Felix at bay. Just a few days. Any more would put the whole pack in danger. Already someone tried to kill me. It was unlikely that the incident had just been an accident. They'd come looking for me. How they'd tracked me this far, I wasn't sure. But running today wasn't going to get me far.

"Finish eating," Liam instructed everyone, then to me he said, "Korissa will show you up to your new room. There's no need for you to be in the safe room anymore." He looked over at his wolves. "The pack and I will be having a meeting." And that sounded ominous enough that once again I was glad I wasn't a wolf. He gave me a small smile. "We meet every Sunday afternoon."

"Right, so you won't be giving them all sorts of instructions about me?" Somehow I doubted that.

"You will be a large part of the discussion. The other part of the discussion will be manners." His pretty blue eyes trailed over the group. No one tried to meet his gaze. "A refresher might be called for, though I really plan on discussing the wolves who attacked you. Perhaps someone will recognize something about them. There was nothing about them that was familiar to you?"

I shrugged. "A wolf looks like a wolf to me." In reality I'd been too busy running for my life to notice much other than the teeth and razor sharp claws. My flight instinct worked really well.

Liam's hand slid off my leg in an almost noticeable caress. "I'll leave you to Korissa then. She'll show you around the house." He got up from his chair and so did everyone but Korissa and I. Once they'd all left the room I could feel the tension ease out of my shoulders.

Korissa gathered up her plate, mood still light and bright. "They're a handful, but you get used to the intensity after a while."

Intensity. Wow. Understatement of the year.

CHAPTER 6

Korissa let me gather up my stuff and take it upstairs. Just as I'd suspected, the house was huge with at least six bedrooms upstairs, each with their own baths. It was far beyond the remodeled tiny camper in which I had lived for years. Though *Apa's* home was almost twice the size as Liam's.

"There's a bunk house outside about a five minute walk away. Sleeps twenty. Mostly the guys only ever stay and sometimes they get rowdy so that's why it's not right outside. None of them actually live there right now, but sometimes if a new wolf joins the pack they live out there until they are stable enough to find a place of their own. Usually it's just a revolving door of members of dad's guards."

"How many wolves does your father have?" I asked her as she opened the door to a bright room decorated in green. This room had two huge windows, one on each of the outer walls, which looked out to trees and the giant backyard. There were no other houses to be seen anywhere from the room. Likely Liam owned several acres with which his wolves could run. The view was pretty, trees and in the distance, mountains, and lots of light.

"Almost fifty, I think," Korissa said. "I know most of them, though some only by first name. The ones at the table tonight were his most dominant wolves."

That surprised me. "The women?" Werewolves treated women about the same as they treated omegas, like they were helpless, worthless, and existed only to be protected.

"Leigh and Stacey? Yeah. They are dominant wolves. Dad doesn't put up with the whole girls aren't as good as boys." Korissa entered the room and went to the windows, sliding open the glass to let fresh air rush in through the screen. "Dad wanted you in this room because it's a long drop to the ground and there's nothing to climb down or up. I told him you wouldn't just leave without telling him. 'Cause that's rude."

Damn alphas and their manipulative children.

"But I like this room a lot. It's away from the noise of the rest of the house, close to the stairs so if you need some air the back door is right there. Dad is down the hall. He wanted you closer to him." She turned to look at me, something in her gaze that made her look older than her young years.

"It's just instinct," I comforted her. She probably didn't like the idea of her dad fawning on some guy. "Alphas have an inherent need to protect omegas, though it's rare they ever even meet one. Apparently the world kills us fairly quickly." Most omegas died in childhood from illnesses or unusual accidents. It was like the universe didn't want there to be enough omegas to allow wolves the strength to grow their packs large enough to rival human reproduction.

"I don't mind," Korissa said. "Mom never treated him nice. You've been very nice to my dad even when he's growly. I haven't seen him smile this much in ages. Not since he took over the pack. When you arrived it was like Christmas. He was excited and relaxed all at once." She shook her head as if thinking back. "It's kind of weird how happy he is. Like he's been waiting for this."

"I'm not interested in your father." I was lying even to myself at that moment. In reality, a man like Liam could never be interested in me. Not legitimately. He was power, wisdom, wealth, and culture. I was just a piece of trash that blew around in the wind.

"You could do worse."

"He can do better. He's an alpha. alphas don't date men."

"Dylan has a boyfriend. He might not be alpha of the pack, but he's pretty dominant. He is third in the pack."

That surprised me. I'd never heard of a gay wolf. Even Felix was bi instead of gay. He was careful to keep me away from the pack after we'd started dating. *Apa* had never mentioned it. Most packs were made up of chest-beating dominant male wolves. Gay was considered weak to them. An abomination for some of the oldest of wolves. Which was just another sin to add to my door, keeping me separated from *Apa's* pack. I wasn't sure what to make of Korissa's statement, so I left it alone.

I stepped up to the window beside her and looked out. It was a long drop. Not that I'd ever been the sort to climb out of windows. There were trees and in the distance water of some sort, maybe a river. Standing there, with the wind blowing on me I could smell lavender. Maybe my sheets hadn't been spritzed with it so much as they'd come from a room with open windows. I closed my eyes and sucked in the scent.

"Where are we?" I asked, opening my eyes to look at her. I still had no idea. There was an island off the coast of Washington that was known for lavender, but I couldn't image how I'd have gotten there.

"Maple Falls. We're not all that close to the lake, but we can hike to it sometime. It's beautiful."

"Washington?"

She gave me an odd look. "Yes."

I needed to look at a map. Other than the mountains which I vaguely knew the placement of, I had no idea where the town was. Close to the Canadian border perhaps?

A gust of wind blew the strong scent of lavender through the room. The need that coursed through me was almost painful. An ache for home. That too was an omega trait. Home was an instinct to an omega the same way violence was to an alpha. Not since I'd left *Apa's* ranch had I felt the pull so strongly.

"Can I go outside? Or am I on house arrest?"

"I can take you outside. Dad took the wolves to the bunkhouse for a meeting. I think he's just being picky about who he lets around you right now. 'Cause you were hurt."

More likely because I was omega and *witchborn* rather than because I was hurt. "It didn't sound like some of his wolves want me here."

"Pretty sure that's my dad's decision, not theirs. Sometimes they argue about me too. Stupid things, like I shouldn't know about them. Or it's dangerous for me."

I agreed on the last part. "I don't want you to get in trouble."

"Why would I get in trouble?"

Because she was taking the omega outside when everyone seemed to want me under lock and key. Likely she was too young to know a lot about wolf politics. It wasn't my job to get her up to speed.

She turned toward the door. "Is there something you want to do? There are benches back there. Closer to the bunkhouse there's a pergola and some lounge chairs. It's a walk to the lake, and I don't think you should go that far.

Dad said you shouldn't put too much pressure on your healing leg."

"Lavender," I said. She probably had no idea what it looked or even smelled like. "I smell lavender." I wouldn't have time to dry it and create tea from it, but I longed to hold it in my hands again.

"Purple flowers, right?" She grinned. "There was a huge mess of that when we moved in. Like someone once had a garden and just let it overgrow. Dad has just left it alone. Sometimes I trim them and bring them in the house."

I followed her out of the room and down the stairs. The house was empty and eerily quiet. "How long have you guys been here?"

"Almost a year," Korissa answered as she held the back-door open for me. "We moved up from Seattle."

"That's a big change for you," I remarked as we stepped into the backyard.

"I was mad at first. Leaving my friends and stuff sucked. But it's nice here. Quiet. Dad is happier. He's thrilled to have his own pack, and now that he has a ton of wolves to care for, he's not always obsessing over what I'm doing."

And for a teenager that made sense. She led me around the side of the house and through a small area of trees to another one of those prairie-like fields, only this one was filled with purple stalks. I had to stop and marvel at the wild beauty of it at first. I'd never had a plot this large to grow my herbs.

Korissa toed at the edge of the plot revealing what looked like tilled land butting up against grass. "That's how we know it wasn't just like this."

I bent to poke at the ground and the nearest stalk, pulling weeds and freeing the base of the plant from a mess of overgrowth. There were a few dead patches, which I pulled free, setting them aside as they'd make good fertilizer down the road. Someone had made an effort to create a useable garden. Tilled up the land and put down nutrient rich dirt. I wondered who Liam had bought the land from and if they'd been tea creators themselves.

I struggled to get to a seat without pulling on my stitches, but I managed, spreading my leg out to my side and half laying on my undamaged hip so I could work. I wished for a pair of garden shears so I could trim some of the flowers and hang them for drying. Just the smell and the familiar feel of earth beneath my fingers helped calm my nerves. I'd been running for so long I'd almost forgotten what it was like to just breathe.

"Don't suppose you have a pair of garden scissors?" I asked Korissa. "I can clean up some of this and trim them back so they grow. With enough work this field could be breathtaking, and worth a fortune if you can find someone looking to buy lavender." The temperature was warm enough that I craved a pitcher of lavender lemonade, or even the honey-lavender scones I used to bake for *Apa*. A thousand things could be done with those tiny purple flowers, even some basic alchemy. It had been forever since I'd done more than a ward or two. All of my skills had gone into creating the tattoos on my arms and keeping out of sight of anyone who might be hunting me. There were plenty of *others* who could track me when I used alchemy. But since *Apa* and Felix already knew where I was, I didn't care as much. The vampires and fairies were unlikely to involve themselves in any wolf pack, so I'd be safe until I left again.

Korissa looked indecisive for a minute. "You won't run away? Dad would be so upset if you ran away. And you're still hurt. Please don't run away."

"I'm not going to run." Not today at least. The stitches throbbed from my movement. The part that Liam had said was my muscle, had been torn. Shifting would tear it open, even if my shift was more magic than anything else. The body shape just wasn't the same. And I couldn't miraculously heal like most werewolves could, which was why I had spells scrawled in ink to help. Even then my wounds still took good old fashioned time to heal.

She looked indecisive for another minute, but finally turned and walked off toward the house. I focused on the ground, peeling away the weeds and layers of dead leaves to reveal rich black dirt. This plot had been intentional. Someone had dug out the land and filled it with soil instead of clay and pine needles. An expensive plan for an area this large. It was easily half a football field if the purple stalks fading into the distance was any indication.

I found neatly planted rows. The first three were lavender, all English, and mostly still in good shape. The third was lemon balm. That was a bit more of a mess as this really wasn't a great climate for it. I cleared a small two-foot-wide area, digging deeper into the garden by stretching out through the stalks of scented growth. The next layer was chamomile. I almost cried with joy. The flowers were tiny, half lost in the overgrowth of the lemon balm, but still fighting for their bit of sunlight.

CHAPTER 7

Korissa reappeared with a basket. She set it down beside me. Inside were several pairs of garden gloves and two garden shears. All of it still had tags on it. "It was in the garage. I remembered dad buying this stuff when we moved in, saying he'd have to replant the flowerbed in front of the house. He hasn't had time."

I picked one of the shears, not wanting the gloves as I needed to feel the dirt run through my fingers, and opened it. I emptied the basket and began trimming the lavender and lemon balm back, filling the basket with the buds and leaves.

"I can help," Korissa said. She put on a pair of garden gloves. "Just tell me what to do." She leaned forward to smell one of the large blooms of purple flowers. "They smell so nice."

"I'm just clearing the weeds so the real stuff has room to grow and trimming the rest."

"How do you know what's real and what's weed?"

"I know all about plants," I said. I pointed out the rows of lavender, lemon balm, and chamomile. There might be more further in, but so far everything seemed to be planted in rows of three, and it looked like they repeated because I could see more lavender on the other side of chamomile. I'd have never planted them that close to each other. Sometimes plants would mingle roots and create odd growths or even just a different scent or flavor. Perhaps whomever had planted the garden had simply done so for a wilder prairie look with useful plants. To most people they looked like weeds, and they were technically part of the ragweed family.

"This is English lavender," I told Korissa and listed out the reasons I knew it was English and its properties, then followed suit with the lemon balm and chamomile.

She began to carefully clear away her small section of garden, adding the weeds to the pile I'd begun, but letting me do the cutting. Some of them I added to the baskets, other cuts were just to trim back overgrowth so the plants could thrive. All of which I explained to her.

"So alchemy is just knowing plants?" She wanted to know.

"More like chemistry. Mixing plants and the like. Alchemy is responsible for the birth of science and medicine. There are a lot of cultures that had aspects of alchemy. Sort of like ancient Druidry and modern herbalism."

"Not like the Japanese anime where the kid loses his arm and his brother's body?"

I smiled, knowing what she was talking about. "There are some similarities. Though I've never really explored the darkest sides of alchemy. I suspect it's a lot like witchcraft, in that the intent is often important. Since its evolution in Egypt, there was a lot of talk about alchemy creating eternal life, and lead into gold."

"Water into wine?" Korissa inquired.

"I think that was Jesus, but maybe he was into alchemy too. Technically you can create a water to wine sort of thing.

Again chemistry. Lead into gold is a bit more complicated, especially if you want real gold and not just fool's gold."

"And eternal life?"

"A myth."

"Does anyone really want to live forever?"

"Sure. Not me, but talk to vampires or even most weres and you'll hear a lot of them fear death the most," I said.

"But they can live forever."

"Not really. Weres die all the time. I think *Apa* did a study and found that weres only live twenty years once changed. Mostly because the wolf takes them over or dominance fights whittle out the rest. Vampires are much the same, though I think they average half a century or so. They also don't reproduce as fast."

"What?" She demanded. "Vampires can have babies?"

I laughed. "Not like that. It takes hundreds of blood exchanges and a lot of blood sharing to change someone into a vampire. It's not like the movies. No three bites and you're done." What I didn't tell her, is that I'd seen enough vampires in my life to know that a lot of their existence had roots in ancient magic not all that unlike alchemy. Which meant they were just a mix of elements that could be taken apart if the right thread was pulled. Soul, spirit, and body. Alchemy was trinity just like every other major religion out there. "Alchemy is sort of where science and magic meet."

"For real?"

"For real." I lifted my arm to show her my tattoos. "The symbols are alchemy, but they create magic, sort of binding spells. Mostly protection and healing. They are written on my skin because they use my spirit as energy. I can also use them to empower a mix of herbs to enhance healing."

She stared at me in awe. "Can you teach me?"

"This is pretty advanced stuff. How about we start with simple chemistry and go from there? Baking is chemistry.

Herbs are a building block. Many cultures use them in their own mixtures. And in fact, modern science takes things from herbs to make pharmaceuticals. It's all about the mixture of elements. Some plants can be deadly if you eat a leaf, but the stem could cure a cold. Combine the leaf of one plant with the stem of another and you can make an aphrodisiac. It's all about the chemistry." The spirit and soul came later. I didn't think I'd be around long enough to teach her any of that. Some people sort of just fell into the spiritual side like I had. Others really had to work for it. It was all about perception and I didn't know Korissa well enough to know which way she leaned.

"What can we do with this stuff?" She held up a handful of the plants we'd been pruning.

"Once it dries you can use it for all sorts of things. Fresh has other uses. It's all about knowing what you need from each plant and how to mix it. Simple is the best place to start. Teas and tinctures. You're probably familiar with lavender oil and chamomile tea."

"I like chamomile tea," Korissa said.

"There was this amazing blend I used to make. Nothing like that sweet tea that people love so much. I like to taste my tea, mull over the flavors." I closed my eyes, remembering the scent of it, the flavor on my tongue and how it used to settle my nerves. "I always had stuff drying. But in Texas, there's not a lot of rain. So I'd pin bunches on clothes lines." I opened my eyes to find Korissa had stopped moving and was looking past me. I turned to follow her gaze.

A werewolf lingered not fifty yards away, making no attempt to hide himself. The fact that he was in wolf form was the first indication that something was wrong. Liam's statement about a meeting didn't seem to indicate they'd be running as wolves, and it was still daylight. Likely we were far enough away from most of civilization for it not to matter, but most packs didn't let their wolves just run free whenever. They really couldn't be mistaken for dogs in broad daylight. They were just too big.

"Don't run," I said quietly.

She gripped my arm. "You're hurt. You can't run."

"I'm fine. If he comes at us, I'll distract him while you get your dad, okay? Maybe he's just out for a stroll." While all the dominant wolves were in a meeting, and I happened to be outside with Liam's very vulnerable human daughter. Right.

She gulped and nodded. "Toby's new."

"You recognize him?" So he was one of Liam's wolves.

She ran her finger down her nose, indicating the white stripe the wolf had in his dusky-tan fur. "Toby is the only one I know with that marking." She paused, glanced back the way toward the house and then at Toby. "His change wasn't right."

I stiffened at those words. A new wolf would often hesitate to attack me because even new, it could sense the omega presence. But if he was new and not quite right in the head…

"Not right, how?"

The wolf crept closer. I gripped the garden shears and put Korissa behind me. There was no way I could run. Even moving around as much as I was made my leg ache, and the hint of a headache marched across my brow from the bright sunlight, echoes of the concussion. The wolf was twice my size, I'd only have one shot if it rushed us, but I would die before I let him hurt Korissa.

"More wolf," she whispered. It happened sometimes. The human got lost in the change, leaving only the animal. Except that unlike normal wolves, a werewolf with the wolf in charge was a destructive thing. It didn't care about home, pack, or food. It only cared about chaos. It would attack anything it deemed a threat to its dominance. Usually such wolves were put down fairly quickly, though I'd heard that sometimes they recovered.

His ears weren't flattened back. Odd as usually that was the first sign of aggression. But he stalked through the lavender, keeping low enough that we could only barely see him above the growth. I could smell Korissa's fear. Probably had a healthy mix of my own fear scenting the air. Coming outside had been a bad idea. But I had thought that Liam's pack would be under his control.

"Stop," I told the wolf. His ears flattened. "Fuck."

Korissa clung to me, her face buried in the back of my neck, breathing labored. Even if I took the attack she'd never get away unharmed. I should have noticed the wolf sooner. Normally I did, since the fire of its aggression should have heated up the spells on my left arm. Why hadn't they? All of them were healing or defense, nothing to attack others, as that went into areas of alchemy that often led down to slippery paths of darkness. The journals I'd read from previous alchemists often ended abruptly when they'd delved into the sort of magic that could injure the living, even in self-defense. I only knew one self-defense type spell, but had tied it into my healing to mitigate the cause and effect. It was something I used very rarely and there was no way it was going to help against a raving wolf.

I frowned at the wolf, then at my left arm only partially visible in the T-shirt. Had someone done something to my spells? The bramble looked okay, and that was the core of the defense spell. Still, it was odd that I'd felt nothing in warning. I raised the shears as it got closer and the wolf growled.

"Stop," I said again.

The wolf snarled at the shears, but didn't get closer. He stood less than five feet away, legs hidden in the overgrowth. He could jump the distance and rip out my throat before I could react. I'd seen that a time or two, never a pleasant memory, and one of the reasons that I stayed away from pack hunts. This wolf seemed more agitated by the shears I held than our presence. I lowered the shears slowly, ready to lift them again if he leapt. I'd wound him if he did. Kill him if I could, before he hurt Korissa.

The wolf watched the shears drop to my side and his ears went up, head tilting, more with curiosity than fierce fangs. His demeanor was almost dog-like and off. After a minute of both of us at an impasse, me not letting go of the shears and him not coming closer, he dropped down to his belly, almost vanishing completely in a row of lavender.

"I hope you're not squashing the plants," I berated the wolf, relieved that we didn't seem to be a source of food for it at the moment. Maybe Liam or Dylan would happen along and take the wolf off somewhere he wouldn't hurt people.

"He's not attacking?" Korissa whispered the question.

"Nope. Seems to just be laying in the flowers. Not sure what he's waiting for. Don't go anywhere. I don't want him to think he can chase you."

"Okay," she agreed. I went back to work, keeping one eye on the wolf and barely able to move with Korissa clinging to me. But the sun felt good on my skin, and I let the familiar smells sooth the edges of my worry. It wasn't until Korissa let out a strangled *'meep'* sound that I realized the wolf had inched itself close enough to touch the foot of my outstretched injured leg. I stared at him for a minute, fearing he'd bite me. But he pressed his nose to the bare skin at my ankle above my sock and below the sweats. His tongue flashed out to deliver a quick lick.

"You better not be deciding I'm tasty enough to be food. I promise to give you the worst indigestion ever," I said. More likely he was sensing my omega presence and trying to understand it. How he reacted would indicate just how *wrong* his transition had been.

He let out a little whine and rolled over, squashing a half-dozen lavender bunches. I stared at him. He stared back.

Almost a puppy-like grin on his face while his tongue lolled out. What the hell? I hadn't even stretched out my senses and he was acting like a cat wallowing in catnip.

"I thought you said he was wrong?" I asked Korissa. She'd pulled away to watch him too.

"He is. Not even dad can get him to stay human, and he attacks some of the other pack members if they come near him in wolf form. He's not supposed to be at the house. Someone should have been watching him."

And yet he'd been allowed to live. Usually werewolves weren't sentimental about death for the *wrong*. When the animal took over a were, it wasn't a wolf like a wild wolf, it was more like a berserker, fueled only by blood lust and fear. It was seen as a kindness to put them out of their misery rather than force them to live existences devoid of love and humanity.

"You're squashing my flowers," I told the wolf. Toby. His name was Toby. "Toby?" I asked him, wondering if he recognized the name at all. Werewolves were not dogs. If there was no human left in him would he recognize his own name?

The wolf rolled back over and inched out of the garden until he sat in the weeds beside us. He laid down in a huff, like we were just too much trouble for him.

Korissa shifted so she was more to my side than behind me, still using me as a barrier. I didn't mind. She was just a kid. Maybe Liam's pack was right about it not being a good idea for Korissa to live with her dad. Kids shouldn't have to live in fear of their lives, and I had a feeling this probably wasn't the first scary wolf encounter she'd had.

"Are you Toby?" I asked again, letting go of the shears, but let my hand hover near them just in case.

The wolf gave an odd nod.

"He understood you," Korissa said in awe.

"I think so, maybe." I put my hand up, careful to keep it a

good distance away from Toby in case he lunged. In reality if he wanted us dead, he was close enough to kill us both without a big lunge, but he didn't have any signs of the aggression I was used to in an uncontrolled wolf. Disguises and pretenses weren't their thing, as they were just not as focused as a human would be.

He lay his head on his paws and just looked at us, big eyes wide, ears turned our way. I waited probably another three minutes before turning back to the plants. It would have been the best chance for him to attack. I was taking my attention off him. If he was going to hurt us, that would have been his moment, and I would have taken the scissors and slashed his throat as he leapt at me. Instead he just lay there watching. Eventually even Korissa pulled away to begin working again.

Toby inched his way closer until he could lay his chin on my thigh. I'd never had a werewolf in wolf form so close and acting so submissive. He even let me stroke his head like a dog, and chuffed happily when I scratched behind his ears. Korissa kept glancing over, and there was no cure for the tension that coursed through her. She didn't address Toby, and kept her voice soft as though she were afraid to startle him. I just prayed that if it was my omega presence that helped him, it was permanent. I always hated to see someone die after they'd physically survived the change.

CHAPTER 8

Korissa created stacks of herbs and bound them with string per my instructions. If we could find a dry place to hang them, they'd be great for tea in a few weeks. "We can make the lemonade later," Korissa said, sounding excited. "We have lemons in the house. You said we can use fresh leaves for that?"

"Yes, fresh is actually best for the lemonade. Dried is better for tea. I can show you a couple of easy recipes. There's even a lavender butter that is amazing on cornbread."

Toby jolted to his feet and snarled. I flinched and had to stifle my own cry when I pulled my leg wrong trying to back away by instinct. The stitches protested as muscles clenched and I had to fight from moving my leg more. Korissa had frozen behind me.

Only Toby wasn't snarling at us. He crouched, teeth bared and snarling at Carl who stalked across the yard toward us, Dylan and Liam not far behind.

"Who let him out? Now we'll have the Alpha's new pet slaughtered by his old one. Christ, can't anyone follow an order around here?"

New pet? Old pet? Either way I didn't like the implication or the way Carl glared at Toby. Everything in his body language screamed violence. If Carl kept coming, Toby would meet the challenge and likely die. And why? For a bit of bluster? The idea that Korissa and I would be caught in the crossfire worried me too.

I reached out and slid a hand down Toby's flank, digging my fingers through his thick fur and sucked in a deep breath full of lavender. The scent filled my lungs, calming me, and centering my energy. I pushed that little bit of calm toward Toby. Mentally whispering "Safe, calm, safe, calm." If he was truly lost it would do nothing. He'd attack, likely we'd all be injured and he would die. If he wasn't lost…

The wolf stopped snarling and actually dropped back down beside me to put his face back against my thigh. My wounded thigh. I winced. Toby whined, reacting to my pain as if he were still feeling what I did. If he really was hearing and feeling what I was, I'd never been that connected to a wolf before.

Carl reached for him just as he arrived to tower over us, but Liam stopped him.

"Stop," his voice echoed over the yard in a way that made even the bugs silent.

Carl froze. Toby dug his snout into my thigh, which really hurt and we both whimpered.

"Tamed the savage beast, now, eh?" Liam said with a bit of a foreign lilt to his voice. Irish? "No debate about that, is there? Not even in the pack a day."

Carl scowled. Dylan stood behind Liam looking amused. Toby rolled over and pressed his belly to my leg. It would have been cute if he hadn't been twice my size.

"Never seen a grown wolf act like a puppy before," Dylan said.

"The lavender is very soothing," I informed them.

"The lavender has been here," Liam said quietly. "The element that has changed is you."

I glanced up to meet his eyes, finding them intense, but not unkind. I recognized that look since *Apa* wore it often when I was able to calm one of the older wolves he feared he'd have to put down. Relief. Liam was relieved that he didn't have to kill Toby today. It made me think better of him. Putting down a wolf like Toby might have been considered kind by the overall population of wolves, but it was a do or die type of action for alphas. To not kill them endangered the entire pack, to kill them meant destroying a wolf they'd promised to protect.

"I am a simple alchemist," I said. "All life comes from a combination of scattered things by the will of the universe." I reached out and rubbed Toby's stomach like he was a big dog. "Maybe Toby hadn't experienced the right combination until today."

Liam nodded then glanced up at the fading sunlight. "Perhaps you're willing to come back inside and leave the rest of the gardening for another day? Now would be a good time to rest and recover."

"Sun and earth are healing," I argued. If I went back inside would I ever be free again?

"And both will still be there tomorrow." Liam swept up our basket full of plants. "Didn't you promise to show my daughter how to make lavender lemonade?"

There was no way he'd been close enough to hear that. I frowned trying to sort through how he knew that. Except that Toby had been sitting in my lap the whole time and all wolves could technically have a mental link to their alpha. Which meant that Liam knew where Toby was the entire time and had not worried one bit about the safety of his daughter or myself. Did he not see Toby as a threat? All wolves were a threat, even the kindest ones, in wolf form.

Their baser natures took over. Or did he just see me as that powerful? He couldn't have just been testing me, could he? Not with his daughter's life on the line. I didn't think Liam was flippant about anything. He just came across as too smart for that. And he didn't know me well enough to know if I could or even would, help Toby. I frowned up at him, more confused than I'd been when I woke up in his house the first time. He rewarded me with a faint smile. Infuriating man.

Korissa stood and chattered with him about the plants and all the facts I'd shared with her. She was very excited to learn about alchemy and began telling him all about the television show which had become popular in Japan some years back before finally making its way to American anime nerds. Liam nodded at his daughter, waiting, listening and ever attentive. No one else tried to get close and even Carl backed away.

"Will you come inside?" Liam asked me again, no strings or guilt in his tone. Just a request. "We will be preparing dinner, and I'd like to check your wound."

I could do diplomacy, at least until I was healed. "If someone will help me up, sure." My leg throbbed and I feared if I put any pressure on it the wound would start gushing again. Too much tension from unexpected wolf visits. Toby got to his feet and nudged me, like I was supposed to use him as some giant wolf-shaped cane. Liam offered me a hand, and after some maneuvering to keep the pressure off the injured leg, I was able to take it and pull myself up enough to lean on the wolf.

"Thanks, Toby," I told the wolf, then nodded at Liam. "I appreciate the hand." When I took a step toward the house, Toby clung to my side. I sighed. Somehow I suspected he wasn't going to be slinking off to wherever he came. It happened sometimes. Especially with the damaged wolves.

Apa had always had to drag them away. After a handful of incidences, the more troubled of the pack suddenly just stopped coming my way. *Apa* was rarely subtle about anything.

Carl stepped forward again like he planned to drag Toby away, but Liam raised a hand to stop him.

"It's on your head then," Carl grumbled and turned to stalk away.

Liam didn't look perturbed. He handed the overfull basket off to Dylan and offered me his arm. "Perhaps you'll let me help you back inside and allow me to look at that leg of yours."

"It's fine," I grumbled but took his arm to help keep the weight off it. It ached. I suspected that was because whatever pain killers I'd been given were wearing off. I had enough lemon balm to make a great salve so long as he had some coconut oil in the house. Now if only I had some white willow bark it would be perfect.

"You're bleeding," Liam whispered, words barely more than a breeze against my ear as we watched Dylan and Korissa disappear ahead of us into the house. "I can smell it."

I didn't feel like I'd reopened the wound, but Toby was pressed hard to that side of my hip. Liam stopped and stepped in front of me. He glanced down at Toby who couldn't meet his eyes and instead looked at the ground. It wasn't that Liam actually did anything, it was just instinct, but it made me feel protective of Toby. I put a hand in his fur to comfort him.

"I like that you protect my daughter and my wolves. Those are good instincts. I wish you had better instincts of self-preservation." He pushed Toby away from my hip to reveal a wet spot in the fabric of my sweatpants. The dark stain couldn't have been anything other than blood. I'd been so lost in the lavender I hadn't even smelled my own blood. "I think you broke a stitch or two."

"Great." I hated the idea of stitching myself back together, and disliked even more the idea of owing him for another visit from their healing witch. "I have enough herbs to make a salve."

"Will that salve stop the bleeding? Reknit torn muscle?"

"Not exactly." I'd need a few other things and some good time in contact with the earth to use some of that alchemy. He didn't need to know the details. There was a faster way, an exchange of energy, but I'd only ever used it twice before and the last time nearly drained a vampire of his *life* to heal. Hugo would have come after me by now if I didn't suspect he was still healing. Vampires didn't have a lot of life to give since they weren't really alive. But I justified what I did to him by the fact that he held me captive for weeks, enthralled by memories of happier times as he fed on me. Heartless bastard deserved what I did to him.

In one fluid motion Liam lifted me again, careful of my hip and stalked toward the house. Toby whined but followed behind.

"I can walk."

Liam just grunted. Up the stairs and back into my room we went. He set me on the bed. Toby tried to follow us into the room but Liam shooed him out and closed the door.

"I promised to show Korissa how to make lemonade," I reminded Liam.

He vanished into the bathroom for a minute and returned with a first aid kit. He set it down on the bed and didn't even ask before pulling my pants down to view the mess of blood, stitches and flesh. I winced. It looked bad. Liam was unfazed as he efficiently cleaned around the stitches with a few alcohol swabs, blotting away the mess and poking at the stitches, which were strained, not torn. He still looked unhappy about them. "Don't your healing charms work for this?" He asked and waved at my tattooed arm.

How did he know? Had his witch told him? I decided to play dumb. "What healing charms?" Not a lie, since he could tell if I lied, more of an *if I have them, point them out,* sort of comment. But I was a master at evasion.

"I could pull the stitches out and re-sew it. Only you'd be awake this time." He was totally calling my bluff.

"I'm fine. I'll stay off the leg."

"You'll rest and stay here then," he insisted and pulled the covers back on the bed.

"I'll rest and stay here," I promised not giving a specific as to how long. It was all in the details.

He stared at me a moment longer. "I should fix the stitches."

"No thanks."

"You are not immune to infection. Not like we are." He glanced at my tattooed arm again seeming to hesitate. Then he knelt before me. "I thought for a while that you were pretending not to know me and was willing to allow for the deception if that was what you felt you needed as my pack is unfamiliar to you. But you really don't remember me, and that's all right. You were traumatized that night. Hurt and afraid. I remember, and I know you can heal this."

His words churned in my head, processing slowly. "What night? I don't know what you're talking about." I couldn't recall ever having met him before. Who could have forgotten a man like him? He could have stepped off a movie set with his perfect features. He also still smelled like fresh bread, cinnamon-sugar, and alpha. I would have remembered him. "We met for the first time at your bakery."

"No. It was a late summer evening over a year ago. I was visiting your pack in preparation for taking over this territory. A dozen alphas were attending the Volkov, hoping for territories. There had been a festival that day. We all gorged on hogs and lavender lemonade. Everyone whispered of the *witchchild,* wondering if we'd catch a glimpse of the child shifter who'd given the Volkov such a headache over the years. Many had been nervous about drinking the lemonade as they heard it was the *witchchild's* creation and feared it was enchanted. It wasn't enchanted, but it was spiked with liquor, which made the boisterous group even louder."

My heart began to speed up.

"The woods in the direction toward your little home were off limits. Many of the Alphas snickered like school children about sneaking away to catch a glimpse. But the Volkov made it clear not to cross the line, and I wouldn't have, if you hadn't cried out."

I shuddered, trying to shove back the rising memories of that night. It had begun benign enough. Life was beginning to settle down after Felix had told me of his latest plans to marry. My rejection of him and his subsequent beating had only served in severing our ties completely. *Apa* had promised to keep him away. There was a grand festival planned. New territories to carve out, and alphas to decide on. I thought it meant he was sending Felix away to be an alpha of another territory. Only Felix would have made a horrible alpha. But it wasn't my decision. Thankfully I hadn't seen Felix in days.

Apa had asked me to prepare enough lavender to make endless lemonade. Since I always had a fresh store it was an easy task. He'd even picked up the supply of herb himself. He'd been in a good mood. Smiled down at me with his pale brown eyes filled with kindness. *Apa* didn't look like one of the scariest men on the planet. He looked like a normal late-twenty-something guy. Handsome, but unremarkably so. Muscular, dark hair, and a disarming smile. He didn't stand out, nor did he really fade into the background. He smiled and others smiled with him. He snarled and wolves cowered, but mostly I just hid. Sometimes I pushed his buttons. But I was growing out of that stage which seemed to please him.

"Promise you'll stay out of the woods tonight," *Apa* had said. "In a few days I'll introduce you to some of the alphas, but for tonight no running."

He never introduced me to alphas, so I found that an odd statement. Usually I just avoided these sorts of events. Too much testosterone and wolf stupidity. "I won't run tonight," I promised.

He'd nodded, accepting my word and leaving. I threw myself into the task of making scones for the morning when everyone would be hung over and begging for relief. The scones had a bit of magic to settle stomachs and break down left over alcohol. It was something I always did for the morning after these festivals. *Apa*'s pack loved to party, but not all were stable enough to endure the bluster of outsiders. Calming food often bridged the growing unease. So I set myself to the task.

Felix stumbled in just after I'd finally finished and headed to bed. I could smell the booze on him before he climbed into my bed. It wasn't uncommon. But he wasn't welcome. "That bitch better give me kids," he grumbled as he tore at my clothes. "Not worth marrying her if she doesn't give me babies."

I pushed him away. "Off. Get out! We're done. *Apa* promised you'd stay away."

Felix hit me. Not a slap but a full punch that sent me flying off the bed and into the wall. I sank to the floor stunned, blinking back stars. Books clattered to the floor around me, knocked off the intricately carved shelves due to the force of the blow.

"You're mine. Not theirs. No matter what my father says. His tests and trials don't mean shit." He reached over, and lifted me up by my hair. I must of have passed out for a minute because when next I came to I was nude, lying on my stomach with him on my back.

"Get off!" I screamed at him. Panic filling my senses. I couldn't do this again. "You said you're marrying another. You don't need me."

"You're mine!" He growled at me, pressing me into the bed with his weight. "You will always be mine. They can't have you. You've forgotten that you are mine. But I'll help you remember."

I'd thought of a thousand ways to kill him and a thousand ways to die as he raped me. I thought of *Apa* looking so happy that evening. I thought of the first time Felix had made love to me. I thought about how I wished I'd never met him. It wasn't the first time he'd raped and beaten me, but it was the last. He'd left me broken and bleeding; returned to the party to drink with men he thought he could intimidate simply because he was the son of the Volkov. Would he jeer and tell them how he'd violated me? Was I just a big joke to them all?

I'd crawled from my home, dragging myself through dirt, to try to reach the garden. It would hurt to drain it of life, but I had no choice. I vowed that once I healed and found myself safe, I would create the largest garden the earth had ever longed for, filled with wilds of all types and the critters that loved them. I promised I wouldn't run that night, and I couldn't have even if I wanted too.

I never made it to the garden.

CHAPTER 9

"You were barely conscious when I found you. Bleeding. I had to strain to hear your heart beat." Liam shut his eyes. "The scent of you still draws me. Honey and lavender fading into the wind as death threatened to steal you."

"I was trying to reach the garden." I'd never intended anyone to be hurt.

"And instead you called to me, and I found you. Do you remember what you said?"

Barely. "I asked if you were a spirit of dark or light."

"Yes."

I couldn't remember his face from that night. It had been so dark and my vision tainted with blood. I'd thought it a dream. Felix had tried to kill me. I knew that now. He'd hit me hard enough that I should have died. He knew I wasn't a wolf and didn't have the fast healing weres did. I should have known better, broken it off sooner. Run before he knew I was considering leaving.

Live and learn. But live was the important part. What had Liam said that night? He would be light or dark for me, whatever I needed. It sounded so romantic and sappy I was sure I'd made it up. He was a stranger. I hadn't even known his name. Yet I had responded with, "then kiss me and share your spirit."

A smile tugged the corners of Liam's lips when I spoke the words out loud. "You do remember."

My heart leapt into my throat. Fear racing through me. No one knew I could do that. Other than Hugo the vampire and that unknown stranger I thought I'd dreamt of that night. Not unknown.

Liam. Fuck.

Was this all a ploy for revenge? For taking his strength without really getting his consent? He hadn't known what I was asking. Hell, I hadn't known. I had only read of it before. Never thought I'd have to steal the spirit of another to heal myself. But my body knew it was dying and my soul acted instinctively.

"I'm sorry," I whispered. Would he kill me quickly? My breath caught in my throat and suddenly I couldn't get any air. Yet I still whispered, "I'm sorry," over and over while the world began to narrow to darkness around me.

He cupped my face with his hands. "Stop. Stop. I can see the terror in your eyes, hear your racing heart. Breathe." It was the last command that had me sucking in a breath so deep I choked and coughed. "That's it." He rubbed my back with one hand while petting my head with the other. Still the terror gripped me and I had to fight to see beyond the fear, and think beyond the mantra of apology.

"Please kill me quickly." I wasn't above begging if need be. If I'd done to Felix what I'd done to Liam all those years ago, the Volkov himself would likely have tortured me to death for daring to use his son for food. It wasn't all that different from what vampires did. Blood, spirit, life, energy, it was all connected.

"Sebastian Volkov hear my voice," Liam said firmly, the

power of Alpha, like he was my Alpha, in his voice. His grip tightened until all I could see were his eyes. Deep pools of endless blue depths. There was no anger to be found in them. He didn't look at me with disgust or rage. "I offered myself to you then to help you heal. I offer myself to you now." He gave me a tight smile. "I hope you've improved since the last time. It took me two days to recover from our single kiss. Your injuries are not as severe this time. Perhaps you'll let me walk away from this with a little sleepiness and not total oblivion. It was difficult back then to explain to your father how you went missing and I was found in the forbidden woods weak as a newborn pup. I was very lucky he didn't kill me, since you smelled of pain, fear, and blood, and I smelled of you."

"Why would you…I don't understand…What…" My brain just couldn't process. He wanted me to use his spirit to heal again. The Volkov knew Liam had seen me that night? Did *Apa* know what I did? Was that why he hadn't fought harder to drag me back?

"I'm telling you to take what you need to heal. You don't have the energy and I have boundless amounts due to my wolf nature. I offered before to be your light or dark, whatever you needed. Let me be your strength, be it in sunshine or storm."

That was too close to the chant of a mating bond. "No. You're not my Alpha. Not my mate."

"No?" He moved one hand to curl around the back of my neck and pull me forward until we were inches apart, lips almost touching. I could feel his breath on my face. The electricity of our touch coursed through my body, making me tremble. This wasn't just the familiar zing of a wolf. It was more. An ache like something that had been lost long ago and finally recovered.

"Didn't you choose me a year ago? You called for me. Not your voice, as you made no sound while you lay in the dark dying. Your *soul*. I heard it. Came running. My soul screaming. How unfair to find you as you were dying? And you were the *witchchild*. Immune to the were magic. Had you been a wolf your father might have been able to help you heal. I felt helpless and you asked for a kiss. I gave it. Life. An exchange of spirit. Isn't that the very meaning of a bond?"

I shook my head even though what he said was true.

"Eleven other alphas shared space in your father's bunkhouse. Eleven, not including those in your own pack. Only I heard you. Only I responded. When your father requested alphas who might be interested in you attend his festival, I hadn't thought much of it. Just that territory would be nice. Didn't think my wolf would be interested in a troublesome child even though I'd always dreamt of finding my true mate. Your exploits were whispered about in every pack, I'm sure. Very few frustrated the Volkov like you. But that night changed everything. *Mine*, my wolf told me. *Mine.*"

"No. I don't belong to anyone. That kiss was just to heal me, nothing more."

"Your soul didn't call to mine? My life didn't restore yours? Haven't you spent the last year feeling the pull in this direction? Trying not to follow it, but failing? It all began that night."

I had no idea. I barely remembered that night. The kiss had been a dream. A fantasy that Hugo had later exploited when he'd been draining my blood nightly for weeks.

"It's all right if you need time. The Volkov said you were skittish. And that was before you ran. He said you prickled when approached with affection, like a porcupine. We'd all laughed at that. But I know now it's true. You're so used to being hurt that you lash out to avoid getting close. It may not be the happiest way to live, but I understand why you needed to protect yourself that way." Liam stared intently at me, like he could see all my secrets written on my face.

"At first your father thought you'd fled because you'd found out about his trials to find you a mate. But you smelled of Felix that night. Of another alpha and sex. I hadn't yet met Felix. When I did, you'd been gone a few days. The Volkov pack was in an uproar and Felix was demanding you be returned to him. When I scented him…realized it was he who'd left you broken and dying, forcing you to flee. What he'd done to you…I challenged him."

He couldn't have. He'd be dead. "The Volkov wouldn't let you."

"It was already done. Your father couldn't stop it. I don't think he really wanted to stop it. Xander is quiet when he's angry. Still like a snake ready to strike. The rage builds in him like some convalescing monster. I've heard legends of when he releases it. Everyone should have been afraid that night of his stillness. Especially Felix. Not because I challenged his son, but because you'd been hurt and ran, not to him, but away."

"No. He would never let you hurt Felix," I said. The Volkov loved his son. Spoke of them fondly and often, and kept them close to protect them. I couldn't imagine him letting anyone hurt Felix.

"I more than hurt Felix. If the Volkov had not asked for mercy, I'd have killed Felix and been justified in doing so. I left him broken and defeated. Your father thanked me with this territory far from his and a blessing that should you and I ever cross paths again, we would be free to bond." Liam's forehead pressed to mine. He closed his eyes and sucked in a deep breath as though savoring the scent of me.

"I've lived a long time. Had many short relationships to pass the years a little less lonely. Never a mate. I had begun to fear I'd never find my mate. My wolf always rejected the others, told me to wait. It was a war between us. Never a moment of peace, until that night when everything changed.

The wolf led me to you. You still smell like honey and lavender. Like wildflowers in the wind and wood smoke on a cool fall evening. Home. Den. Pack. Mate. I've spent a year dreaming of your scent and your lips. Waiting for you. The Volkov assured me, eventually you'd arrive in my territory. Fate would eventually steer our paths together again."

The entire past year of running had been in a zig-zag across the country. Every time I veered too far to the east or south something cropped up that made me run again. Always north and west until I'd almost run out of road. "Have you been stalking me? This whole time?"

He opened his eyes, the blue of his gaze intense. "No. I had a pack to run and a territory to build. I worked to build a home that would be ready when you arrived. The Volkov planted the field before I had even chosen the territory. Said you'd need it someday. I created the bakery with room to expand it into a tea shop."

"You're insane. Fate isn't real." None of this was logical. How could *Apa* even know? Had he known? Had he been pushing me in this direction for the past year? Or had it been longer? I hadn't even known Liam's name that night. Remembered very little of him appearing in the dark, though my fantasies had taken the kiss and replayed it a million times over. Had *Apa* planned to mate me to an alpha? But alpha's didn't mate with men. Likely they'd all been more interested in territories than me. Had I been a tool then? Something to barter to gain a pack? My head began to hurt. There was just too much. For the last year I'd felt pulled in this direction. Some internal compass saying go northwest. Fate? Liam?

"But when I arrived you just let me go," I pointed out.

"Because I knew we'd be drawn back together. The second you drove away I knew it was a mistake. The bond between us tightened and I wanted to follow so badly. I raged a war with my wolf that day. Dylan sent wolves up the highway to make sure you were safe. Dylan found your car and reported it to me. I asked him to stay and watch for you. By the time I arrived, he was already chasing the other wolves, trying to save you."

I couldn't breathe again.

"I ask you again, Sebastian Volkov. Can you heal this?" He moved one hand to my injured thigh. "If I give you my strength? I don't want you to have a weakness while someone stalks my pack. My wolves will guard you day and night if necessary, but I need to know you can run if your survival depends on it. Can you heal this?"

"I don't know," I told him honestly. "It sort of just happens when I'm on the verge of death. I have books on it back home, but haven't had access to them to look. I've done it two times, accidentally. Not sure I can direct it purposely." Never had the chance to really try. Stealing energy, or life force from another, just didn't sound like a very nice thing to do.

"Twice?" His eyes narrowed, growing dark and serious. "Who else?"

"You don't get to be jealous when I barely know you."

He snarled, baring teeth a moment, then he crushed his lips to mine, drawing a startled gasp from me that fell into his mouth. His fingers dug painfully into my thigh as he drew out a kiss. I closed my eyes to keep from staring into the intensity of his and just let him take the kiss where he would. I should have been afraid. He could have forced me down on the bed and done to me the same things Felix had. But his hand on my throat was caressing, soothing, fingers sliding from my hair, down my neck and back to trace my throat. His tongue surveyed my mouth, searching out the heat of my own and exploring every bit of me he could reach.

The pain in my leg pulsed. Reminding me of the injury.

Liam touched the still tender spots of my head, and I almost cried out again. Pleasure teetered just beyond the edge of pain, and I couldn't reach it. True desire pooled in my gut. Building in pressure until something cracked between us. Like a door opening with the speed of a flower bud waking to the sun. At first the energy was a trickle, just tiny zips of electricity rising in strength as the bridge between us built. Brick upon brick of energy, light, and electricity until finally power rolled through me in a wave of heat, soothing away my aches in some places and making others burn. Pleasure crashed through me, overriding the pain, swallowing it and sending me on a wave of floundering emotions of desire and need. I clung to him, returning the ferocity of his kiss, and flailing for stability in his embrace.

The kiss went on until I was gasping at the warmth of the power flowing between us. Like a boat oar-less in the ocean we swayed, back and forth, back and forth. A swinging cradle of power that I knew we could build into something large, something more. I yanked myself away, trying to catch my breath and sagging in Liam's arms. I felt like a ragdoll. Boneless. Aches gone. Tired, yet pulsing with the continued flow of Liam's energy. It shouldn't have stayed after I broke the kiss, yet my muscles twitched and pinged with the sensation of his strength running through every cell. Home, my body sang, completion, mate. Fuck.

He cupped my face in his hands. "Much better this time." He kissed my cheeks gently, thumbs gently massaging my temples. "Now you smell like me, and I haven't even claimed you yet."

My heart skipped a beat, and I wasn't sure if it was from excitement or fear. Was he lying to me? He hadn't mated with me, right? I knew enough about it to know how rare it was that a wolf actually tied themselves metaphysically to their significant other. It was so rare that it was only whispered about in stories. Mostly I'd read that when a mate died, so did their wolf. Tying themselves to mortality didn't appeal to a lot of wolves.

"You really didn't bond with me?" I searched through my head, wondering if I would feel some sort of tie, or link to him. I could still taste him on my lips and feel his power zinging through me. It was unnerving, though not painful.

"There will be no question when we bond."

"Really? Have you bonded before? What does it feel like?"

Liam sighed like my questions were exhausting him. Or maybe it was the fact that I'd used his energy to heal myself. "I've never bonded before, but knew a couple who were."

"Where are they now?" I would love to question them. Maybe even look at them through alchemy. Would the bond be visible that way? Golden strings tying them together perhaps?

"They passed some years ago." Liam sounded sad.

"I'm sorry," I said automatically.

"It's in the past. For now, we have time." Liam released me to tend to the stitches and I immediately missed the warmth of his breath on my face. "You've healed enough that the stitches can come out." He dug through his first aid kit again and began to cut them away and tug them free. I barely felt anything as every nerve in my body pinged with electricity. It was almost uncomfortable in its intensity. If this was what it was like when we hadn't even bonded, I wondered how intense it would be when we mated.

Wait. Not when. If.

Hell, not even if. I'd had more than enough werewolf trouble in my life. The whole reason I'd needed to be healed was because some werewolves had tried to kill me, again. No matter how much I wanted the dream of forever that he'd dropped in my lap, my life never gave me the good stuff.

"Felix will come for me eventually. With or without your permission." Now that I was healed, I could run.

Liam paused and was quiet for so long that I looked up to meet his gaze. "Don't make me chase you. I will if I have to. Don't make me. I've waited a year. My wolf has been pacing and fighting with me for a year. Begging to bring you home. Don't make me chase you."

"You can't read my mind. We aren't bonded. You said we aren't."

"I can read your face and body language. You've wanted to run since the moment you woke up in my home."

"Your second doesn't seem to want me here."

"Carl doesn't run the pack. I do."

"And since you have a pack to run, you really shouldn't be chasing after me," I pointed out. "Protecting them should be priority."

"You are part of my pack now. My wolf won't let me wait another year. He'll insist that we follow you." He paused, then continued, "Only after last year did I know that it was you my wolf was waiting for. He's very insistent on this. Mine." He sucked in a deep breath like he was battling his wolf right that second. "Ours."

One kiss. One great near orgasmic sharing of supernatural energy did not give us wedded bliss. I was a distrustful bastard who'd been through a lot and there were powerful monsters on my tail. "Wolf metaphysics aside, you don't know what you're asking for. Felix isn't the only issue." Though if the Volkov had given Liam the A-okay, maybe the wolves weren't such a hurtle. But I had vampires after me, a handful of the fae, and more than my fair share of witches who thought I'd make better use as a spell ingredient than a living being. *Witchblood* was common enough. Omega somewhat rare. The combination was unheard of.

"I can handle your issues," Liam said dismissively.

"You don't even know what they are."

He just shrugged. "As I said before. We have time. My wolf knows you are my mate and will do what it must to protect you. In this, we are in agreement. If I had met you before the attack, would I feel the same? I think we'd likely be mated already. The Volkov invited only the alpha's he trusted and knew would be interested in you. I'm sure he tempted some with territories, but he weeded out those fast enough. Every alpha in that group had eyes for the Volkov's little prince. I went with thoughts of territory and curiosity about the prince. I'd long since lost hope that my wolf would pick a mate. Now I'm thrilled he forced us to wait. I could not have chosen a better match."

"I'm not a prince." Was barely tolerated in the Volkov's pack. "And how…we are nothing alike. I don't understand you at all."

"Men often forget in the boisterous noise of other men that what they say can be overheard. There was many a discussion about the spirited *witchborn* omega. Your father crossed half of them off his list that first night because they spoke of you as a possession, a thing to be bartered and traded. He made it very clear that you were to be treated as though you were royalty. We all knew before arriving that we were on a short list of alphas the Volkov considered trustworthy enough to care for the *witchchild,* but put alphas with other alphas and the stupid really shines." Liam shook his head. "I am thankful I didn't say anything regretful, but I heard enough from others to really change my views on some of the alphas I had once respected."

"There aren't that many gay alpha werewolves," I said. There couldn't be. Statistically I guess it could be, but in reality, being a werewolf was a brutal life. "And not that would want me." A possession made sense. *Apa* having to bribe them with property sounded more accurate.

"I don't think all or even most of them are *gay*. Not in the terms that the western world deems it. Most of us predate current ideology. For some that is good, for others, not so much. I don't consider myself *gay*. The term didn't exist when I was born as it does now."

That irritated me. Just like Felix. "Too good to acknowledge you like dick while you've been staring at me like you can't wait to get into my pants. No straight man kisses another man the way you kissed me."

Liam laughed. It was a bright sound. "I like dick just fine. The parts don't matter so much. I've indulged in my fair share of genders." He nodded as if thinking about something I said. "I've actually been in your pants. Helped you dress and undress. Helped you shower, washed your flesh and held nearly every inch of you in my hands. Still I crave more. I want to explore your passion. Discover the sounds you make when your skin is under my lips and your body submitting to mine. I've had others before, but my wolf has rejected everyone until you. The wolf is the most basic and primal part of us, and yet he wants you. *Demands* you. Your gender doesn't matter. The wolf doesn't see gender, never has, no matter who I've brought to my bed. It sees mate or not mate."

A hint of jealous rolled through me while my brain registered what he said. He'd been with men before? The parts didn't matter? Was that a cop out? "How many other men have you been with?" I didn't really want to know the answer.

A smile crossed his lips. "Do you really want to know about past lovers? You strike me as a jealous man. Part of your prickly nature perhaps." Liam met my gaze, his pale blue eyes looking amused. Was he teasing me? He had to be teasing me.

I shrugged. "Since you know about mine. It seems only fair that I know about your past lovers." And I knew almost nothing about him. Was he a player? He was handsome enough to have dozens of lovers lined up. He was also overbearing and overprotective like most alphas. The fact that he hadn't stopped touching me since our kiss, which kept the power zinging between us, only proved just how attached he was to the idea of having me. Maybe he didn't want a mate and just wanted a night with the *witchchild*? Maybe I was just another conquest? Maybe the magic appealed to him? How much of his words could I trust as truth?

"I know about all yours?" Liam inquired. "I know of Felix. Was he your only? He isn't an ideal example for relationships. I've heard stories even if I haven't heard all of yours. Aren't there other *issues* with past lovers who might come to call? I can't imagine so many could resist the temptation."

"Of an omega?" I asked because that was usually what alphas wanted from me. To possess an omega. *Witchborn* was more of a curse than a blessing, though some may want me for magic they thought I had. Others might want me just to try to influence the Volkov. They'd have been disappointed to learn that I had little sway over him.

"The fire of your temper with your hair to match. The honey of your lips, and the scattering of freckles across your nose." Liam ran a hand through my hair, letting the strands fall from his fingers like it fascinated him. "In the dark it looks brown, but the red…" He sighed. "I really like the red. Not the orange like some redheads, but more like sun-ripened strawberries, rare steak, or fresh blood. My wolf loves the latter two more, though I've been known to enjoy all three."

If I hadn't known he was an alpha wolf, his words might have scared me. But wolves loved blood almost as much as vampires. Usually they preferred it attached to some fresh meat, but his comparison told me he'd been a wolf a long time. When the balance between human and wolf began to blur, a wolf showed his age.

My red hair came from the bleed-through of the fox to my human side. It was a trait of the *witchborn*. I had met two other *witchborn* in my life, and they too had traits of their spirit animal. Without the fox, my hair would likely be black as night, instead of interwoven with red which made it look brown. The older I got, the more injuries I healed, the more magic I used, the more my fox bled through. My hair was more red than black now. I'd always hated it. Even tried to dye it, only to have the red bleed through like some horror movie death stain. It wasn't even a normal shade of red. Many complimented me on a dye job I'd never had. At least it wasn't clown red. More that dark oozing color of blood like Liam had pointed out. Not fresh in my opinion, more the sort of brown red of drying blood.

Felix hadn't liked it either. He'd required me to wear it in a ponytail so he didn't have to touch it. I'd cut it a few times in my life, short like a normal guy. Only then the very vulpine and sharp shape of my face became more pronounced. More of the fox bleeding through. Keeping my hair long made me feel more human and the fox less noticeable. Though maybe I was fooling myself.

"I hate it," I whispered. "Everyone hates it." Mostly because I'd been a fox living among wolves. Never really accepted by the pack, but always longing for it. I never minded being a fox when I was actually in the fox shape. It was the human that overthought everything and condemned every little difference. Too long living in the shadow of others' judgement had broken me. "I hate not being like everyone else."

"I don't," Liam assured me. "You're..." He let out a long sigh, fingers still curled in my hair. "Exactly what I need."

I squinted at him. "A mutt of mixed heritages and blood magic? You're a bit twisted, aren't you, Ulrich?"

He laughed. "Maybe. So other lovers? You never did answer from who else you borrowed strength."

"Hugo?" Was he actually a past lover? I couldn't remember if I'd actually had sex with him or if it had been an elaborate fantasy. "Umm… It's sort of complicated. And I wasn't really his lover so much as a juice box. He's probably not coming around any time soon." Not unless it was to deliver me to a painful death.

Liam's eyes narrowed.

"It was all sort of a big misunderstanding to begin with," I rambled. "I helped a little girl who wasn't really a little girl, but before she could bite me, Hugo came along. It really was a bit too much like the movie for me."

"Vampire?" Liam's voice became really soft and dangerous. "This Hugo is a vampire?"

"I didn't know the girl was a vampire. Didn't know Hugo was either. I mean I knew that vampires existed, but *Apa* never let them near the pack, so I never met one. They smell different, but it doesn't scream *vampire smell* to me. At least it didn't. Now I could probably detect them a mile away. He was a smooth talker and looked like one of those Nordic gods you see on romance novels."

"Nordic gods?" Now he sounded mad.

"You know, with the flowing blond hair and goofy clothes? Well the clothes were just a little off century is all and I was sort of shocked from having a curly sue attack me. Didn't suspect that I was jumping out of the frying pan and into the fire when he *rescued* me. Then he kept me locked in my own head while he fed from me. I guess he couldn't thrall me like he could other humans, so I dreamt while he ate."

"Is he still alive? Hugo?" He drew out the name like he was debating on ways to kill the vampire and keep him dead.

"I guess. I drained him of energy to escape. That was a few weeks back. He's probably healed by now. I'm not sure you can kill a vampire that way. Their magic is renewed each time the sun sets. I suspect they also draw power from death, which is why most of them are mob bosses dealing drugs. Hugo led me to believe he was pretty powerful, but I haven't met a lot of vampires. I do know that by the time I'd escaped him, I'd lost two weeks of time."

Liam's expression was so intent I had to look away.

CHAPTER 10

Some things were better left unsaid, I guess. "Enough about me. Your turn. How many Hugos do you have in your past?"

A few heavy minutes passed before he seemed to be able to get a hold on his feelings. The tension in the room eased. He pulled out the last of the stitches and swabbed at my flesh with alcohol pads. "I've never been used as a juice box. I tend to bite back." He flashed me a bit of a grin. "Where to start? Before I became a wolf? Only the most recent years perhaps? Categorize them by quality of lovers they were?" Now I knew for sure he was teasing.

"How old are you?" I asked.

"Older than you."

I growled at him. "If you think you're going to have any sort of relationship with me, you'll need to stop being evasive."

"*I'm* being evasive?"

"Yes. I just want to know stuff about you." Because he might be my mate, even if my heart was terrified of the very same idea. It was also intrigued. My heart hurt with how fast my mind leached on to the hope of actually having someone, of being important to someone.

"We have time. I have much to learn about you as well."

"Because the Volkov didn't tell you everything?" I scoffed.

"He didn't," Liam assured me. "I heard stories from the wolves in your pack, but how much of those should I believe? If I were to take them at their word you'd be the most dangerous man on the planet, tricking the Volkov and controlling the world's werewolf population with your mysterious tea, pranks, and smiles."

I gave him narrowed eyes to show him just how much baloney I thought he was trying to feed me.

"Seriously," he said. "Child of legend, stories sung as in days of old. I am nothing in the shadow of such greatness."

"Now I really know you're teasing me," I told Liam. "And being evasive about yourself. Are there songs that the bards of old used to sing about you? Broken hearts and battles won? That sort of thing."

"Hmm. Bards, I don't think so. I have heard others sing me a song or two about you while I was there. Teasing things, embellished to sound ridiculous and funny. Though there's always some grain of truth to those songs, isn't there?"

"Like?" I prodded, trying to think of anything I'd done that had been worth *Apa* creating a song.

"Eggs in shoes?"

I laughed. Yeah, I'd done that. "*Apa* insisted I do chores, one of which had been collecting the fresh eggs from the chickens every morning. We took turns cooking them, but somehow there would never be enough for me. Wolves eat so much. *Apa* never said anything, though I knew he'd disapproved. He'd been waiting for me to do something, stand up for myself, I think, and so I had. Instead of bringing the eggs to table one morning, I cracked the whole lot of them over everyone's shoes. Probably hundreds of dollars of expensive shoes ruined, but I'd been eleven. *Apa* had taken the egg collecting job away from me and given me the garden to tend instead. That worked out just fine for me."

"Dyeing everyone's clothes bright orange?" Liam continued laughing.

I nodded. "Okay, yeah, that was me too."

"Tea that gave the whole pack the runs?"

"Now that's going a little far and it wasn't the whole pack." It had just been a handful of wolves who enjoyed picking on me. "Careful, I still have the ingredients for that tea memorized. Should you have any incontinence issues, let me know."

Liam laughed. He had a great laugh. It wasn't fair that I wanted to hear the sound more often. "You know a lot about me, and I still know so little about you," I complained.

"Okay, but we have time. I can't possibly tell you everything in one night or even a year. You still need food and rest."

"Sure, but we gotta start somewhere right." If we were starting something, and dammit if I didn't hope we were.

"Okay, three burning questions for right now," Liam consented. "However, the way I answer is up to me."

"Fine. First question, where are you from?"

"Maple Falls, Washington."

Grr. "You know that's not what I meant. Where you are now is not where you are from."

"It is now. But if you must know, I was born in Ireland."

The hints of accent could have been Irish. I'd not heard it outside of movies enough to know, and his was interlaced with a hint of a Southern drawl and his very modern American TV standard. I'd be listening for it now. Not that it mattered much where he was born.

"Second question, how long have you been a wolf? And you better not say since some asshole bit you." It actually took more than a bite. It took death. Much like vampires, wolves had to die to be reborn. Unlike vampires it didn't take years of blood exchanges, just one horribly bloody moment and their world could change.

Liam shook his head. "I choose how I answer, remember? Anyway, I am not as old as the Volkov, but substantially older than you. It makes me feel old just to think about it."

No one really knew how old *Apa* was. I suspected over a thousand, but no one talked about it. The fact that Liam wouldn't give me a straight answer meant he was really old. Older than Felix, I wondered. Was he on the verge of losing it too? Is that why *Apa* had chased me into his territory? "Older than Felix?" I whispered, not realizing I was really asking a question.

"No," Liam said gently. "I believe last I heard, Felix was a half millennia or so old. Not as old as Oberon, who is almost as old as the Volkov himself. I am not as old as Felix."

I wouldn't ask if he were crazy. The crazy couldn't really answer that truthfully. He hadn't attacked me yet, and that was something. But he was really possessive. "Last question for today. Do you have any lovers or other kids lingering around that I should worry about?"

"No. Korissa is my only child. And I've already told you about her mother." He didn't point out that I'd already had my three questions. I had a million more. He could have a little time to sort out what to tell me. Getting information had never been hard for me. Part of being an omega made people just want to talk to me. If he was telling the truth, then maybe, just maybe he wasn't like Felix. I didn't want to be anyone's dirty little secret.

"Would you hide me from everyone? Your pack? Other packs? Regular people?" What I didn't say, but so wanted to ask was: Would you be ashamed of me? I didn't expect him to answer.

"No," Liam said, looking me straight in the eyes. "My pack already knows. The world can know. I don't care what they think."

"About us being mates," I clarified because everything was still just so complicated. We'd just met. Sure I felt this pull toward him, but I'd felt drawn to Felix too. Liam was dangling a dream in front of me, and I was too afraid to reach for it. Instant love didn't happen in the real world, only in storybooks. My life might have been filled with fantastical monsters, but I couldn't see a happy ending coming any time soon. It was better if I just left. Before I began to hope and maybe fall in love again. Definitely before I began to trust again.

Liam sighed, once again seeming to know what I was thinking because he said, "What will you have if you run again? I'm offering you a place to rest. A home with protection."

"And strings. You want me to be your mate. Which I still don't get. You're an alpha. Alpha's don't do men. Won't it make other alphas think you're weak? Have other men challenging you?" It boggled the mind. "I have nothing to offer you. The Volkov doesn't listen to me, so you can't use me to control him. My magic isn't that powerful, and I have no money or power to help you build your pack. The omega thing isn't really a power. You'd be better off finding a human woman to serve as omega."

"I tried that. And while I love my daughter, the relationship was a nightmare. Fighting my wolf every day because the world accepts my marriage with a human female? Wasted years. Endless battles. I've spent too long trying to fit in. Now I just embrace what and who I am. My wolf rejoiced when he first scented you. Exclaimed: Mine! Mine! Finally, mine! You are more than just the value of what you can do for me. You have worth just being you. I understand if you don't believe it yet. You've been running a long time, before you even left your pack, I believe. The Volkov is to blame for that. As your Alpha it was his responsibility to provide you with safety, love, and a home. I offer no strings, just safety, and home. Wishes, yes. Again, what will you have if you run? Is that freedom? Or a cage of fear? Always running.

"Omegas are ingrained to want roots, a home, and a pack. You'll never have any of that if you continue to run. And what of your alchemy? The gardens and the tea? The things you love so much that you've given up to escape? What if stopping here will let you reclaim that part of your life?"

Damn him for seeing so much of me in such a short period of time. He searched my head, likely for damage. His hands gently massaged my scalp. He also seemed to be enjoying the way my hair cascaded through his fingers. It had been a long time since I'd felt sexually aroused by anyone. His continued touch burned into me with need, building something in my gut I'd never felt before, a longing to be claimed, to submit. But I couldn't.

"It's not safe. There's Felix, and *Apa* and maybe Hugo."

"There's not. The Volkov has declared you mine. He recognizes our bond. Felix has no claim. And while I won't force you to mate me, it does give you a safe place to rebuild. Heal. From more than just these physical wounds. If Hugo comes, I will deal with him." He ran his fingers over my scalp. "Are there any tender spots? How is your vision?"

He was too close again. My brain warred with the thought of begging for another kiss and screaming at him to stop touching me. I just grunted. Liam sat back on his knees, finally releasing me completely. Immediately I missed the warm of this touch. Stupid contrary nature.

"Your word you won't run?"

"That's not fair."

"I give you my word as the Alpha of this territory. I will protect you. I will not harm you. I will not let my people harm you."

"That's a lot of promises." Unrealistic really. And werewolves weren't bound to the truth like the fae were. He didn't smell like he was lying, but believing something was true was different than it actually being true.

A phone rang and Liam frowned as he pulled a cell phone out of his pocket. My hearing wasn't as good as the wolves, and he must have had the volume turned way down because all I could make out was Dylan's voice. Liam simply replied, "Yes," after a moment and hung up. Then there was a knock at the door.

"Enter," Liam called. Of course it was Dylan, who stepped into the room and shut the door behind him. He was carrying a box, like the sort of thing UPS left on people's doorstep. He didn't seem bothered by the almost subservient position of his Alpha in front of me. He just crossed the room, dropped the box on the bed beside me, turned and left without another word.

Once the door was closed, Liam reached for the box. I took the opportunity to pull out of his touch completely, wrapping myself up in the top blanket. It was a flimsy barrier, but so was my resolve not to touch Liam again. How long would the taste of his lips linger on mine? When would his power stop rolling through me? Was this what it felt like to have a mate? I'd never felt this haunted by Felix's touch. I'd also never felt the need to roll in his scent, revel in his kiss, and beg for his touch. I sucked in a deep breath and focused on calming my body.

"The box is for you from the Volkov. It smells like the Volkov." Liam hesitated. "Perhaps I should have one of my wolves take it outside and open it."

"If *Apa* wanted me dead, I'd already be dead," I told Liam. Though I wasn't sure that was true. Felix might want me dead, but Liam said the box smelled like *Apa*. I wasn't close enough to tell. It could have been an elaborate ploy by Felix to hurt me, but I couldn't really see him setting a bomb or something. Maybe he wanted me dead now that he knew he'd never get me back. Or maybe he just wanted to kill me himself. But it would never be from a distance.

Liam ripped at the tape on the box and opened it. Inside was a wallet and a cell phone. Both items I had abandoned when I'd run from the Volkov's territory a year ago. The contents of the wallet hadn't changed. My driver's license, cash, credit cards, business cards, everything. Liam examined the phone, first taking off the backing to look at the battery area, then putting it back together and holding the ON button. It took a moment for the little Apple symbol to fade and my old background photo to show up. It had been a picture of my garden, one taken to hastily replace the one I'd once had of Felix.

Then the phone started ringing. Across the screen in large letters it read, *Apa*. I took the phone from Liam and hit decline. How had *Apa* known? Not only when I got the phone but when it had been turned on? Was there some sort of tracker in it? Was he really in my head? Able to find me anywhere just like he led everyone to believe? He denied omniscience, but he always seemed to know everything about everybody. It was unnerving as hell.

The phone began to ring again. Liam took it back and

accepted the call, hitting the speaker button. "Hello," Liam answered.

I clutched at the blanket waiting for anger, rejection, and painful words. At least this far away all he could do was talk me to death.

"Liam?" *Apa's* voice came through the phone, soft and uncertain, which was unusual. "Is Seb there? Is he safe in your territory?"

Liam's eyes flicked up to my face, and I don't know what he saw there, but he answered, "He's safe."

Apa let out a sigh. "Small favors," he grumbled. "Does he plan to stay?"

"We're working on that," Liam answered.

I frowned at him.

"I've had Oberon check all of his accounts and everything is as it should be. He put some sort of tracker on the phone that alerted me when it was turned on. Kevin should be arriving before nightfall with the trailer, but he'll call before he arrives. I hope that providing all his things will help." Kevin? I tried to recall if I knew a Kevin and should be worried. "How is he holding up?"

"He's skittish," Liam said, humor in his eyes. "Prickly. More like a porcupine than a fox."

Jerk, I mouthed at him. Hopefully even the Volkov wasn't powerful enough to hear my heartbeat through the long distance line of a cell phone three years out of date.

"That is actually normal, and reassuring," the Volkov replied.

"Felix has called several times demanding entrance to my territory," Liam told the Volkov. I felt my heart begin to pound. "If he persists and crosses into my land…"

"Understood. I've warned him myself. He may be too far gone to make any reasonable decisions. I take the blame for that. I will deal with him directly if I have to." *Apa* was quiet for a moment as if thinking. "Seb?"

Could he hear me? I gripped the blanket tighter and tried not to breath.

Again he sighed. "I understand."

"Time," Liam said.

"Is often a luxury," the Volkov finished. "Make use of it the best way you can." Then he hung up.

"I don't know anyone named Kevin," I told Liam. Why was he coming? What trailer?

"Let's go get dinner," Liam said instead of answering.

"Evasive," I pointed out again, but my stomach growled.

"Change the pants," Liam instructed. "No need to smell wounded among wolves."

I growled at him as I let go of the blanket, slid to the edge of the bed and then stalked to the dresser to grab a clean pair of sweats. My leg still hurt a little, the edge near my stomach being the worst of it. The wound looked healed, a pink scar tracing the path through my flesh, but the skin still tender from regrowth. I suspected when I brushed my hair I'd feel much the same tenderness in my scalp.

"Thank you," I said. "For helping me heal. You're really not angry?"

"Not at you."

I looked up to see there was a tightness to his eyes. Maybe anger, maybe frustration.

"You look mad." But he hadn't lied. If he was mad it wasn't at me. "Are you mad at the Volkov?"

"That would be stupid," Liam said, though he didn't deny it. "I'm not suicidal." He was quiet another minute before adding, "He should have protected you better."

I didn't disagree as I tugged on the sweats, feeling Liam's eyes on me the whole time. Not predatory, but not innocent either. When I glanced back his way there was heat in his eyes, amusement, and pride. Pride?

"I don't get you," I told him.

"What is to get?" He asked.

I waved a hand at all of him.

He quirked a brow at me.

"Nevermind. Let's get food." Because I could go for another bacon sandwich, that would be fantastic, and maybe I'd stop tasting Liam's lips on mine.

CHAPTER 11

No bacon. Dinner was roasted chicken with vegetables. Apparently Stacey and Leigh had taken over the kitchen, deciding to once again feed the pack. My lips ached as though Liam's kiss had bruised them, and I felt like everyone was staring at me. Did they all know their alpha wanted a guy for a mate? Did they care? Maybe the *witchborn* thing bothered them more. I'd heard of packs hunting down *witchborn* and wiping them out. It wasn't a sanctioned practice, but some packs took out vampires too. *Apa* didn't regulate them so long as they kept off his radar and out of the news. Oberon dealt with the ones who didn't.

"Kevin called," Dylan said as he walked into the kitchen with the first tray of four roasted chickens. "He's just about to town. He was hoping to make it by dinner."

"Has the trip been eventful?" Liam inquired. He stood only a few steps behind me, staying in my bubble. It should have bothered me since it normally would, only I kind of liked his presence at my back.

"Nothing that he brought up."

"Who's Kevin?" I asked again.

"One of our submissive wolves," Stacey answered absently as she prepared some sort of potato salad.

"One of your submissive wolves? How many submissive wolves are in the pack?" I asked. Submissives were rare in general among wolves as wolves were dominant by nature. Not as rare as omegas, but not much more common either. Most packs had one if they were lucky to have one at all. I'd never heard of a pack having more than one. Not even *Apa*'s pack.

"Four," Leigh answered this time. "Liam has a hero complex. Rescues strays a lot." Her eyes flicked over me. It wasn't a disapproving look, more an unimpressed one. "Submissives usually spend a lot of time jumping from pack to pack until they find their mates. The ones who find their way here just stay."

Four was a lot of submissives. Four submissives and an omega. Was Liam trying to set himself up like the Volkov? Dominant wolves surrounded submissives to protect them. It was their nature. Instinct. It also kept them from fighting amongst themselves as they had a duty to create a solid and safe home for the submissive wolves. Having four would draw more dominant wolves to the pack. Liam had said it was a growing pack. The Volkov's pack was the largest in the country with over two hundred wolves. Packs were usually fewer than fifty. Hard to hide a large pack in the modern world.

The more dominant wolves in one place, the more fights and death there was. Only no one in Liam's pack seemed to be fighting. Except maybe Carl who happened to be missing from the dinner set up.

The sound of a truck pulling into the long drive interrupted the chatter. The mysterious Kevin, perhaps? Liam glanced my way only once before leaving the kitchen to head for the front door. The feeling of his warmth leaving me, made me shiver. I caught the glimpse of a giant Chevy pickup truck from one of the front windows, but couldn't see much about it until I followed Liam out the door.

The man getting out of the driver's side of the truck was unfamiliar. He was ordinary looking enough, mid-twenties, with sandy brown hair and chocolate brown eyes. He dressed like a college student but stood stiff through the shoulder like a soldier. His submissive presence preceded him and distracted me so much that it took me a full minute to realize there had been someone in the passenger seat. This time it was someone I recognized.

The second man got out of the truck, a large black man with rows of beautiful half-bleached braids that flowed down to his shoulders. His skin wasn't as dark as my grandfather's, but only just. He was almost six foot five and broad through the shoulder, a big enough man to make anyone pause. His dark black eyes sought me out, but were wary. I'd know him anywhere since he'd been a mentor to me for years. Oberon, *Apa's* second.

I must have made some noise because when I turned to run, Liam was already there, arm around my waist, pulling me against him. His heat surrounded me and sent the power pulsing through me again. Liam's scent, body heat, and touch soothed the instinct to run. Calming me as an alpha should not be able to do. Not unless he really was my mate. Instead I clung to him trying to breathe. His presence just rolled over me like a wave of protection, home, and safety.

"You sure you didn't mate me?" I grumbled, lost in the comfort of Liam. It wasn't fair that his touch could unravel my sense of self preservation. Oberon could snap me in half without breaking a sweat. Running was a good idea, snuggling with Liam…

"Oberon is no threat." Liam held me tight.

"I'm wounded, little fox. I have never offered you harm,"

Oberon called. "And after all the work I did to bring home to you, I'd think you'd be more welcoming."

My mind still screamed: Trust no one! While my body said: Liam is home, mate and fuck! But slowly the calm sank in. Liam overtaking my senses with his quiet strength. I'd heard alphas could do that sometimes. Seen *Apa* do it a time or two in his pack. He'd tried it on me more than once, but it never worked. Omega overruled alpha. I didn't have to submit. But in Liam's arms, I *wanted* to.

It wasn't fair or safe. Not even Liam could stand against the Volkov. And why would he? We barely knew each other. Just because some year ago trauma had called him to me didn't mean we were mates. It didn't mean Liam had to die for me. And he would die. I felt that like a knife in my gut. Oberon was bigger than Liam. More dominant? Oberon's was easily the second most powerful wolf in the country. Maybe one of the strongest wolves in the world. If *Apa* had ordered Oberon to end me, no one could stand in his way. I didn't really want he and Liam to fight. Fights meant death, and I loved Oberon like a brother. Liam I barely knew, but wanted to bask in. The war of my emotions storming inside me, made it hard to breathe.

I had to close my eyes and just suck in air for a minute. Center myself. Even if I ran right this second, shifted to my fox and just bolted, Oberon could catch me. He wouldn't need to shift. As big a man as he was, he could move. His ease with people made everyone underestimate him. I'd seen him fight. I'd seen him kill alpha wolves who stepped out of line without hesitation. Had wondered a time or two why he hadn't tried to take out *Apa*. I thought *Apa* might send Felix to kill me. I never thought he'd send Oberon. This hurt more. Was so much more overwhelming than I'd ever imagined the moment to be. A thousand scenarios I'd imagined, and not once had Oberon been the one to end me.

Liam turned me into his embrace so his arms encircled me completely. I was trembling. Freezing. Heart pounding in terror while ice poured through my veins. Liam whispered something. I had to work to hear him, fighting through the noise in my own head, my own stabbing voices, to hear his. "You're safe. Breathe. I will protect you. Breathe. That's right. In…one, two, three, four; out…one, two, three, four. Does your arm hurt? Breathe. You told me when someone means you harm, your arm hurts. Breathe." Had I told him about the wards on my arm? I didn't remember telling him. "You talk in your sleep," Liam whispered. "Breathe. That's good. Slow down your breathing. Focus on my voice and your breath. Much better." I still struggled for breath, gasping for it in huge gulps, but I could work at making each one a conscious effort.

"Is this new?" Oberon asked. "These panic attacks?"

"I suspect it has something to do with his departure from your pack," Dylan said as he took a couple of bags from Kevin. "Since he's ours now, we'll sort it out."

"Watch it, pup," Oberon growled at Dylan.

"I've seen you fight," Dylan said. He dropped the bags just inside the door and came back out. "I know I can't beat you. But death doesn't scare me. Boss has declared the omega his. Even without them being mate-bonded the whole pack feels it. Not everyone will like it, but we will all defend what is ours. We're not a large pack, but we are close. A family. He needs a family to help him heal. The Boss just has to convince him to stay. What you do to me won't change that."

"Not yours," I grumbled into Liam's chest, though the words felt like a lie. Liam's chin rested on the top of my head. He'd practically wrapped himself around me, becoming a physical shield against my emotional monsters. At least I could breathe again, even if all I could smell was how fucking fantastic Liam's natural scent was. I tried to mold my breathing to his, focusing on the movement of his chest against me. He didn't respond to Oberon or Dylan, didn't focus on anything but me. Counting breaths with me, while I tried to calm my racing heart.

"I'm going to move the trailer since we've got the pad set up. I'll pull it around," Dylan said. He must have been talking to Liam because he was close again. I had to work to pry myself away from Liam's warmth. I felt him nod. The truck restarted, engine making that distinct Hemi sound. It was only after it started to move that I could see what was attached to it. A camping trailer. My camping trailer. There was no mistaking the silver bullet-like body, and technological upgrades I'd made. I'd remodeled the whole thing, adding a few windows, which hadn't been in the original design, but it still looked like the 1960s era family vacation hauler on the outside.

I shoved away from Liam's chest while still clinging to him just to be sure. I told myself it was just to push him at Oberon if Oberon decided to attack, but that was also a lie. If Liam went anywhere at that moment, I'd likely go with him.

"Is that my trailer?" Really, a dumb question since I didn't know anyone else to have an ugly beast with modern additions like retractable awnings, solar panels, and satellite dishes.

Dylan pulled it off the drive and around toward the lavender field. Kevin walked past us, stopping only long enough to nod to Liam before disappearing into the house. Oberon kept his distance. "Your third assures me he knows how to set up the water and power connections," Oberon said. "If not, I'm sure Sebastian does."

Apa had sent Oberon with my things. They'd given me back my home, even if it was across the country. Did that mean they didn't want me dead, punished, or humiliated? I was so confused. This whole day had been madness. Waking up in the middle of a pack with an alpha who was claiming to be my mate. Calming rabid wolves, cowed by little girls, healed with a kiss, and confronted with my past. Too much. It was all just too much. I should have let Liam go, gone back into the house, or followed my trailer, but I couldn't. I didn't know what to do. Move or stay still? Run or hold on?

"Seb?" Oberon asked.

"He's processing," Liam said. "Lots of thinking. Your father warned me that he *thinks himself into a corner and back again.*"

Oberon snorted. "Made him really good at alchemy and herbalism. Was always testing and hypothesizing. He and Felix were always a bad match. Felix doesn't think, just demands. Anyway, the inside of the house is untouched. The wards wouldn't let any of us go inside. Wouldn't have the wallet and phone if they hadn't just one day appeared on *Apa's* desk. Hopefully everything didn't get tossed around during the drive. It took eleven witches and a shit ton of wolf strength to get the camper unrooted from the spot it'd been parked. *Apa's* pack witch was furious that Seb had a ward that strong, and she couldn't figure out how to break it. If someone hadn't suggested we dig up the trailer we'd have never broken the ward that bound it to the earth. You were always good with wards, little fox."

"Not good enough," I muttered. Should have kept Felix out. Redone the ward. Something. I was suddenly exhausted. The energy I'd borrowed from Liam drained away and I just wanted to sleep. My trailer was here. Home. Safety. I would need to sleep soon if any indication of the last two times I'd used someone else's power to heal was. Already my emotions garbled in a mix of chaos. Exhaustion and vulnerability were never a good combination.

"You can let me go now. I'm not going to run," I told Liam. Seeing my home so close made me long for it. It wouldn't be the same, would it? A year was a long time for the world to change. For me to change. But it was warded. No one could get inside but me. I could lock even Felix out with little effort now. A year of practice casting wards on my car had done me a wealth of good. They couldn't even burn the trailer down around me as the wards made it inflammable. It wouldn't survive a bomb strike and it would take a while to rebind it to the earth to make it unmovable again, but it would be safe. Safe on Liam's land. Being close to Liam was okay. Would he let me stay? Was it too much to hope that what he wanted from me was real? Maybe I could just live here for a while. Work at the bakery, make some tea, rebuild a life without the Volkov's pack since they hated me anyway. The pack didn't have to accept me. Liam didn't have to mate me.

"No strings," I said. "You promised no strings."

"I did," Liam acknowledged. "The house is movable, and Kevin's truck can move it to wherever you'd like, but for now it will be hooked up here. Kevin needs some sleep and time with the pack. He's been away for almost a week. You promised to show my daughter how to make lavender lemonade. I'm sure that will take a day or so at least."

The effort it took to finally get my hands to release their death grip on Liam's shirt had me sweating. Soon I'd collapse in a dead sleep for at least a few hours, my hunger completely replaced by exhaustion. I turned away from Liam and followed the truck and trailer across the property. On the other side of the lavender field from the house, Dylan was parking the trailer. He jumped out of the truck and began unhooking the trailer from the truck. Liam followed me at a subdued pace when he could have beat me to the camper a hundred times over. Vaguely I could feel Oberon at our backs, but was too tired to care. Not when home was this close. Safety…

CHAPTER 12

I reached the door of the trailer and just stood there, soaking in the sight. When I put my hand to the door, the sensation of the wards rippled through me. Welcoming, awakening, almost like a sleeping cat, they recognized me. I turned the handle expecting resistance for some reason, though I'd never needed a key. The door locked just fine from the inside. I just never used it as the wards provided better security.

I flung the door open, fearing a mess of a home left to time and flight. Only everything was in its place; clean, dust free, and quiet. It was a little stuffy so I stepped inside to open some windows. In the hottest of Texas summers there was a tiny central air unit that ran on solar energy. The whole camper ran on solar, was connected to satellite, and could store enough water for a week's use without a fresh water hookup. I'd had rain barrels too, but they weren't part of the actual camper and I suspected they'd been left behind.

"Can't get the door to the hookups open," Dylan said from the doorway. "Some kind of ward?"

"Yes," I said. I put my hand to the wall and closed my eyes, centering on the wards, letting my senses breeze over them, testing each one and smoothing out gaps, removing axis points. A year of practice and I could even out the kinks with little effort. The wards on the camper were years of trial and error patched together. Only now could I meld them into something seamless. At least the year on the run had taught me something. I'd have to spend some quality time making them permanent and etching wards under the floorboards, but I could enhance what I had for now. I added Felix to the non grata list. He could pick the trailer up and throw it, at least until I could get it rebound to the earth, but he couldn't get to me when I was inside it.

"The house was unhooked and buttoned up. We noticed it a day or two after you left. Didn't think you'd been in the right mind to close it down before leaving, but *Apa* said it was probably a ward. Never known a ward to unhook lines and close doors. Barriers, yes, but wards aren't active like that," Oberon said. "No one could get in. Xander wouldn't allow Felix near it. But I swear sometimes I see lights on in there."

I quirked a smile at Oberon's tone. "It's not haunted." Though many in the Volkov's pack had often whispered of it. When I'd bought the trailer it had been a mess. Only gutting it and recreating it had made it what it was today. But I'd never have purchased it if I'd sensed something as dark as death had taken place inside. Now it was a place of safety. Felix couldn't enter, neither could Oberon or even *Apa*. His entrance had always been temporary and very careful.

Liam couldn't enter either. He stood in the doorway looking resigned. "At least let us help hook it up and come to the house for dinner. You're hungry. Your stomach was growling earlier." He glanced at Oberon who hadn't gotten closer and was standing off to the side so he wasn't behind Liam. I could see him through the window, with his arms folded across his chest, expressionless. Why had they brought me my home? Were they trying to lull me into a false sense of safety? Had they done something to the wards?

I touched the wall again, testing the wards. Everything was secure, though the ties were old and not as strong since it was no longer bound to the earth. I was pretty sure I could improve the wards, but it would have to be over a few days. Just the feeling of standing in my own space made me feel calm, safe, and exhausted. I relaxed the wards on the hookups and heard the little supply closet outside pop open.

"That worked," Dylan said from the other side of the trailer. "Hooking everything up now."

"Seriously haunted," Oberon grumbled. "Wards don't close doors and unhook powerlines."

The trailer wasn't haunted like Oberon seemed to be implying, and I was just tired.

"I just want some rest," I said to Liam who stood right outside the door with his hands touching the side of the doorway. He couldn't enter, and he might as well have been staring through an unbreakable glass window.

"You won't eat dinner first? You'll need the strength from all that healing." He would need the food more than I would though he didn't look tired at all.

"One skipped meal won't hurt." I'd gone for days without eating before. Having my home back just overpowered every other need. I looked around my little camper. It was a 21' trailer with the kitchen right inside the entryway and the bedroom in the back. All of the area for seating and traditional camping setup I'd removed and added custom shelves. All of my books, herbs, and equipment was where it should be. Walls full of tiny roll-out shelves for tins of herbs, mixtures, and supplies. It was a wide open space, with only the bathroom closed off. The bed was made with fresh linens. Something that should have been impossible if no one could get inside.

I'd run that last night, leaving the house in disarray. There had been dishes to wash and the bed had been a mess of blood and fluids. I even vaguely recall a dent in the wall near the bed from Felix throwing me into it. Yet it was all gone.

Not haunted. Not really. It was a little more complicated than that.

Dylan stepped up beside Liam. "Everything is hooked up." He glanced from me and back to Liam. "You sure you won't come in for dinner?"

"I just need…"

"Time," Liam finished. He nodded and stepped away from the trailer. "Good night, Sebastian. Remember, if you'd like to start in the bakery, we're up early." He walked back toward the house without another word. Dylan returned to drive the truck back, and Oberon stared at me through the window. I closed the door and locked it. Not that the lock really mattered.

"Tomorrow then, little fox," Oberon said.

"You're not going home?" I called through the window.

"Not yet. I have unfinished business here." He walked away, leaving me with those cryptic words. I closed the blinds near the sleeping area and dropped down on top of the bed. It smelled like home. Lavender and chamomile, of den and safety. I was asleep before I even realized I'd closed my eyes.

CHAPTER 13

I dreamt of Felix. He'd brought me flowers. Just some scrap of half-dead buds he'd gotten at a grocery store. An apology for something I couldn't recall. He did that a lot. Not that it mattered. I'd been annoyed by the flowers as I grew better myself. Thought and all that, I'd tried to remind myself. The dream version of him was kinder, until he suddenly shifted into his wolf and leapt to tear out my throat.

I jerked awake.

Only a pale sliver of moonlight eased through the trailer. All the window shades were closed, though I couldn't recall pulling them all before I'd fallen into bed. The gentle dance of bugs in the night soothed my anxiety a little. If something like Felix was stalking the darkness, the night would be still.

I lay there for a bit, willing myself back to sleep. Only it didn't come. Instead uneasiness rose. Nothing around me seemed off. My arm didn't hurt and the night sang. Still my body ached with a need to get up and run. Fear. I'd been running from myself for almost a year. Running from voices in my head that told me I'd never be safe again.

Pointless.

I dragged myself out of bed and went to the fridge, expecting molded food or an empty space. Only it was full of freshly brewed tea, stacks of veggies and even a package of eggs with a current date on them. At least someone had missed me, I thought, as I poured a glass of lavender lemonade. The taste of it was slightly sour, the bitter edge of magic always seeped through.

The night outside went silent. I froze, listening. My heart began to pound.

Not again. I wasn't going to keep running. Even when my body told me to run, that death was imminent if I didn't. If Felix stood outside my door he'd regret coming here. I wasn't powerful, not in the way a werewolf was. But I was done looking over my shoulder. My supply of books was categorized by type. I had plenty of dark magic books I'd barely touched. Things with alchemy so dark it would have made that anime Korissa knew of look tame. It meant giving up part of my soul for safety. Maybe I was ready for that.

I opened the door and stared out into the darkness. There was a wolf laying at the base of the step-down. He turned his head to look my way, and I caught a glimpse of the stripe of color running down his nose.

"Toby," I grumbled. He looked back out into the night, but didn't appear alarmed, just alert. "Someone out there?" Hey Lassie, is Timmy down the well? I thought as I leaned out the door.

I caught Liam's scent before I saw him so he must have purposely gone upwind. "I thought you said you had to be up early? You should go to bed."

He materialized from the darkness as though called by magic. "I did. Couldn't sleep. Had my guards patrolling, but decided to take a shift myself."

"Guarding me or guarding your people from me? And since when do alphas do guard duty?" I waved a hand at him. He made no sense.

He stepped up to the door, letting just Toby's body and the strength of my wards separate us. "Can I come in?"

"Absolutely not."

He frowned. "You're afraid I'll hurt you."

Yes. "No."

He turned and paced for a minute, back and forth in front of the door. "I'll sleep out here then."

I shrugged. "Okay. Night." I closed the door on both of them, put the lemonade pitcher away and went back to bed. It took me a while to fall back to sleep, but as soon as I did, I dreamt of fangs again and bolted upright. Dammit. I threw off the blanket and stalked to the door. Toby hadn't moved. Liam sat on the ground, not touching the trailer, but close. He looked up when the door opened.

"If you agree to let my wards lock down your power, you can come in," I told him.

"Lock down my power?"

"It binds your alpha strength. You won't be able to shift while in my home and your strength will be no more than human level. You'll still be able to feel your pack and their bond with you, but you won't be able to borrow energy or power from them." It had taken me months to perfect the ward, and I'd used it on my car and every hotel room I'd ever stayed in. The ward even worked on fae. It's only real limitation was that it had to be bound to a place. I'd tried small objects like lockets, but those failed. I could exclude people individually from the ward, so it didn't block my ability to shift or use magic, but it would for just about anyone else. The only other alpha wolf I'd ever used it on was *Apa*. He'd visited often, and after the initial shock of the wards wore off, he seemed to enjoy spending time being almost human in my home.

Liam took a minute to decide, but finally he jumped to his feet and approached the door. "I agree. Inside your home, your rules, so long as I'm not truly separated from the pack."

I put my hand out, palm up, through the doorway, offering it to him. He took it and let me pull him inside. Toby whined. I felt Liam slide through the ward with my consent. When he was inside, I let him go. He stood blinking, and shaking his head a little, like he was disoriented.

"If you step back outside the feeling will go away," I told him. "I've been told it's very unnerving for older wolves. If it's too much for you, I understand." I left the door open, walked toward the bed, and glared at it. "Inviting you into my home does not mean I'm having sex with you." Even if I had only the one sleeping space. Maybe I should shift and sleep as a fox. But he'd consented to the ward that virtually stripped him of his otherness. He was still an alpha, still leader of his pack, but inside my trailer, he was little more than human. He'd still be bigger and stronger than me, but here I had power. I was also no longer afraid to use it. No one would ever hurt me in my own home again.

"It's odd," Liam said after a minute, "for my head to be so silent. I never realized how loud the wolf was, the pack, and the responsibility as alpha. It's still there." He pointed to his head. "Just muted." He reached out and shut the door, sliding the lock into place. "Can anyone enter? Like if someone just wandered up who had no magic?"

"No. No one can enter without an invite. It would be easier to grate a rock into dust than to get through my wards." I made my way back to the bed and actually pulled the blankets back. It was a queen-sized bed, the largest I could fit in the space. Right now it felt really small. Maybe Liam would sleep on the floor. I could tell him to sleep on the floor since he'd sort of demanded entry into my home. He kicked off his shoes and followed me to the bed, grabbing the blankets and holding them up for me.

"No sex," I said again. Determined to convince him, even if my body was saying, hey okay, let's do it.

"Agreed," Liam nodded. I curled up into the wall at the back of the camper, away from the doors and windows. This end of the trailer I'd reinforced with steel interlaced with silver coated steel, so it kept wolves, vampires, and fae alike, out if the wards stopped working. Liam crawled beneath the blankets, giving me space, but blocking me in, so his body was between me and the door.

"My wards are enough to protect me," I said quietly.

"Hmm," Liam said. That annoying sound of acknowledgment but disagreement. I turned my head away and closed my eyes again. Liam's body heat close enough to warm me, even while I pretended I didn't want him to hold me while I slept.

I woke again, not sure what had actually roused me, since I couldn't recall a dream. My body felt good, sated, warm, and sleepy. Safe. How long had it been since I'd woken up feeling safe? Was it being home in my own bed? Or the fact that Liam's scent surrounded me, much like his body spooned me. He'd flipped us, somehow, or maybe I'd done it, but my back was to the open space and his to the wall. I glanced up, expecting him to be sleeping, but he was staring across the room, a troubled expression on his face.

"It's not haunted," I muttered at him.

"The glass of lemonade you left on the counter is gone."

I couldn't help but smile. Even big scary alpha werewolves were afraid of things that went bump in the night. "You said we have to be up early. Is it time already?"

Liam glanced at his watch. "Three hours."

"I can sleep three more hours."

"What about the ghost?" He didn't sound afraid, but he watched the room warily.

"Not a ghost."

"I heard that was something you can do. Talk to ghosts."

"Sadly that is just one of my very limited super powers. Trust me. You don't talk to ghosts because if you do, they never shut up. Mostly I ignore them, and they ignore me. If I stay here long, I'll plant some things that will keep them moving should they stumble across the area."

"Are ghosts mobile? I thought they were tied to places and things."

"A little of both really. Depends on the ghost." I yawned. "Sleep. Even alphas need sleep."

"Hmm," he grumbled, and this time it did sound like he disapproved. He could stay awake and keep watch if he wanted. Nothing in this little camper would hurt me. He tucked his arm around my waist and pulled me closer. For a minute I was frozen in fear. Only something about Liam trickled through my senses, calming me. His scent maybe? The warmth of his touch? I wasn't really certain, except to know it was nothing tangible.

"Is it okay to hold you while you sleep?" He whispered softly. He didn't loosen his hold. "I should have asked first."

"It's okay. Just keep your hands above the border," I grumbled at him, like he was putting me out. In truth, he was being the perfect gentleman. No erection poked into my belly and his body kept a careful distance while still lending me a semblance of protection and heat.

"Hmm," Liam said again. I was beginning to really

wonder what he meant by that disagreeing noise. "Sleep. You're safe. Just sleep."

He made me feel safe, even while my brain screamed at me to trust no one. In his arms my physical anxiety vanished, leaving just my over active brain to compensate.

I closed my eyes, and told myself to sleep. Seconds later I drifted off. It was a gift.

CHAPTER 14

The sound of Liam's watch alarm woke me the next time. He silenced it quickly, but I was already moving out of his warm embrace, and toward the bathroom. Had he slept at all? Since he was the manager of the bakery, maybe he could stay home and sleep, letting his minions take care of things. Though that didn't really seem to be his way of dealing with things.

I wondered if leaving my little camper was a good idea. Oberon was still around, and Felix might be stalking me. Neither of them had actually tried to kill me since entering Liam's territory. Unless the wolves who'd attacked me had been theirs. Oberon did the dirty work himself, so I couldn't see him hiring some random wolves to hurt me. And Felix... he didn't inspire loyalty in anyone. Not really. He had money, so maybe he'd hired them. Perhaps that was why Oberon was still here.

Getting up to work a few hours for Liam made me feel better about all he'd done for me. Repayment of some kind at least. I'd learned long ago to suck up my pride and allow myself to accept the charity of others. If it didn't turn and bite me in the ass so often I wouldn't fight it so much. Liam had given me a lot. Healing, safety, food, and rest. Those things were worth more than a few hours of labor, but I'd give him what I could while I was here.

I did my business, brushed my teeth and combed my hair. When I stepped out of the bathroom to dig in the drawers built beneath the bed for all my clothes, Liam was sitting up in bed, staring at a large gray cat who perched on the top of a shelf. The cat was dark gray striped in black. The tail was thick and striped more like a raccoon than any cat I'd ever seen. Its long fur gave it bulk, and the flattened ears made it look angry and judgmental. Was that look for me, or for the wolf I'd let in my home?

"Morning, Robin," I called to the cat. My clothes sat where I'd left them, all clean and neatly folded. I chose a pair of jeans and a t-shirt, with a hoodie to help with the morning chill. Liam didn't correct or direct what I needed to wear for the bakery, so he either didn't notice or didn't care. That suited me just fine. "I'll be going out for a bit. Do you want me to bring something back for you?"

Robin leapt down from his perch with delicate grace belying a cat his size, glaring at Liam the whole time. He stalked across the open area with his tail held high, displaying his asshole for Liam to see. Tactful was Robin.

"He'll be leaving with me. No one in without me, I promise." I set the clothes aside, trying to decide if I was going to strip and change in front of Liam or not. He had seen me naked, helped me shower, and held me in his arms. I guess it didn't matter much, so I stripped and changed into the new clothes. Everything was a little bigger than I remembered. Or maybe I'd just lost a little too much weight.

Robin's disapproving look increased. The narrowed eyes and lowered ears were a dead giveaway even to anyone who didn't understand cat body language. He stood in the kitchen, tail flicking back and forth like a snake. His gaze went from Liam to me and back again. "This has nothing to do with him," I said, putting my hand on my too loose jeans. "Just too much time on the road."

I went to the kitchen, debating food. Since Robin was filling the pantry, everything would have that magical aftertaste. Most people wouldn't notice it, but I would. Maybe I'd eat at the bakery.

"It doesn't smell like a cat," Liam said. "Never seen a cat like that outside of a zoo."

"It's not like he's a lion or anything. Just a European wildcat." I hadn't known what he was until I'd looked it up online. He was bigger than a housecat, but smaller than a bobcat. He also never left the camper. At least not as a cat.

"A cat who lived for a year in an unopened trailer with no water, food, or litterbox," Liam pointed out. He was much more observant than I thought he'd be. *Apa* never talked about Robin, though I knew he'd noticed him a time or two. They seemed to have agreed to ignore each other. Liam and Robin, however, appeared to be sizing up the other.

Liam finally got up and headed to the bathroom, keeping a wary eye on the cat until he closed the door to the bathroom. "Be nice," I whispered to Robin. "He's letting me park on his land for now. His pack is protecting me from Felix."

Robin stalked toward the door and back again, tail swishing fiercely. All attitude was Robin. My heart hurt with how much I'd missed him. There had been so many lonely nights on the run that I'd just hoped he'd appear, a friendly face if nothing else.

"It's safe. I promise." I put my hand over my heart, because promises were power to fae like Robin. "I have some new wards to try and will get us rebound to the earth soon." I dropped to my knees in front of him and scratched his chin. "Sorry it took me so long. Been running from my own shadow it seems. A little afraid this is all a dream I'm going to wake up from soon. I've missed you terribly."

Robin huffed, but his head sought my hand for more scratches until he finally turned and nipped my fingers.

"Yeah, well, right back at you." I got up.

Robin jumped to the top of the refrigerator. A normal cat would never have been able to jump that high. He loved being up high. I reached up to scratch his ears. He closed his eyes for a minute and relaxed into my touch. A year was a long time to be alone and untouched. "I'm going to work at a bakery for a bit. Maybe earn some cash." Robin flicked his tail, uninterested. "Maybe I can work long enough to buy a truck. Then we can travel around anywhere. Explore the world. Well at least this side of the world. I suppose you've seen all of Europe."

He never talked about his past. Not that he talked much at all. Never as a cat as that was something that would garner attention. I had known the little boy I'd picked up on the side of the road late one night a few years back hadn't been human. The shape of his face tipped a little too ethereal, and his eyes glinted in headlights with magic. He'd worked to look human for me. The thought that he might be trying to lure me into something had crossed my mind, but far away from everything, on a road in the middle of nowhere, his presence didn't make sense. Fae weren't common in America. Sure they popped up once in a while in areas the old spirits of the land had faded. Most who did travel to this new world stayed in the big cities where they could syphon energy off the huge bustle of people.

I'd driven halfway across the country to attend a small alchemy conference. *Apa* had argued for ages about security before finally giving in and letting me go. Not that he could have stopped me. I suspected he had someone tailing me, though I'd never seen them. And then I'd found Robin.

Hadn't expected him to stay. He'd vanished at one of the hotels I'd stopped for a night of sleep, only to reappear three days later in a completely different state, waiting beside my car. Traveling with him would be fun, though I suspected I'd miss Liam. Maybe it was a good idea to leave now, before I got even more attached. Who was I kidding? Liam said pretty things. But I *felt* something when we touched. Almost whole...

"I'll try to pick you up some chocolate," I told Robin trying to get my brain off Liam. Robin loved a particular brand of highly processed, sugar laden, chocolate. And while he seemed to be able to create just about anything out of the ether, he never did the chocolate. Maybe he could taste the magic too. Robin nipped at my fingers again and I let him go.

Liam stepped out of the bathroom. He didn't look any different, but I'd heard the water running, and I'd left him a spare toothbrush on the sink top. If he'd barely slept, he looked fine. Good actually. I could look at him every day and think he looked good.

"Do you need to run back to your house to change for work?" I asked.

"I have clothes at the bakery. I've had a lot of late nights negotiating pack business and still get to work each morning."

I opened the door. Toby no longer sat at the base of the step, but a few feet away. "You do know that's a perk of being alpha, right? Having minions to do all the hard work?"

"Is it?" Liam seemed amused. "I'll have to get on that. Having minions do all my work. Bet Dylan would love that." He stepped past me and out the door. I knew when the wards left him because he stopped. I could see the tension of his wolf roll back into him. The oldest weres often thought they'd beaten their wolf into submission, only in reality they'd trained it to be quiet and deadly, waiting for a chance at control. I'd never bound Felix inside my home for that very reason. He had always unnerved me a little. The tiny glimpses I'd seen of his wolf left me afraid. In public, he was the poster boy for control. I was one of the few who knew the truth. If I'd bound his wolf to allow the man silence, they'd have died when they stepped outside my wards. The wolf would have used that half second adjustment to rip him apart. It was a wonder we'd lasted as long as we had. My delicate dance around his ego had progressed over time to terror. Not a good thing to base a relationship on.

I stepped out of the camper and closed the door. Liam still hadn't moved. He couldn't shift faster than I could get back inside. His wolf didn't seem out of control either. Near the surface, yes, much like *Apa's* was, but not crazy like Felix. For just a second or two I could almost see the shadow of it moving around him. An edge of light displacement, waves or whatever, flickering the ether. Was he safe? Would his wolf hurt me? Even though it had claimed me as mate?

"You can't get back in without me pulling you through again, so you don't ever have to feel like this again," I told him.

"It's fine, just…different." He looked up to meet my eyes. His were their normal blue, no hint of the wolf luminescence in their depths.

"Peace and then madness?"

"More like quiet and then noise," Liam corrected. "Inside I could feel the ties to the pack but didn't have them tugging at me in small ways like they do. Out here, their tugging is stronger. They don't realize they do it, it's just a need of being a part of a pack. Most of the time I don't notice it. It's like a radio always playing that you just tune out. Having the silence inside made me realize how much I've tuned it out. The Volkov warned me, the larger the pack, the more *noise* they make. I will have to speak to a few of them and find out if they felt any differently when I was inside. I'd hate to be cut off from a wolf who needs me, even if it is for a few hours of peace." He glanced down at Toby. "You didn't seem bothered."

Toby bumped my leg. Liam sighed.

"Why doesn't he change back to human?" I asked Liam.

He turned and headed toward the giant parking area in front of his house. I followed and Toby trailed me. I wasn't sure if we could or even should take Toby to the bakery, but Liam didn't tell him to stay behind.

"Toby was injured in a car crash. He's a family member of one of our wolves. They thought to change him instead of letting him die."

Becoming a werewolf wasn't a cure for death. Usually if someone was already dying, trying to change them would only speed the process along. "I'm surprised he survived at all."

"As am I. Toby is a good kid. I understood why they wanted to save him."

"But when he wouldn't stay human you didn't put him down."

"No," Liam agreed, "I didn't."

"Because you thought I was coming?" Wasn't that just a huge weight on my shoulders? How many times did I have to prove to people that I couldn't save anyone? Not even myself.

"No, because I believe in Toby. He is strong willed. I can feel it in him. His wolf is very strong. His human side more agreeable, less argumentative. I was thinking that over time they could come to an agreement. His wolf doesn't want him to die, and Toby doesn't want to die, so while they still argue about who gets the reins, they both behave. I think that much like you, they both need time. I can give him that."

"Korissa said he'd attacked other wolves."

"Sometimes. Our pack has a lot of dominants as most

packs do. Most of them see Toby as weak. His wolf takes offense to that. Not a good way to survive, but the wolf is a simple animal. He isn't a submissive wolf. His human is just more…relaxed than most dominant wolves."

Liam strode toward a black SUV, paused and frowned down at Toby. "You can't come, even if I'd like to have you around to guard Sebastian. You don't look enough like a dog to pass around humans."

"Sebastian doesn't need a guard," I said indignantly. Toby huffed, then stalked back to my camper, apparently finding the bottom of my entry as his new favorite resting spot. "That's what the wards are for." He didn't need to guard my home. I wondered how Robin would react to having a werewolf, in wolf form, keeping an eye on unusual happenings. "It's not haunted," I told Toby, just in case he saw something move in a window that made him try to get in. "I have a cat. He's not really dog friendly."

Toby just dropped down in front of my door again, putting his head on his paws.

"I feel like no one listens to me," I said to the air. Liam opened the passenger side door of the SUV for me. "I'm not a princess," I grumbled. "Opening doors and posting guards…" I stepped to pass him and climb in anyway, but he stopped me, first with a hand on my arm and then a grip on the back of my neck, pulling me to him. His lips met mine in a kiss that was sweet, quick, and yet mind blowing. I sputtered for thought when he let me go.

"Sometimes I think you talk, want people to hear you, but you distract others with your words. You never actually say what you feel. Toby feels safe around you, at peace. Let him be peaceful. I desire you. It's okay if that makes you uncomfortable right now. We have time. I will only take the steps that you're ready for." His lips touched mine again, only this time it was a graze. He rested his forehead against mine for a minute, staring down into my eyes. "I listen. Both to what you say and what you don't say, Sebastian Volkov."

Liam stepped away and went around the truck to get in the driver's side. I finally cleared my sleep and kiss addled brain enough to get in and yank the door shut. I clicked the seatbelt into place and stared at Liam as he started the SUV. He didn't look at me, though there was a small smile on his lips.

My mind raced with the things he said and so much more. The idea of making a life here…

But first we had to figure out what was really going on here. Would I ever feel safe without knowing? Was it Felix? Or something else?

"I've been thinking," I told him after we'd pulled away from his house and the fog of desire from the kiss had faded.

"About?"

"The wolves who attacked me. You would have known if they were yours through pack ties and Felix doesn't seem to be the type to inspire loyalty. So what is their roll in this?" Why come after me? Had it been a fluke?

"We don't know they are involved with Felix at all," Liam pointed out. "Just because he knows you're here, doesn't mean he did before the attack."

"So it was just my bad luck to have run into them?" I really tried not to be paranoid and think the world was out to get me, but somehow it kept working out that way.

"Maybe."

"Or maybe not." I'd been wondering something for a while. *Apa* often set up packs in territories where there were a lot of wolves. Unfortunately, sometimes that meant displacing an alpha who'd already taken a pack for himself. Not all of them were fit for the job, or so *Apa* assured me. Ousting them wouldn't make friends for the new alpha, unless he happened to be strong enough to make them all submit and the other alpha was looking for someone to guide them. Alphas in general didn't take orders from others well. "What happened to the alpha of this territory when you came?"

"He challenged me," Liam answered.

"And you won," else he wouldn't be sitting here. "Did you kill him?"

Liam glanced my way, a frown creasing his brow.

"You didn't kill him." Alpha fights for dominance usually ended in death, especially when a pack was on the line.

"I offered him a place in my pack. He refused. I gave him twenty-four hours to leave the area."

"And others left with him?" Or had he found other strays to rule?

"A few," Liam agreed.

"You didn't recognize them when they attacked me?"

Liam snarled then. "You were dying. *You* were my priority." He sucked in a deep breath and let a few long moments pass. The tension faded as his shoulders loosened. "My wolf went a little wild, seeing you hurt, dying, *again.* I don't remember much of the fight or the wolves. Dylan was with me, but he was still recovering when I fought Warren in the challenge. Carl never met Warren either."

Liam's wolf had been in control. Revealing that little secret could get Liam killed. The Volkov killed weres who let their wolves take control. *A wolf in control kills not like an animal, but like a raving beast. Not for food or protection, but simply because it craves the taste of blood.* If that were true in all cases, Liam would have killed Dylan, Carl, and me as well. Did true mates supersede that logic? Had his wolf's need for me held him back? Or was *Apa* just wrong?

"You think Warren and his bunch attacked you to get to me?" Liam asked.

"How long have you been talking about me coming to be your mate?"

He let out a long sigh. "This is my fault."

"I didn't say that. Do you know why he was displaced?"

"There were rumors," Liam said. "Nothing I could confirm."

"Of?" I pushed.

"Him eating people."

Yeah, that happened sometimes when weres went rogue. With the strength of the inner beast, some decided they were the dominant species and everything, *everyone* else was just food. "*Apa* felt there was enough of a reason to give you his territory, to ask you to clean up the problem."

"No proof. None of his wolves could confirm it. I fought him. He yielded. I've never cared to kill a man begging for his life." Liam's voice had grown soft, almost as if he were ashamed that he'd let the other wolf go.

"My only point in this is that as a wolf, mercy makes other wolves think you are weak. *Apa* reminded me of that often. It's why the rules are strict, punishment almost always death, and decisions are made by alphas."

"An alpha takes on all the errors of his pack. It's his duty to protect and guide them. If they fail, it's his failing. His weakness is their weakness," Liam recited as though it were some werewolf mantra. And it sort of was. Just another thing ingrained in all wolves as they learned to live as human beings again, rather than just raving animals. "My compassion is a weakness."

It was. But it also wasn't a bad quality to have, if he hadn't been a werewolf alpha. "I like your compassion. It's what drove you to save Toby, even when everyone else has turned their back on him. But it may not be this Warren guy anyway. It could be unrelated. It could just be Felix fucking with me."

He nodded, but looked buried in thought. "You have good perspective. Let me think. I'll call around and see if anyone has seen Warren lately. Perhaps the Volkov knows where he is."

"If I got close enough, I could tell if he was the one who attacked me by smell alone." Another part of my *witchborn* curse. Hyper senses looked cool in the comic books. In real life it just meant I could smell when the guy three rooms down farted or not.

"Not a chance," Liam said. "If it's Warren, it's my battle to deal with."

"And if it's Felix, then it's mine," I pointed out.

Liam growled again as he pulled into the lot for the bakery.

"It's okay to be irritated with me for making sense. *Apa* was all the time too. Sometimes it takes an outside view to see common sense when we're too close to something." I flashed him a smile. "Now show me the dough. I need to bake off some of these nerves."

CHAPTER 15

The Sweet Tooth was a quiet little place this early in the morning. I'd expected a handful of cars, employees to create the flurry of pastries that people would line up for the next day, but only two other cars were in the lot. Liam parked the SUV and got out. I followed, tired, but a million questions and thoughts running through my mind. I also couldn't help that the taste of him still lingered on my lips.

Inside already smelled like sugar and yeast. I sucked in a deep breath. All we needed now was some tea and lavender scones. Liam disappeared into another room for a minute, only to return in different clothes, a hairnet, and an apron. He held an apron and net out for me too.

"Racks or mixer?" Liam called out, apparently not talking to me, but the two other wolves I could smell moving about the bakery.

"Mixer," said one voice.

"Three racks ready," said another.

Liam pointed me toward the back. The mixer was a monster of a bowl. There were laminated cards with recipes on them. "Just tell me what's up next and I can start mixing," I told them.

"Orange raspberry scones," said a voice from the back again. I thumbed through the recipe cards until I found that one and took stock of my ingredients. Everything was clearly marked and organized. I read through the card twice more, just to be sure, before starting. The first giant bowl of mix was ready before I realized Liam had vanished only to reappear moving carts of trays around. I found a tray to let the dough rise, moving it to a shelf and on to the next.

The scent of sugar, flour, and yeast filled the air. I finished the second and third mixes of different scones, setting them to rise before taking the first to be rolled out and cut. Liam reappeared and took charge of the rolling, going so far as to roll and cut them into triangles fast enough that I was in awe.

"Can you mix some muffins? All the bread is in the oven or resting, we do those the night before so they have time to rise. Sour dough is done every two days. Scones are huge in the morning. Muffins for midday, and bread all day. Adair is working on the pastries." Liam told me as I filled the baking trays with his cut scones. He rolled and cut, rolled and cut. First batch was done and then I handed him the next.

"Are they on the recipe cards?" I returned to the mixing area to clean up again and sort through the cards. Yes, muffin recipes. Though they were a little dull. "You have three amazing scone recipes but all you have for muffins is blueberry, banana nut, and chocolate chip? Are you competing with Starbucks for lack of originality?"

"Adair is too busy making pastries to mess with muffin recipes. So we always just make the same. Adair is our only pastry chef. I can follow a recipe, but bread is my specialty. The scones are more popular."

Because the scones had character. I began to put the first recipe together and decided to see if I could spice it up a little. If they didn't sell, or everyone hated them, did that mean he'd fire me? Decide I wasn't mate material? Not that it mattered. I knew these recipes well enough to know how good they were. If people didn't like the change, the bakery could go back to the mass market crap tomorrow.

The first batch was lemon blueberry with a streusel top. It smelled like heaven and I couldn't wait until they were finished baking to try them. I portioned them out into the giant muffin cups and put them on the baking rack. The chocolate chip recipe was another easy one to manipulate flavor so long as they had the correct ingredients.

"Do you by chance have avocados in here somewhere?" I asked Liam. He was finished with the scones and onto kneading and prepping bread in trays for the oven. He really was a pro, very intent on his work.

"Produce fridge, if we do," he replied absently as he shaped another loaf.

I hadn't noticed it when I'd gotten the blueberries and found the lemons, but I'd look again. Sure enough in a lower drawer were avocados. I rescued them and hoped no one had a particular plan for them since I'd need them all. This recipe was a gluten free double chocolate fudge muffin. Easy to make and super fudgy in the middle, laced with dark chocolate chips on the outside. If someone didn't know they had avocado in them, they'd have never guessed.

The last muffin was a harder reboot. Banana nut was just so dull. Instead I made gluten and dairy free banana, walnut, cranberry muffins with a streusel top again. Another fudgy and dense muffin, with a refreshing pop of flavor. The first two sets of trays had already disappeared, likely to be baked. Liam moved like a ninja around the kitchen, filling up the glass display case in a dance with the other two bakers.

An older looking man appeared in full chef detail to take the muffin trays from me. He didn't more than glance at them before whisking them away. Colleen, the woman from the register the day I'd met Liam, appeared in the doorway. Her eyes rolled appreciatively over Liam and gave me a tight smile. "Morning, Liam," she said.

"Morning, Colleen. You get the coffee started?" he asked without looking at her. Technically we both knew she hadn't because we'd have smelled it, but maybe he had issues with her follow through in the morning.

"About to start it now." She lingered a moment longer before disappearing back out into the main part of the bakery.

"I don't know what these are, but they smell good," the second as yet unidentified voice said as a woman walked out of the very back with a tray of the lemon blueberry muffins. She was younger, maybe early twenties, with red hair swept back in a braid, and big brown eyes. Her smile was warm.

"Lemon blueberry with a streusel top," I told her, then looked at Liam. "Can I eat one? I'm starving."

"Sure." He reached for the tray. "I want to try one too." Everyone tried one except Colleen. The display case was filled, and the muffin shelf which was normally shared with the pastries was overflowing with new flavors and hand-written signs. I'd gotten a little bake happy and made larger batches. Liam said nothing, and ate not just the lemon blueberry, but one of each of the others as well. Werewolves. I wished I had their metabolism.

Melanie, the other baker, walked me through how to run the register, though it was pretty straight forward. Liam programmed in the new muffin flavors with only a handful of keystrokes. The entire system was all touch based, and very high tech, but I was hoping they wouldn't just throw me to the proverbial morning wolves. I could handle the computers. Filling orders, computers, and coffee was a little much even for me.

"I'm going to open the doors. Everyone ready for the morning rush?" Liam asked as he headed to the front. There really was a line forming outside.

"Is that normal?" I asked.

"Oh yeah. Just wait till you see the Monday morning crowd," Melanie said as she patted my back. "And holidays. Holidays are insane. We start taking pie orders in August every year."

The doors opened and rush wasn't even the right word. I felt like a robot, punching things into the computer and spitting out orders for Melanie, Liam, Adair and Colleen to fill. Everyone moved like their hair was on fire, making coffee, tea, or bagging up pastries, moving out empty trays to fill new ones. Racks of bread came and went. The customers smiled and chatted with me like I'd been there for years. Everyone loved the new muffin recipes. Several buying up boxes full of them, until the shelf was empty and had to be restocked with scones instead.

It was almost nine in the morning before there was finally a break. Two other employees showed up, Rick and Joel. They gave me a friendly smile, and got right to work restocking the baked case and filling orders.

"Can you make more of those muffins?" Liam asked.

"If there are more ingredients. I used the last of the avocados and am not sure about the rest."

"Make a list and I'll call the grocery to send over supplies."

"Okay." I took a spare bit of receipt paper and began to make a list while Melanie filled a large pastry order, then took an order for a custom cake. The Sweet Tooth had no cakes on display, which I thought was odd. If I had my own little bakery and tea shop, I'd have a delightful display of the most heavenly cakes in one of those twirling cases to draw people inside. Apparently the bakery did special order cakes for weddings and such but not just every day cakes. I had over two dozen cake recipes which had been perfected before my world had imploded. In that moment I realized just how much I'd missed having others to bake for, and to craft tea for, and to make smile with the most decadent of desserts.

"Take a break," Liam told me as he carried another tray of bread out to the shelves. He hadn't taken a break either. He snatched the list out of my hand as he passed again with the empty tray. "Eat whatever you want from the case. Food and drink are on the house for employees. I'll get this list over to the grocery. Break, now," he commanded, and disappeared into the back.

"Um, sure? And kettle, black, but you're the boss." I stripped off the hairnet and apron, stretched my back, listening as it popped several times, then headed out the front door.

CHAPTER 16

The sun was shining and the weather cool as the wind blew through the trees. The area was pretty enough. Quiet. The scent of fresh bread still filled my nose and it felt oddly like home with a little something missing. Tea would fix that, I thought. I could have really used a cup of fresh lavender tea sweetened with just a hint of honey. A slice of strawberry lemonade cake topped with candied lemon rinds would have made the bright morning perfect.

A couple walked by me, nodding their heads in greeting as they entered the bakery. I took a minute to examine the street. I hadn't noticed much about it the first time I'd come through. Really just about it being some tiny main street in a middle of nowhere town. And it sort of was, only it was cute. Filled with small shops in old buildings, all with small business names instead of big box store ones. Liam's bakery was The Sweet Tooth, which was a bit of irony since it was run by wolves. There was a small hardware store, a general shop, a grocery store, a couple of antique stores, a furniture store, a bookstore, and a handful of small boutique clothing shops. The bakery shared space with another building area which appeared to be unoccupied at the moment. I wondered why Liam hadn't just expanded into the space and enlarged the bakery. He could have done an entire sit down area to get people to linger over pastries and coffee and tea.

The windows were covered in paper on the inside. Maybe someone was already working on doing just that. I didn't know enough about Liam to know if he handled all the financial and business planning or if he had people do it for him. So far he'd been pretty hands on, but only so much could be expected from one person. Even if that person was an alpha werewolf.

Would being his mate mean I had a say in those decisions? With Felix that had been a definite no. Most alphas treated omegas and mates like something to be sheltered and protected. Liam did try to throw his weight around, giving orders and such, but he didn't really make them stick. His words might not have the full whammy power on me that they did on others, but any alpha could compel anyone to obey. Just because I didn't have to obey, didn't mean I didn't feel the pull of it. Liam pushed, but not so hard that it felt he was stripping me of my will. Not like I imagined most alphas would treat their omega mates.

Mates. What the hell was I thinking? I couldn't mate with Liam. There were just so many things wrong with the idea. He was an alpha wolf. I wasn't even a werewolf. I was a guy and a mutt with some messed up lineage. He was a successful businessman, and I was a homeless wanderer running from my past.

The morning had been peaceful. The first time in a long time I could recall just being okay with myself and my surroundings. The panic in my head quieted finally and just let me breathe. I'd worked without analyzing everyone and their reaction to me. For a few hours I'd felt *normal*. And just thinking about it made the weight of fear return to my chest.

Fear of when the quiet would end and the world would erupt into chaos again. I'd been running for so long from the voices in my head that I'd forgotten they were just voices. But thinking about them made the panic well up in my gut, physical sensations running through me just as much as the mental ones did.

I put my hand to my chest as the familiar weight of anxiety rose and worked hard on my breathing. Online courses taught me some basics in anxiety management, but having a little security and less stress would help so much more. Staying with Liam had dangerous appeal. But if I stayed just to use him to fight off the demons in my own head, what was I really doing for either of us?

Sometimes I wished my metaphysical gifts ran a bit more to precognition. Sadly, like everyone else in the world I stumbled my way through bad judgment after bad judgment. It was hard to weigh a decision when I felt like I kept making all the wrong ones. Running always seemed easier, if a lot lonelier.

I wandered toward the edge of the building, trying to focus on something positive, like maybe the bakery expansion. Even if I didn't stay, I could offer Liam the ideas. He could take or leave them as he wanted. In the meantime, it was something to focus on that didn't have me dwelling in my shadowed past.

There was space for an outdoor area when the weather was nice. The cool breeze caressed my skin with the scent of the bakery and coffee. An expanse of grass stretched out for several yards between the bakery and the next building, green and lush. It would be a tragedy to let people trample on the grass that someone had worked so hard to thrive. Maybe a small section of pavers, or a minor expansion into the parking lot. Not that it mattered. The empty part of the building might belong to someone else completely.

I turned to head back inside and caught the glimpse of something moving across the edge of my vision, which, of course, made me look. A small boy flashed me a devious grin before opening a side door and disappearing into the empty building. For a minute I thought, wow, weird that someone working on it would let their kid just run around like that. Only it wasn't just any kid. The almost white hair, which could have doubled as spider silk, and translucent skin, gave him away. It'd been a while since I'd seen him like that, and it took just that long for me to realize what I was seeing. But when I did, I stalked for the door, almost expecting it to be locked.

"Robin!" I called as the door swung inward. "You best not be breaking into other people's places. You'll get us kicked off this land, and I don't have a way to move the camper." Plus, I didn't really want to go. Not yet. I sort of wanted to see if Liam was for real. If I had to leave the camper again, it meant leaving Robin again. I wondered if this was payback of some kind. Maybe he was mad because I'd been gone for so long. The fae were like that sometimes, their rational a bit skewed. He could get back at me by making me run, but that would only hurt him. I didn't really want to leave him again.

"Robin? Please don't play games," I said. "I just want to rest a while. A few days at least. Please." A chance to find out if Liam was for real. Could a fox mate with a wolf? Was this all just an elaborate dream? If so, was it created by the vampire or perhaps the fairy? Was I still asleep in my camper? My head spun with questions as I followed the possibilities inside in pursuit of answers.

Light filtered through the paper over the windows to cast a gray shadow on the space. A long counter with a bar like space covered in a thick slab of wood took up a large part of the room, and an entire sink area behind it was carved out in stainless steel. There were empty narrow shelves that lined the walls as though waiting for tea tins to fill their length. No chairs or actual appliances had been placed. Perhaps they'd just finished the plumbing. The open space left enough room for several tables and chairs along the covered windows. It did look a little like a tea shop might look if it was attached to a bakery, but that could also have been wishful thinking on my part.

No sign of Robin.

He wasn't in the store room, or either of the bathrooms. Would I get in trouble for being in here? There were permits taped to part of the window. I'd seen them from outside and could make out the outline near the front door. Construction permits, but where were the workers? Maybe they didn't work during the peak bakery hours to minimize noise and dust? Either way I decided it was a good idea to get the hell out before I got found somewhere I wasn't supposed to be.

I turned to leave, only to run right into Liam. "Fuck!" I cried, jumping back a few feet with my heart pounding in my chest. "Visions of lots of horror movies here," I grumbled at him. "Warn a guy."

"Says the man sneaking into locked buildings." He didn't look mad, or even alarmed, but his gaze was a little intense.

"The door was open," I protested.

"By Robin, your cat who is not a cat?"

"You saw him?"

"No. But I heard you call his name."

"Dammit. He never leaves the camper. I'm sorry, Liam." I made to step around him and leave. "I shouldn't be in here. I shouldn't have followed him. He just messes with me sometimes. I hope whomever owns this isn't angry. It's a pretty space even if the colors are a little bland." Maybe they just hadn't painted the walls yet. Everything felt very gray, cold, though that could have just been the filtered light on whitewashed walls.

"I'll try to keep Robin out of trouble." Though that was a little more wishful thinking than anything like I had power over him. Maybe if I offered him something. Working a few days would earn me money to buy him chocolate bars. That was a start at least.

Liam caught my arm. "It's safe to rest here. More than a few days. I want you to stay."

He didn't mean here as in inside the building. He meant here with him. With his touch a rush of heat rolled through us again. I closed my eyes a minute just to feel the warmth of him. "I don't trust anyone," I told him and opened my eyes to stare up at him. He was close now, towering over me, but not in a threatening way, more like he was my shield.

"Especially yourself, right?"

It wasn't fair that he knew me so well already.

"Are you willing to try? I can't promise to be perfect. And I'm an alpha, so domineering asshole comes naturally, just ask my daughter. But I want you. I want what we could have together. I want to try." He leaned forward to rest his forehead against mine.

"Because your wolf wants me for some reason?"

"He doesn't want you. He proclaims you mate, no matter what. Has been fighting me since the night we met, to go after you and bring you home. My rational, human brain, reminds my wolf patience is necessary when pursuing skittish prey." He let out a deep sigh. "But late at night, when I'm alone in bed after solving everyone else's problems all day, all I can think about is how nice it would be to not be there alone."

"You could snap your fingers and have anyone."

"Yet I have dreams of us. You and I."

"Fantasies of things I'll never be." Submissive and dependent. Never again.

"I dream of small things," Liam said. He kissed me gently

on the forehead. "Like holding you while you sleep. That dream has come true already. I hope to repeat it over and over again. I also dream of having tea with you. Of waking up every morning to see your face. I dream of running with you, my wolf and your fox. Chasing each other playfully through trees and brush until we change back to human and make love under the moon. You've already given me more peace than I've ever experienced in my life. My wolf is no longer raging for control. He sees you and says *mine*. I agree. *Ours*. Even if it just means arguing with you over whether you'll eat properly or not."

His words gobsmacked me. His words, his sincerity, and his amazing eyes that looked gray in the pale light. "I worry that *I'm* dreaming this and still stuck with Hugo while he drains me dry." Hugo had a gift for dreams, making them seem so real, like that movie with the goblin king I grew up watching on repeat.

Anger flashed across Liam's face, but he didn't pull away. "I need to find this Hugo. Have a *talk* with him."

"*Apa* doesn't like the wolves fighting with the vampires. Too many opportunities for norms to catch something on camera these days." I tried to pull away, and he let me, only to trail closely behind as I made my way out the door. "He meant nothing to me. Just a bump in the road."

"Another past to run from."

"Well yeah. You don't stick around vampires. They kill you." I waved a hand at the room around us. "If I'm dreaming all this, he's killing me slowly. Can take years sometimes, from what I've heard." But dreaming of Liam for a few years as I died under a vampire's fangs didn't sound so bad.

"What can I do to make you believe this is real?" Liam asked.

I didn't really know how to answer that. Him kicking me

to the curb or betraying me to Felix would feel more real than all the happy, touchy-feely stuff. "I don't know."

He gripped my hand. "I don't feel real? My touch? My kiss?" He yanked me back into his embrace. "My scent?" Liam bent to capture my lips and I let him, closing my eyes to delve into the warmth of him. "My taste?" He asked when we came up for air. He tasted like the muffins I'd baked. "Could the vampire fake all of that?"

Had he? I thought back to the memories Hugo had strung out for me. His power, or perhaps just his knowledge or lack thereof, of my herbs had been what had clued me into the dream last time. One of the tea brews had been wrong, the smell and the taste, though I knew I'd made it with the right herbs. Other things had smells and tastes, textures, and emotions. It had been so real. Just that little blip, like a Matrix de ja vu, had alerted me to the mind trap.

Was there anything off here?

Robin.

But how would Hugo know about Robin? All the dreams I'd had under his care had been about Felix. No instance of Robin. That was something I should have noticed at the time. Likely Robin had some sort of magic to keep others from pulling information about him out of me. Okay. So other than Robin being out of place?

Liam sighed deeply, pulling away again, but keeping my hand as he tugged me out the door. "Time. I have to keep reminding myself," he said as we stepped back out into the sunshine. "I'm more impatient than I thought I'd be now that you're here."

"I'm sorry," I apologized immediately. Habit from years of trying to please the unpleasable. "If this was a dream I'd probably be less suspicious, but maybe Hugo caught onto that too."

"Where was this Hugo again?"

"Chicago."

"Hmm."

We walked toward The Sweet Tooth, hand in hand. No one stared or commented and I wasn't eager to pull away. His touch was warm and soothing. If others didn't know, they would soon. Gossip traveled fast in small towns. Yet Liam made no move to create distance between us.

"What colors would you prefer if the space was yours?"

"Huh?" I asked, lost in savoring his touch and not thinking about his words.

"For the shop next to the bakery. You said it's bland. What colors would you have chosen?"

"Depends on what the space is used for. Cool tones for a tea shop, I think. A soft green or even a blue/green like the ocean on a spring day. Warmer ones for a bakery. Dark for a bar."

"Cool tones." Liam nodded. "Tell me about Robin."

"Not my story to tell."

"I think it is. Fae are dangerous."

But I'd been dancing the edge of that danger with Robin for a while. I knew how to be careful because Robin had taught me by being patient when I'd been young and stupid. A thousand times he could have trapped me for saying or doing the wrong thing, only he'd only ever clucked and offered wisdom instead. "I'm safe with Robin."

"A puck…"

I squeezed Liam's hand. He was more observant than I thought he'd been if he'd devised that much about Robin after only meeting him once. "He's like family to me."

Liam pulled us to a stop and gazed down at me. "You trust him more than the Volkov?"

"The fae can't lie."

"But they are really good at bending the truth," Liam pointed out.

"You've met a few fae in your time then? At least with them you know to sort of expect betrayal. They look out for themselves first. Most won't lie to your face, even if they are twisting the truth. It comes out as a poetic brush off if they are avoiding telling you something. With the wolves it was always pretty lies until the claws came out. I prefer knowing to always watch my back." I'd never felt safe among *Apa*'s pack outside my wards. "Instead of waiting for someone I thought loved me to stab me in the back." Plus I always felt like Robin hid in my presence somehow. Maybe the other fae couldn't find him if he were surrounded by wolves or even *witchblood* like mine. We never talked about it. I just knew I had his back and he had mine.

"Are you talking about Felix or someone else?"

I said nothing. Liam was right about me running from a lot of my past. I wasn't ready to share that yet. Not even with Liam. I'd been too young, and the past year made me too raw.

"What did they do to you? There are no stories of anyone hurting you. In fact, it was always the opposite. Tales spread about how the *witchchild* fooled the Volkov again, or got away with another prank."

"You shouldn't believe everything people tell you. It's a lot like a game of telephone. By the time it gets through to the other side, nothing is actually as it was."

Liam seemed to just examine me for a minute. "The Volkov loves you. Anyone can see that."

Did he? I wasn't so sure. Not after Felix. But perhaps *Apa*'s affection had more stages than most and Felix just ranked above me. Biological bond and all that.

"Hmm." Liam huffed after being rewarded with silence again. He tugged us back toward the bakery. Another line was forming. "I need you to make more muffins."

Not a smooth subject change, but I let it go. "Okay."

"And eat something. There's fresh bread and cold cuts in the freezer."

"Yes, sir," I said as we entered the shop and went off to attend the crowds. Thankfully he was leaving me alone to brood for a while. Maybe the next time he asked me something personal I'd be able to share something. Or maybe I should just go with my gut instinct and run before I got us both killed.

CHAPTER 17

The day flew by in a flurry of customers, baking, and conversations with the locals who were a very chatty bunch. I'd ended the day by giving a boy who appeared to be around four years old, a free cookie from a sample batch I'd thrown together during a lull. The shop didn't have cookies regularly. Much like their cake rules, cookies were special request. Liam's comment was just that they couldn't do everything, though the bakery would be expanding and eventually have more variety. His pointed look at me while saying that did make my heart pound a little. I dabbled in baking, but tea and alchemy had been my passion. Liam didn't push when I didn't reply. Maybe he was getting used to my silent brooding.

"What's your name?" I asked the little boy. He had a mop of brown curls and rich burgundy colored eyes. His mother stood a few feet away talking to Liam about something to do with an upcoming meeting. She wasn't a wolf, didn't smell like wolf, and neither did her son, but maybe they were related to one who didn't come around much.

"Nicky," the little boy told me.

"Nice to meet you, Nicky. I'm Seb. I'll need you to give me your honest opinion of this cookie. It's a new recipe." I'd already asked his mother if the boy had allergies and she'd indicated he could eat anything I gave him.

"I like cookies," Nicky told me.

"All kinds of cookies?"

"Yes."

"Well then, as a connoisseur of cookies, I must have your opinion." I held out the plate of cookies and waited as he carefully selected one. A chocolate chip cookie was a chocolate chip cookie, but I'd worked hard to balance the white and brown sugar ratio for the perfect chewy snap. Nicky took a giant bite, nearly shoving the entire cookie in his mouth all at once. I had to fight to keep from laughing. In less than a minute he was covered in chocolate, but the grin was worth it. The cookies had his stamp of approval.

"Sorry for the mess," I told Nicky's mother when she came to retrieve him.

"Kids attract messes. It comes with the territory. Thanks for distracting him while I got my work order placed. Usually he's pawing the glass and begging for everything in the case," she said.

I grinned down at the little boy who was busy licking chocolate off his fingers. "Now that's understandable. I want everything in the case too."

Liam handed her a bag of cookies and a stack of napkins, thanking her again for her business as he escorted her out. Since it was almost four in the afternoon, I was beat. Not that I hadn't done long shifts before, but I didn't have the stamina of a werewolf, and I was still healing.

"Dylan's going to drive you home," Liam said as he came back in.

"What about you? You've been here all day too." Shift had changed for everyone else. Liam had tried to get me to go home at lunch time, but I'd been in the baking zone by then and not willing to leave batter unattended. My leg hurt and I'd been nursing a headache most of the afternoon. If he could keep going, so could I. I tried not to think too hard about how safe I felt with him close.

"I've just got to prep the evening crew. We're only open another two hours anyway. Maybe once next door opens up we'll run later, but right now it's just easier to put everyone on the morning rush than linger for the few who trickle in late." Liam never stopped moving. He didn't wait for someone else to do any of the work. If the shelves needed to be stocked he did it, he mixed batches, ran the checkout, and even brewed coffee. I couldn't help but stare at him in awe. In my entire life I'd never met an alpha so involved in everyday normal things. It was like *life* wasn't beneath him. He wanted to live in the here and now, even if that made him sweaty and tired.

The door opened and Dylan stepped inside. He looked good, dressed up like he was going out. His blond hair had even been pulled back into a ponytail. The pale blue button-up looked good with the black slacks and shiny shoes. I couldn't help the wolf whistle I gave him. "Look at you. Hot date tonight?"

Dylan actually blushed. "Yes, actually. Once I get you home I'm taking my man out for dinner."

"Yeah? So when do I get to meet him?" It would be nice to know another gay man who had to deal with werewolf bullshit. Was he a wolf too? Somehow I didn't think so. "We can bond over the dominant wolf lover thing."

Dylan looked away, smile fading.

"He doesn't know," I affirmed.

"It's law. Mates can't know," Dylan agreed. Technically they could know, but they had to meet certain criteria. Being another preter like me was an option, or from a were family in which a wolf was an immediate family member. Couples were more complicated. Like they had to be married for at least five years, had to vow to tell no one, had to have the alpha's approval, and most often the Volkov's approval. Since the wolves didn't recognize homosexuality in their own ranks, I wondered if they would even acknowledge a relationship like Dylan's. Or like the one Liam wanted with me. I felt my cheer evaporate too.

"Are you married?" I asked, thinking at least that was a place to start.

Dylan ducked his head. "Nah, only together a few months. Figure that's a little fast."

"Almost a year," Liam interjected. "And Dylan is very cautious."

"I'd still like to meet him," I said. Even if we couldn't talk werewolf crap.

"Sure. He knows Liam pretty well. He'll be tickled to finally meet the guy Liam has been fawning over for the past year," Dylan shot back like he was trying to goad Liam.

Liam didn't even have the courtesy to look upset. He just shrugged before yanking me into his arms and kissing me breathless again. When he released me, I stumbled, dazed and hard instead of sleepy. Damn.

"Not fair," I grumbled. "I'm too tired to fend off your advances with rational thinking."

"Your rational thinking is more along the lines of survival thinking, fight or flight. Relationships should not be survival training. You're safe here. Get some rest. I'll stop by your camper when I get home," Liam said and walked away as if he hadn't just kissed stars into orbit in my head.

Dylan chuckled and tugged me toward his car. Unlike

Liam's SUV, it wasn't new and shiny black. Instead it was an ancient but well-loved Oldsmobile in dark red. Old fashioned steel. Wow. The spells this car could hold for me. I wondered if he'd sell it to me. I'd have to have money first.

"Nice car," I told him.

"Yeah? Sean keeps her running. She's his baby. That's why she's so clean. Mine is a bit of a mess. So I figured I'd take his car tonight."

"Sean is the boyfriend?" I clarified as I got into the car. The upholstery was immaculate. In fact, the entire vehicle could have just been driven off the lot for how well it was maintained.

"Yes." Dylan started the car and pointed us back toward Liam's. He was quiet for a minute. "Never thought I'd have a chance at love, or even a pack, you know. Spent so long as a lone wolf, fighting to survive every day, that I'd convinced myself love wasn't necessary." Lone wolves lived outside packs but only by the sufferance of the packs that surrounded them. The Volkov kept track of them. Part of Oberon's duties, if I recalled correctly, was to monitor them. Most lone wolves were just men who couldn't function in a community where rules were strict and the penalty death. Men who hated having someone else rule over them, but weren't strong enough to be alphas. And apparently gay wolves.

"Did Sean change all that? Meeting him?"

"Partially, but I'd never have met him if it weren't for the Volkov, Liam and you."

"Say what?" I glanced his way. "Have we met before?" Maybe Hugo had messed with my head more than I'd thought.

"Not directly. I was brought to the Volkov's pack not long before you left. I'd been set upon by a group of wolves and badly injured. They tried to kill me, but I'm a tough bastard."

He threw me a wide smile full of teeth. "Spent a long time learning to fight dirty. I survived. Someone dragged me to the Volkov, who set me up in his safe room under his protection and fed me medicinal tea made by his mysterious *witchblood* son."

"Seriously?"

"Seriously. I was healing, slow, but healing. Too much damage…"

I nodded having seen it a time or two. Sometimes even the wolf metabolism wasn't enough to save them. "I didn't know. *Apa* made me stop seeing any of the injured personally years ago. None of them ever hurt me, but the other wolves protested." I wasn't pack. Never had been pack, no matter how much *Apa* had tried to include me. The free access I'd been given to the alpha's den was enough to set most wolves' teeth on edge.

"I heard a lot of talk of you while I was lying there. Even the Volkov planning the feast in which he was going to find you a mate. I thought that was the answer for a while. That I'd be strong enough to be alpha and mating with the *witchchild* would give me a territory to build my own pack, safety and home. It would make it okay to be a wolf and love men. A stamp of approval from the Volkov himself."

"Oh," I said. "I'm sorry."

He steered us through the pretty countryside filled with trees. "Nothing for you to be sorry about. I wasn't strong enough to be in the running. Barely able to walk by the first day of the trials. When word rose that you'd run, the whole place was in an uproar. Alphas blaming alphas. Fights and chaos. Yet in that storm of testosterone bullshit Liam stood unfazed. He admitted to seeing you, to feeling you call his wolf, claimed you to one and all, and the world stopped. Not just for me, but for everyone. They all looked at Liam and the

Volkov, like they expected the Volkov to attack him for daring to claim the *witchchild*."

"Liam said *Apa* approves." *Apa* hadn't sounded upset with Liam when he'd called my phone.

Dylan nodded. "Oh yes. The Volkov was not upset at all. More pleased than anything else. He laid out a dozen territories and let Liam choose, then sent me with him."

"What?"

"It made sense to me at the time. Liam would become the first gay alpha. It only made sense that I be a part of his pack. He could have turned me away, spurned me for being something he hated in himself."

"He's not like that." I hadn't known him long and I knew that.

"No. Though it still took me a while to warm up to him. Since he's not really the gay alpha."

"Not waving the rainbow flag, you mean. Anyone looks at him and thinks straight."

Dylan shrugged. "It's you he wants. Gender doesn't matter to him. I didn't know him before all this, but now, women throw themselves at him and he's unfazed. Men flirt, wolves sneer, yet nothing bothers him. Especially now." He threw me a wide smile.

I nodded because there was no such thing as a private conversation around most preternaturals. My hearing might not be as good, but it was better than ordinary humans.

"He couldn't be bothered with games even when Carl goads him because he was eager to get back to you."

"He knows nothing about me. Just what his wolf tells him."

"And that's not enough?" Dylan glanced my way. "I'd kill to have a true mate. To feel a call like that and know it had just been for me."

I looked away, out the window and into the distance, uncomfortable. "I'm not sure that's what it was."

"What else could it have been?"

"Desperation. My soul didn't want to die and he was the closest alpha?"

"Not true. He ran past a half dozen alphas, including Felix that night. No one knew why until later. None of those alphas felt the call. None of them responded. Several of them called out to him as they attested the next day." Dylan turned into the long rounded drive that made up Liam's driveway. "And now that you're here he's drawn to you. Until you truly mate bond he'll be clingy and unreasonable about your safety."

"It can't be undone," I reminded Dylan. "The mate bond. If I die, he could too, and vice versa. True love, dying for each other, really is just poetry. In reality it's very scary."

Dylan nodded as he pulled up a few feet away from my camper. Toby was gone from the foot of the stairs so I hoped he was somewhere getting much needed food and sleep. Maybe even working out an arrangement with his wolf that would keep Liam from having to kill him.

"It's early yet for you. Liam has had a year to accept your bond. You've only had a few days. Makes sense," Dylan said. "Give it time. You look like you could use some rest and time to adjust to our pack. We're a little different than the Volkov's pack. Not as formal, closer knit. That's Liam's doing."

"He could do better than me," I told him as I got out of the car.

"We'll have to agree to disagree on that one. He wants you. Think on it for a while. Ask yourself what you want. Him? Freedom? Love? Maybe you'll surprise yourself with the answer because maybe it just doesn't have to be that profound. Happiness is not perfection. In fact, most days I think perfection just gets in the way. It's more about perception. Sean isn't perfect, and neither am I, but we work. Liam is not perfect, no matter how much he might seem that way sometimes. In fact, he comes across as somewhat cold most of the time. More like a soldier than a person. I suspect he's served in several wars, though you won't hear him talk about it. Your presence has chiseled off the ice. Just be you. I think that might just be what you both need."

Maybe. "Thanks for the ride." And the stuff to think about, though I didn't add the comment. My brain would stew on his words for a while at least. I shut the car door and headed inside. The familiar rush of the camper's protection made my nerves ease as the wards settled around me. Dylan didn't leave until I waved to him from the doorway. Robin sat on the middle of my bed, tail curled around him, looking less perturbed than he had the last time I'd seen him.

"Why were you messing with me today? It's not like you to leave the camper." He just stared at me, tail flipping nonchalantly like any content cat's might. I didn't bother taking off my clothes, just kicked off my shoes and plopped down on the bed beside him. I buried my hands and face in his fur. He purred. For a little while I thought about pushing for answers. Only that's not what we needed. He needed me, and I needed him. Even if it was just for company. He snorted into my hair, and licked me for a little while. It was gross but familiar enough that I sighed happily. In that moment I knew if there had been any trouble between us, it was forgiven.

"We can be home for a while, yeah?" I asked him.

He chuffed at me.

"Liam isn't so bad." I rubbed the fur behind Robin's ears, enjoying his closed eyes and obvious happiness. "You can share right? If he treats me better? If it's just Felix all over again, then we leave. I'll figure out how to take the camper.

Even if it means stealing a truck." It wouldn't be the first time I'd taken something and run. I just prayed I didn't have to.

Robin nipped my fingers. I let him go and curled around him. I fell asleep dreaming of Liam's arms wrapped around me while I baked cookies for the entire population of four-year-olds in the state of Washington.

CHAPTER 18

Once again it was the silence that woke me. Living on the run had taught me a lot about noise; what to tolerate, and what was normal. People by their very nature made a lot of noise. Animals and bugs made noise. The wind made noise. The world in general was a loud place. The ability to tune out the background sound most people learned at an early age. Being homeless taught me the nuances of each noise. From a sign creaking in the wind to the blast of a car horn, to a particular owl hunting its prey. All of them spoke of life, movement, even a hint of safety. Silence meant danger.

It was dark. Robin was gone, and no sign of Liam, which made sense since I'd have to invite him in again. I hoped he was getting some sleep. He'd promised to stop by when he got home. Was he even back yet? Maybe he'd changed his mind. Either way I missed him badly.

Dylan had said to ask what I wanted. If I went with my gut, it was safety that I wanted the most. Love, lust, and the whole mate thing seemed so grand and romantic in novels, but none of it mattered when you were always running for your life. I'd been in Liam's pack less than a week and already they'd made me feel more at home and safer, than I ever had in the Volkov's pack. Liam's presence? Or just the pack?

I sighed and stretched, wondering again why everything was so quiet. It would have been nice to wake with Liam wrapped around me, though he'd never have gotten in without me pulling him through the wards again.

Still everything was too quiet. Were there guards outside? Maybe they had startled the night to that eerie quiet.

I peered through the front window. No Toby or anyone that I could see. The lack of noise didn't have to mean someone was out there. It could have been a bird or another animal startling the night critters. Robin's absence shouldn't have made me uneasy. I'd survived without him for an entire year. Sometimes he vanished for days at a time. Gone to whatever other world the fae had, I often thought. It was unlikely to be him prowling around outside. Maybe Liam was out there somewhere, keeping an eye on me without coming to the door like he promised he would.

I turned to head toward the bathroom and it was then I noticed a picture taped to one of the windows facing away from Liam's house. My heart leapt into my throat.

Please let it not be what I thought. My brain whirred on high speed of all the terrible things it could be. Liam hurt or dead. Dylan injured, Robin slaughtered, Toby bleeding, all at Felix's machinations. Only it wasn't any of those things.

The picture was of the little boy I'd fed cookies to earlier that day, covered in blood, but alive and looking scared as he crouched in the corner of some unknown room. Nicky. Someone had Nicky. What about his mom? Had they killed her? I trembled with indecision. Run to Liam? Was someone waiting outside? What about Nicky? Would they kill him if I went for help?

Why take the little boy at all? Dumb question. Anyone who knew me at all would know I'd give up a lot to protect an innocent child. A spark of irritation flickered through me. It was all a game, wasn't it? The one person who should have known me the best, but always seemed oblivious. He had some things right, but often forgot just how hot my temper could run.

I thought for a minute of how Felix had begun his courting of me and huffed a deep breath across the window. Memories of better times. In the fog the words "Come out back" appeared for a few seconds before fading. Anger welled up in my gut, spark kindling to a full fire.

He knew he couldn't get to me inside so he wanted to lure me out. Using a child of all things. The Volkov would kill him if I didn't first. That little boy's momma had better be okay too. I'd never really been the type to let someone else suffer on my behalf.

Felix was a monster. Blind, stupid, and dumb, but a very dangerous monster.

I stomped toward the door half wishing I had a weapon other than basic magic and a lot of alchemy. Without enough time to brew something all I had were my wards. It would have to be enough.

Nothing moved when I stepped out of the camper and carefully went around the side to the back which faced out into a vast distance of fields and scattered trees. There wasn't a lot of cover out there, but enough to hide more than a few weres. My wrist burned, the wolf hidden beneath the bramble design lighting on fire in my skin. Felix stepped out from behind one of the nearest ones, and panic began to rise in my chest.

Physical terror, I reminded myself, was uncomfortable, but couldn't really kill me. I thought of Liam and how he would tell me to breathe, count, rub my back and hold me tight. I could do this. Felix was stronger than me, but I didn't have far to run for help. I wasn't alone anymore.

Felix looked the same as always, a well-dressed 6'2 with dark hair and piercing blue eyes. His handsome face had won him more than a few lovers over the years. Rumors of his mother, whom the Volkov never spoke of. She'd passed not long after Felix had been born. A couple hundred years ago the mother fatality rate giving birth had been sky high from infection and complications. *Apa* never talked about her.

Felix's outer beauty did not match his insides. Seeing him with moonlight streaming over him reminded me of that night he'd almost killed me. If I could turn the fear to rage perhaps I'd have a chance of making it through this night. I prayed he hadn't killed whatever guards Liam had on rotation for the night, or Toby, who might not have been willingly away from my door.

"What do you want?" I demanded. "How many times do I have to tell you we're done? I don't want you anymore."

"I just want to talk. Explain some things," Felix said.

"There's nothing to explain. You chose someone else."

"She means nothing to me."

I huffed out a laugh. He never changed. "No one ever really does, do they? Where's Nicky?"

"Who?"

"The little boy you took, asshole!"

"He's safe." Felix took a step closer. "I'll bring you to him."

"Stop," I commanded him, putting the pull of the earth in my words. It wasn't much, and didn't work at all on a shifted wolf, but it almost always gave a human pause. He did take a few seconds longer to complete his step. Then he sort of shook himself and narrowed his eyes. "We're done," I reminded him. "Even the Volkov agrees."

"You're not Liam's. You'll never be Liam's. I've told *Apa*

that time and again." He took another step. I should have kept the camper to my back so I could draw on the wards.

"Stop," I said again pushing a ward through the ground again. To him, he'd feel like he was walking through quick sand or really deep snow. "Just give me Nicky and we'll forget this ever happened. You'll go home." And I would be free of him forever. Only that was just a dream, wasn't it? "Oberon is here looking for you." And saying it, I realized it was true. Oberon wasn't there for me. He was there to put Felix in line, drag him home and out of Liam's territory.

"I'm not afraid of Oberon. He won't hurt me. *Apa* loves me too much to ever let anyone hurt me. My mother was his true mate. He would never let anything happen to me."

"Liam hurt you," I said. "Beat you in the challenge."

"It wasn't a fair challenge. He didn't have the right. Never had. You belong to me anyway," Felix said.

"I don't. Never have and never will. No matter how many times you beat me or rape me, I will never be yours." I was Liam's. My heart stuttered at the thought, which rang true. The memory of his arms around me as I slept, giving me safety even in the warded confines of my trailer. Maybe he couldn't always keep me safe. That was impossible. But he would try. I knew that down to the very core of my being. I wondered where he was. A thousand reasons for him not being at my side at that moment crossed my mind, but I was pretty sure Felix had done something to keep him away. "What did you do to Liam?"

"He doesn't want you, Sebastian. I'm the only one that ever has."

What wolves? Not Liam. Of that much I was sure. "You're so full of shit you've got flies coming out of your ears. How did you even find me here?"

"*Apa* said you'd be drawn here, so I had those wolves keep an eye on the area. They told me you were here." When he took another step I pushed as much power through the ground as I could.

"I said stop."

"No more games, Seb. You belong to me. You've always been mine. I knew by the time you'd hit ten that you were meant to be mine. *Apa* demanded I wait. Those years…I think you became too independent in those years. Now it's just lost time."

"What?" Ten? What kind of sick bastard was he? *Apa* had known?

"You've spent years refusing to bond with me. I should have just convinced you to do it as a child. Would have saved myself all this trouble."

"You've got to be fucking kidding me," I said. Of course I'd refused to bond with him. I might have thought I'd been in love with him, but I'd never felt a bond to him. Had thought it a myth until Liam. Fuck, Liam…What had he done to Liam? "Go home, Felix. We're done."

He reached for me. "We're not."

"If you've done something to Liam I will tear you apart."

"You can't hurt me, Seb. We belong together. I can prove to you we are true mates. Just let me bite you. Once I come inside you and feed on your blood you'll see. Liam is nothing. You'll see."

The idea of him holding me down and raping me again just ripped the control right off my anger. I flew at him with all the rage the last year on the run had bottled up. My fist met his face and he staggered back. It couldn't have been the punch; I wasn't that strong. Surprise then. Fine.

No mercy, I thought. He'd never had any for me. Before I even realized what I was doing, he was on the ground beneath me as I pummeled him. Blood coated my fists and splattered on my face. His and mine.

"Enough," Felix growled at me.

I caught a glimpse of his eyes as they flickered in the moonlight with that eerie luminescence that animals shared. Then he hit me back. His punch equaling about a thousand of mine. One second his fist was barreling toward me, the next the world fell into oblivion.

CHAPTER 19

Old blood has a sort of rusty, spoiled smell. Like a package of beef set out too long. It's a distinct odor. Even my dreams couldn't filter out a reason for the scent. Instead I just woke, groggy, in pain, and smelling blood. Mine or someone else's?

My head throbbed. Another concussion? Probably not a good thing since I'd still been healing from the other one. My stomach roiled with nausea from the pain and the smell. I was careful not to move my head too fast. Throwing up all over myself would have only made the churning in my gut worse.

A lone window bathed the room in pale moonlight. Same night or had I been out that long? It took a while for my eyes to completely adjust. One was swollen enough that I knew it had to be quite the shiner. With my one good eye I could make out a small room, with a twin-sized bed, and happy cartoon animals stuck to the walls. They'd left me in the bed, and from what little I could see from the window, I was on the second floor. No trees nearby, just the vast darkness covered with pinpricks of stars. Which meant they didn't expect me to jump out the window to my death, and probably had guards on the door.

Was this Nicky's room? Had Felix followed them home just to use them as hostages? The shadows mixed with the shades of darkness of the room, leaving it hard to tell if blood stained anything, or if it was just me I was smelling. Though old blood had a different smell than fresh. Maybe I'd been bleeding and out for a while.

I sucked in a deep breath and tried to center myself through the monster weight of anxiety rising in my chest. Panic got me nowhere. Liam would be looking for me. I wasn't alone anymore. Dylan made it clear that the pack wanted me here. Even if not all of them agreed, whatever bond Liam and I had made them all sit up and listen. Or at least be open to accepting a fox in the wolf den.

Felix's words came back to me. *Apa* had known how troubled Felix was long before our relationship began. Yet he still allowed it. Once again I felt betrayed. The only man I'd ever had as a father figure and he'd let his son abuse me. For what? To keep a crazy wolf alive? Simply because Felix was one of *Apa's* blood sons? He had others. Had even put others down in the past. Why had Felix been so different?

I closed my eyes and ground my teeth, trying to yank myself out of the self-pity. Now was not the time. Freedom first. Safety first. Hadn't I spent the last year in a non-stop battle for just that? Maybe it was time to stop running. Was I ready to face the monster? My stomach roiled again with the thought. Memories of that final beating and rape rose in my head. Faded, but never gone. I rolled instinctively, as if to escape the attack again, and covered my head as though I could push the feelings away.

I hit the floor with a thud, shoulder stinging with the pain. The throbbing in my head intensified for a minute until I thought I'd pass out, then finally subsided enough to allow me to breathe without pain. Tears leaked from my eyes. Not from the memories. I refused to keep crying over what had happened to me. But I lay there for a while, curled up in a ball, listening to the world around me, and crying. I waited for them to come from the noise of my fall. Muffled voices trickled up from below. None moved closer. The smell of death surrounded me.

The stench was close enough to touch. I cried harder. I didn't have to open my eyes to know my sacrifice had been for nothing. The kindness of giving a child a cookie had stolen his life.

Not my fault.

Living surrounded by monsters had never been my choice. I'd run from them for a year and still been unable to escape. Nicky hadn't stood a chance.

I opened my eyes, having to see, though I knew it would be something I'd never forget. He looked peaceful. Like he was sleeping. If it hadn't been for the blood drenching his clothes, I'd have shaken him awake. His face stained with dirt, blood, and streaked with tears, looked so innocent. I lay there a while, lost in sadness, vaguely listening for approaching footsteps and hearing myself breathe.

Only it wasn't me I was hearing. I frowned and stared at Nicky, watching him intently for the rise and fall of his chest. I couldn't hear a heartbeat, but he was also several feet away. Though my hearing was better than most humans, it wasn't as good as any werewolf. Finally, I saw it. A tiny blip of movement. I held my breath until I caught it again. He was alive!

I crawled beneath the bed and wrapped my arms around him. He startled awake instantly, and I covered his mouth with my hand before he could scream. His eyes were wide and terrified.

"Shh," I whispered. "Nicky, it's Sebastian. The man from the bakery who gave you a cookie. Do you remember me?"

He nodded a little.

"I need you to be very quiet. I'm going to get us out of here."

Another nod. He wrapped his arms around me, clinging. In that short minute I'd become his savior. I just wasn't sure if I could get us both out of there alive. The drop down from the window was a long way. I could probably run past guards in my fox form if they weren't expecting that, but couldn't get Nicky out that way. Likely Felix would have them watching for my change if the attack at my car and subsequent change hadn't already tipped them off.

I crawled out from under the bed with Nicky wrapped around me like one of those wire monkey dolls. I whispered soothing things to him as I checked the door and the hall. The hall was empty. I could see a set of stairs that led down into lights and movement below. Close enough that if we made a step toward the stairway the whole group would be on us. I didn't need them to use Nicky as another bartering tool. "Is there another way downstairs," I whispered to Nicky.

He shook his sobbing face into my neck.

There was a second doorway, but the smell of death wafted from there strong enough that I knew someone was dead in that room. Likely Nicky's parents. Had he seen them die? Was that why he was covered in their blood and the reek of death?

His room didn't even have a bathroom attached, it was across the hall, empty, unused and clean, at least. I wasn't going to chance using it and bring the masses up, even though we both stank. He had a small closet for all the good that did. It was barely large enough to fit the two of us.

Robin talked about closets a lot. Doorways really.

Legends of Narnia and such, which were all plays on the fae secrets. Doorways weren't just entries to rooms, Robin had often reminded me, they were structures built into the earth allowing energy to flow, connect, and stop. I'd never been the child to be afraid of the monster in the closet. In my life they'd lived in plain sight. But I could understand the reference.

"Doorways frighten children because sometimes things come through them that are unexpected," I'd reasoned to Robin one day.

"It's not always frightening." Robin motioned to himself. *"Sometimes a game of trust is played."*

"Tricks," I whispered.

"You see a child when you look at me," Robin said to me once while I brewed tea and he sat in his youthful form on the edge of the counter, swinging his feet. *"You think it's a trick?"*

I still wasn't sure. At first when I'd seen him on the side of the road, I thought for certain he was trying to fool me. But it had been years. I'd only seen two forms. The cat and the little boy. "Why do you look like a child?" I had asked him.

"It makes you more comfortable."

It did and it didn't.

"Humans in general trust children. Though their innocence isn't really a strength. A child is easily led astray, abused, or murdered. Why do you think adults trust children? Is it only because an adult can overpower a child? Are humans so broken, that trust only comes from what they feel they can control?"

I didn't know. Trust had always been hard for me, even as a child. Too many bad memories. I'd never had a place to run. Did a lot of my running through the different worlds in books. Tales of people who could open doors and disappear into another world.

"It's an escape," Robin had told me. I had agreed at the time. *"Not all fiction. Doors open and close all the time."*

"To other worlds?" I confirmed.

He shrugged. "Nothing is as linear as humans think. The world feels flat but appears round. In reality it's fractured into a billion dimensions interwoven with doorways. Though it may sometimes look like a window or even a wall."

It was the most he'd ever spoken to me about the other worlds he'd seen. That had surprised me. Over the years I'd questioned him many times, only to have him deftly avoid giving me answers. Nothing was ever direct, but what I'd devised over the years, was that the fae loved the purest of heart. Not for kindness reasons. No, the fae liked to eat them. Doors to Underhill opened for the pure of heart all the time. It was a bit like ringing a dinner bell. The pure of heart opened a door and walked right into the snare of the nearest fae. Those who made it back to write about it, or dreamt about surviving it, those were rare.

I always asked how it happened. Did the pure of heart just find the doors by accident? Did the fae seek them out? Was there a way to bring a doorway to them? Robin had been vague. My impression was that the fae couldn't control the doors. Underhill did.

"So no one really opens a door. They just have to find them and pass through it?" I'd been thinking about it a long time. Alchemy was a set of rules, if *a* was added to *b* they equaled *c*. It was a law of the universe. The human eye could not detect atoms, or viruses, or even the true path of light without many tools of divination. Maybe that was the reason for the doors. Pure heart aside. Maybe it was more about finding the rift in dimensions, or at least a way to divine them. Doors. Physical doorways were bound in place, but opened into space. A room, a closet, whatever.

Maybe it was more than that. I could really use a door right now, even as terrifying as the thought of falling into some dark corner of Underhill and never getting out was. Certain death, or maybe a little wandering? Could I find a door to Underhill if one existed?

I was certainly not a paragon of virtue. I'd stolen to survive, among many other misdeeds. But I was desperate. Facing this pack of rogues again would be suicide. Life with Felix would be torture, and getting caught would lead to Nicky's death. I had to at least try to get Nicky out. All of this was my fault.

I opened the closet door, examining the contents. A handful of stuffed toys were strewn across the floor. Otherwise the closet was empty. Nothing special about the closet at all. No monsters, handles built into the back, or glints of light through cracks in the wall. I nudged the toys aside until we both fit and closed the door, sitting us down in the corner.

"I need you to do something for me, Nicky." This was all theory, and my head really hurt. Too much movement, which meant I had another concussion and would likely pass out soon. I hoped I wouldn't have to ask Liam to share his strength to heal me again. I also hoped I'd get to see him again. "Did your mom ever read you fairy tales? Like Peter Pan or Cinderella?"

He nodded again, wiping his nose all over my shirt. I tugged up the edge of my shirt and rubbed some of the blood off his face. His tears helped wash most of it away.

"Remember the fairy godmother and Tinker Bell?" I asked. He nodded. "I want you to think really hard and ask them for help. Pick one. I'm going to think and wish with you too."

"Wish?"

"Remember the fairy godmother helped Cinderella go to the ball? She gave her a dress and a car to get there? Tinker Bell gave Peter Pan the ability to fly. We want to wish like that, only we want to wish for a way out of this house."

"Mama doesn't wake up anymore," Nicky told me solemnly. "The monsters downstairs ate her."

I nodded and swallowed back bile. "Let's not think about that, Nicky. Close your eyes with me and let's think about a way out. It can be a door to the outside, or even a door to the bakery. We can go there and get cookies. We just need to get out first."

"M'kay," Nicky said. He shut his eyes really tight, and his little fingers dug into my sides. I closed my eyes and thought of Robin. He came and went from our trailer to Underhill without a door most days. Sometimes if he was being flashy he'd open a cupboard door and walk through. I knew it was a rare gift among the fae to open doors. Mostly because it wasn't really their power. Underhill liked Robin. I saw that time and again every time I planted a garden and he blessed it. Wild things could happen. Plants that didn't normally grow in the human world sometimes popped up. Robin often took control of them, and the plants would vanish back to the ether from which they came.

It was to Robin to whom I wished. We didn't keep a tally of favors. Robin might have at first, but the time had worn us down. The many little gifts I gave him became the norm, when to others of his kind they would make him beholden to me. There was enough give and take on both sides that I thought we were even. I was willing to owe him if necessary. A thousand years of serving the puck didn't seem all that bad an option when faced with probable rape and death. I could see buying a lot of chocolate bars in my future if we made it through this.

I thought hard of Robin. The smell of him, the feel of his fur, or the rare occasion when he wrapped his thin arms around me, much like Nicky was doing right this minute. The sound of his voice, and timber of his purr. He was home to me. Had been for years. I let my mind open up to memories of us, all while whispering, "Please open a door to home."

Nicky whispered about cookies and seeing his mom

again. The moment narrowed into thought, the feel of his weight on me, and the smell of blood, but it all began to fade. Almost like falling asleep. One minute everything was vivid and defined, the next fuzz invaded my thoughts and pulled me toward oblivion. I didn't want to dream of being free, so I struggled with the heaviness of my limbs and the crashing weight of exhaustion.

In the end, the world vanished from around me more like a door was shut in my face than having one opened. At least the darkness soothed away the last of the aches and fears.

CHAPTER 20

I dreamt of *Apa* and my mother. Of course it was a dream because there was no possible way I could have remembered being the baby that was swaddled up in my mother's arms. My current self seemed to be looking on from the side of the room, seeing them all, instead of from that baby's point of view. *Apa*'s living room looked the same as it always had. Barren and sparsely furnished as it was used for pack meetings. When the occasional fight broke out, he lost less furniture.

He also was unchanged. Looking young, late twenties, strong, and wide through the shoulders. He wasn't large, likely close to Liam's size if they stood side by side. The Volkov was a bit more muscular, though the added strength was very smooth and unnoticeable if he smiled your way.

His hair was a sweep of dark hair left long enough to fall around his eyes. No one would look at him and think ugly. He was handsome enough, but only just slightly more so than average. He wasn't movie star beautiful, or the kind of man who could stop a room with his looks. No, his presence is what made people hesitate. The weight of him could smother anyone with all the subtlety of concrete when he was in a sour mood. His clear, pale gray eyes, looked calm, focused on the child several feet away.

My mother rocked and soothed me, all while I fussed and wiggled. Then I leapt from her grasp, shifted into a tiny baby fox, and made to dart across the room. Only *Apa* caught me.

"I see what you mean," *Apa* told her. He struggled with the squirming fox but held tight. "An infant should not have the ability to shift, and even if he could, his fox is far more advanced than his human side…"

"My mama used to tell me stories," my mother said. She had been young when she had me. Seventeen, I think. She was one of the most beautiful women I'd ever seen. Her skin so delicate, features dainty and feminine. Her hair styled up in a black bun with ringlets of curls around it. Her clothes were worn, tattered, and too large, but the bag full of baby supplies at her feet were brand new. "Tales of mythical creatures in her grandparents' time. None of them will answer my calls now, even if they are alive. My mother passed a dozen years ago. I'm not sure who else to call."

"What about the baby's father?" *Apa* asked. He held me firmly in his arms, but carefully stroked my fur. His eyes drooped and his shoulders slumped. I stopped wiggling and seemed to settle into place in his arms, with my nose pressed to his chest above his heart.

"Dead. Killed in a car wreck before I even knew I was pregnant. Haven't been able to track any of his family down either. Heard they came from Nevada somewhere, maybe Texas."

Apa snorted. "That's always the case." He let out a long sigh and gave in to some unseen pull, collapsing into the chair behind him. "He's *witchblood*."

Omega. I could hear *Apa's* unspoken thought in my head just as clearly as if he'd said it out loud.

"I hear that a lot, but don't know what it means. No one in my family has ever been a witch. Is it because he can change," my mother asked. She didn't try to take me away from him, but did reach out to stroke my back. "Never seen a fox so bright red outside a kid's book."

"*Witchblood* just means magic in the blood. Usually there is fae somewhere in the family line. The term came from the Christian revolution like much of the rest of the Western world's beliefs. There could have been a fae ten generations ago in your family line and the taint in the blood just showing up now could be a coincidence. Or you might have a dozen relatives with little powers that they brush off as good intuition or luck. It doesn't always manifest as shape-shifting, and to do so this young is unheard of." *Apa* sat transfixed, staring at me, running his palm down my back, eyes shut as though he was about to fall asleep. The stroke of his hand down my spine was slow and made me sleepy just watching it. Almost like I could feel it. "If the baby's father had a drop of fae in his blood as well, that might explain the intensity of the power now."

My mother flushed. "I didn't know much about him. Just that he was handsome. Like one of those men from the romance book covers. We were only together a couple days. Just some fun was all it was supposed to be. We both came from families with obligations. He mentioned a grandfather, but I can't find him. We didn't talk much…"

"If you give me the little information you know, I'll have someone do some research and see if they can find out more about him. Perhaps more of this is from his line than yours. I don't know of any creature that is born with the ability to shift other than fae."

"He sees things I don't," my mother said. "I'm sure of it. He stares off at nothing all the time. Babies don't do that."

Apa shrugged. "Since he already has the ability to shift he could have other abilities. He could be seeing spirits or auras or just have really good vision and be examining the dust flying through the air."

"My daddy had a friend who referred me here. Said you knew a lot about his kind. Shifters and the like. I won't tell no one." My mother burst from her seat and paced the room. "Would never put Sebastian in harm's way. It's just so hard to keep him hidden. I never know when he'll shift. And he doesn't act like a normal baby. Doesn't cry for food or play with toys. He just rocks and looks around the room like he's seeing people I don't. People ask questions and I don't know how to explain. I've had so many people give me sympathy and tell me that I should have him tested for autism as soon as possible."

"He's not sick," *Apa* agreed, "just not average. I can find a place for the two of you to stay. Close to the pack." *Apa* offered. "Guide him as best I can. Wolves aren't born. They are made. We've never had a child survive the change."

My mother looked down at me with a sad expression. "I can't stay. I have to help my daddy with his shop. He doesn't have anyone else. We're barely making it…" She trailed off still staring at me. "I can try to send money to help with his care if you'd be willing to look after him. I'm thinking you'd probably know better how to raise a boy who can change into a fox."

Apa opened his eyes, his face was still neutral, calm, but something in him tensed. "You want to leave him with me?"

"Can't you shift with him? Teach him how to be normal?"

"Miss…" *Apa* swallowed back whatever he was going to say. "This is normal for him."

"And that's the problem." My mother paced, not looking in my direction at all. "I want him to be safe. I still love him."

"But you don't want him with you."

"Maybe if you can train him not to shift?" She looked hopeful now. "I can come back and get him then."

"You want him to hide what he is."

She just shrugged. "Being different isn't safe. You know that's true for anyone. Werewolves, half-Japanese black women like me, and that baby fox in your arms. We do our best to not be seen. Not make waves."

"I can teach him control," *Apa* offered. "Though as young as he is, it may take years."

My mother stopped pacing again. "I could come see him sometimes?"

"Anytime you wish," *Apa* agreed. He sat back in the chair, cradling me in his arms and closing his eyes again. "Thank you for bringing him to me, Starla. I promise to do my best to care for him as if he were my own."

"Thank you, Mr. Volkov. Thank you so much. I will try to send money…"

"Not necessary," *Apa* cut her off. "I have plenty of money. I will have my second, Oberon, speak with your father about investments that might help his business."

Appearing as though summoned, Oberon stepped through a doorway, a frown etched on his face. My mother didn't notice. She just nodded her head. "Thank you so much. And please take good care of Sebastian. I probably should have been smarter about making a choice of bringing him into the world, but I didn't know…Does anyone really? And what if I'd given him up for adoption? Those poor people would be so confused."

"Sebastian is in good hands," Oberon told her. "Let me walk you to your car." He led her out, barely throwing a glance back at the Volkov who didn't move. It was like he'd fallen into a trance.

It stung a little to be reminded of how little my mother wanted me. She said nice things, echoing what I'm sure she'd heard from a television show instead of what she felt. Her eyes spoke the truth. She'd looked at me with disinterest when I'd been a baby. Maybe even horror for what she'd been stuck with. Recently, her eyes said I was an obligation, almost a bad memory of what she could never really escape. She had three other children now. Was happily married to a man I'd never even met. All of the other kids were normal. It was just me who'd messed up her life by being conceived too quickly and born to the *witchblood* curse.

Apa rocked in the chair, looking as young and unassuming as always. Especially holding a baby fox in his arms, eyes closed, and body relaxed as though he were nearly asleep. No one would see him walking down the street and think he was the deadliest werewolf on the planet. In fact, a lot of wolves didn't believe it either once they'd met him. Dangerous, that assumption.

Oberon returned and stopped with the door open behind him. "Xander?"

The Volkov froze, tension whipping through him, cording his muscles in an instant. A dark wind swept the room. Something I'd felt only a handful of times in my life and knew enough to run far away from. The Volkov's eyes opened a slit to reveal a glowing yellow so bright that Oberon immediately dropped to the floor and bowed his head in submission.

"Volkov?" Oberon asked again, this time his voice in a high pitched whine I couldn't recall ever hearing from him before. The baby version of me shifted, changing back to human and began to cry. Some instinct within me reached out to soothe the baby. Not physically, more an emotional touch like the day I'd calmed Toby. The same thoughts, *Safe, calm. Safe, calm.*

The Volkov's eyes shut again. The dark wind vanished. He began to hum and rock me. His touch once again soothed away the baby cries until the baby version of me was nestled against his chest, fast asleep. Oberon still knelt at his feet, prostrated to a power I couldn't feel. His ragged breathing told me he was fighting to stay still and not startle the Volkov.

"Omega," *Apa* whispered.

Oberon let out a deep sigh as though he could finally breathe, and so did I. "Like Felix's mother," Oberon agreed, an edge of warning in his voice.

"My control is much better now," *Apa* said.

"You haven't been tested in centuries. There's a reason we don't keep omegas in this pack. They make the men lazy and stir the wolves into a frenzy of ownership."

"He's just a baby. His *witchblood* should offer him some protection."

"Yet you hold him in your arms as if there could be nothing more precious in the world. What does your wolf say? Mine? Claim him?"

The Volkov looked at his second, eyes bordering on that yellow shine again. Oberon bowed his head. Then it faded. "I'll teach him to suppress it. By the time he's five he won't even realize he has the power."

"And how will you keep him alive that long?" Oberon demanded. "I'm three feet away and want to rip him from your arms. Hold him. Bite him. Claim him…"

The Volkov closed his eyes again and bowed over the baby version of me. "It's time for me to take a little trip."

"He's an infant. It could take years to teach him control. You can't leave the pack that long," Oberon protested.

"They will be in good hands. Both you and Felix are here."

"Felix is not well."

"And if I have to put him down right now, I won't be either. Find out what you can about the father. This isn't just a random hiccup from an old bloodline."

Oberon let out a long sigh. "As the Volkov wills."

The dream did a weird shift and I was no longer in the room, but in a wide open field. I remember running with a wolf as a small child, but only in vague memories. This time I was the little fox. Gleefully jumping after the nearest beetle, or chasing a dragonfly. Happier years. Glimpses of catching rodents, fish or small birds for food. Memories of sleeping in a cave-like den. Days filled with carefree fun and joy. Until a stranger came to disturb all of it.

This day was a vague memory, so I knew it had been pulled out of my subconscious somewhere. Specific things like time and place had long since vanished into the depths of the abyss of my memory. But smells: the woods, pine and maple, grass, dirt and wildflowers; the warmth of the sun on my fur; the sound of a gurgling stream nearby; home to me. Familiar.

In memory the human was little more than a shape of a person. An outline of noise and separation of space. Only now, transposed over my young self, did I see him clearly. Felix.

Apa slid to a stop and growled, so I mimicked him, being the good little fox he'd trained me to be. Sometimes a big black wolf showed up to play, but mostly it was just *Apa* and me.

"Oberon has been spewing lies for years now. You're visiting other packs. On a diplomatic mission across the ocean. Only I find you here, playing games with a fae fox." He flung his hand in my direction.

I snarled and bared my teeth at him.

Felix bared his human teeth and snarled back at me. I felt a wave of some supernatural energy sling off him, smacking me hard enough to throw me and roll me several feet. My yelp disappeared in the grumbling rage of *Apa* attacking Felix. One moment it was wolf on man, then next it was two wolves, larger than most ponies, battling with claws and fangs.

I darted back, remembering *Apa* telling me to make myself small and invisible. Sneak away from an attack if I could. My fangs and claws couldn't tear a man in two. Not like *Apa* and this other wolf.

How real it felt to be nestled in the cradle of a bush, watching, terrified, yet fascinated, as I'd never seen anyone fight *Apa* before. The other wolf dwarfed him, looking almost awkwardly large. The dark gray in contrast to *Apa's* white-spattered gray helped me track the fight. The new wolf wasn't winning despite his size, but he also wasn't giving up.

Apa leapt at his throat, catching him hard and shaking him. The other wolf made a strangled sound. The movement slowed. *Apa* tore at the other wolf, shaking it, trying to break its neck. I could feel the rage pouring out of him, growing like some sort of monster. I tried to soothe it with natural instincts, sending waves of it outward. For a minute everything froze. The wolves, the sounds of the stream far off, and even the air seemed to stop.

Then both wolves dropped to the ground. *Apa* breathing hard, the other wolf shaking and foaming at the mouth. *Apa* whined. The other wolf staggered to its feet, swaying, almost drunk. It peered into the brush where I hid, eyes finding me without trouble. There was nothing calm or safe in those eyes. He took an unsteady step in my direction. In that blood-spattered face I saw madness, rage, and my death. Whatever had been human in him was gone, leaving just the blood-crazed wolf.

Apa growled again.

Another step.

Blackness began to ooze from *Apa,* pooling into another shape in between the wolf and me. It grew and grew, mass upon mass of liquid darkness built until it was something I couldn't begin to comprehend. Not then with my little baby fox brain, and even not now, seeing it again. It was some sort of dragon, perhaps. *Monster,* my brain affirmed, having nothing else to compare it to.

In this memory, I was nothing more than Sebastian the baby fox. Tiny and helpless with baby teeth, and baby claws. I must have made a sound because it turned my way, and suddenly my world was terror. Any other thought was swallowed into the darkness of absolute fear. My heart raced in my chest until I couldn't breathe from the speed, my body refused to react to my brain screaming "Run!"

All that remained was darkness, pain, terror, and oncoming death. I dropped to my belly, too terrified to do more than submit to my extinction. The high pitched whimpering sound dripping from my throat sounded foreign even to me. If I could have dropped dead of fear alone right there, I would have.

A bright light surrounded us and the calm dripped over everything like a blanket of snow. Only the terror remained and I could feel energy coursing through me, demanding release. I responded with an explosion of something within me. A searing heat poured over me, making my fur light on fire. I screamed, a keening wail. Terror all around. Burning up from within.

A dark form leapt over me, shoved me away hard enough to send me rolling down the hillside and into the creek. The cold bite of water doused the fire and snapped me free of the terror that had kept me immobile and my body finally reacted, running as I'd never run before. With no thought to direction, other than *away*, I ran until there wasn't an ounce of strength left in my body.

That memory was vivid. The exhaustion. The hopelessness. The loneliness. The release as I let my fox take over when my human brain succumbed to the absolute emotional exhaustion.

I crawled into the rotted innards of a fallen tree and was asleep before I even had a thought to where I might be. Both in that time and in whatever dream world I'd been dragged into.

CHAPTER 21

Werewolves lost most of their humanity in their animal form. It was what made them so deadly. Instincts of a wolf, and the niggling sensation of being human. It was enough to drive a lot of wolves mad after their first change.

As a fox I was always me. I could let the fox to the front when we hunted or had to den outside, but the human mind was always present, functioning and planning. It made me slow to react to most other animal threats, but more cunning overall.

Like waking from a dream I found myself lost in confusion, trying to separate reality from distorted memory. For a minute it was like my human brain struggled to catch up with the fox. Which was why I stumbled groggily to a stop, chasing a squirrel of some kind, even though I subconsciously knew my belly was full.

Never before had I felt such a strong sense of a separate being bound together with me. The familiarity of it let me know this was the fox part of my *witchblood*, but I'd never experienced it as a full awareness before. It thought of food and den, while I was confused as to why I was a fox at all.

Stupid. The fox seemed to think. *What else would we be?* the fox snarled at me, trying to rip the control back. I held tight and hushed it.

I tried to will myself to change, only it wouldn't come. Where was my human half? Where was I, at all?

Trees and plants grew in tall stalks of green and brown, larger than anything I'd seen in my life. Just the leaves from one bush was bigger than I was. A sound in the distance, movement through the grass had my ears perking up. As my human brain settled back into place, so did the terror from the prior memory. We zipped, the fox and I, across an expansive distance of foliage to find a tiny den of wood and brush. Too small for bigger predators, and barely big enough for me, I curled in, nose to tail, making myself as small as possible. The fox in agreement with me. Our heart pounded in tandem, racing with the chase and fear.

Safety came first. Battling for control and shifting back could wait.

Nothing moved for a while. I didn't dare put my nose close enough to the opening of my den to attract attention, but I could *feel* it. A very subtle presence. Danger. Something moved through the underbrush close enough to silence the bugs and birds to a stillness.

We struggled to breathe, the fox and I. Would it hear us? Could it hear our heart beat? Was it the monster? The darkness that eats everything? Or something else?

We trembled with the fear. But no one can stay vigilant forever. Our tummy was full and we were in our den. Safety, as much as it could be found, was what we had. My eyelids grew heavy. Though I wasn't sure how they could in a dream, but they did. Finally, they didn't open again, neither of us really noticing.

A warm rumbling against my back eased me awake. I should have been alarmed, only I was warm and feeling safe. A large furred body had shoved itself into the den with me, taking up every spare inch. It wasn't a wolf. That much I knew from the striped tail flicking slowly by my nose. It didn't smell like a wolf, yet something familiar tugged at my senses…

The face that appeared in my sight a second later was that of a round cat with small ears and a somewhat angry looking face. He licked my head, purring a comforting rumble. The fox was a jumble of images, scattered bits of emotion tied to small clips of life. We'd seen the cat before. Slept in the same bed, shared food, and even an occasional hunt. It took my human brain a long while to click into place since labels weren't a fox thing.

Robin.

I blinked away the sleepiness. Was this still a dream? My body ached, a little sore from running, if I read the muscles right. My brain felt vaguely detached, and foggy. I wiggled out from Robin's warm cuddle and the den. Outside the world was filled with the normal noise of a forest, only it looked more like a jungle than a forest. Trees towering into the sky, leaves and foliage a hundred times larger than I'd ever seen in my life. I couldn't recall any of these plants being native to anywhere in the USA, but my brain wasn't working all that great either.

Where the hell was I? What had happened? I couldn't still be dreaming, could I?

I stretched my fox form out and tried to tug at the human shift again. Nothing happened. Instantly I began to panic, sending my heart racing. I sat down and forced myself to breathe. A panic attack would not help the situation. Robin appeared behind me, pressed his nose to my back and kneaded my side, purring. I knew he was trying to comfort me, but I suddenly felt claustrophobic and couldn't bear to be touched.

With a quick roll away, I bounced to my feet and darted into the undergrowth. The sound of Robin's low growling meows chased after me even as his chittering faded into the distance.

That last memory of seeing *Apa* change into something when he tried to protect me from Felix replaying in my head. The darkness so vast and yet impossible to fathom. No shape, or perhaps too horrific a shape for a human brain to grasp. The terror it set into my bones felt just as raw right that second as it had years ago when I'd first experienced it.

How deeply had I buried that memory to forget so much? The power I'd used that day was so much more than I had even now. Where had the fire come from? How was that possible? Had my terror over meeting *Apa's* monster face-to-face awakened something only to suppress it when I escaped?

I ran like the devil was hot on my trail, no thought to the path, just feeling the need for distance. Even Robin's small sounds vanished into the greenery. Something had arisen inside me and it needed out. It was bigger than me or the fox. It rose like the anxiety always did, twisting my body with tension and fear. I felt like I was going to come out of my skin if I didn't keep running.

The forest, or jungle, or wherever the hell I was, had no rhyme or reason. One moment I'd be following a stream, only to have it vanish off a cliff into a vast ocean and turn around to find I was on the top of a mountain with snow pouring down on me. I backtracked a dozen times, the landscape shifting around me like a living thing, until I could find my way back to the forest-like place in which I began.

I ran until I could barely breathe and my ribs ached with the strain. For a while I felt like I was running in circles. Finally, I had to drop down into a lush pile of grass and just catch a break. Either this was some really vivid dream, or I was lost in Underhill. Underhill, the world of the fae. Human rules didn't apply here. Hell, I was pretty sure wolf rules didn't either. It was the place of nightmares. I'd read some of the original fairy tales and knew enough about the fae to know the originals were probably much more gruesome than the writer had recorded. And yet here I was, trapped in Underhill. The mere idea of it terrified me.

How had I gotten here? I vaguely recalled a fight with Felix. Everything after that was a little hazy. And when I tried harder to think through the maze that made up a jumble of images, my head began to pound with a throbbing pressure that made even my eyes hurt. Then the feeling would rise again. That monster inside me. Cold fire. Fear. Pain. A need to let something free. Had what I'd seen come from *Apa* attached itself to me somehow?

For a moment I was completely lost in terror again. Overwhelmed just trying to breathe. Out in the open like this wasn't safe. Even in a normal forest it wouldn't have been entirely safe. If I really was in Underhill, it was likely there would be a giant troll or something to happen along with a taste for fox shifters. I'd heard rumors once that the fae find *witchblood* to be a delicacy. But I needed a minute.

A stream glowed with vibrant red leaves pooled across the top and trees straining to reach the sky. I sat transfixed for a while, lost in the kaleidoscope of color. The wind echoed a trilling sound. Shuffling of feet. Something big coming toward me. My gut clenched in terror, senses screaming to run, again. The sky had changed. Darkening a little. How long had I stood there captivated by a magical earthen landscape? Long enough to become the worm on a hook for some mythical monster.

Shuffle, shuffle, whoosh, whoosh. Snap!

Nearby a tree seemed to splinter without anything touching it. I let out a yip and ran. There was a snarl as something gave chase. A wolf? It sounded bigger, clumsier than any wolf I'd ever heard before. *Apa's* beast perhaps? Not his wolf, but the other thing that lived inside him.

The scent of blood wafted through the air, bitter, copper, and old. Again that spoilt meat stench that stirred a memory of a room decorated with child-sized furniture and happy animal stickers on the wall. I cowered with the memory of fear and pain, not sure which way to run as the sounds surrounded me now. The smell overwhelmed my senses, blocking out everything else. Like something large, but imperceivable, leaned over, basting me in its foul breath.

The explosion happened within. A blast of light and heat, followed by searing cold. I suddenly felt larger, towering over the trees and meadow, and looking down on something my eyes couldn't focus on. Some sort of bug? Multiple legs and body segments glistened in the sun, giving away a reflective and almost chameleon-like coating. The vision lasted only a few seconds before the light and cold overrode my senses.

The monster howled a sound that hurt my ears as the brightness that illuminated and nearly destroyed my vision expanded, devouring the creature. Then it was over. The meadow silent, monster gone. I was small again and so tired.

Another small shuffle echoed in the distance. It was the fox that said run and made my body respond. My human brain just couldn't fathom the last few minutes of my life. At least the fox was fast on the uptake. We dashed through more woolen looking trees, feeling like things were reaching out to capture us.

Danger! My fox kept telling me as our body protested with the strain. I struggled to breathe as we sped so fast it felt a bit like flying. The scenery didn't matter so much as the fox seemed to know where it was going. I hoped he didn't guide us off a cliff or something.

We stumbled to a stop at another stream. The water burbling and cheery. It smelled okay, and I was dying of thirst, but I sat, watched, and waited. The movement of the waves certainly wasn't normal. It lapped the shore for a while, then seemed to crawl forward a few inches, before sliding back.

The little light filtering through the trees made the stream glitter like diamonds. The water smelled sweet and clean. It sang of my thirst, tempting me closer. Only there were no fish. Why would a stream have no fish?

It inched toward me. A living thing with its odd snake-like movement. *Slither.* Side to side. I backed away twice before watching a bird land close to its edge. The water rose up and slapped the bird like an invisible hand. The bird vanished into the depth of the water. I trembled. The cold fire began to lick at my gut again, draining my energy.

No. Not again. I didn't think I had enough strength to survive that again. Whatever it was. I leapt away from the stream. Keeping my distance, but following it, hoping for some place safe to rest.

Some ways down the stream I found a pile of rocks, collapsed around in an odd triangle. They were some space from the stream. The grass around them covered the opening, but when I investigated I found no scent of anything other than grass and wind. What an odd place. The fox nudged me to rest. Too tired, it protested. I wiggled into the opening. Happy that it provided a good view of the whole area, even though I was straining to see through the tall grass. I listened intently. Body throbbing with unmatched pain. We were waiting, the fox and I. For the next attack.

CHAPTER 22

I must have half dozed from complete exhaustion because the smell of cinnamon, vanilla, and cardamom wafting through the air startled me awake and to my feet. For a while I sat peering through a very densely overgrown field of grass for any sign of movement. The scent was so out of place, and exhaustion had me disoriented, all I could do was blink into the distance, confused as to whether I should run away or pursue the delicious flavor in the air.

Silence blanketed the field, enough so that I felt I had lost my hearing completely. The grass sat still. No wind. The stream still present, but completely absent of sound. The sky overhead was an odd teal more like an ocean color than any sky I'd ever seen. Not a cloud to be found. There were trees, twisted and dark things that reminded me of artisans' renditions of gnome-like faces carved into the knobby sides of trees. Faces, dark and angry stared out at me. They didn't move either. Though I hadn't remembered them being there when I'd fallen asleep.

The smell intensified. It curled around me like a living thing wrapping me in a warm hug and begging me to come.

A fae trick? Perhaps another monster? One with a lure of sweet home and memories? I could almost see someone's face attached to the memory of the scents, but couldn't quite make it out. Like something blocked the memory, or slowed my thoughts. Maybe it was because I'd been the fox too long? I'd never spent more than a day or so as the fox. I vaguely recalled that werewolves lost their humanity very quickly when forced to stay wolves for extended periods of time.

The face almost appeared in my mind again. A cloud of darkness hovered over it. Frustrating me because I felt like I needed to see it right that second. Just finishing the memory would clarify my thoughts. I was sure of it.

I dropped back down, trembling with the need to follow the pull tugging at me. After a few minutes I heard it. My heart beat in tandem with someone else's. The idea should have terrified me, except that it just made me listen harder and feel for that other half I'd somehow been missing. More than just a smell now. A feeling of home and safety. A *need* for something so profound I couldn't put it to words. It was like my very soul would rip itself out of me to follow the sensation if I didn't move. So I got up.

I followed the tugging, reveled in the scent, slowly at first, cautious, until a few dozen yards' distance showed no ill intent. Then I was bounding across the vastness, racing toward the feeling of home, the *need* burning in me like I'd been lit on fire. I'm not even sure how far I ran, since I was already long beyond exhausted.

At one point I felt as though I'd hit some sort of invisible wall. I raced back and forth alongside, not sure why I couldn't pass through when I saw across to the other side just fine. I nipped and clawed, digging into the ground a little. Nothing worked.

The invisible wall ran along the edge of the stream for some ways. I followed it, keeping my distance from the stream, kicking rocks toward the wall only to watch them bounce off. It wasn't just me who couldn't pass. The stream was different there as well. Less vibrant and clear, more mobile and full of darting fish. How strange.

I followed them for a time. The wall and the stream. Saw the splice in the water, where the barrier seemed to cross, dividing something. The fish just couldn't pass one area, and everything beyond the wall where I stood radiated menace. Warning. The chill of it sank into my bones.

I doubled back toward the fish filled side of the stream. It meandered on for a mile or so it seemed until there was a bridge. Built from stone, it was narrow and covered in green and brown moss. The water rushed beneath it like a real stream. Sounds of water over rocks and fish darting about were still a bit muffled, but I knew they were there. Life existed on the other side of that bridge. Though I wasn't sure anything had crossed it in decades. Would it crumble beneath me?

Then there was the barrier. I could see it here too. A swirling thing, like too much sun over a tar road. Wiggles of color that solidified into the distance, but over the bridge looked a little weak.

I sat staring into the swirl for a bit. Trying to think through my options. Stay in the unknown with monsters chasing me, or try to get to more familiar ground? I made up my mind with a huff, rose to my feet and paced a good distance away. That inner cold fire rose up again, rolling over me like flames eating oxygen in a newly opened room.

Maybe I'd break my neck, but I planned to run at the wall to break through the weak spot. If it was someone's magic, perhaps I just needed a little force. I took a few bounding steps before pushing my tired body to run. In the last minute I closed my eyes, expecting to be eaten or run headfirst into a rock. But something just seemed to pop and I tumbled through, ass over teakettle, landing in fallen leaves and pine needles. At least this little forest area looked more like what I was used to. No gnome-trees in sight. The stream was gone and I could hear birds and insects again. The wind blowing through the trees chilled my skin. I forced myself back to my feet and ran on at a slight tilt upward.

It wasn't until I found a small cave that I slowed.

The delicious scent curled into the space. My heart leapt forward as though demanding I proceed. But a dark cave was not what I thought an ideal hiding place in Underhill. A million things could be waiting there to eat me. The smell was so strong. That heart beating with mine. That call of home. I trembled with the need of it and approached the entrance slowly. If it was a trick, it was a good one. I could barely breathe through the need to be in that cave right that second.

A light flickered inside, far enough away from the entrance to cast shadows. Nothing moved through the dance of the flame. I expected some sort of trick to befall me the second I set foot inside the cave. Only nothing happened. Still I strode forward as though my feet were covered in molasses. The panic ever present, just on the edge of my consciousness, ready to overwhelm me at the slightest hint of something out of place.

Further into the cave an old fashioned oil lantern sat on a small rock ledge. A bedroll had been spread out a few feet away with a pile of blankets and a bag beside it. A man lay on the roll, his stomach pressed to the earth and his face turned away. His back was presented to me. I froze, too afraid that moving would wake him, or bring an attack. Was he trying to make himself look vulnerable?

The silence brought back that echo to my heartbeat. Fast, but not racing. I cocked my head and studied the man. His breath even and strong, though his eyes were closed. He didn't look injured. Intrinsically I knew he wasn't asleep. His breathing was too focused and not slow enough to symbolize sleep.

Thump. Thump. Thump. Our hearts beat, together. I shuddered with the need to touch him and verify it was his heart I was hearing. His that mimicked mine. His energy that danced in unison with mine. His cool calmness that tamed the fire burning my soul while igniting the heat in my gut. His body that I wanted to wrap around me.

There wasn't enough light to see him clearly. Just a mop of darkish hair, blue jeans and some sort of sweater over the top, which made sense since the cave had a bit of a chill. My fur kept me warm enough, but humans didn't have that luxury. I took another step toward him. Still he didn't move. Was it him who smelled so divine?

That pull of need kept dragging at me, urging me closer, one strained step at a time. Until I stood over him, close enough to hear his heart clearly. Beating with mine. Not a trick. Couldn't be a trick. Not this close.

A touch of tension strained his shoulders, like he was trying to keep himself still. I touched a paw to his back, expecting him to leap up and try to catch me. Only he didn't. Instead he let out a long sigh and the tension melted away. I couldn't stop trembling. Touching him drained the last of the energy out of me and I collapsed on top of him, my entire body racked with spasms.

"Sebastian," He whispered, voice soft, familiar, yet my memory was still so fragmented. He heaved a heavy breath and rolled over, careful to catch me and hold me against his chest. Not confining like he'd captured me, but more like he held something precious. I didn't have the strength to run anyway. And now as my heart settled over his, I could finally breathe.

The change poured over me without conscious thought.

One moment I struggled with being the fox, run into the ground and nearly lifeless with exhaustion, burning with an unseen cold fire, to becoming the man I'd lost for a few hours, and frozen as though I'd been dumped in a subzero lake. Still my head swam with confusion and a jumble of scattered images. Only now I knew whose arms I was in and whose heart beat with mine.

"Liam," I breathed his name like it was a magic word. He reached out and flicked a blanket over me, protecting my naked body from the chill wind, and helping me feel less vulnerable.

"There you are," Liam said, as he ran his fingers over my face and through my messy hair which hung loose over the both of us. It looked dark and tangled in the pale light. I could barely see his eyes, clear and pale blue, though little more than ice in the darkness. I trembled against him. Freezing and detached, needing to be closer to him, needing every part of him to cover me.

I leaned down and captured his lips, diving into the taste of him, as though I were trying to crawl inside him. He returned my kiss with just as much ferocity, hand wrapped around the back of my neck, locking me in place against him. I gripped at his arms, nails digging into his biceps. "Please, Liam, please…" I begged when I released his mouth.

"Anything, baby," Liam whispered, "Anything. I'm here. Let me be your home, provide you protection, and love."

"Please," I pleaded, not even knowing what I really wanted. Just that I needed him. Had to have him. He was the raft in the sea of chaos weathering the storm of madness that had taken over my brain. Something had awakened in me. A lightning rod of energy, desire, and power. It was like the monster I'd seen *Apa* become had been absorbed into my skin and needed release or it would eat me alive from the inside out.

I began tugging at Liam's clothes. "You. Please. I need you." I tore at them then, shredding the sweater, though he helped by peeling away the last piece and shucking it off with a small flex to lift himself and me off the mat. His chest and stomach bare, I pressed myself to him, curling myself against his searing heat. Still I shook with the cold power throbbing within me. "Liam…" I whined. Needing him to do something, though I wasn't sure what. He was so cautious.

"Anything," he repeated.

"I'm c-cold," I stuttered. "Help me."

His hands knotted in my hair and pulled me down for another kiss. It helped a little. Like the warmth of him leaked into my mouth, but it wasn't enough. "I don't want to scare you," Liam murmured between kisses. "Please don't run again. I won't survive."

"I won't," I promised, shoving at his pants, needing his skin against mine, his heat to wrap around me. I couldn't imagine being any place other than with him. Forever. "Please." I was so cold.

He rolled us then. A smooth shift of space and he was on top, out of his jeans, skin against mine and the blanket over the both of us. I should have been terrified. He could have held me down and hurt me. My heart did skip a little beat, but it wasn't in fear. His weight poured heat into my limbs, awakening them to the tingles of energy, mine and his. That monster inside continued to paw at me, demanding freedom.

Liam was hard against my stomach. The length of him radiating heat like a furnace. I suddenly wanted it so bad. Wanted him, like I'd never wanted anyone before. My cock ached with the need to be touched and all I could think about was what it would feel like to finally have Liam inside me. Would his fire drive away the cold? Could it quiet the monster? Soothe the madness of energy swirling through me?

He wrapped his hand around my cock and began to stroke me slowly. His palm was slick with something, but warm and beyond heavenly.

"Anything," Liam whispered, stealing kisses as he found a smooth rhythm. I thrust into his grip. It was good, but not enough.

"More," I demanded of him, feeling bold.

Part of it was the fox, only that small bit seemed more relaxed, ready to pounce if necessary, not afraid. The fox assured me that it was okay. We were in the right place. Right where we needed to be. He wouldn't hurt us. *Mate.* The fox decided even if I was still confused. I felt my eyes roll back in my head as Liam's hips bucked against mine, creating more friction.

"Please, please, please," I couldn't stop the word from falling from my lips. I knew what I wanted. But part of me was still terrified. Not of Liam, but of my reaction to the act. No. I wouldn't think of it that way. It wasn't just a separate action. This was Liam. I was in his arms, wrapped up in his energy, begging for his touch as we made love. Yes, that was okay. That felt right. "Take me," I whispered into his lips. "Make love to me."

"You're sure?" He asked, his eyes searching mine. I probably looked like a mad man beneath him. Writhing in pleasure, begging for more, yet terrified of getting exactly what I wanted.

"I need you inside me." The energy was too much. Whether it was us, or whatever had awakened within me, something needed to break. If it didn't happen soon, I would shatter. "Please. In me. Warm me."

"I have lube," Liam said, "but no condoms." He ran his grip down the length of me again, twisting a bit and tightening at the base before sliding back up again. "I can make you come like this."

"No."

"Sebastian, I only want this if you're ready. If we do this and you run…I can't…"

"I'm ready." So fucking ready I was about to push him over onto his back and ride him. "I can ride you, if you prefer. I just need…" Oh God did I *need*.

Liam's stroking eased a little as I heard him fumbling with the tube of lube. "I need to prepare you. I know it's been a while."

But that wasn't what I wanted. I didn't want sweet and gentle right that minute. I just wanted him surging into me. *Claiming* me. Fuck. Was that what this was? This gut-wrenching need? The fire and ice? He cooled the energy flame, all while warming my soul inside and out. Yes, that felt right.

"Claim me," I demanded.

Liam stopped breathing. His eyes were all over my face, searching for what, I didn't know.

"Claim me," I demanded again. "I am giving myself to you. Just you, Liam. I am yours, you are mine."

His blue eyes flashed yellow and he stuttered back to life, shoving me down and pushing my legs up over his elbows as he steadied himself above me.

"Mine," he growled, the wolf rising to the surface at the chance to claim its mate. He wasn't gentle with himself as he covered his cock in lube. He used one finger to probe at my hole, slicking the entrance with lube and gently slipping inside. It had been a long time, but the discomfort was familiar enough, brief as it might be. He didn't try to add another, or stretch me, just slid the finger out and pressed the large head of his cock to my hole. He pushed in and I pushed out, telling my body to let him in. I needed this like I needed air.

The burn lasted a little longer than I remembered after he

was finally fully seated. Now we both trembled. Him with the resolve not to move until I was ready, and me with need for him. He was so warm. I could feel his heartbeat in two places, in his chest against mine and in the throbbing of his cock deep within me.

"Move," I begged when the pain eased. Pleasure began to pool in my gut, rising with the heating of his skin spread against mine.

Liam let out a slow hiss and pulled back, sliding himself almost all the way out, before pounding back in.

"Yes!" I cried. That was what I needed. "More." He pulsed with heat inside me, like a branding iron, warming me from the core on outward. Sweat trickled down his chest. My body leeched warmth and strength from him. I panted, pushing back into his thrusts. Needing more. Something just out of reach. I wasn't sure what, but fuck I needed something. I kissed him again, devouring his lips and nearly cutting my tongue on his teeth, which had sharpened.

Fangs. Only alphas could do partial shifts, and it was for one reason alone. To mark their mate.

"Mark me," I begged into his mouth.

He shivered. Together we both must have looked like we were dying or something with the way we shook. "Sebastian," he whispered.

"Now," I demanded, the fox in more control than I was. But it was okay. The fox assured me, we would be okay. Liam was mate. He was safety, home, and love.

Liam roared a primal sound and pulled out just long enough to flip me over onto my stomach. He held me up, balanced on my hands and knees as he surged back into me. Deeper this time. The heat plummeting to the core of my being. It was just this side of pain, but so good I wasn't sure whether to moan or scream.

"Mine," he growled as he pumped into me.

"Yours," I agreed, enjoying his strength, his warmth, his grip and the pulse of his heart against my back. His heart was mine. "Mine," I growled at him. I was so close. "You're mine."

"Yes," he agreed, lips against my shoulder, nipping a line to the base of my neck. He set his teeth there, waiting, his body slamming into me hard enough to lift me off the ground. Yet he held me tight and I took every bit of it wanting more, to be closer to him, to have him inside every pore of my being. Heat burst from me, not the kind that had burned my fur, but the familiar song of release as my cock spurted while I screamed Liam's name.

His teeth sank into my flesh, breaking skin and drawing blood. I saw stars and shuddered beneath him as my blood filled him and he finally released his seed deep within me. A fire, sweet and comforting, soothing as it warmed my soul while it cooled the energy that had been gnawing at me.

For a minute I was dizzy. Liam was everything. Overlapping my soul. Encompassing my heart until all I could feel was him inside me, over me, all around me. Even our labored breathing was an echo of each other.

He eased us onto the bedroll, not letting any space separate us. I was too exhausted to move. Boneless. Satiated. The fox curled up inside me to sleep, content in our mate's arms. *Safe*, it told me. I agreed and shut my eyes.

"Don't leave me," I muttered to Liam as sleep began to pull me into its embrace.

"Never," Liam promised. He licked at the teeth mark on the back of my neck. The whole idea of the mark should have terrified me. We were bound. If I died so did Liam. But in that moment, I didn't care. As long as he was with me. For the first time in my entire life I felt like I mattered to someone. I wasn't alone. I fell asleep praying I'd wake up to experience the feeling again.

CHAPTER 23

Novels glorify sex and claiming. Make it all hot and sexy, and it was when it was happening. But sex is messy. Both physically and emotionally. Books often fail to give truth to the morning-after sort of emotions. Lying wrapped in someone's arms is great, if your brain isn't thinking stupid things like *does he think I'm a wanton whore?* or *I hope he doesn't think I like it rough like that all the time,* and *wow, I hope he doesn't think I do that with just anyone.*

Truth be told. I was more than a little embarrassed. I couldn't recall a time in my life I'd been so demanding. Not that Felix would have ever allowed me to be selfish with my needs. He'd always come first. Liam…

Mate.

The word was almost visceral inside me. A claim written on my soul. I could feel him, not just physically, wrapped around me, but some part of his presence tucked into my chest like he'd taken up residence where my heart should be. And while I was embarrassed, there was no regret. He was mine and I was his. It felt right.

I also felt sticky, and like I really needed a shower.

No condom. Hmm. It didn't worry me since as a werewolf, Liam couldn't carry human diseases. Not that sort at least. They could get cancer sometimes, but it was rare. However, no disease didn't mean no mess.

I shifted a little, moving my legs so I wasn't completely pinned under Liam. He grumbled. I groaned. Yeah, rough sex. The whole feeling it the next day wasn't as sexy as the books made it sound. My thighs burned and I had barely moved them and my ass…

"Ow," I whined.

Liam moved, appearing over me for a second before running his hands through my hair and over my face, finally he traced the bite on the back of my neck. I could feel the bruise and his broken touch as his fingers drifted over the scabbed over portion. It would scar and that was the point. If you'd asked me a year ago if I would ever wear someone's mark like a brand, I'd have told you how crazy the mere idea of it was. Now there was Liam and he had really become everything very quickly.

"Where do you hurt?" Liam asked. He didn't look completely awake, but wow he looked amazing scruffy, with lines of sleep etched across his face.

"Um, where men hurt when other men ride them like a pony."

He snorted out a laugh and kissed the tip of my nose, then he reached over me and pulled a small package of wipes out of a pile of what appeared to be supplies.

"Those better be industrial strength," I told him. "I'm pretty sure your come is cement now."

"Are you always this funny after sex?" Liam asked as he began to gently wipe me down. Again, not as sexy as the books make it sound since I was covered in both of our spunk and sweat.

"A total comedian," I promised. I whined in pain when he lifted my right leg to wash between all my folds and junk. My face felt like it was on fire. I was so bad at this morning after thing. "Probably good that I was never into one night stands. I'm so bad at this."

"Bad at what?" Liam asked. He massaged my thigh, working into the muscle, which hurt. I scrunched my face in pain until finally the muscle relented and it was heaven.

"Okay, that's good. Do the other one too, please. Bad at mornings after. Felix…"

He cut me off with a kiss and his fingers digging into my left thigh causing more than a bit of pain. "Not in bed with us," he said after he was done ravaging my mouth.

"How do you not have morning breath," I grumbled at him. "Can you be more perfect?"

He grabbed a small tin out of the stack and popped it open to reveal some mints. I opened my mouth and he put one on my tongue, then went back to his work of cleaning me up. At least the wound in my thigh had healed. And I didn't feel any of the familiar throb of a lingering concussion. Magic from Underhill maybe? Liam massaged the other thigh until the pain eased, then began to work on my butt muscles.

"That's totally not going to work where it really aches," I promised him.

"I offered to prep you," he reminded me.

I sighed. "Stupid fox brain."

"Was it the fox who decided to mate with me then?"

I frowned at him, not liking the tension that suddenly tightened his shoulders even while he tried to play cool and calm. "I wouldn't have mated with you if I wasn't on board. It was all a little bit more over the top than I've ever experienced in my life, but hey maybe that was the mating thing. I've never mated before. Next time we'll start with some kissing and a couple of hand jobs, okay?" Yeah, I was so going to die of embarrassment. "Maybe some frottage. Save the surprise ass pounding for special occasions like Christmas or the election of a democratic socialist leader."

He laughed again, the tension vanishing. "Anytime." He spread my legs apart.

"Hey, warn a guy. Not really ready for another round," I griped.

"I'm just going to examine you. I'm worried I may have hurt you." He prodded a little bit, even easing a pinky inside. It ached but nothing stung. "No blood. No tears that I feel."

"See, all good. Nothing broken. I'd feel it. Just sore. Maybe we can put some clothes on and talk?" Anything to make me feel less embarrassed and vulnerable. "What are you doing in Underhill anyway? I thought it was hard to get into?"

"We aren't in Underhill." Liam dug through his pile of goodies and found a hoodie and a pair of sweat pants. The hoodie must have been his because when he tugged it over my head, I could have fit at least two other people in it. He finished wiping up my legs and cleaning all my private parts very clinically, before he tugged a pair of warm wool socks onto my feet and then the pants over them. "Your father arrived and tried to find you. Something went really wrong there because until that moment I could feel a link to you. Faint, but I could almost follow it if I could have gotten through to Underhill. Then it was gone. Like you'd vanished completely. Robin went in after you. Said Underhill would likely pull the fox to the surface. Something to do with your *witchblood*. Took him forever to find you. I went a little...*mad*. Like crazy mad. Have been camped out here for a while, away from the pack, to protect them."

"Huh?" I replayed his words in my head. "What do you mean took him forever? I saw Robin right away. He appeared after a nap."

"You'd already been gone awhile. And then you ran from him and he lost you again. Oberon suggested that I use the mate bond to try to call you. Appealing to your omega side instead of trying to find the fox spirit like Robin was. I called. You came. You got through without Robin's help and found your way to me."

"I smelled you. Then I felt your heart. And I was on fire. All while being lost…" The whole thing felt surreal, like a really bad dream. Was I awake now? Maybe this was another fae trick? "I was so afraid and alone."

"Never again." Liam kissed my forehead. "Just promise the next time you run, you take me with you." He cleaned himself off. I had to admit to staring open-mouthed in awe the entire time. Liam's lean muscles, covered in tan skin looked tasty. The couple days beard scruff was hella sexy.

"Next time I get to lick all of you," I said without thinking.

He paused for a minute and rewarded me with his dimpled smile. "Anytime."

I shook myself, I had questions. "How did I get to Underhill again?"

"Even Robin isn't sure. Though he felt you. Said all of Underhill felt you cross over. A ripple through the layer of magic or something." Liam pulled on his own pair of sweats and a long sleeved T-shirt.

"Sounds like he's talking to you a lot."

"To me. Precisely. He won't talk to anyone except me. Oberon wanted to question him, but Robin just turns cat and disappears into the furniture like the Cheshire cat or something. Your father didn't even try."

Apa was here in Liam's territory. My stomach sank. "Is he going to make me go back to Texas?"

Liam squinted at me. "Robin?"

"*Apa*," I corrected.

"Of course not. You belong to me. This is my territory.

You are my mate. He wouldn't dare try to separate us. No one separates a true mate bond. Especially not one between an Alpha and an Omega."

"He can do whatever he wants. He's like the king of werewolves."

"A president at best," Liam said.

"If you think his rule is democratic you've got some surprises ahead. No one gets a vote on his decisions but him."

Liam yanked me into his arms. For a minute I just stood there with his warmth surrounding me and his heart beating against my chest. I nestled my face into his shoulder, breathing in the scent of him. Here the bakery smell of him was faint. More a hint of the vanilla combination I'd followed out of Underhill than the nearly overwhelming siren call it had been last night. But it felt good being that close to him. It felt like home.

His sigh was long and deep as he rested his chin on the top of my head, not easing his hold on me one bit. "I know exactly what the Volkov is and can do. He's scary, yes. But not invincible. Anyone who knows him well knows his weaknesses are few. And his biggest weakness is his heart. That's why his family fears you so damn much. He loves you more than he loves most of them."

I sucked in a breath like I'd been sucker punched. "He knew about Felix. Knew Felix wanted me." Liam held me up and let me bask in his warmth, plus my thighs weren't quite up to carrying around my weight. "If that's love, it's a twisted one."

"Perhaps. I also know that your father has been trying not to kill Felix for the last fifty years for fear that he himself will be lost to madness with the pain. There aren't many who would be strong enough to face the Volkov face to face when he'd gone berserk."

The monster. I remembered the feeling it invoked so clearly, but not what it looked like. Just that gut-wrenching terror. I'd read once that a person couldn't die from fear. The body's reaction to fear, however, could kill a person if it made the heart stop, or lungs freeze up.

"I think he was hoping that you could ground Felix. Only that didn't happen. Felix got worse. Now I think the Volkov prays that you can stop his beast from ripping us all to shreds. There is no choice but to put Felix down. I think the only reason Oberon hasn't done it is because he fears the Volkov will go mad without you nearby."

"I'm not a wolf. I'm just a little fox," I reminded him. Compared to Oberon, I was a gnat on the Volkov's back. If *Apa* killed Oberon in his madness, would there be anyone who could stand against him? Surely not Liam, the baker, who had a beautiful teenage daughter and a pack who loved him fiercely. Not Liam, who spared the man who'd previously run this territory. Not Liam, who held me like I was the most important person in the universe.

"You're an omega. Even more than that, you're a *witchblood* omega. I felt your energy last night running at me from the darkness. I knew it was you, but couldn't help worrying how much of you remained after your trip to Underhill. What if it had stripped away your humanity, I thought to myself? But it wouldn't have mattered. I would have lain there until you ripped me apart if that was what you wanted." He trembled around me. "Don't leave me again. I nearly didn't survive the madness the first time. Now that we're truly mated, I'd be little more than a raving beast without you. Volkov be damned, the world would live in terror of me trying to find you."

"Fuck." Strange how amazing it felt to be needed so badly. Even if it was some weird magic or something. Hadn't Dylan said something about figuring out what I really wanted? To be loved. To be needed. To be part of something. To not be alone anymore. Wasn't that exactly what Liam was giving me? A home, a pack, a family, and his heart? "Fuck," I repeated.

"Indeed. I think it's best we head back to the house and see if we can calm some hot heads?"

"Yeah, Dylan probably has his hands full."

Liam swallowed hard. I felt a ripple of something run through him. An emotion I was chasing to try to place. Worry. Fear. Despair.

"Liam?" I stared up into his clear blue eyes and didn't like the pain I saw there.

"They have Dylan."

"Who?"

"The rogues and Felix. They took him to distract me so Felix could take you."

I blinked at him in horror. "Is he okay?" Oh wait, everything was beginning to flood back in. The bakery. Cookies. And Nicky. "Wait. What about Nicky? Where's Nicky?" Had I vanished into Underhill only to accidently leave him behind for the wolves to kill?

Liam pulled away a little and tilted my face up to look at him. "You've been gone a while, Sebastian. We all assumed Nicky was dead just like his parents are."

How long was a while? "I had him in my arms when I fell asleep or into Underhill, or whatever happened." Had I pulled him into Underhill with me? What if he was still trapped there now? I began to panic.

"He wasn't at the house." Liam held me tighter. "Breathe, Sebastian. We'll figure it out. We will find him." His will soothed the panic like a cooling gel over flames.

"It's my fault."

"It's not."

"They took him because I gave him cookies," I pointed out. Liam rubbed my back fiercely, his touch grounding me like nothing ever had before. The fear still lingered at the edges, panic flickering like flames on my consciousness, but I could think through it now.

"He was convenient. It had nothing to do with you. Their choices are not your fault. It could have been anyone. They took Dylan because of me. Should I blame myself? What would that accomplish?"

"Nicky is just a kid…" If he was in Underhill, he'd be so helpless.

"Anything could have happened to Nicky. Oberon found the house after Robin had told us you'd been pulled into Underhill. He said he cleaned up the situation. I know there was a fire and a memorial. I'll ask him about Nicky."

"But if you know where they are, you'd have Dylan back, right?" A memorial? How long was I gone? A few days? It felt like a few hours, not days.

Liam shook his head. "We knew where they were, not where they are now. Oberon is scouring the countryside. Your father, Robin, and I were looking for you. After the Volkov tried and failed to bring you back he retreated. He's locked himself away in my bunkhouse, refusing to let anyone but Oberon enter. Oberon suggested I try our matebond, though we hadn't sealed anything yet. It was too muddy a link at the house. Too many scents and wolves to get in the way. Then the Volkov did something to our bond and you vanished. I went a little nuts. Carl suggested this cave since it's far enough from the pack to keep them safe and give us space for a mating."

Carl. He'd been oddly absent that night. Of course it was my gut that instantly thought him suspicious for disagreeing with Liam. That didn't mean he was a bad guy. But getting the pack's other two most powerful wolves away from the pack would give him an opportunity to get the rest on his side. Whatever that may be.

"Do you really trust Carl? I mean, if we're out here in the middle of nowhere, and he's in charge of the pack, what's to keep him from taking over?"

"I trust Carl," Liam told me. He let go and began to pack up all the supplies. He was done in little more than a minute, surprising me with not only his speed but his efficiency. "He's saved my life more than once."

"Doesn't seem to like me much," I muttered.

Liam glanced my way as he hauled a full hiker's backpack onto his back and reached for my hand. "He doesn't like anyone much. It's probably *the* reason he'll never be alpha of his own pack. He just doesn't like people. It's nothing personal."

"Even you?"

"Even me. Plus, I am tied to my wolves," Liam reminded me. He pointed to his head. "I can feel them, hear them all the time. I'm sure they can hide some things from me, but something as big as betrayal? Carl would have to be a lot stronger of a wolf if he thought he could hide that from me."

I let him tug me out of the cave. He had a pair of hiking boots that he stepped into, which had been shoved off into a corner. I did not glory in the idea of walking back through the woods in nothing but socks. Especially not when I was still sore and really tired.

Liam leaned over and pulled me into his arms in a bridal carry. "Nap if you want. It's an hour or so hike back," Liam informed me. He paused as if thinking something. "My head is clear and focused. I need to check on the pack now that my head is lucid. But I need you in my den, too."

"We'll work out sleeping arrangements later," I told him.

Though my gut suddenly ached with the idea of not having him in my bed wrapped around me for even one night. "Maybe spend a few nights a week in your bed and a few nights in the camper."

Some tension eased from his shoulders, though his hold on me tightened. "Rest. It's a long walk."

CHAPTER 24

I did fall asleep, though it was one of those odd light sleeps in which I felt like my brain just wouldn't shut off. I jolted awake twice after dreaming of having Liam vanish, only to find him still holding me and still walking. "Nap dreams are the worst," I remarked to him before I fell asleep again.

It was the weight of darkness that startled me to full wakefulness as we approached Liam's home. The sky edged toward dusk, but that wasn't why it felt like light had been stolen from the world. How anyone could miss the heaviness in the air astounded me. Liam's steps slowed. Did he know why *Apa* had locked himself away? Liam had known well enough to keep a distance from his pack when he was struggling with the darkness. How were they not drowning in it from the Volkov even now?

"Liam?" I whispered, feeling the terror rise over me. Again his cool calm washed over me.

"You are safe."

"Even from *Apa?*"

"Especially from the Volkov." We were close enough to

see the backdoor of the house now. The oppression of darkness wafted like black smoke from off in the distance. The bunkhouse. The backdoor opened and Carl stood in the entry as though called. Liam walked by him and into the house. It was weirdly quiet. The subtle warmth had also vanished. It no longer felt like a den, but just a house, cold and unwelcoming.

A small growl escaped Liam's lips. "You're not leaving me."

"Not going anywhere," I told him.

"Your emotions shifted. Like you suddenly didn't want to be here." Liam scowled. "Fuck. Is this always going to be such a jumble?"

I thought he was talking to me, though I had no clue, but it was Carl that answered. "Time will smooth the edges. Eventually you won't be able to tell whose thought is whose."

Did Carl have a true mate?

He continued, "I've sent everyone away. Korissa is at Leigh's. The Volkov and his assassin are still out at the bunkhouse. The only guest left in the house is Dylan's man. The Volkov's message was that you would deal with him directly. I've been feeding him, but he's been driving me nuts. Pounding on the walls and screaming to be let out." Carl looked bored. "Didn't matter that I explained that no one was around but me."

"I'll take care of it," Liam said suddenly sounding sad. Take care of what? Dylan's man. Sean? Dylan's human lover was here? Had he found out about the werewolves? He had been on a date with Dylan. Maybe Dylan had been taken in the middle of it. Was *Apa* expecting Liam to kill Dylan to keep the secret?

"Go home and get some rest," Liam told Carl.

Carl frowned. "There are no guards or anything on site. I should stay."

"With the Volkov's black cloud hanging over us? No. Go. It's late." Liam commanded.

"I'll be back in the morning," Carl conceded, like he could somehow contradict his alpha. He turned and headed toward the front door. A minute later he was gone, and I could hear a faint pounding on the wall.

"Put me down," I told Liam.

"Sebastian…"

"No."

"I don't like it any more than you do. But he made threats."

"What kind of threats?"

"To talk to the police, to get media coverage."

Words spoken in desperate fear. I could sympathize. "The love of his life is missing. I know I'd make all sorts of threats if it were me."

Liam's expression softened. I gripped his shirt and tugged his face close to mine. He offered a kiss, which I accepted, enjoying the simplicity of just us. When the kiss ended, he set me carefully on my feet. Liam didn't want to *take care of* Sean. He cared about Dylan. Dylan loved Sean. Hell, Liam might even like Sean too. But he was a practical man. Now he was mated to me, and I didn't have to follow werewolf rules any more than a fae would have to.

I headed for the safe room and opened the door.

The man inside stopped banging on the wall the instant he saw us. Sean wasn't at all what I expected, though I'm not sure what I expected to match the thin, blond Texan that was Dylan. But the tall, very beautiful looking Asian man was not it. I didn't know enough about Asian men to tell if he was Japanese or Korean, but I knew he wasn't Chinese. Just something in the face. He was tall. Over six feet, even towering a few inches over Liam. Thin, but more of a runner's sort of build than that super high metabolism waif-look some men had. He had high cheek bones, large dark eyes, and a perfect top-long, sides short, haircut.

"You can't keep me here forever," the words came out of him in a huff, like he'd been yelling for a long time. He seemed to slump like he was just too tired to keep fighting. Was Carl feeding him enough?

"Will you put together some sandwiches for us?" I asked Liam.

He frowned down at me as I stepped into the room. Sean stumbled back a few feet and sat on the bed.

"I'm fine. Hungry and tired, but fine." I gave Liam the shoo away gesture with my hands.

"Are you sure?" Liam asked, a loaded question. Was I sure about what? Him? My lack of fear of Sean? My lack of concern for what *Apa* would do when he found out about what I was going to be telling a human? Was I sure it was okay for him to leave my presence after being so recently mated? The last part was probably the worst. Because I really didn't want him to stop touching me. It felt like a dream that would evaporate the second he left my sight, but I wasn't a coward. Not anymore.

"Don't you trust me?" I asked.

He smiled. The expression filled with warmth and peace. "Yes," he breathed.

"Food first, then we can see if we can fix this den situation," I told Liam, and closed the door, locking both Sean and myself in.

After I heard Liam walk away, it took a minute to regain my composure. Odd how strong I felt in his presence. Like nothing could touch me. Only to fall into worry again the second he left. I steeled myself for whatever anger Sean would rightly throw my way and turned to face him.

He looked beat. Bags around his eyes, lips drawn in a

strict line of worry and shoulders tensed up almost to his ears.

"Can you do me a favor first?" I asked him.

"I owe you nothing. I don't even know you."

"True enough. I'm just asking for a few minutes of your time. I'd like to sort this whole thing out." Without bloodshed, I thought. "My name is Sebastian. And you are Sean. Dylan's boyfriend."

Sean went very still. "You're *the* Sebastian."

"You make it sound like I'm famous or something."

"You are. At least around here. Liam's been waiting a year for you, only for you to show up and vanish again. Dylan was so ecstatic when you showed up. Practically glowing, saying that Liam was thrilled." Sean shook his head. "Their relationship is confusing enough, and then there's you. I couldn't get why he wanted you so bad if you wouldn't just show up already. And if you couldn't, why he wouldn't go to you. It's like he'd walk around in this love sick daze whenever anyone brought you up.

"Where the fuck have you been? Can you rein in these crazies? Dylan was telling me that you calmed Liam. Whatever the fuck that means. This whole place is a madhouse. They act like he's a mob boss only he hasn't been here and all the times I've met him he's always been very polite and unassuming. He owns a bakery. And Maple Falls doesn't seem like a big enough town to have a mob. Since he's not taxing my auto shop for *security* fees when it's only two blocks from his bakery, I don't know how this all fits."

"He's not a mob boss," I assured Sean. "Dylan isn't doing anything illegal." Not technically. I didn't think there was some obscure constitutional amendment that banned anyone from being a werewolf, or even worse, a gay werewolf.

"Right. So tell me why I've been stuck here for a month

like I'm in some b-rated drama flick while Dylan is God knows where?"

"A month?" The words hit me like an iron fist in the gut. That wasn't possible. Liam said I'd been gone a while. A while. A month was longer than a while. "Holy fuck!"

Sean looked alarmed. "Why are you so surprised?"

"I've been gone a month? Dylan has been missing for a month?" Nicky had been missing and presumed dead for a month. No wonder there had been a memorial. A chill began to rise in my gut. Something awakening, slow, and delicate. I barely held back a tremor.

"Why does this surprise you? Where the hell were you anyway? Is Dylan there? Is he being held hostage? No one will tell me anything. They threw me in here a week after he walked away with some strangers that last night. My business, my life, my family, probably all think I'm dead." He paled. "That's it, isn't it? They plan to kill me?"

That sort of was the original plan. Standard operating procedure for werewolf politics. Only I was going to do my best to throw a monkey-wrench in that ideology. "How much do you love Dylan?"

Sean narrowed his eyes at me. "Why?"

"Because I need to gauge whether I can trust you or not. Last time he and I spoke, I could tell he was crazy about you. I'd hate for the emotions to not go both ways." Or to put myself on the Volkov's shit list when he was already in a bad mood by telling a human about werewolves.

"I asked him to marry me," Sean whispered. "That night was great. He dropped you off, arrived for the date. We danced. I asked and he accepted." He let out a long sigh. "Feels like a dream now. A lifetime ago. I could have grown wings and flown when he said yes, if you'd asked me too. Then when we went out to the parking lot there were men waiting at the car. Dylan told me to go back inside."

"He was trying to save you." Because I knew Dylan loved this man and would never let anything happen to him.

"I didn't need to be saved. Never understood that myself. I have martial arts training. My dad owns a dojo in Portland. Spent most of my life winning competitions and matches. Dylan is smaller than me, but those guys showed up and it's suddenly like he's larger than life. Not how he physically is, but just something. I don't know." Sean laid back on the bed and reached for the blanket like he was cold. Likely it was more from the memory than any real temperature since he was in the usual unisex sweats and fuzzy socks.

"Can I show you something?" I asked because I had a feeling that a guy like Sean wouldn't just believe me if I told him. Really, would anyone? Hey werewolves are real and your boyfriend is one? He can probably bench press you without breaking a sweat so your martial arts training doesn't mean much. He acts like a caveman sometimes because werewolf programming makes his wolf demand your safety. Werewolves functioned a bit like a cult to those who could see the workings from the outside. It didn't sound sane to most people any more than fanatics ever did.

Sean glanced my way warily. "Can I stop you?"

I shrugged, trying to keep my teeth from chattering from the rising batch of liquid ice cycling through my blood. Was it Liam that kept it at bay? What was it? "It's your choice. I just thought you'd want the truth about Dylan."

"Shouldn't he tell me?"

"He can't."

"Won't."

"Can't." I reaffirmed. I raised a hand when he went to speak again. "Let me show you something and then I'll explain. Just don't freak out."

"I'm way beyond freaking out," Sean told me. "Pretty sure I'm five stops passed the freaked out station of Crazyville.

I'm not even sure I'm talking to you right now. You could just be a figment of my imagination."

I smiled, liking him a lot. No wonder Dylan had fallen for him. Sad that everyone treated him like he was delicate just because he was human. Sean had a backbone of steel. He wouldn't have survived a month locked up in an alpha safe room with his sanity if he didn't.

I lifted up my borrowed hoodie and tugged it off, dropping it on the floor. No need to strip fully, but the shirt would distort too much.

Sean raised a brow. Not at my half nudity and tattoos, but what I now realized was my skinny chest covered in love bites. When had Liam done that? I felt heat rise to my face.

"Not that." I waved a hand at him. "Pay no attention to that. New boyfriend and all that. We sort of mated last night. Long story…" Then I shifted. Instantly from man to fox. My pants and socks pooled around me.

Sean sat up in the bed, eyes wide and shaking his head like he was trying to convince himself it wasn't real. I hoped I hadn't mistaken his personality. Sometimes it happened. A spouse found out about their werewolf lover and spurned them for being *unnatural*.

I shifted back to my full human self, adjusting my pants back into place, then grabbed up the hoodie and tugged it back on. The cold intensified. It felt a lot like a tide lapping at the edges of my soul. Each wave rising a little higher as though the tide were about to come in. Like being too far from Liam was just not possible anymore.

"What are you? Am I awake?"

"I'm a shifter. Obviously."

"Obviously…" His tone dripped with sarcasm. "'Cause that was my first thought. Still thinking maybe I'm not really seeing things. Or…" He glanced back at the bed. "Maybe I'm dreaming?"

"You're awake. About to get woke, really. They call me *witchborn*, but I'm not a witch. Just a fox shifter. There is a whole world of *other* things that humanity is taught to believe is all fantasy."

He looked around the room and I could almost see his brain racing, coming up with questions and answers all at once. "Others like what? Vampires, ghosts, and zombies? Dylan is a shifter too?"

"Sort of. He's a werewolf. I was born a shifter. It's a little different." I'd spent my entire life being reminded just how different the two were. "Werewolves aren't born. They're made. He was made a werewolf by surviving an attack." I waved away the question I could see Sean begin to ask. "I don't know the details of that. You'll have to ask Dylan when we find him. The attack is always brutal and nearly fatal. Most survivors don't talk about it much."

"Past trauma," Sean mumbled. "Explains a lot."

I agreed. Wolves in general began a little broken due to the violence of their change. "Werewolves live in a pack structure. Liam is Dylan's Alpha. He leads the entire pack here in Maple Falls, but there are alphas and packs all over the country. Probably all over the world." I'd have to ask Robin sometime about the non-American wolves. "Right now you are in the pack house. The werewolves have rules in place to keep their secrets. Dylan wasn't allowed to tell you. In fact, for most wolves, when it's an order from their alpha, they physically cannot do what they are commanded not to. It's a bit of magic, I guess. If he tried, he wouldn't be able to get the words out." I shrugged, not sure how it worked, though a lot of wolf magic seemed to run toward geas rather than magic spells. It was sort of black and white that way.

"Another pack of werewolves, a rogue pack, took him to distract Liam from protecting me. I'm sorry about that." I was really sorry. For getting Dylan kidnapped and losing

Nicky to only God knew what fate. What about Toby? He'd been missing that night from outside my camper. Had he been taken too? I'd forgotten to ask. So many deaths on my hands. All because I'd chosen the wrong man once upon a time. Would I ever be free of his madness?

I was suddenly freezing again, shivering, anxiety cascading over me so fast I could have drowned in the wave of panic. The fire erupted in my gut again. Cold fire, burning me with ice, crackling from the inside out.

The door opened and Liam stepped inside with a giant plate filled to the brim with sandwiches and several bottles of water tucked under his arms. The sandwiches smelled heavenly but I wasn't sure I could eat and keep it down.

He set everything on top of the dresser as though he'd done it a million times and then wrapped his arms around me. I didn't realize I was crying until he soothed away my tears with his thumbs running down my cheeks. My throat hurt, and I struggled to breathe.

"I lost a whole month. Nicky and Dylan..." I blubbered feeling heavy and tired. So fucking tired, guilty, and hopeless. Who was I to think I could save anyone? The Volkov would likely kill both Sean and I now. Nicky was probably already dead, Dylan too. The weight of self-doubt poured over me. I could barely breathe.

His arms became a shield of radiating warmth around me. "Shhh, it's okay. Everything is going to be okay."

Liam's arms tightened. His warm breath caressed my face and neck. He swayed a little, as though moving to some unheard tune in his head. His heat surrounded me, while he kissed my face, hair, and ears, whispering words that took me a while to comprehend. That panic attack had come on so fast I hadn't even noticed it until it was already in full swing. My brain had narrowed to nothing but pain and worthlessness, while Liam whispered about calm and air.

Liam was counting again. In fact, Sean counted with him. Voice soft and careful. The fear and panic began to recede along with the icy fire. I didn't realize until my lungs finally loosened and I could breathe again, that Sean had been gently rubbing circles over my back and shoulders. I had thought it was Liam, but Liam was holding me too tightly for that. Funny that he didn't freak out about another man touching me. Perhaps the mating made a difference.

"That was unreal," Sean whispered after the counting had faded. I lay sprawled like a rag doll in Liam embrace, fire gone. I just didn't have enough energy to deal with anything right that minute. Why was I so tired? The sex shouldn't have worn me to the bone, but that was how I felt. Every muscle in my body had turned to jelly. If not for Liam, I'd have been sprawled on the floor helpless and weak as a newborn baby.

"It's new," Liam replied.

"The panic attacks or the whole giant fiery fox shadow that surrounded him when it happened?" Sean wanted to know.

"You could see it?" Liam asked. I was so lost. What giant fiery shadow?

"You can't?"

Liam shook his head against my shoulder. "I can feel it, both through our mating bond and as a werewolf." He must have heard everything I'd told Sean. I really hoped he wouldn't undo my good work and kill Sean.

"Mating bond," Sean said.

"Yes. Sebastian is my mate."

"I assume that's more than just the standard boyfriend speak when it comes to werewolves."

"Our souls are married. Intertwined now that we have bonded." Liam said. Yes, that was how I felt too. Him wound around my soul. When he touched me it was a near perfect melding. Separated, it was like something else wanted control and gnawed at the bonds.

"Another magic thing? So that's for real. Dylan is a werewolf?"

"Yes."

"You can change? He can change? Like what Sebastian showed me?"

"We are nothing like Sebastian." Liam said.

Those words stung because I'd been hearing them my whole life and never expected to hear them from the man I'd mated to. I tried to muster strength to pull away, but Liam held me tight.

"He's far beyond anything we could ever be. We are just men who change into raving beasts with a little pack magic thrown in. Werewolves die and turn into monsters who learn to be human. When you watch Sebastian shift it's like a flower petal opening. Beautiful and natural life. When you watch a werewolf shift you will see fear, horror, and pain. Sebastian is a being of spirit magic. More than wolf or man could ever be. He is light and dark. Fire and ice. Yin and yang. His time away unlocked something that I believe had been buried deep within him."

"A kitsune? Like a real kitsune of legend? His eyes are Japanese, right down to the color. My grandmother has eyes like that. Windows into eternity. And that shadow… I've seen pictures in stories and legends." Sean let out a long sigh. "I wish Dylan were here to hold me like you're holding him while I sort this all out in my head. The whole 'werewolves is real' thing, is a lot to take. And seeing a real kitsune…They are bad omens sometimes. Tricksters. Mayhem."

"Mayhem does seem to follow them. Their fault or just an unfortunate circumstance of fate? I prefer the latter. Sebastian never really asks for trouble, it just always finds him," Liam affirmed.

That at least was true. Trouble found me everywhere I went. All the way across the country and back I'd run into mayhem, if that's what they wanted to call it. Was that my *witchblood* nature at work? Or bad luck?

I thought about my years sequestered in *Apa*'s pack. Lots of tricks and ill-fated events had befallen me there as well. Even leaving home once had brought Robin into my life. Was I doomed to this chaos forever? Would Liam aid that curse just as he eased my panic? What the hell was a kitsune anyway?

There was so much spiraling already, I couldn't fathom another puzzle. I needed to find Dylan. And Nicky. And *Apa* was going to be so mad, but all I could think to say is, "What is a kitsune?" I copied his pronunciation. *Kit-soon-eh*.

"Fox spirit," Liam told me, lifting me into his arms to carry me in the bridal style again. "I have a couple books I've found on the mythology. When things quiet down a bit I'll lend them to you."

"Don't kill Sean," I told Liam, like I could make him listen to me.

"Yeah, don't kill Sean," Sean echoed.

"I need to find Dylan," I grumbled, suddenly too tired to think straight. He could talk sense into Liam.

"No one is killing anyone tonight," Liam told me. He glanced at Sean.

"No protesting here."

CHAPTER 25

The door to the room opened and Oberon filled the doorway. Maybe Liam was wrong and we were all dying tonight. But Liam met his gaze steadily. While Oberon loomed large as always, he looked tired.

"I sensed Seb," Oberon said. He looked at me like he was searching for the answers to all the universe's questions. "He smells like you."

"He's mine," Liam affirmed. "How is the Volkov? If you sensed that Sebastian was back, he must have as well."

"I'm glad to see you've finally bonded. You sound more rational than you did the last time I saw you. *Apa* is...struggling. When I felt Seb's presence there was a flicker of humanity. I called out to him, but he just growled at me."

The idea that *Apa* was lost permanently to his beast made my heart hurt. Yes, he scared me, and I wasn't sure he always made the best choices, but he was the only man I'd ever known as a father. He'd also been the one to hug me without hesitation, smile and encourage my interests, and let me run free enough to make my own mistakes.

"We can go see him," I whispered, almost too afraid to actually do it.

"Are you sure?" Liam asked.

"You said I was safe from him," I said. Would Liam be safe from him? "Now that we are bonded..."

"You smell like me. Like pack," Liam agreed.

"I'm not sure if that will make him angry, or pleased that Seb finally has a home to take care of him," Oberon interrupted. "Mated omegas have a different feel than unmated ones. Seb has always been a bit of a loose cannon with his pheromones though. So maybe we should wait a few days. See if the return of Seb's presence can help at a distance?"

"What pheromones? You want me to sit around while Liam's whole pack suffers?" I sighed. It would sort of be better to pull the Band-Aid off, right? *Apa* had hosted some sort of trial to find me a mate, and here we were, bonded. If he didn't approve of Liam, why would he have given Liam this territory? Why set up the land for my arrival with a giant garden?

"It's your pack too," Liam reminded me.

"Not yet," I told him. But they would be soon. It would take rebuilding the den and linking myself into Liam's pack bond, if that was even possible. I had heard of some human women managing it. Most mates weren't true mates, even with a pack's support. Maybe ours would be different. "Let's go say hello," I said. My stomach growled loudly. Liam chuckled and grabbed a sandwich off the plate, handing it to me.

"Eat," he ordered me, like his command would work. I ate because I was hungry. "The human is under my protection," Liam told Oberon.

"He knows about us," Oberon stated.

"I told him, Liam didn't. Blame me. Sean won't tell anyone. He loves Dylan. Wants Dylan back."

Sean sighed again, "Yes, please." He grabbed a sandwich off the plate and crawled into bed. "I'll stay locked up here forever if you just bring Dylan back to me. I can work on pack cars or something."

"Tomorrow, after I've had rest and my head is clear, I'll try to use the pack bond to find him," Liam said, both to Sean and Oberon.

"Carl tried that," Oberon pointed out.

"Carl doesn't like anyone," I said, remembering what Liam had told me. Only the alpha could access the whole pack unless they'd all truly bonded. It didn't sound like Carl cared enough for anyone to feel that sort of link.

Liam pushed past Oberon. "Tomorrow is soon enough to start putting out fires. Will the Volkov's sanity last that long?"

"Maybe," Oberon allowed. "He's not hearing me anymore. Figured I'd spend the night in the house and see if I could actually sleep myself." He glanced at Sean.

"Under my protection," Liam repeated. He didn't take us to the stairway, but back toward the outer door. "You really want to see the Volkov?" Liam asked me.

Not really, but I needed to. If I could stir him back to humanity, that was enough, right? Even if it was a bit of a reminder as to the madness of the current state of affairs. If *Apa* was in control again, instead of his beast, maybe we all had a chance.

I clung to Liam as we crossed the distance between the house and the bunkhouse. Liam was tired too. I could feel it. It was a bit like I was draining him. Maybe this struggle with the kitsune spirit or whatever it was inside me was draining him. I prayed *Apa's* control returned fast enough that no one had to face off with the monster. We trudged forward, the weight of the Volkov's darkness like wading through molasses. Slow and sticky.

"Do you want me to walk?" I asked him. Maybe seeing

Apa while I still smelled of Liam and sex wasn't such a good idea. Arriving wrapped in Liam's arms also seemed like a screaming declaration. But *Apa* had approved of Liam, or so he'd led Liam to believe.

"You're too tired. Rest. We'll say hello and head to bed," Liam reassured me. Like it would be that simple.

"I don't know why I'm so tired. Is it the mating?"

"I suspect it's the fox spirit draining you."

I muddled over the thought of that. "Why now?"

"Why did it change? You'll have to tell me. Was it Underhill?"

For a moment I remembered the giant bug-like thing and the explosion of something large and fiery from within me. "I think maybe it protected me when I was in Underhill." Though that had already been after the memory of *Apa* and Felix fighting had awakened something within me.

"Then it's not a bad thing. Just something we need to better understand," Liam said. "Plus the mating is only mostly complete. We have to solidify our den before we can unify the pack. They are scattered and tugging at me, and in turn. I'm pulling energy from you, and you're pulling energy from me. It's a vicious cycle."

"Werewolf chaos," I grumbled at him as though he wasn't the best thing that had happened in my life. "I really hope you're not too good to be true."

"I'm sure I have plenty of bad habits to displease even the most generous of fox shifters," he teased. "Like leaving dirty socks on the floor, or not shaving for a week."

"I vote for not shaving," I told him gravely. "It's a sacrifice I'm happy to make." I reached up to run my hand over his scruffy cheek. "Maybe trimmed a little."

"Hmm," he acknowledged. "It's been a couple decades since I had a beard. If it pleases my mate…"

I grinned at his phrasing. "I like the sound of that."

"I will consider a beard so long as you don't cut your hair."

I narrowed my eyes at him.

"Mating is a partnership, you know. Give a little, get a little. I've spent the past year talking to every mated couple I could find," Liam informed me. "I've never been a man who likes being unprepared."

"But you said you know about as much as I do about this whole mating thing. And I haven't spent any time researching it," I pointed out.

"Mating is so varied that no one can give me definite answer. However, love, life-long love, the answer to that is two Cs. Communication and compromise."

"Great sex in the top five at all?" I wondered out loud.

Liam laughed. "It was in there somewhere. Right above negotiations over facial hair."

"Hmm," I mimicked his half-committed reply. Wait, he said love. Life-long love. He couldn't love me. Not yet. We barely knew each other.

He stopped for a minute to stare down at me. "Why are you suddenly a mix of chaotic emotions? Your heart beat picked up and then fear, confusion, hope…Might have been more, but it's different sorting out someone else's emotions."

"You can't love me yet," I said. Because that was the chaos that whirled in my mind. Did I love him? I needed him. That was unmistakable. My soul needed him wrapped around it like I needed air to breathe.

He stared down at me, his expression guarded. "Does it scare you?"

Love was scary. It wasn't even real. Not really. So many people said they loved you, then turned around and stabbed you in the back. I didn't want him to love me like that. Empty words. Broken hearts.

"Time," Liam said, sucking in a deep breath. He continued

toward the bunkhouse. "We can debate facial hair later. Right now we have a demon to confront. Even if he's just one made up in your mind."

"He's real," I insisted. I'd seen the dark thing that could take over *Apa*. It was not a wolf. Or at least not just a wolf. Having seen some of the monsters of Underhill now, all I could think of his other being was *demon*.

"He is," Liam agreed. "But you are no longer alone, nor are you a defenseless child." His grip on me tightened, and I wished we were headed back to bed instead of into the lion's den. Maybe this would be fast. Though the lingering tension in the air made it hard to breathe.

As we stepped up to the doublewide doorway, the cloud of gloom vanished. The evening sky went from black and ominous, to cool and filled with stars. Birds chirped and crickets danced. The change made Liam pause. I think we were both unsure what to do, but it was Oberon who stepped around us and opened the door. I hadn't realized he'd followed us out.

The bunkhouse had one large main gathering space filled with giant couches and several comfy chairs, all gathered around a large screen television. There was a small kitchenette off to one side, with a fridge and a single burner stove. The TV was off, and the door that must have led to the beds beyond was closed. *Apa* puttered around the kitchen, heating water in a large tea kettle and searching the cupboards for what, I wasn't sure.

"No tea cups?" The Volkov asked Liam. *Apa* was trying hard, but his jerky movements, and foot-tapping energy told me he was agitated. Normally the Volkov was contained, still like a river before the rapids began. This movement was startling. Unlike him, though not the raving monster I'd feared him to be. Perhaps he was not as bad off as Oberon had led us to believe. I hadn't done anything to try to calm him, and he was coherent enough to be talking to us about tea.

The shadow monster that sometimes hovered around him had vanished. Though I wasn't dumb enough to think it couldn't reappear in an instant. His agitation could have come from knowing Felix had caused this mess. Or from the fact that Liam was holding me tightly in his arms.

Overall, *Apa* just looked tired. Different from the last time I'd seen him. The put-together, quiet man I'd grown up to think of as *Apa* had become a somewhat scattered and lost seeming young wolf, barely holding his wolf back. Was this what it was like in the end for old wolves? The few times they'd gone wild-eyed like this, they had been quickly put down, leaving only whispers behind them just hours after visiting the Volkov. My heart hurt with the thought.

"No teacups out here. Too much gets broken. At the house there is a large selection," Liam responded calmly, though his grip tightened on me a tiny bit. He talked about the cups as though it were as uninteresting as the weather. "Sebastian can make us some tea in the morning. How about we all get some rest for the night?"

Apa looked a little wide-eyed for a minute. Almost afraid. Was it my presence that was holding him together somehow? I didn't feel like I was doing anything. Just being me. In fact, barely that, since Liam was holding me up. I could have slept just about anywhere right then.

"Liam's got room in the house since no one else is home," I said. "Why don't you and Oberon join us? Tomorrow I'll make breakfast and tea." I glanced at Liam. "As long as we're not needed at the bakery."

"It will be fine," Liam assured me. "We could all use some rest." He didn't meet the Volkov's eyes any more than Oberon did. It was a non-verbal queue. No challenge here, even if the territory was Liam's. No need to stir up the monster. "Why don't you come up to the house?"

Apa's hands tightened into fists for a minute as Liam shifted my weight in his arms. I don't think Liam was tired from carrying me, more like readying himself in case the Volkov's façade disappeared and he came at me, Liam would be ready.

"*Apa*," I called and reached out to touch him. Liam took a step closer so my hand fell on *Apa*'s upper arm. "Come to the house. Rest. Tomorrow morning is early enough to enact a war council."

I looked at Liam. He was tired too. I'd been gone a month. He'd been battling psychological demons the whole time, while trying to keep his territory from falling into chaos and the Volkov went mad just feet from his doorstep. No wonder Liam had felt the need to camp in a distant cave just to find me. I'd been lucky to have caught his scent through all the muddled magic lingering around his home.

Once we re-established den magic around the house, I'd have to smudge away the rest of the negative energy. There was just too much *other* floating around.

"Will you come to the house with us?" I asked *Apa* again.

He nodded slowly, as his eyes began to droop. Was my touch doing that? I carefully drew away, fearing he'd change in an instant. Only he just slumped forward like he was tired. Oberon turned off the stove and moved the kettle aside.

"Are you going to Liam's room?" Oberon asked.

"Yes," I answered for the both of us. We both needed to sleep. The house had lost the sense of home and safety Liam had spent a year building due to the Volkov. It would take some work to restore, but that could be another chore for the morning.

"Your camper would be safer," Oberon pointed out.

Because the wards would protect me from *Apa* if he went mad. But it was also a long way from the house.

I looked up at Liam. "Your bed." He needed that. I could feel it thrumming through him. A need to put me in a space he considered his. A need to give me a home, with a safe place to sleep. Somehow, Liam had become everything in such a tiny space of time. I barely knew him. Yet I felt like I could barely breathe without him.

A dimpled smile lit up his face. "The way you are looking at me right now…"

I tilted my head, wondering how I was looking at him. "What do you mean?"

Liam shook his head and left the bunkhouse, not seeming to care if Oberon and the Volkov followed. "Our den is where my mate feels safe. Right now that is only two places I know of: my arms, and your camper. I'll put the two together and we'll both get some much needed rest. Now that my brain isn't being ripped into shreds of madness anymore, I can slowly rebuild the pack bonds. Tomorrow."

"The pack should be first," I grumbled at him. "*Apa* needs us close."

"He can sleep in the house or at the foot of the stairs of your camper. The camper is less than twenty yards from our backdoor." He took us out toward the camper. "My mate comes first with me. Pack second. If I can't make my mate feel safe and happy, how can I possibly hope to give those same feelings to my pack?" Liam asked. "Do your wards stop the Volkov from feeling your presence?" Liam asked.

"No," *Apa* answered. He veered off toward the house.

"Don't hurt Sean," I called after him. Sean belonged to Dylan and since Dylan was Liam's and all that was Liam's was mine, that meant Sean was mine.

"I don't even know who that is," *Apa* muttered.

"The human mate," Oberon reminded him.

Apa nodded. "Right." He looked up toward the corner bedroom that faced the purple field and my camper. "I think I'll sleep there. Tomorrow we'll have tea and speak of important things." He blinked as something dark flickered through him, only it was swallowed just that fast. Then he turned and headed toward the house. Oberon followed but threw a meaningful glance our way. The Volkov was scaring everyone lately.

Liam carried me toward the camper. "Carl is right; our tie is less muddled when it's just us. You're worried. Probably about Sean. He'll be fine."

"I'm worried about everyone. Dylan, Sean, *Apa*, Oberon, your pack, Nicky..." I let out a long sigh. "I am so tired."

"I'd lend you energy if I knew how. The mating is new. It will take some getting used to."

"What about the kitsune?" I asked him. "You have books about it?"

"Mythology mostly. So it's probably about as accurate as most legends of werewolves are." Meaning not at all. "Asking the fae for anything isn't recommended, but Robin may know more. He might have met others like you."

Kitsune. A fox spirit. That sort of made sense. "What about the cold fire?"

"I know as much as you do. But we can start asking around. Researching. Perhaps Oberon and your father know more than they let on."

I recalled *Apa* telling Oberon to research my family when I was an infant. If that had been real, did that mean they had known all along? Had *Apa* taught me to suppress it subconsciously? I was too tired to rationalize it all.

We approached the camper and I reached out to touch the side, running my fingers along the shiny edge as we walked to the door. I opened up my senses to the wards easier than I ever had before. I could see them in my mind, almost like cuts of paper layered one over another, edges smoothed down in places, loose in others. It was a bit haphazard, and that was okay since it felt familiar. The wards stretched around me, expanding from my touch out and over Liam, recognizing him as part of me. I didn't even need to change the wards, they just recognized him as a part of me. He hesitated a moment at the door, but carried me right through, no shuddering and closing off of his senses that I could tell by looking at him.

Robin lay curled up on the bed, a ball of warm fur. The second he saw us he jumped up and darted across the room to tangle around Liam's legs. His low growling mews brought tears to my eyes. Liam carried me to the bed and set me down.

He closed the main door and the rarely used inner door, locking them both. He then began shutting all the blinds, leaving only narrow dots of moonlight filtering through the slats. There were blackout curtains too, but he didn't pull those. Instead he crawled into bed beside me. He wrapped his arms around me and spooned against my back.

I felt Robin jump up on the bed, march around our feet for a minute, before finally settling down to lie against my shins. The sense of calm settled over me like a wave of warm water, soothing the last of my worries. Right that minute, we were safe. *Home*, my gut told me. Even if it was just my little camper. In Liam's arms, with Robin safe and close, protected by wards, I shut my eyes and let sleep take me where it would.

CHAPTER 26

Erotic dreams weren't something I experienced often. In fact, it was so rare, that I thought it strange to be dreaming about sitting on a beach, sipping iced lavender lemonade from a cup with a tiny umbrella sticking out of it, and feeling like I needed sexual release right that second.

I'd never even spent time on a beach. So the idea of relaxing on one was almost foreign. And my body was keyed up, engine running at full speed, which was something I could only recall from early puberty. The intensity of the feeling made it hard to sit still.

Touching myself in the dream did nothing to ease the need. In fact, it seemed to get worse. I groaned. The warmth built between my legs, cock pulsing with heat, and I panted with desire. Someone needed to touch me. My body ached with it. Only in the dream I was alone.

That wasn't right.

My brain slowly shuffled through memories as it sought an explanation. I opened my eyes while it was still sorting to see my pillow, with a tan hand wrapped around it attached to an arm that stretched over the top of me. Tan skin, yet still lighter than mine. The arm was muscular and sprinkled with light blond hair almost imperceivable to the eye. It made a great anchor. Settling my soul in peace even if my body *needed.*

Liam.

His breathing was steady and deep. Sleeping.

Dammit. Just because I woke up needy didn't mean I was going to jump him. Having experienced that a time or two in my life, I knew waking up with someone pleasuring themselves with your sleeping body, wasn't the stuff of romance. It was actually somewhat disturbing. Not that my experience with men was vast. Maybe Liam liked that sort of thing. I didn't really know him well enough to make that call.

He left no wiggle room under his arm for me to try to reach down and quietly take things into my own hands. The need burned in my groin like a fire begging to be quenched, and hell if it didn't make it even worse to know that it was Liam who was wrapped around me. Liam who touched me. Liam whose body was pressed to my back. His scent and presence that surrounded me in blissful safety and happiness.

The need hadn't gone away when I awoke like it often did with dreams. And this wasn't normal morning wood. I couldn't feel Robin at our feet anymore, and didn't hear his breathing. Had he left? I hoped he was gone or he'd be getting an eye full.

Liam's soft breaths told me he was deep into sleep. As much as an alpha could sleep deeply. With the perpetual threat of being attacked for his place in the pack, alpha's were in general light sleepers. Now that he was mated, and in tune to my emotions, I was surprised he wasn't already awake, boring a hole into my backside with his cock. The idea made my hips jerk. I swallowed back a cry and fought to keep still.

Pale rays of light filtered through the edges of the windows. Was it really morning? Why was I so rock hard?

What if I woke him slowly with a blow job? I'd read about it in books. Been told I gave a great blow job, but never had it reciprocated. But the idea of touching him like that, before he'd given me consent, just made my heart hurt. Never would I violate Liam's trust like that. Hell, I felt weird about just being held by him at that moment and being so turned on while he slept, oblivious.

I sucked in a deep breath and tried to think of non-sexy things. Pie crust with no butter. Lemonade without the lavender. Burnt baked goods. But all I smelled was vanilla and cardamom. Liam's warm body wrapped around me made me throb. Fuck.

Liam tugged me closer, arms like steel around me, but body warm and pliable. "What?" He mumbled into the back of my neck.

"What, what?" I asked quietly, trying my best not to jump him. He was tired and deserved sleep too, even if I was irrationally horny.

He pushed himself up to an elbow and leaned over me. His hair stuck up in a dozen directions. Lines etched across his face from the pillow. He had a dark 5 o'clock shadow that had seen enough days to almost make it a full beard, and his eyes were half-lidded. Fuck. Okay, so imperfect, sleep-tousled Liam was even hotter than put together Liam.

I couldn't stifle the groan. He frowned and rolled me beneath him to examine me. Hands all over me, which was both bliss and torture at the same time.

"Are you hurt?"

"Not really…"

"Sebastian?"

"Are you really awake?" I demanded.

"Uh, yeah." He glanced around the small space. "Pretty sure I'm awake now."

"Good." I leapt at him then, rolling him over onto his back and pressing my hips into his. He hadn't been hard, but with my cock pressed to his, that quickly began to change.

He looked up at me, a little shocked. But so damn sexy with a tiny smile curving his lips.

"This okay?" I asked him. I did a quick glance around the room, searching for Robin, but he must have gone to wherever it was he went when he left this plane of existence. At least we were alone.

"Yeah," Liam grinned up at me. "What do you want me to do? Can I touch you, or do you just want to be in control?" He glanced around. "Now I'm wondering if I'm really awake."

"You can touch me," I assured him. "Please touch me. I just need…" Him. Fuck, I needed him so bad. He was what had been missing from the dream. Him sitting beside me at the beach, willing to reach out and kiss me if I just turned my head. "Is this because we're mated?"

"I know about as much as you do about mating," Liam said. He reached up to cup the back of my neck and draw me down for a kiss. It started slow, just a meeting of lips, teasing of plump flesh and soft nibbles. Then the intensity grew as he licked the seam of my lips for entry. It shouldn't have been so hot. We'd been kissing a lot. Liam really seemed to like it. I'd never been a fan before him. Now it was a battle of tongues, nips and exploring caresses.

He let go of the back of my neck and ran his hands down the length of my body until he reached my hips. He shoved aside the fabric of the hoodie and sweats until his palms slid over my skin. Then he lifted my hips, shifting them until we were more comfortably gliding against each other as we kissed. One hand slid around to my butt, easing between my cheeks. A moment later one of his fingers was tickling the rim of my asshole.

"Liam," I sighed into his lips. The sweet sting of passion building like an inferno between us.

"We are wearing too many clothes," Liam muttered.

I didn't care as long as he kept touching me. He yanked the hoodie up and off, over my head. I threw it to the side and pushed his shirt up. "Don't stop," I grumbled into his mouth, diving in for another taste of him. It wasn't even the flavor that mattered. The warm wetness of his kiss, and the knowledge that it was him was everything. "Touch me."

Liam shoved the front of both of our pants down. Hot flesh met hot flesh. I hissed as our precome mingled, adding slick between us and increasing the heavenly friction. His fingers returned to my ass, massaging the entrance, teasing around the edge and down between my thighs to press on my taint. I squirmed into him seeking friction and more of his touch, but certain I'd become unglued any second.

"Holy…" I breathed, sucking in his breath as my own.

He wrapped a hand around both of us, not really moving his hand, just adding friction as we ground our hips together. I trembled with the growing burn of need. He panted and demanded more kisses.

His finger dipped inside, and I could barely breathe. It was just the tiniest of pressure, so close to exactly what I needed. Not him fucking me, but a release to the desire that made my body scream for him.

"Please," I said into his lips. "Make me come."

The edges of his lips turned up in a devious smile. "What if I want to tease you a little?" His hand on our cocks loosened and his fingers drifted away from my ass.

"No!" I groaned into his lips, demanding another kiss as I pressed my hips against him. "I'll die if you tease me right now."

"But I can tease you later?"

"Maybe?" I wasn't sure. My head swam with lust and little of the normal survival instinct that kept me cynical.

He tightened his grip again and I sighed, nearly coming right then. And his finger probed me again, the press on my taint better than anything I could remember experiencing with a little frottage.

"Close," I whispered to him, my hips moving against him wantonly.

"Yes," Liam agreed.

He rolled the heads of our cocks together, mingling our precome, adding to the slickness. I bit my lip as the fire rolled through me, passion and heat pouring out in a release that covered Liam's chest in white ribbons.

"Don't bite back your cries," Liam told me. "Give them to me. I worked hard to hear them. Give me your pleasure." He sealed his lips to mine, swallowing my whimpers as the pleasure rolled through me in waves. Multiple orgasms. Liam's hand was still wrapped around us, and his thumb pressed into my taint, giving me something to grind against.

I let out a long sigh as the fiery need finally eased, though my hips and thighs still twitched from the force of my release. It was everything all at once, and too much, but so necessary.

"Fuck," I breathed, my whole body trembling with the aftershocks of my orgasm.

Liam growled and seconds later he was painting me with his own hot come. I collapsed on top of Liam, who accepted my weight and the mess of come between us as he wrapped his arms around me.

"I could wake up like that every day," Liam said.

"We're gonna get stuck together again." But I was too satisfied to move. Liam's warm body made the greatest pillow. "I was going to wake you up with a blow job, but didn't want you to think that I was forcing you into anything." And queue the awkward brain train of thought. As our spend cooled between us, I felt my cheeks heat in embarrassment. "Sorry," I told him, trying to pull free from his embrace.

"For what?" Liam asked, sounding genuinely confused. He didn't try to keep me against him, but he did reach up and brush my hair out of my face. "Feel free to wake me up for anything. A blow job, a cuddle, a noise that scares you, to let the cat out, whatever."

"I should clean up," I looked away. Holy fuck what had I been thinking? What was it about Liam that set my motor running at two-thousand percent?

"Why are you embarrassed?"

"I'm not," I denied.

"It's just us here, Sebastian. No pack to muddle things. I can *feel* your embarrassment and…fear. Do I scare you?" He frowned.

I picked up the hoodie off the floor and mopped at my chest, then pulled up the sweats. Liam made no move to cover himself. "I…" I began but didn't know what to say. I'd woken with desire unlike anything I'd ever experienced before. Only to turn over and use Liam like some sex doll. It wasn't fair to him at all. I wasn't sure what was going on with my body, but I suddenly wanted to cry.

"Hey," Liam said. He was just there, standing in front of me. The hoodie pressed between us as he held me to his chest. "I'm not getting it all, you know. Just emotions. You're freaking out."

"I'm not," I insisted. Which was a total lie. We barely knew each other and now I was tied to him 'til the real death did do us part. What would happen when he realized I really wasn't what he'd hoped for? Did he understand that mating me had substantially shortened his life? *Witchborn* didn't live longer than normal humans. At least none that I'd heard of. It came with a lot of banter about curses. Cursed blood, cursed fate, always bringing mischief, or maybe that was just the kitsune spirit in me.

"Sebastian," Liam said, lifting my chin so he could look at my face. I could barely see him through the swimming vision left behind by tears I hadn't realized were falling. He stroked away the tears with his thumb and kissed each of my cheeks. "Tell me what's going on in your head. Share so I can sort some of this out."

"I practically raped you," I muttered. "You were still asleep and I jumped you." How many times had it happened to me that way? Asleep, groggy, and someone suddenly all over me. I'd learned quickly to play along else there would be anger and resentment aimed my way.

He snorted. "Not asleep. A little groggy, but more than on board. No rape. Full consent. My come is all over both of us in case you forgot."

But this wasn't like me. How long had I worked to hide my emotions? To not let myself be seen as needy? Emotions made me vulnerable. The feeling in my gut every time I looked at Liam, terrified me. Sure there was lust. He was an attractive man. But this was deeper. How much I needed him…that was not normal for me. "I don't know what's wrong with me. I've never been like this before."

"Like what?"

"Sexually needy," I said in a tiny whisper, feeling horrified. Needy in general. Because, by God, I needed Liam like I needed air to breathe. If he abandoned me now I wouldn't survive. Who would have thought, after a lifetime of being battered and told I was worthless, that the one man who told me I wasn't, could turn my world around. Not just words, I reminded myself. He'd spent a year building a stable pack for me to come home to. He'd waited patiently while I ran across the country, afraid of never finding a home. Now we were mated. His soul draped over mine in some metaphysical magic that I couldn't begin to fathom. Two lives intertwined and inseparable.

"Why is that a bad thing?"

"'Cause we barely know each other?" I asked, unsure. I'd only had one other real lover in my life, and he'd frowned at any dominance coming from me. The entire pack I'd grown up in, hadn't liked me doing anything different from them. I'd clung to Felix for validation he would never have given me. No one ever had. I'd never been the sort of guy to jump from bed to bed. Too many trust issues. Now there was Liam. Carved into my soul with a fine point blade. His presence sharp, but it didn't hurt. Instead it soothed.

Odd how I'd spent my life trying to know and please Felix, only to fail and fall into Liam's lap. A man I felt I barely knew, but connected to like I never had anyone in my life. We had small things in common. Would it be enough?

"We know plenty about each other, and we have time to figure out the rest." Liam took the hoodie from me, wiped us both clean, and pulled his sweats back up. He stripped off his shirt and pulled me back down onto the bed. He snuggled into the wall, the pillows and blankets mounded up around him and cradled me in his lap. The skin to skin contact was nice, warm and cozy. When normally I would have been in a full on panic attack, instead the feeling of safety and home settled over me.

"I don't know anything about you."

"Not true. You know where I was born. You know I have a daughter I adore, you know I like to bake, and you know that my compassion gets me in trouble as an alpha." Liam ran his fingers through my hair, carefully untangling knots he found.

"That's not much to know when we're stuck together forever."

"You worry about odd things," Liam said.

"Why is it odd? Mating is a big deal." I'd heard the pack members talk of it with silent fear my entire life. People married, but never mated. It was the kiss of death, as everyone said they knew a mated couple who now were both dead. And wolves never mated humans. Even if the secrecy wasn't an issue, humans lived short lives. Wolves could live a very, very long time.

"I'm not worried at all about our mating. We are meant to be together."

"Because your wolf says so."

"More than just my wolf. *I* need you. The way you react to me says you feel it too. When I'm with you, everything is clearer, calmer, yet I have a burning need to touch you. I want to learn everything about you. I want to memorize the noises you make when you sleep, and the taste of your skin beneath my tongue. I want to argue with you about the best yeast to put in a doughnut, and kiss you until you agree. Your soul is nestled against mine. They fit together perfectly, two halves of a whole. The mating was the hard part. Learning about each other as our love grows is worth spending the rest of our lives exploring. That is what our mating means to me."

Once again this man made me breathless with his words. "You're too good to be real." I leaned my head against his shoulder.

CHAPTER 27

"I'm also temperamental, territorial, and an alpha asshole. Ask anyone in the pack," Liam said.

"You've done pretty well with *Apa* and Oberon being in your territory," I pointed out.

"I haven't. That's why I needed to go to the cave up the mountain. You weren't there as a buffer for me focus on, and I just wanted to rip them both apart for thinking they had any right to come and defend you. You're mine." He sighed. "That sort of caveman thinking probably scares you."

It didn't. Which was odd because Felix's thinking hadn't been all that different. Or had it?

"I've worked really hard to push my boundaries. Sometimes the possessive bastard in me rises up when someone says the wrong thing. Carl and I have fought about that a lot in the past year. Many a time I wanted to go looking for you. He always backed me down, reminding me that you'd run if I stalked you. No matter how much my wolf needed you, I had to wait. Dylan saw the worst of my temper crop up after you arrived, but he's always been good at sensing when to back down. I can't always stop myself from growling when someone else touches you. He's a dominant wolf, and attractive, so my wolf bristles at the idea of him being close to you, even though he's my friend and third. I try to rein in the dominant asshole raging through my blood."

"You were okay when Sean touched me."

"Sean is Dylan's. They are practically mated. He smells like Dylan. You smell like me now. So it's easier to restrain the wolf. Sean also doesn't ping my wolf's radar as competition. He might have an independent personality, but he's not a dominant wolf like your father, or Oberon." Liam stroked my back lightly. "It's easier to face them with you in my arms."

He made me braver too.

"But I'm not a possession to you," I affirmed. Not like to Felix. I was not just the little fox. I wasn't something to be hidden away or condemned. He'd held my hand and walked through the town's little main street with me. He'd even introduced me to the most powerful members of his pack like I was more than just a useful omega to him.

"You're my life. You possess every part of me. My mate. My love." His arms tightened around me, reaffirming his words. His body warmed mine even if his touch made me crave something much hotter. I sucked in a deep breath, realizing what he'd just said.

"Too soon?" He asked. He didn't sound worried or apologetic, more curious.

"I don't know," I told him honestly. "You've had a year to work this all out in your head." I told him, reminded of my conversation with Dylan before the madness began. "I'm new to this mate thing. Is this us or just some weird pheromones? Some metaphysical pull created by fate?"

"Does it matter?"

Maybe. I hated the idea of him being forced to like me because his wolf was attracted to some metaphysical scent my fox was producing. "Do kitsunes produce pheromones?" I sniffed my arm pit like I could smell some if I was. I just smelled like me, thankfully not ripe, though I could use a shower.

"You smell like lavender and honey. Like forest and wildflowers. I'm not the only one who smells those things. The whole pack does." He lifted my hair, like maybe it was the scent of my shampoo. "It's not something you use, it's just your scent. Over the past year I'd get glimpses. Like a ghost of the scent drifting through the window. I'd remind myself you'd find your way home. The pack sometimes said they smelled it too."

"So do they smell you? Vanilla, cloves, and cardamom?"

Liam squinted at me. "No. To them I just smell like a dominant wolf. Maybe you smell that on me because of the bakery?"

"Have you been to the bakery in the past month while I was gone?"

"No. I wasn't sane enough." He ran his fingers over my cheeks like he was memorizing how my skin felt. "For a year I battled the wolf. But the moment you stepped into my territory, he decided he was done fighting me. Then you vanished. He became enraged. Holding him back took everything I had. There was no time for the bakery, my pack, or even my daughter. Though Carl has often assured me they are all fine."

"Sorry," I whispered. Feeling bad about taking him away from everyone.

"You didn't do any of it. I'm just glad you found your way back."

"I followed your scent out of Underhill. Vanilla, cloves, and cardamom."

"Hmm."

I growled at that answer. He laughed and leaned in to kiss my nose. "I'm not imagining your scent. It's real."

"I believe you," he agreed. "All that matters is that I smell nice to you."

"You're a little cheesy," I told him.

"And you are beautiful. More than just a little. Did you know?"

It was my turn to snort. "You might want to have your eyes checked. Can werewolves go blind?"

"Never met one who has. I see just fine. And I see you. All of you. Your mixed heritage that you hate so much. The fire of your hair, and the skin you hate because it's not white. The ink you use as a shield both metaphysically and physically to warn others away. I see the trauma in your past that makes you doubt every word I say. But do you know what gets me every time I look at you?"

I shook my head, trying to fathom if I could believe all the things he was telling me.

"Your eyes. Huge brown eyes filled with so much eternity." His gaze was intense, like he really could see into my soul through my eyes.

"They're just brown. Lots of people have brown eyes."

Liam used his thumb to trace the outline of my brows and down around my eyes. "Not like yours. You've experienced a lot of pain and neglect. Yet your eyes still shine with hope." He sighed, breathed in deeply and leaned forward to press his forehead to mine. "I'm not sure why this is only going one way. I can feel your uncertainty. Your hesitance. Can't you feel the truth of my words? I think our bond is supposed to go both ways."

I tried to think for a minute, see if I could sense anything from him as he seemed to be able to do from me. Only there was nothing. Just me and my ever over-thinking brain. I'd always had an internal wall against the outside world, blocking off emotion because someone was always on the verge of hurting me. Had I blocked Liam off too?

"I was hoping the two of us could figure it out if we had a bit of time. Carl said it would be less muddled with the two of us. But my being an alpha might mess things up a bit. Oberon said the den was important, only he couldn't tell me why. And your father is clinging to his sanity by a thread. The only woman he ever mated produced the son he now has to destroy and almost killed him with her death." Liam rubbed my back. "He's not in a good place mentally, asking him would only add fuel to the fire. I think some parts of his wolf identify you as his. Even if he thinks of you as his son. It's a battle between them that I hope your *Apa's* human half wins."

I sucked in a deep breath at that revelation. *Apa's* wolf thought I was its mate? That couldn't be right. He'd never looked at me that way. Never said a word to make me think he did. Perhaps it was proof of just how separate *Apa* and his wolf were. No unity, not like he taught young wolves. And then there was Felix. "Felix told me his mother was an omega, but I didn't know *Apa* had actually mated her." No wonder *Apa's* hated talking about any of his children. "He seemed okay last night. Scattered, but okay," I pointed out.

"I think that was you."

"I didn't do anything."

"You don't have to. Just be you."

I scoffed at the idea. The pack had made it clear that I would never be beneficial to them, and especially to the Volkov. After all, what use was a child omega to the most powerful wolf in the world?

"You may not see it, but your father loves you. Everyone sees it when he looks at you. Something about you helps him be in control. I don't know if it's the kitsune spirit in you, or just knowing that you, his youngest child, is nearby. That's why he let you have the camper, and drop out of school to bake, make tea, and study alchemy. That's why he searched to find you a mate who would interest you more than his destructive son did. He's always loved you for just being you. Not because of any power you give him."

I frowned, trying to think of a reasonable rebuttal. But Liam went on, "I think he's always battled the will of his wolf when it conflicts with your power. Omegas bring peace, but only to those willing to accept it. Your father can't let his wolf be at peace because it would mean the destruction of both of them. It's a delicate dance of power, him and his wolf. Which is why I don't think his affection for you is because of your power. It's because you're you. Because you made him tea, and called him father even when you could have run in fear like everyone else does. Why isn't that enough?" Liam asked.

And wasn't that the question. The wolf pack had all treated me like they expected something bigger to come from me, and when it didn't, they beat me down for being weaker than them. I'd always thought it was because *Apa* had invested so much time in me, but maybe it was more the kitsune spirit. Had they all known and never told me? Did they hate me so much because *Apa* loved me? Or perhaps because I'd kept him sane? His pack had always been twisted in a way. Old wolves, a lot coming to him for the chance to die at the Volkov's hands. It seemed a lonely existence, and one from which *Apa* had often tried to keep me separated. Alienated. Alone. Though I wasn't sure that had ever been *Apa*'s intent.

My childhood had taught me that if I wasn't useful, I was worthless. Not because of anything *Apa* did. More due to how everyone else treated me. If I made a mistake everyone had to know and berate me for it. No one gossiped like a wolf pack. The scrutiny built character, *I* had been told more than once. A wrong decision could leave me stranded and alone in a bad situation. I'd spent the last year running from bad decision after bad decision, afraid of more choices, but never at a loss for them. Every road I'd taken had eventually burned until I'd ended up here. Was this just another bad decision? Maybe not just for me, but for Liam also?

"Everything I do, turns out badly," I spoke my fear. Did he realize what he'd gotten himself into? "I'm some weird *witch-blood* shifter adopted by wolves and raised like every day meant survival of the fittest. I'm messed up. And you're stuck with me. Fuck. Do you get how bad this is for you?"

"Sebastian," Liam grumbled, the argument starting in his tone even before he could get his thoughts in place. "You're so cute."

"I'm not cute! I'm being serious."

"You are cute. Especially when you're being serious."

I scowled at him. "You have no idea how long I'll live. You know that half the world of monsters is after me for one reason or another, and that everyone hates me just for being different. By God, why did you ever even want me to show up here? If I were you, I'd have cursed my name and hidden so I could never have found you." What horrors had I brought down on his pack. This whole thing was my fault, after all, wasn't it? Felix looking for me, likely ramping up the rogue wolves just for a chance to get back at me. *Apa* was here in Liam's territory with Oberon, the second deadliest wolf on the planet. We'd been mated less than a day and Liam's pack was already falling apart. If I hadn't feared it would kill me, I might have run from him again, just to save him from all this madness.

"I would never have run from you. You were mine from the second you called for me in the dark. Before I'd seen you, or even knew you were the *witchchild*. None of it mattered, and none of those things are things you could control. How others feel about you, how much mayhem follows you, I don't worry about any of that. Not now that you're in my arms. We belong together. The schematics will work themselves out."

My heart hurt, but I wasn't sure if it was pride or fear. Liam had pretty much told me he loved me, though he barely knew me. Could I utter the words back? No. And I hated myself for it. The mistrust, fear, and self-loathing. It wasn't that I didn't want to. I wasn't sure it was the truth yet. I felt something for him. Something I'd never experienced before in my life. Sure lust was part of it, but my gut ached at the thought of not seeing him every day. I couldn't imagine not hearing his stupid *hmm* again. Or never having the chance to search those clear blue eyes for truth. If I hadn't been so broken…

Would he understand? Even I didn't understand. Sure I'd had it rough for a few years. What didn't kill a person made them stronger, right? More cynical for sure.

"Liam, I'm trying, I promise," I told him. Fearing he'd be hurt.

"I understand," Liam said. Sure he did. Maybe I could make him understand.

"We're mated," I reminded him.

"I know." He sounded pleased by the fact.

"Soulbonded." Wrapped around each other so neatly I wondered if I could breathe without him. Yet still, something separated us. An invisible barrier of some sort. Maybe there was still a chance to save him.

"Carl," I suddenly thought of a question I'd been stewing on before bed. Distraction. I was good at that. I needed him, while wanting so badly to run from everything. My heart couldn't take another break. Not like this. Was it even possible to separate a mated pair and not go mad? "Was mated."

"Yes," Liam agreed.

"But she's gone and he's still here." Was that even possible. *Apa* could survive, maybe. He was the strongest werewolf alive, but just an ordinary wolf? Carl didn't seem crazy. Just a little anti-social. Well anti-people if Liam's observation agreed with reality.

"Yes. He'll tell you every day he regrets surviving. I think he's still here because he's got shit to do yet. He says he can't imagine losing his Emma to be my second was much of a brilliant plan of fate. He was in your father's pack waiting for his turn to be put down. Yet when I offered a place in my pack, he agreed. I wanted to know all about mating. Your father wouldn't talk. Both Oberon was good at deflecting your father's attention away from his lost mate and he lost her centuries ago. Carl lost his Emma less than five years ago. I thought he had to know more." Liam traced his fingertips over my face. "He warned me it's not the same for any two mates, while being overwhelming for every single one of them."

The answer stumped me. Carl had been mated. She'd passed, but he was still here. Sane. Sane enough at least to be allowed to move to a pack outside of *Apa*'s at least. That said something about Carl's state of mind. No wolf could fool the Volkov.

"They were true mates?" Like us? Liam was strong, right? He'd survive being stuck with me a few years.

"Yes," Liam agreed. "Mated over a hundred years."

"That's not possible. Was she a wolf too?"

"No. Human. He thinks his life extended hers. Has a picture of her before she passed. She didn't look older than forty. Lost a battle with cancer." Liam looked into my eyes, searching for something. "He didn't have a pack. He'd been exiled for mating a human. Everyone was just waiting for him to die."

Only he hadn't. He'd beaten the odds. Had a mate for over a hundred years. It was sort of good news. "That means you won't die when I do."

"Not true," Liam said. "There would be no point for me to live without you."

I stared up at him. "Do you realize what you're stuck with?" Was he hearing anything I said to him?

"A beautiful yet infuriating man who was not taught that his true self-worth is his heart?"

I frowned at him. "Don't go all Hallmark card on me. I'm trying to help you realize I'm not all the balloons and the little stuffed animal too. I'm more like the rubber snake in a box of confetti that sends people screaming *Lord Jesus have mercy!* An unwanted surprise."

Liam laughed. "You're not just funny after sex. Good."

I smacked his shoulder. "I'm being totally serious."

"Self-deprecation aside, I want you. All your quirks, included. I'm glad you're funny. Your father never mentioned your sense of humor. I was a little afraid that life had beaten it out of you as it does to us old wolves." He hugged me tight, then loosened his grip.

"When I became a wolf, that first pack had a mated pair. I dreamt of having what they had. The way he'd look at her and she'd look at him. They were everything to each other. Saw the world through each other's eyes. When she passed, so did he."

"I heard that happens a lot."

"It doesn't. True mates aren't that common. A handful of wolves among thousands experience true mates. Just like in the human world, so few find true love. And often, like storybooks of legends, it ends tragically, ending up as the story that everyone repeats. Never mind the others who went quietly into the night after a long happy life."

"But all the couples you know who were true mates are

dead or separated because one of them is dead," I said. "That doesn't not scream happily ever after to me. What if I've made your life shorter by letting you mate me? Or if you go mad after I die?"

"I will take that risk. I will take every moment from now until the sunsets upon our time together to enjoy your presence in my life. I can't wait to learn everything about you." He let out a long sigh. He wrapped his ankles around my legs, cradling me tight against him, while still managing to keep me from feeling confined. "You're so afraid of losing someone, of your heart being hurt again, that you're terrified to let yourself feel joy or hope." He let out a long sigh. "Your *Apa* did not protect you well from trauma. He really wasn't well enough to raise you. Should have found another, much more stable pack. The Volkov's pack is not known for being a sanctuary. I blame him. He could have had Oberon take you somewhere else. You should not be so cynical of the world at such a young age."

"I wouldn't be me if I were innocent and trusting. I never would have found my way here. If you're looking for Susie Homemaker because I'm an omega, you've been bamboozled."

He laughed again. "Totally bamboozled. The fact that you left me unconscious in the woods just steps from your father's backyard was the first indication you weren't going to be the submissive mate most alphas salivate over."

"Assholes," I agreed.

"Good thing I'm not most alphas."

"Do they get that submissive mates aren't all that fun? Do this, do that, yes sir. Well that's boring." I pointed out. "Would they show up at your work in the middle of the day to surprise you with sex? Probably not."

"Would you?" Liam wanted to know.

"Maybe. If not sex, then at least to share a cupcake."

"Cupcakes and sex would be a good combo."

I narrowed my eyes at him. In some ways we were a really good match.

He laughed lightly. "I've read lots of romance novels. Was waiting for my wayward mate to find his way home and trying to keep my wolf from playing the worst game of chase ever. Some of the most unusual ideas of food sex…"

How one little kiss had started all this, I couldn't fathom. If Felix had not raped and nearly killed me that night, would I have met Liam? *Apa* had been trying to find me a mate. A true mate, or just someone he thought could better care for me?

"See. Your mind is a whirl of questions, doubt and confusion. I don't worry about our mating. We are meant to be together. However it happened, it did. We met. I heard your call and we kissed, sealing us to a bond that would eventually pull us back together. That worked out just fine."

If he had any idea how the last year had been…

"Vampires and things aside," Liam said as though catching my thoughts as they began to scatter. "Everything else will work itself out." He wrapped a hank of my hair around his fist, rolling and unrolling it like it fascinated him. "Touching you makes me feel whole, even while I can feel your unrest. It hurts my heart to know that you're not as settled as I am."

"I'm sorry," I said automatically. "I'm not sure how to fix it."

Liam nodded. "Might not be your doing at all. My pack is in disarray. I can barely feel them. Toby is sitting right outside your camper door and he feels like the whisper of a shadow."

Had mating with me broken something within his pack? I was happy to hear Toby was okay. "How would you fix that if I wasn't here?" I asked. *Apa* didn't speak of his connection to the pack, though I knew he had it. Many wolves complained of him giving them orders mind to mind, so they couldn't argue back. I'd always believed the times I thought I heard his voice in my head, that it was just some memory coming up. Maybe it was more to it than that.

"I have to reestablish the den."

"We should go to the house then." I tried to pull away, but Liam wouldn't budge.

"The pack den is not a dwelling. Not really. It's easier if it's tied to a place, which is usually the alpha's home. But the pack den is really a state of being. Security and happiness for the wolves in the pack. Only an alpha can create it, though it's a fragile thing. It's why alpha's don't challenge each other often. Once a den is established, it's difficult to reform it after killing the alpha who created it. The pack resists the change even if they support the new leader. When a pack member is lost, often there is chaos in the bond. Grief can gnaw away at the unity of any pack."

"So your den is messed up cause your wolves are scattered to try to get away from *Apa's* black cloud?"

"Something like that. Dylan's disappearance has a lot to do with it. As my third he's a strong part of what makes the pack feel safe. Though if I'd been sane while you were gone, I could have held it together by will alone. Distance doesn't matter." He shook his head as though trying to shake away the memories. "I was so lost in pain and fear of never finding you again. My wolf howled non-stop, fighting me for control, claiming it could find you. But the wolf is a simple creature. He'd have taken over, and when I was too weak to fight, likely killed someone while searching for you."

"When I touched you it changed?" I wondered. Remembering him in the cave and how vulnerable he'd left himself. The wolf probably hadn't liked that.

"Yes. The wolf stopped and we both waited like we had spotted skittish prey, and feared chasing you away. He let me have control, saying my human brain was more capable of calming the fox and claiming the man, though he was on board for both." Liam tugged my hair. "I want you to try something with me," Liam said.

"Okay." At that moment I probably would have helped him take over the world if he'd asked me to. As long as he didn't let me go. Hope was what he gave me, and somehow I couldn't think of a better place to start.

CHAPTER 28

He let go of my hair to wrap his arms around me, and then pressed his cheek to mine. I sighed at his warmth. "Close your eyes," he instructed.

"Okay." I shut my eyes.

"You say you smell my scent. Focus on that. Follow that in your head. See if you can follow me as I touch each of the pack members. It's a bit like guided meditation."

"Are we going somewhere?" I wondered, doubtful. I had never been good at meditating. Too much noise in my head.

"You're the alchemist, and you scoff at magic?" His tone was teasing.

"Alchemy is science, not magic."

"This is magic. But small magic. Trust me. We alphas do this with new wolves to establish a connection. You just have to let me through. Now breathe me in."

I focused on the scent of him. It was warm and sweet, like fresh bread, which was sort of how I felt in his arms. Pillowed in a warm cocoon of safety. With his cheek pressed to mine, chest to my back, I could feel his heart beating. It was soothing and steady, like a river. I flashed back briefly to the river in Underhill, and how it had been divided in the middle. Dangerous on one side, and full of life on the other. A glance back into the woods and a light flickered off of iridescent legs, the scrape of glass against glass, the feeling of terror. The memory so vivid it startled me. I reached for Liam's warmth, his smell, the feeling of his soul wrapped around me, seeking peace, or at least a minute to slow my racing heart, only to fall.

The sensation was so abrupt I gasped and opened my eyes to find myself in a giant bakery kitchen, alone. Was I back in Underhill? What if I'd never left? The panic arose whip fast, but a timer beeped and the smell of vanilla, cloves, and cardamom filled the room calming my fear.

I turned to try to find Liam, only instead of Liam, there was a door to a proofing room. The proofer was a large warming room to help the dough ferment and set properly before being baked. Most large bakeries had proofing rooms. It was an essential part of the baking process. Some bakeries had small proofing boxes, but this room was large enough to fit easily fifty or more racks filled with loaves.

The door hung open and racks of dough were scattered about haphazardly. Some racks were only half full, others appeared ready to be baked.

I stared at the giant space for a few minutes, trying to decide what to do. The kitchen seemed to go on indefinitely in both directions. Like a long shotgun kitchen built to feed an army of a couple million. Not an oven in sight. Just tables and sinks, racks of bread on wheels and cabinets with shelves open to cooking utensils.

The room itself smelled like Liam. It was warm and made me sleepy as I stepped inside to examine the space. Plenty of room for all the racks. I shoved the first rack inside, lining it up beside the wall near the door, and breathed in the warm vanilla scent of my mate. Was he here somewhere and I just couldn't see him? I grabbed the next rack, though it was only a partial, and began to push it into place.

A dizzying rush flowed through me, and I could see Toby sitting at the bottom of my camper stairs, guarding it, head on his paws. Somehow I could tell he was happy. Wolf and man. His thoughts were simple. Just of alpha and alpha's mate. Home. Safety. He closed his eyes to sleep and I was dropped back into the proofer.

I blinked around me, seeing all the racks a second time. Pieces of the whole, needing a place to rest, to grow and settle. That place was Liam. I examined the room with awe. Was this some sort of dream he was leading?

I moved another rack, then another: Stacy, Leigh, even Korissa. Each one clicked into place and I could feel them. Just a glide over the top of their consciousness. I knew Korissa was worried about her dad. Most of the pack was more worried about the Volkov's presence in their territory. I touched over Santa Claus, whose real name was Benton, and Marlow. Then there was Carl.

His rack of bread seemed a little over proofed, so I hesitated. If left in the proofer too long it would come out hard and more than a little chewy. Yet I couldn't leave him out. Once I pushed his rack into place I could feel him too. Awake. Sitting in his truck, watching the camper and the landscape around it with a shotgun in his lap. He was not leaving his alpha to fend for himself. Not even for a few hours of much needed sleep.

Once all the racks were in the proofer I tried to shut the door, only it wouldn't close. Which meant the racks by the door wouldn't rise properly or might even flatten. That would leave Toby and a lot of pack vulnerable.

I huffed in frustration, trying to understand what Liam

was telling me. I couldn't feel him like I could feel the others. With each of the pack it had been a full visual roll of emotion and personality. Even members I had yet to meet. But Liam remained elusive, when all I wanted was to feel the connection he was experiencing.

I'd close the door and it would swing open. Packs didn't work like that. Liam's pack would have a set bond, with a full ceremony of blood and flesh for pack members to join. There was no reason for the pack bond to stay wide open. Was it because of me? I entered the proofer and tried to close the door behind me. It swung open again.

I stomped out of the room and glared at it again. It was then that I saw another rack off in the distance. In fact, it was so far away, I was shocked that I'd seen it at all. The silver metal finishes on all the shelving made it hard to distinguish that rack from the shelving around it. I raced toward it, heart pounding as I got closer. The loafs on the rack looked over kneaded, mounds of battered dough, left to flatten in the cool breeze of the kitchen.

I reached for the rack, hand grabbing the handle, and was plunged into pain, hunger, exhaustion, and hopelessness. Dylan settled around me. Battered, living, but just barely. Why were they keeping him alive? Dylan seemed to ask me the question as I asked myself.

Where? I demanded from him. But his confusion only told me he wasn't sure. He was tired. Starving, and half mad with pain. There were horrors in his memory he tried to hide from me, only it made me search them out, pull them forward. Memories of things done to him in the past month. Similar to my own pain, I let the rage swell in me. Felix would not survive this. I'd never killed a man before, but he deserved to die. The whole mess of rogue wolves. Seven in all if Dylan's memories were correct.

Sean? Dylan asked me through his fog of pain.

"Safe," I told him. Not sure if he could really hear my words. "He's ours, you know. Pack. Because he's yours." I knew that for a fact because I could feel Liam's agreement. His hand over mine on the rack, like he too had been searching for his missing loaves only to find a wolf in need of help. It was his guidance I was using to link to all his wolves. His alpha power that let me into Dylan's mind more deeply than anyone ever had a right to be.

A smile ghosted over Dylan's face. I could almost see him in the dark. Shoved away from light, restrained with the weight of something heavy and metal. The room stank of blood, piss, and sex.

Keep him safe, Dylan requested. Like he was giving up.

No.

"Don't you dare give up!" I shouted at him, then looked around like I could see where he was just by examining the walls. Only it was unremarkable. Just a dark room.

Not that it mattered. I couldn't see where he was, but I could *feel* where he was, like a beacon pulsing on a map in tune to his fading heartbeat. We'd found him, only for him to give up as soon as he knew Sean was safe. Not on my watch.

I opened my eyes, not realizing they'd been closed, to find myself back in the camper, staring into Liam's intense gaze. I leapt free from Liam's arms, shifting from man to fox, pausing only long enough to shake off the pants, and bolted to the door.

Should have thought ahead. Foxes can't open doors. Paws don't work on handles. Dammit. I glanced back at Liam, but he was changing. His shift not as fast or delicate as mine. His was a breaking of bones and reforming of muscle. Painful.

I whined. His pain lingering on the edges of my senses. Dylan's pulse was far off, but I could feel it and needed to follow it. Only not alone. Wait, that was Liam's voice in my head. *Do not go alone! Wait for me.*

I paced. Could have shifted back to human and opened the door while I waited, if I'd thought of it. Only I was too intent on the hunt. Find Dylan, kill the wolves who'd hurt him. I knew the first part was me and Liam, but I was pretty sure the second part was Liam. I'd never killed anyone in my life. Though at that moment the blood lust raged in my gut. It wasn't even just a wolf thing. Vampires and fey experienced blood lust too. My omega blood had always made me immune. Only now I could feel it tugging at me. An emotion that might have been mine, or might have been Liam's. I still wasn't sure if I was feeling him like he was feeling me.

The fire began to build around me as I watched Liam get closer and closer to completing his change from man to wolf. His sleek dark gray coat erupted from his skin, covering the terrifying muscle-coated bones just a moment before it all became too horrific. He was so dark a charcoal color I knew why he'd looked black at night. His coat blended well with shadows. If I hadn't been filled with blood lust, I might have admired him for a minute or two.

Cold fire lapped at my feet, and I felt larger than my normal fox. Would I fit through the door? I hated the thought of breaking it since it would take longer to reseal the wards afterward.

The door opened. An unfamiliar young man opened the door, with a blanket huddled around him. His hair was a mix of sandy dark blond. He had wide blue eyes, and wore a bewildered expression. He flicked his eyes over me, beyond, until he found Liam, then he stepped back. He held the door open and out of the way.

Toby. Liam told me as his change finished. He shook out his fur, casting off the last lethargy and pain of the change. I felt the young man's link to the pack at the same time Liam established his identity. Toby lowered his head and his eyes so he wouldn't accidentally challenge Liam's wolf. With the wolf at the front, there would be less of the logical and calm man I was coming to crave.

Not that it mattered. Finding Dylan was my focus. Saving him for Liam and for Sean. With Liam changed and ready, I leapt through the doorway and into the light of the morning, sprinting at a speed I'd never imagined possible before.

CHAPTER 29

Liam raced behind me, the sound of his breathing a warm balm on my soul. Not for one second had he thought to leave me behind, or tell me to wait out the rescue. No, he just wanted to be by my side when we ripped the rogue wolves apart and brought Dylan back into the pack where he belonged.

The distance flew by with little recognition on my part. Not that I knew the area well. There were roads and trees and houses. I wondered if we looked odd, a fox bathed in cold fire, which froze the ground with each step, followed by a giant wolf so dark grey he looked black.

Pack magic could make people believe they saw large dogs instead of wolves nearly the size of small cars. Would it extend to me now that I was mated to Liam? Not that it mattered. Let the world film this if they wanted. Most wouldn't believe. The supernatural beings of the world had been dissuading humans for centuries. The advances in digital technology helped all *others* hide in plain sight.

At least this time the fire wasn't eating at me. It almost seemed to loop between Liam and I. When it got too cold, a blast of heat would explode around me, singeing the air as I sailed through brush and trees. Nothing caught fire, so I wondered if it was some sort of metaphysical fire.

Soul fire. I liked the idea of that, and hoped it did something more spectacular than make me cold, hot, or crave jumping Liam's bones.

We raced into town. Down the main street which was mostly absent of people this early in the morning. There was the usual line outside the bakery, but no one even glanced our way as we passed. Beyond the grocery store and even down the road past an auto shop that I thought must have been Sean's.

How many miles had we covered? I wasn't even sure where I was going. I was just following Dylan's heart beat on my soul radar. Or whatever this weird link was. Maybe it was Liam who was feeling it and I was just following him. We were side by side now. Dashing through trees and brush, zig-zagging through yards and around parked cars, though those things grew further and further apart.

Liam's pace quickened and I struggled to keep up. We were close. I could feel Dylan now like a beacon throbbing in my mind. Internal GPS. At least it didn't have that annoying electronic voice. *Turn left here. Recalculating...*

Sounds filled the darkness around us. Pack, wolves running, claws digging into wood and dirt. *Ours.* Liam told me.

And there was something dark ahead of us. Something not unlike the Volkov's black cloud.

The house appeared an unremarkable two story farm-style surrounded by a dilapidated barn and massive groves of trees. An apple orchard perhaps. I had a brief moment of wondering if there had been people here, or if they might still be there, injured or held hostage. But wolves burst out of the front door like a startled hornet's nest spewing its angry inhabitants. More than seven. At least a dozen, large and very deadly wolves flew at us.

Liam leapt over me, catching one by the throat seconds before it reached me and broke the wolf's neck with little effort before tossing it aside and heading for the next foe. I darted around raging claws, thinking hard about the cold fire that lapped at me. I imagined it extending over the wolves surrounding me, freezing their lungs until they couldn't breathe and stopping their hearts.

Cold blanketed the area like an instant blizzard. Snow dropped around us and ice slicked the ground. The wolves didn't fall over dead, but they did slip and slide into each other, comically. One leapt only to have its back feet slide out from under it and land in the rapidly rising snow. At least that was a start. The one closest to me coughed, a thick, mucus-filled wheeze that sounded like it hurt. He backed away from me, turning to go after Liam, but I gave chase. Latching onto his back leg with sharp teeth and shaking it, trying to break it.

The wolf snarled at me, turned to shred me with its claws, but Liam arrived a second sooner and ripped out its throat. *Find Dylan!* Liam commanded me, mind to mind. There were so many wolves for him to hold off, and I hadn't even seen Felix yet.

A giant black wolf leapt into the clearing, landing on two wolves who'd been trying to get behind Liam. This wolf made Liam look small and was so black in color he'd have a hard time blending into shadows. Life wasn't usually that absent of shades of gray.

Oberon.

A smaller gray wolf, slid into the field, taking out three wolves back legs and turning at the last second to tear another wolf open from tail to nose with claws sharper than butcher knives. *Apa*. There was a fury in him I hadn't seen in a long time. His eyes glowed with a demonic light. It scared me, but bolstered me as well. Liam had backup. I needed to find Dylan, and I was the only one who could change shape back and forth instantly.

I scurried around the battles toward the house, expecting another rush of wolves to come at me. Or at least to have Felix emerge like the demon he was. Only nothing happened as I nosed my way to the door, carefully peering inside. Nothing moved. I listened hard, straining to hear around the violence behind me.

The place stank. Death, booze, defecation, and sex. It was almost overwhelming. I heard nothing from inside. Not the sound of anyone's heartbeat, or the breathing of a mouse. Though my ears were not nearly as sensitive as Liam's, I had to focus on the tie to Dylan again. Had he died in the time it took us to get here? Maybe they'd felt us coming and had killed him? Was that why I couldn't feel him?

More likely it was the stench that made it hard to focus my senses. I wandered room to room, searching for life, trying to ignore the gore at my feet. The rotting smell wasn't all from takeout bags. Pieces of things littered the floor like forgotten morsels. Not all of it identifiable. There was the hind leg of a cow in one corner. Something that looked suspiciously like a dog head had been rolled into the bend of the couch. I identified a finger or two in a huge pile of discarded bones.

Nothing about this was normal. These weren't wolves or men. They were monsters. I wondered briefly if Nicky's remains lay scattered about this nightmare somewhere. My gut rebelled, and I fought the need to vomit. Now was not the time for weakness. I could sob and be sick later, reflecting on the horror and terror. Liam battled a pack of wolves to buy me time to save Dylan. The pack needed

Dylan. Of that I was positive. Me…well, I wasn't sure the pack needed a fox omega.

But Liam needed me. Of that I was positive, even if his wolf drove the desire. I needed him too. Something metaphysical, yes. Just this weird tingle in my brain that began to panic at the thought of him not being close. But there were other things, too. His scent, the way he held me, the way he looked at me sometimes, like I mattered. I let out a long sigh.

Liam needed his pack whole and at his back. I could give him that. If Dylan was still alive. We could work on the mate thing. I still wasn't positive I was the best thing for Liam, but hope had planted a seed. Maybe if I nurtured it a little instead of jerking it out by the root right away, we had a chance. A lifetime of getting stabbed in the back would make just about anyone shy away from affection. My gut kept telling me that Liam was too good to be true, while my heart said wait. In reality, I needed Liam now. Not just because he said pretty things to me, and had wrapped his soul around mine, but because he'd given me hope for the first time in a very long while. He loved me. Said so, with no trace of lie in his voice. Fuck, he was too good for a mute like me.

I could be useful at least. Find Dylan, I chanted to myself. Liam was counting on me. Sean needed Dylan back. I was pretty sure the whole damn pack needed Dylan more than they needed some little fox shifter messing up their den. Dylan first, self-doubt later, I reminded myself.

Finding the first floor empty, I headed up the stairs, dreading again that feeling of not being able to escape. As a fox I could probably jump from the second floor and live, but I'd likely snap a bone or two trying. Werewolves were more unbreakable than I was. I really hoped that was true of Dylan.

Where are you? I asked into the pack bond I could still feel through Liam. If I thought hard enough I could feel the tiny ping of their presence in different directions. Some closer than others. Like Liam outside, and Carl racing our way in his truck, trying to hurry yet still obey traffic laws, as he tracked his alpha through the same pack link I was using.

And then faintly…

I followed the tiny ping down a long hallway of doors. The stench of death overrode everything. Maybe the alpha Liam had taken the territory from hadn't been deranged when Liam took over, but he was now. My sensitive nose wondered just how many horror novels would be written about the events in this house. Made for TV mystery stories of the serial killer no one knew haunted their little backwoods town.

How many had died? Would Oberon cover it all up? How would they explain the missing? There had to be a lot of people missing.

A cow or a dog wandering off was easy enough to explain away. But the number of dead here reminded me of a ghoul nest I'd stumbled onto once. Ghouls weren't ghosts as some legends thought them to be. They were a sort of spirit. They'd taken up residence in an old cemetery outside this tiny town in Iowa. Ghouls didn't really need the old bodies, since it was flesh they craved. The softness of the ground appealed to them. Recent death would draw them in, just like the group of four teens who'd died in a car when the driver had been texting, had drawn these ghouls in. Once the cemetery was infested, it was only a matter of time before the ghouls started finding food the good old-fashioned way. Hunting for it.

Usually they started with deer, or dogs if the area was too urban. It always ended in humans though. Humans were too slow, dumb, and meat covered, to be left by something as simple as a ghoul.

The whole house, its rooms filled with stench, blood, and

discarded bits, looked like a ghoul den. Except for one thing. Normally ghouls piled bodies up to eat later. It was almost organized, like an ant farm might be. They'd carry them in, set up a hoard of food, and hunker down. Here the bones and bits were thrown about, nothing whole to be found anywhere. But many choice pieces left at random. Hearts, livers, a thigh with most of the meat still on it. Even as I forced my eyes to take in the horror of every room I passed, I catalogued the memories. Maybe I'd be able to help a family find closure after this. Rescue enough pieces of someone to put them in a proper grave.

Fuck.

Monsters. This wasn't instinct or a dominant species making a claim. This was slaughter for the sake of blood lust.

When wolves go mad, they are nothing but killing machines, Apa had told me more than once. He'd done his best to scare me away from his aging wolf pack when I was very young. *They lose what it means to be human. They forget how to feel. They become nothing but hunger and rage. They feed on life because they have lost theirs.* He'd always sounded like he'd spoken from experience, and I had assumed he'd seen it from a lot of his wolves. Only now did I wonder how many times he, himself, had gone mad, lost in blood lust. How had he come back? Was the madness permanent for most? If an alpha went berserk did that mean the whole pack followed?

Were the rogue wolves berserk? Or just Felix? Perhaps both?

I found a room in the back of the house which despite all the cast off body parts and blood, still pulsed through my borrowed pack senses with something alive. Though when I entered the room it was just as empty of life and desolate as the rest of the house. The sounds of the fight had faded into the distance. I could still hear the shrieks of wolves, and prayed they weren't any of the ones I cared about.

My heart throbbed, a sluggish beat. I focused on it, trying to link the feeling of exhaustion and pain to something. Was Liam hurt? I almost turned back. Would have if I hadn't heard the faintest scuffle of sound.

A door off to the side, looking much like a closet had been shut tight. It wouldn't open when I pushed at it with my paws or nose. I hated to shift in the middle of the mess, but had to. The change flowed over me like water. Smells that had started to fade from overexposure returned with a vengeance and I sneezed for a good minute. I had to fight back a gag as stomach acid backed up in my throat. My eyes burned with the intensity of the smell.

Find Dylan, I reminded myself and reached for the door.

It was a walk-in closet. Or had been in another life. I was surprised when the light switch worked and filled the room with a brightness so intense I nearly went blind for a minute.

Dylan was chained to a metal chair. Rungs of the chains had been slung through the floor of the house and around what looked like a large wood beam. I blinked at the set up in confusion. It took a minute to realize that the arrangement was new. The chains, as thick as they were, were only locked with a single small lock. Though they were wrapped in a way that would make a shape change near impossible. A werewolf of normal strength could have broken the lock or even some links of the chains without much effort.

After a month in captivity, Dylan was far from at normal strength. Both of his eyes were swollen shut. His face limp on one side, like a bone in his cheek had been broken. He was nude, covered in bruises from head to toe. Cuts everywhere. He appeared gaunt, skin sunken and stomach caved inward. I could hardly look at him and not shudder at what they'd done. Kept him alive just to torture him? Why?

To get back at Liam? To lure me here? None of this made sense to me.

"Dylan," I whispered. I hadn't heard anyone else in the house, but that didn't mean there wasn't someone I missed. When I reached Dylan's side, he flinched. "It's Sebastian, Dylan. I'm not going to hurt you, I promise." I wouldn't be able to free him either. Super strength was not one of my magic powers. Though I wondered briefly…

"I'm going to try something to get you free. Okay? Liam and the Volkov are downstairs fighting the other wolves. You're safe now. We have Sean back at Liam's." I tried to tell him soothing things as I squatted beside the lock. Could I make the cold as a human? Or did I have to be fox? Maybe I could break the lock that way. Shatter a chain or something?

I focused on the sensation for a minute, trying to bring the cold with me, but nothing happened. No snow, no cold, just me and Dylan. Both naked, and terrified. I changed back to the fox and tried again. Still nothing. Fuck.

"It's okay," Dylan whispered, voice barely audible, but raspy like it had been ages since he'd had water.

I glared at the chain, the complicated weave of it around the chair, him and the beam, then the wood beam. A full strength werewolf could have shredded that wood with its claws in a few minutes. Sure he'd have to hope he could get Dylan free before the weight of the house caved inward due to the broken support, but hey, minor technicalities. If I could get Dylan out of the chain, maybe he could change and start to heal a little.

I began to rake my tiny claws at an area near the chain. For a minute or two, it seemed to be working. Only I wasn't a wolf and my nails just weren't that sharp. The first broke and I cursed, pain traveling through one toe and up my arm. I must have whined at the pain because Dylan jerked at the sound.

I dug at the beam until my paws bled, front and back. Nails torn to the quick, but still no more than an inch or so through a thick slat of wood. I leapt onto the beam a few times, trying to crack it with my weight, but neither fox nor human was enough to do anything but wiggle it a little.

Twice more I tried for ice and even fire, but nothing happened. Neither human nor fox worked, and I just exhausted myself with all the shape changes. Even I had a limit. Maybe I needed Liam close to use this new power. Maybe I just had no real clue how to use it at all. That was the more likely answer.

The sounds of battle had faded, and I wondered if they were waiting for me, or would be coming into the house.

Liam? I tried calling through the pack bond. Nothing. Frustrated, I found my way to a nearby bathroom and prayed the water worked since my hands ached. It wasn't warm, and it burned like acid on my mangled hands, but I rinsed away some of the blood, then found a small cup to bring Dylan water. He sucked it down quickly, choking the first time. Three times more I brought him water and prayed Liam was coming.

It was my third trip to the bathroom that I thought to look under the sink. Cleaning supplies plus alchemy. Within minutes I had an arm full of bottles that could help me break the chain. Starting with a toilet rust remover, a lot of bleach, and some basic alchemy. The stench made Dylan flinch.

"Sorry," I told him. "Just trying to weaken one of these links." I worked on the one near the lock, soaking it with chemicals that made it hard to breathe and tugging. The metal began to give a little where the chain had been welded on one side.

"I know you're weak, but if I direct you to tug on a section of the chain, can you try?" I asked Dylan. He nodded weakly, his breathing labored. I struggled to get the chain to a place he could reach that wouldn't strangle him if he tried to pull.

"Okay," I told him. He pulled with one hand. I watched the muscles in his whole body go rigid with the attempt. The chain began to buckle, but then he stopped, wheezing like he'd run a mile.

"Sorry," Dylan whispered.

"It's okay," I assured him using my foot and a well-placed towel to try to tug more at the loosening chain. "It's starting to break. I'll just work on it a little more." I worked in silence for a few minutes. Tugging and praying the metal moved, though if it was, the shift was so gradual I couldn't see it.

"You should go," Dylan said. "He'll be back."

"The wolves are out front fighting Liam, Oberon and *Apa*," I told Dylan. "I'm sure Liam will be up soon."

"And Felix?" Dylan asked, a slight tremor to his voice.

Felix had not been in the rush of wolves. I'd know him anywhere. His wolf was dark gray, more like soot, than the near charcoal of Liam's wolf. Was he in the house somewhere? Wouldn't I have sensed him? Heard him? I listened hard for a minute, wishing my ears were as good as the werewolves were. But I heard nothing.

Nothing.

Not the sound of the fighting out front. Not a peep from birds or bugs. Or even Dylan's breathing as he seemed to be holding his breath. Much like I did right at that second. The darkness of the shadows expanded. The lightbulb overhead shattered, spraying glass shards over us. A supernatural wave of energy seemed to suck all the air from the room. For a moment I was certain it was *Apa's* monster finally set free after it had killed Oberon and Liam. I didn't have a second to be sad because everything in me screamed in terror.

It *felt* like something otherworldly. Demonic even, if that was a real thing.

Only it was a mostly human hand that grabbed me by the throat and threw me out of the closet and into the other room. I landed hard on my right shoulder, rolled through sludge, then smashed into the wall, blinking stunned into the darkness for only a second. Then I was lifted by my hair, pain scorching through my scalp, and turned to face darkness.

I screamed. Couldn't help it. What had once been a man named Felix was now some sort of skeleton with flesh stretched over it. His skin clung to bone, as though no muscle existed beneath, and his eyes had become giant pools of swallowing darkness. His fingers ended in claws, and parts of his body seemed to be half stuck between the change. I could count the ribs protruding from his bare chest. He had wolf fangs in a partially human mouth. Inhuman. Monstrous.

Panic roared to life, but instead of freezing me up like it normally did, it gave me a fire to fight. Liam needed me back. I had to save Dylan. The pack needed Dylan whole, even if that meant distracting the monster long enough for Liam to come to our rescue.

I began to kick, punch, and wriggle as much as I could against Felix's grip. I slammed my thumbs into his eyes. The wet pop would have horrified me at another point, only now it was the crawling darkness that gave rise to terror. Transferred from his face to my hands. It curled around my fingers, gliding up my arms, like a parade of stinging fire ants soaked in liquid nitrogen.

Felix shrieked in agony and tossed me into the wall again. There was an explosion of pain through me. Darkness lingered on the edge of my vision, just teetering on a tightrope over unconsciousness. I lay stunned for a moment, hands burning with a terrifying tingle of pain. Like ice running through my nerves, licking its way up my arms. I couldn't get my fingers to do much more than twitch as I tried to roll over, crawl away, something.

Then Felix was back, smacking me into the floor, hand on

my neck. Claws inches from ripping the life out of me. He dripped blood, which burned my skin like acid. I flinched and yelped, trying to kick him away, while cursing my now useless arms. The ward spells and warnings did nothing. I couldn't even feel my hands anymore. The tingling kept moving upward. Like it was eating through my nerves. What would happen when it hit my core? My lungs or heart?

I sucked in a deep breath to scream again as Felix's fingers dug into my throat. His mouth opened to something out of a horror movie, giant, dark and filled with teeth. Then something large and dark smashed into him, dragging us all tumbling several feet in a mass of limbs and gore. Felix let go.

I rolled into a pile of discarded bones and tried to stop my face from landing in the mess with no arm strength. Felix got up, shaken, but still mad and blind, yet somehow able to face his opponent as though he could see. And then there was a giant dark gray wolf launching itself at him.

One moment I was joyous with relief because there was Liam. Alive and fierce. The next came horror as the wolf collided with the monster that was Felix and the both of them stumbled backward, into and out the second story window.

CHAPTER 30

The sound of glass shattering seemed to happen after they fell, like the noise of life suddenly returned to the room. I could hear Dylan's mewling cries from the closet, growls and snarls from below, and in the distance a wet chewing sound. I shuddered, arms not working, but heart pulsing in fear as I found my way to the window to look out.

Below a fierce battle was going on. Not just Liam and Felix. But *Apa* and Oberon too. Liam was trying to fight Felix, while *Apa* and Oberon fought. Well Oberon wasn't fighting so much as trying to keep *Apa* out of the fray. The yard looked like an explosion of bodies had taken place. Blood darkened the grass as far as I could see and pieces of wolves and some humans were strewn everywhere. The grass squelched beneath the raging battle, but Liam seemed to be holding his own. I heard a chain rattle and pop, then raced back to Dylan's side. He'd broken the link, but was unable to unravel the chains.

There was glass everywhere, which I found by stepping too close. "Stay still," I begged Dylan. "Fuck." My arms were completely numb. My feet throbbed from my broken nails and glass shards. It took a little ingenuity, but I was able to nudge a few choice links free with my toes until the chain began to loosen and Dylan crawled free. "There's glass," I told him.

"Not strong enough to walk anyway," he said grumpily.

From outside came a furious growl, followed by a howl that chilled my blood. Pain stabbed into me. Like someone had raked their claws across my entire body, from my face down my gut. It hurt so bad, and I felt the warm rush of blood. Thought for a minute that somehow Dylan had found the ability to change and attack so quickly. Only he howled too, in pain, writhing as though he'd been cut open.

Yet neither of us bled. I felt like I was dying. Pain intensely blinding. There could be only one reason.

Liam!

My heart screamed as his blood began to pour out of him. He was dying. The link stretched between us. His soul wrapped around mine, but he seemed to be trying to unravel it. No. Not after I'd just found him.

I won't take you with me, he told me through the bond. But I wasn't going to stand by and let him die. He'd waited a year for me after one kiss. He deserved more than the five seconds this insanity had given our relationship. And I had so much I wanted to tell him, even if the words were damn near impossible to say. He was mine, dammit. The universe chose him for me, it was only fair it gave me a chance to know and love him.

Love. Fuck. Yeah. Not there yet, but so close. Need. Want. Hope. Dream. All of it rested on Liam being for real. I watched Felix dive toward Liam, intent on the final kill.

The fire ignited in me, like Liam's spilling blood was kerosene. A moment I was human, the next I was fox. The pain in my arms vanished and warmth spread to every bit of my body. Hot, this time. A raging fire, and real flames lapped at my feet, engulfing the dried dead.

I was bigger again. So large this time that as I tried to exit out the same window Felix and Liam had, the wall shattered around me in a splinter of wood and siding.

I was weightless, then I landed on the ground, on all four paws. Unhurt, and unfazed. It was Liam who lay in the grass, gutted and bleeding, his face a mass of gashes. I shrieked a sound of warning that hurt even my ears. I wasn't fast enough. Felix was already on Liam, claws digging in.

A shot rang out. Sharp and loud, echoing through the darkness.

Felix paused as though confused. A hole appeared in his forehead, oozing darkness even as the bullet pushed free and it began to heal. Yeah, the old often couldn't die that way, Oberon had once told me. It was why alphas had to put them down. Only they were strong enough to rip them apart and give them permanent death. The werewolf healing kicks in too fast. Though brain damage could be permanent.

Everything froze for a half a second as Felix tried to parse what was happening. It wasn't long. But enough time for me to charge forward with speed I'd never experienced before and take a massive swipe at Felix, hitting him at neck level.

If I'd been my normal fox I'd have done little damage to him. Maybe annoyed him a little, but not hurt him. As this kitsune or whatever the hell I was now, my hit slid fiery blades through him. His skin burned but didn't bleed. There was nothing left in him but darkness. My claws weren't like the fox anymore, small and delicate. Instead they were something similar to talons, large and thin, curved and sharper than razors. He may not bleed, but my claws ripping his head from his body was enough to stop his movement. Felix's head rolled in one direction, body collapsing at my feet. *Try to heal that, motherfucker*, I said to myself in Samuel L. Jackson's voice.

I caught a glimpse of Carl in the distance, rifle raised, though not pointed at me. He stood very still and focused. I could feel him pouring some metaphysical power into the link of the pack. A warm energy, sort of like a cup of hot chocolate on a cool fall evening. I wasn't sure what it was until I felt the whole pack streaming the energy through Dylan, Carl, me and finally, Liam.

Liam stopped tugging so fiercely at the ties between us. I worried it was because he was finally succumbing to the loss of blood and massive wounds, but when I looked down at him, he was healing. Wounds visibly closing. I gasped and pushed my own energy into that guided pool Carl was directing.

I had never seen a pack heal its alpha. Maybe the Volkov's pack was just too broken to even try. I could feel them all through the link though. Even Dylan was healing, cursing at the speed at which his body demanded fixing, but still healing.

The house behind us began to crackle, and I glanced up to realize it was on fire. Blazing, in fact. I had a moment to worry about Dylan, before he leapt out of the hole that I'd made in the side of the house, in his wolf form. He landed less than gracefully, but he didn't seem to be more hurt than he had been.

A glimmer of joy rolled through me. It was over. Everyone was safe. Felix was dead. We'd slain the metaphorical demon and I'd grieve over my actions once I knew everyone important was safe.

The reverberating grumble of something huge seemed to make the ground shake. The dark sludge of the Volkov's beast rolled over us all, flattening the wolves to the ground as if gravity wouldn't let them move a muscle. Darkness blanketed over the sky, plunging us into an unnatural black stillness, devoid of life. I struggled to breathe as the panic began to rise in my gut.

Like that day so long ago when I'd been a child and I'd seen something I couldn't fathom. An evil so great that most went mad from its sight. Once again that raging madness hovered over me. Like it could touch me, rip me to shreds and not even blink an eye.

Another shot went off, flying wide, beyond me and into something I hadn't yet had the courage to face. I heard Oberon's whimper a second before something leapt the nearly forty yards over our heads to lunge at Carl.

I thought to protect Carl since he belonged to Liam, but while I wasn't forced to bow like the wolves seemed to be, I found myself unable to breech the wall of fear. My labored breathing kept me hunched to the ground, frozen. Panic coursing through each cell of my body.

In that second I finally saw the thing that the Volkov struggled to control. Not unlike Felix, it was an emaciated creature with talons instead of claws. But the Volkov wasn't human at all. Part wolf, perhaps part bat, but all thin flesh pulled taut over bones, it looked almost dragon-like in the head. Yet not. Snout elongated and filled with razor-sharp fangs. I couldn't focus on it, the more I tried, the more the terror filled my belly. It seemed to morph from fear to fear; if I thought too hard about one fear it became that only to meld into another until I was left paralyzed, trembling, and terrified.

CHAPTER 31

The Volkov reached Carl and slashed at him. An action slowed down by my mind like the sort of things done in movies for effect, only this was all too real. Blood and more visceral things flew. A spray of gore spattered the ground in a wide arc around them.

And a half second later, Liam was on the Volkov's back, claws digging into that wiry monster and teeth tearing at the back of his neck. No one else had strength to move. Not even Oberon.

Carl lay in the grass unmoving. I tried to reach down the pack bond to find him, but all I could feel was Liam's panic. He had to save the pack, save me. Stop the Volkov from being set loose on the world. Impossible tasks set before him as he faced down a monster I wasn't sure even the legendary terrors of old could measure up to.

The Volkov slashed at him, trying to rip him off, and bleeding Liam with every touch.

Liam. I thought hard at him, begging him to stop with one word, to run. He was frantic now. Both in his attack on the

Volkov and his pulling on our bond. He knew he was going to die and didn't want to take me with him.

I trembled, unsure how any of us stood a chance if Oberon, the Volkov's own right hand man, couldn't stand up to him.

With a yelp, Liam let go under the Volkov's tugging. It was that or let himself be ripped in half. He was flung away, like no more than garbage, landing hard in the grass, a few feet beyond Carl, with a heavy thud. He didn't get up either. I still felt him. Liam's life wrapped around mine. His body damaged, bleeding, bones broken, bruises arising from every crevice of his body. He'd fight until he died before he gave up one of his wolves.

He struggled to pull himself up, wobbling, swaying, dripping blood. The Volkov focused on Carl, readying another pounce. Only a dusky-colored wolf flew from the second floor of the house and landed on the Volkov, hallowed in fire, like an avenging angel.

For a second it worked, even knocking the Volkov back several paces. Liam and Dylan tugged Carl away. But now it was another wolf in danger. One much younger and less experienced.

Toby.

I almost ran to him. It was Liam's voice in my head that commanded me to stop. *The Volkov won't see you right now. All he sees is prey.*

Toby shrieked when the Volkov's claws slid through him. A sound so unghastly and terrifying, I was certain I'd hear it in my sleep if we somehow made it out of all this. I paced a few feet away, uncertain.

Toby flew into the trees, launched like he'd been spit out of a cannon. Liam returned to cut off the Volkov's pursuit even though Liam was in rough shape. How was he even still upright? I didn't understand why the Volkov was chasing

Liam and the wolves. Carl had shot Felix, but it hadn't been fatal.

I had killed Felix. Sliced into him with some otherworld power I couldn't have imagined having just a few weeks ago. Is this what everyone was expecting out of me? Some vengeful spirit with the power to kill the bogeyman of the werewolves. Was that what I wanted? The Volkov to die?

I knew I didn't want to lose Liam. I'd known him only a handful of days and yet dreamed of things I'd never thought to hope for before in my life. He gave me fantasies of home, happiness, and safety. A place to finally belong. Were they really fantasies? Or did I have a chance to experience those things with Liam?

Liam protected his underbelly with fast turns and low dives, but his back took a lot of damage. Blood matted his fur until he looked coated in it.

This was a fight we weren't winning. I wasn't sure what the strategy was, but the Volkov didn't look any worse for wear. Liam, however, only stood from sheer willpower. He wobbled and the Volkov barely had to swing at him before he'd fall over again. It was all a game now wasn't it? The Volkov playing with his prey before he tore us all to shreds.

I'm going to sever our bond. Run, Sebastian. Go to another continent if you can. I'm not sure there is anyone strong enough to defeat him. Liam whispered through my mind.

No. I wasn't going to run. And his tugging at the bond hurt. Genuinely hurt like he was cutting something inside me. The pieces of himself, I supposed. Pieces that had melded with mine. But we were two halves of a whole now. Inseparable. Isn't that what I'd feared most? Being Liam's downfall. Yet here he was battling the monster of all monsters to try to save me.

Run. He told me again. *He's not your Apa right now. He's just a mindless monster.*

The words stung. I'd been thinking so hard about the Volkov's monster and how it was a separate thing from *Apa*. *Apa* who had loved and cared for me like I was his own. Who'd given me the chance to stand on my own, while quietly protecting me in the background. *Apa* who had fought this monster inside his soul for so long I wasn't sure he even knew how long.

Oberon lay bleeding only a few feet away. His battle with *Apa* having failed. He was alive. I could see his chest rise slowly, strained, but visible even in the black shroud we'd been thrown into. Had *Apa* spared him? Or had he simply not noticed that Oberon was alive? Who was strong enough to destroy a demon if Oberon wasn't?

Pain tingled along my entire bond. Liam wasn't tugging at it anymore. He didn't have the strength. I wasn't sure how he was still standing. And then he wasn't. He toppled over onto his side, breath labored, blood pouring from him, eyes narrowing.

Run. Liam commanded again. Not just me, but the reverberation ran through the entire pack. A true command, even if it was from their dying alpha.

Okay, I thought and ran toward the Volkov. I expected him to slice right through me, even in my larger fox form. We collided in a spray of limbs that sent us tumbling. I dug my claws into his torso for half a second before leaping off and landing over the top of Liam. I dug my nails into the dirt and growled at the Volkov who appeared momentarily confused. His eyes went in and out of focus, like the light pouring off me was too much for him. Not the Volkov. *Apa*.

I had no desire to kill him. He'd been the only parental figure I'd ever known. Was there a choice? A way to get him back? Liam was dying at my feet and I knew the pain of his death would kill something in me. A will to live perhaps. And if *Apa* was gone too, what did I have left?

Nothing to look forward to, and no safety net to fall back on.

I'd spent the last year running, telling myself I'd been fleeing from *Apa's* failure to protect me from Felix. In reality, I'd been running from self-doubt. A fear that no matter what I did I'd never be happy. Never be safe. Never fit in. Never find a home.

Only *Apa* had given me a home to the best of his ability. He'd been broken long before I was born. Now there was Liam. Offering everything I'd ever wanted, and willing to die to give it to me.

I could run and maybe survive. Or stand my ground, which probably meant death. But at least I'd die in good company. Liam's eyes were dark as he lay at my feet. I wasn't sure he could see me anymore, but I felt him. Funneled my energy into him like I'd felt Carl do before.

Apa leapt at me, claws outstretched. I shifted, fox to human. Fire demon of some kind, to vulnerable, tiny, me. Matted red hair, dusky skin, Asian eyes, and freckles. Unremarkable me. Would it be enough?

The jump floundered, falling short and landing hard, confusion on the morphing creature's face. For a moment I thought I saw *Apa* in there. His calm features flowing through the monster's before being replaced by a nightmare again.

"*Apa*," I called to him as I knelt beside Liam. His bleeding had stopped but his breathing still labored. Silently I slid through Liam's bond to feel the pack and call them back. Liam needed healing and his pack was strong even if the den had been weakened by the Volkov's madness.

"Enough. It's over." All of it was over. Felix was gone. His madness finally silenced as it should have been years ago. Our relationship had been a blunder all the way around. *Apa* grasping at straws to save a son he'd already lost, and me enamored by the first person who ever spoke pretty words. All that was in the past. The fading of Felix as he lost himself to the monster. His many attacks on me, the final one which had opened the door to this new life.

Liam.

One kiss. A breath of new life. Hope.

Books often spoke of love being the greatest power in the universe. But love was a fragile thing, battered by emotions, pierced by pain, and often shifting to those who gave us hope. Liam gave me hope.

So I opened my arms and held them out wide. "*Apa*," I called. "Come back to me. I forgive you. You've brought Liam into my life. Provided me with someone who will take care of me and bring me happiness. Isn't that what you wanted? To save at least one son?"

How many of his children had he had to kill over the centuries? How many pack members or rogue alphas? He'd spent hours hanging out with me while I gardened or made tea. Often just humming and watching me work.

Perhaps it was the omega in me he felt. Or simply the lack of violence or anger within me. I didn't battle my fox for dominance. We were a team, and most of the time that worked just fine. As much as his pack had taught me that being different was undesirable, it was who I am. Liam had asked me why it wasn't enough. Maybe because I hadn't let it be enough. No matter how long I'd run or how far I'd gotten. I'd never been angry with *Apa*. Hurt. Confused. Afraid. But never angry.

"*Apa*," I called again, watching the creature writhe before me like it couldn't keep a grip on the shift. Another horror story they tell young wolves, that losing control can get them stuck in the middle of a shift. Perhaps the monster truly was just a malfunction of being an out of control werewolf.

I held my arms out and closed my eyes, hoping for all of

us that he was strong enough. That, as Liam had stated, *Apa* loved me so much the rest of his pack feared he cared more for me than them. It didn't matter to me. So long as I was with Liam in the end.

Liam who rested his head on one of my bare feet. He was healing. The pack racing closer and funneling energy into him. He was more than a little disgruntled that I'd overridden his command. Perks of being the mate of the alpha, I thought. Better than just getting the big house with the needy wolves attached. He must have caught my thoughts because a warmth wrapped around me. A hug of energy that smelled like Liam. Hope.

The sound of movement crunched through the grass and leaves. Something coming closer. I didn't open my eyes to look at the death that was *Apa*. He'd either kill us or he wouldn't. His choice, not mine.

Then real arms wrapped around me. Human ones. Naked and icy cold, but strong. Tears flooded over my shoulder as *Apa* lay his head down into the bend of my neck, breathing me in, with long deep sighs and trembling.

The darkness lifted. Sound flooded back into the world. I sucked in a deep breath, letting the tension ease away. I could feel them all now. Liam, Dylan, Carl, Toby, and even Oberon. All alive, exhausted from the power struggle, but breathing.

I dug into my soul and found that deep edge of peace that Liam had given me when we'd slept after I returned from Underhill. A well of safety and warmth which eased the last bit of tension in my soul. I let go of that feeling, which rolled outward, imagining a wave of sanctuary pouring over the field flooding the entire pack. Calm, peace, safety.

Whatever power I had, it was enough. For once I was enough.

I opened my eyes to see *Apa's* blood-stained hair while he clung to me. The wolves began to rise, healing enough to move. Liam pressed into my hip, steadying himself against me. I looked down, first seeing all the blood that still covered him. Then realizing my own hands were covered in it.

Felix's blood. I blinked at the light of the day which had illuminated everything with its return. Far too much. Felix's lifeless body separated from his head looked like a rotten thing, dead already on the inside, green rot creeping to the outside. His blank eye-sockets stared sightless at me, mouth open in a snarl of hideous teeth. It was all I could take. I shoved *Apa* away, stumbled two feet away, then dropped to my knees and vomited.

It lasted so long I was almost sure I'd purge an intestine or two. *Apa* stood at my back, holding up my hair, and Liam pressed into my side. Comforting. I collapsed backward, letting Liam's warm bulk cradle me to the ground. *Apa* ran his hands over my face and whispered things I couldn't understand. My vision went a little dark on one side, and I blinked hard at them. I didn't remember anything else before I blacked out.

CHAPTER 32

I awoke in an unfamiliar bed. If it hadn't smelled like Liam, I might have panicked a little. He wasn't in the bed with me, but I could feel him moving around the house with the same sort of radar ping I'd used to track Dylan. Which meant I was in the pack house.

The whole pack seemed to be in the house. All of them echoed with tiny blips on my psychic scanner as they moved. A swirl of bees buzzing around the colony. Toby, Dylan, Marlow, Stacey, Leigh, and even Carl. There were more I couldn't really put names too. And distantly, I felt two others, not part of the pack, but something similar. *Apa* and Oberon.

Everyone had survived. Except Felix who I had killed rather icky-like. My stomach rebelled again, and I bolted across the room to the open door that I could see was a bathroom.

Nothing came up but bile. My stomach didn't stop trying for a while though, so I admired Liam's clean, large bathroom. He had a nice cushy mat at the base of the toilet. The bathroom attached to the safe room had been nice, with the big stand shower and double vanity. This was more spa like. Was that a jetted tub in the corner?

My tiny camper bathroom shower was hardly large enough for one person to stand up in. Liam's shower could probably fit a half dozen people. Yet he'd chosen my little camper to sleep in after a month away. I sighed at the implications of that. A lifetime of betrayal and being an outcast didn't lead easily to trust or affection. But man, did I want to be everything I could with Liam. All I could do was give him me, and pray it was enough. I'd been enough to bring *Apa* back. I could keep Liam's interest, couldn't I? Not like Felix…

Another wave of nausea rolled through me. I dry-heaved a bit longer. Someone had seen fit to dress me in a cozy, if a bit oversized, jammies-top. They smelled heavenly, like Liam. It was the button-up shirt type and large enough to fall past my knees. Warm and fuzzy socks were on my feet, and someone, Liam I hoped, had put a pair of undies on me. I was going to have to break it to him that I was a boxer-brief guy, not bikinis. Though I'd have liked to see him in a pair. Bikinis did have a nice way of hugging a butt. Liam had a fine ass worth framing. Maybe a g-string would be better.

I got up, found a spare toothbrush and some paste, and began to wash away the nastiness. It took some work to keep pushing the memories of the house and of Felix aside. Wolves weren't bothered by gore. It was just meat to them. The violence became ingrained into their lives by the end of the first year after their change, desensitizing them to it, or else they died.

I'd never been the apex predator. And as an omega, blood always bothered me. Violence held no interest at all. I didn't crave that battle to reach the next level of bullshit. I preferred to make my own way on a road of less resistance.

Half a bottle of mouthwash and four brushings later, my mouth tasted about as minty fresh as it was going to get. A hairbrush had been set out next to the sink. One identical to the one in my camper, and hair-free, so I picked it up and began to run it through the mess that was my red mop. Surprisingly, the brush slid through like a warm knife through butter. My hair was clean and untangled. Had Liam done that? I must have slept like the dead for it to still be untangled after sleep.

I heard the door in the other room open and close. Did I smell bread? A pause, then footsteps headed my way. Since I could feel him, it didn't alarm me at all that Liam stepped into the bathroom. He was dressed in fitted jeans and a blue t-shirt that brought out the blue in his eyes, and a slim cut to it that accented his nicely toned arms. His hair looked lighter, almost as though it were touched by gray instead of the blond kisses he'd had when I'd met him at the bakery.

If he was still injured I couldn't tell. He moved fluidly, swiftly wrapping his arms around my waist from behind and hugging me close enough to rest his chin on the top of my head.

He let out a long, happy sigh. "I'm so happy you're awake."

"Hmm," I grumbled at him. I needed coffee before I could hold coherent conversations. Maybe a decent scone or two as soon as my stomach stopped flopping around like a dying fish. Did he have to be so hot every second of his existence? Would anyone notice if I just ripped his clothes off and dragged him into the ginormous shower stall?

His smile was radiant. "There's my prickly mate. How's your stomach?"

"Wriggling." I shuddered at the idea of meat of any kind right that minute. Memories of the gore still dancing through my head.

"I brought you a peanut butter sandwich on fresh baked bread, and coffee."

I gaped at him. "You seriously *are* in my head."

He put his hand over my heart. "I'd rather be here."

My cheeks heated because I knew what he wanted. I just wasn't sure if I could say it yet. He was something to me, practically everything I'd placed my hope on, but I was terrified if I said the words it would all shatter. A lifetime of learning couldn't be changed in a handful of days. "Liam…"

He shook his head. "No strings. But no, our bonds have settled now that the pack has settled. Having Dylan back helped a lot. I feel you wrapped around me, in every pore, but I'm not getting all that's in your head. Just guessing at something to ease a troubled tummy and waking up after a long sleep."

"Thank you," I told him and put my hand over his on my heart. "I feel you too, wrapped around me. When you tried to cut our bond it was like you were cutting me apart."

Liam looked stricken.

"It's okay. I know why you did it. But hey, let's not do that again, okay? We did this mate thing and I'm committed. Even if we want to play it up like we're both a little crazy, 'cause I sort of think we are. Just know we're a partnership in this."

Liam nodded. His arms around me tightened and it felt so fucking amazing to be held. I looked at the two of us in the mirror. Him breathtaking, suave, and sexy, and me…

"You're beautiful," Liam said. "Handsome if you prefer." He smirked at me.

"Jerk." I said.

He kissed my hair and ran his fingers through it for a minute before taking the brush from me and combing it into a ponytail, then braiding it. "Eat, then maybe you can have a visitor?"

I looked down at my bare legs and the long nightshirt.

"There's clothes for you in the left side of the dresser. I bought it with room for your stuff. Was going to get some of your stuff out of the camper, but then he appeared," Liam said. He swept his arm up to motion at a large armoire. Robin sat on the top, tail waving like he didn't have a care in the world. His kitty judgement face was gone and replaced with just sleepy cat. No wonder Liam hadn't been in bed with me when I woke up. Apparently we had an audience.

"Your side of the dresser and closet is filled with clothes," Liam said. "But eat first. You've been asleep a few days. You need the calories."

"Days?" I squinted at him.

"A little over seventy-two hours. Dylan said you did a lot of changing back and forth to try to get him free. I think that plus the big cold-fire fox thing probably drained a bit of energy out of you." His cheeks pinked. "Not to mention how many times you pushed energy into me to help me heal during the fight."

My stomach began to grumble again as memories of the gore and terror cropped up. "Don't remind me please. I'm trying to get my stomach to stop its spin-cycle impression."

Liam turned me to face him and kissed me. Okay, I could live with that forever. His lips, his body against mine, his passion flowing over every cell of my body. I returned his kiss and thought briefly of closing the bathroom door to give us privacy. But I had questions for *Apa*.

Reality had a way of throwing a bucket of ice water on excitement. I pulled away and sucked in a deep breath, savoring the lingering feel of him on my lips. "Raincheck?"

Liam glanced out the door to the cat, then back down at me. I could almost see him making the same deduction I had. He sighed. "Business before pleasure, right? Life 101."

And, wasn't that the truth. "Coffee, first. It's been three days. I'm surprised I woke up at all and didn't die from lack of caffeine in my veins." I tugged free of his embrace and found my way to the sandwich and coffee. Okay, I don't remember tasting the sandwich, or really the coffee, not until

I'd had a second cup and Liam was handing me a set of clothes. "I thought you wanted me with my clothes off?" I teased him. The sweet nectar of java felt good flowing through my veins.

"For all your love of tea, I've never seen anyone need a coffee so desperately they drank an entire pot, black, in under five minutes," Liam remarked. "And yes, naked is great, *after* I get your father out the door. The sooner he leaves my territory the better."

Or his monster at least. "He came back," I reminded Liam. Felix hadn't.

"This time," Liam agreed.

I understood what he didn't say. There may not be a next time.

"Is he first on the docket then? I get to pretend to be the royal prince, with lords of another nation visiting to curry my favor?" I asked with a total straight face as I tugged on a pair of soft black jeans, and a gray Mario Bros T-shirt. The clothes weren't lord of the manor, but nothing I owned was.

"It is a bit like that," Liam confessed. "Since you're Alpha Mate now. You have always been a prince. Even if it was of the Volkov's pack before. Now you're the gem of the Northern Cascades pack."

I squinted at him. Ready to rail against white glove coddling that would drive me nuts in sixty seconds flat.

"Does it help that you're my prince?" Liam asked, sounding amused.

"Not if you're going treat me like I'm incapable of taking care of myself."

"I saw the big fox thing." He grinned at me, "I know how sharp your claws are. I'd rather enjoy the brush of your lips than your fangs. Is it okay if I run interference?" Liam wanted to know. "To move things along?"

"God, yes." Especially with *Apa*. The Volkov sometimes

made it a habit to linger even when I'd tried several times politely to kick his butt out the door. I was not a diplomat. Not when blunt worked just fine, even if it offended some. Hopefully Liam was a bit more careful with other's feelings than I was. Most of the time I found it easier to say nothing. It was the option that got me into the least amount of trouble. "I can smile and nod with the best of them."

"Good." He swung the comforter over my legs after I'd settled back on the bed, and refilled my cup of coffee. "Sit there and look tired. I think it will get them moving faster." He sighed. "Some of the pack want to see you also. Tradition mostly. Since you're alpha mate now."

I knew well of the tradition and thought it silly. But I just waved my hand. "I'll survive a little awkward staring and glaring," I promised. "Bring on the Volkov."

CHAPTER 33

Liam took me at my word, leading *Apa* in alone a few minutes later. I wondered where Oberon was. *Apa* looked okay. More like himself than I'd seen in a long while. He sat down on the edge of the bed and looked me over. Still, the loneliness and pain emanated from him. He did his best to cover it with false smiles, but I could feel it like the lingering smell of burnt bread.

"You look good," I told him. Better than the monster thing he'd become. I had a million questions I wanted to ask. But in reality, didn't want the answers. If what he became happened to all werewolves when they got old, I didn't want to know. I'd just pray that Liam left this world after I did, so I'd never have to see him eaten away by the darkness, feeding on any source of life he could reach. "How are you feeling?"

Apa gave me a strained smile. "My head is clear, if that's your worry. Oberon is waiting in the car. I wanted to stay, Oberon insisted we have matters at home to attend to."

I'd need to send Oberon a thank-you letter. I loved *Apa*, but this was not the place for him. Everything here was new. Mostly untouched by memories of failures. I wanted to know if it was a place I could thrive in, and if Liam really was all he promised. *Apa* was not anywhere in that vision. "Like?"

"I'll be moving the pack around. Sending some out to packs who can better care for them, and alphas to put down the others who can't be saved." A touch of shadow crossed his face that wasn't from any light source. I did my best not to acknowledge it or act frightened. "I'm breaking up the Volkov Pack."

I gaped at him. "What?"

"It was an idea I had years ago. Oberon has been bothering me about it. I'm too old to lead the pack properly and take care of the young. Oberon suspects it's why none of my wolves get better." He paused, his gaze roving over me for a minute. "Except with you in the pack. I was putting down more than two dozen a year before you came to me. The omega in you or the *witchblood*? No one knew."

I gaped at him unable to believe it. In all my years with his pack, I only remembered three deaths of pack members. Two the Volkov had put down, and one that Oberon had. None of which I had witnessed. Only heard about later. The Volkov's pack liked to gossip. There had been no secrets, so if more than the three had died, I'd have heard.

Apa's smile was sad. "My selfishness kept you in my pack. It's not your responsibility to save my wolves. That was my burden."

"An alpha's pack can only give back what they are given," Liam spoke up from his place beside the door. That made sense. *Apa* could only give them madness and so they couldn't get better, not without me to calm him.

"So you won't be the leader of wolves anymore?" I asked.

"More leadership guidance. That will leave me no time to care for the rest. Oberon has already been handling most of those things for years."

"It will invite challenge. Other wolves may see you as

vulnerable," Liam pointed out. "There are plenty of power mad wolves who'd love to take down the Volkov and declare himself king."

The black shadow crossed *Apa*'s face again. "Let them try. It will help weed out trouble among the packs."

I shuddered at the idea of some rogue alpha werewolf wanna-be pulling the monster out of *Apa* again, just for power or greed. Unfortunately, there was a lot of the special kind of stupid among wolves.

"Oberon will handle a lot of the challengers," *Apa* said. "He has already been doing it for years." He sighed. "I spent too long focusing on the mess that my pack was to lead, or to care for anyone really. This way I can focus on the alphas, who in turn will care for their packs."

Liam lingered near the door like he wanted to open it and shove *Apa* out. "Not all Alphas take care of their packs," he pointed out, tone a little bitter. "The pack here was a mess before I came. I've heard of others. Some of my pack have run from other packs to join mine. Just because a man can be king, doesn't mean he should be king."

Apa nodded. "I plan on sending Oberon out to visit all the packs and assess. I have endless alphas waiting for packs. Some fit to lead, others who will have to be removed. Part of it is politics. Part of it brute strength." *Apa* sighed heavily. "Your pack healed you, Liam. I'd thought we wolves had lost that ability centuries ago. Only I learn that it's not the wolves who have lost the abilities, it's the packs who have lost faith in their leaders. My fault. I will take blame. I will fix it. Starting with dissolving my own pack."

"But then you'll be all alone," I said.

"I need to spend some time fixing myself before I try to change others. Rebuilding the packs to be cohesive units will be priority. We live to protect our omegas and submissives. We enjoy a healthy play fight. All the infighting was a disaster. They never should have looked at you and thought *prey*," *Apa* said to me. "You are a kitsune. The whole pack knew. I made it clear to them the day I took you in. We live in harmony with the spirits or they destroy us. It's always been that way, whether in Europe or here in the New World filled with its vast array of power. I thought it would be enough to protect you." *Apa* glanced up at Liam. "Your mate has been very clear about my shortcomings."

I raised a brow at Liam. He'd berated the Volkov? I totally needed to talk to him about his death wish.

"If it makes you feel better, Oberon says I've actually gotten better at parenting than I was with my own."

"How did they survive?" Liam asked bluntly.

Apa flinched. How many hadn't survived? "Anyway. I have much to do and you have a mate to care for. If you'd like I can have Oberon contact a wedding coordinator to make everything official for you. We could invite hundreds, make it grand and memorable like days of old."

My eyes must have gone huge because *Apa* frowned, then glanced back at Liam. "Mates usually marry not long after the mating."

"We are far from the traditional couple," Liam said. "Our mating is new and we'd like to spend time exploring what that means for us before having to follow social norms to make others more comfortable. If we do wed in the human courts, it will be a small ceremony, limited to pack and family."

Smooth was my mate. So little time together and he already knew me well. I needed him naked and on top of me soon.

"Less marriage," I told *Apa*. "More walks in the woods, and baking of lots of stuff. A soul bond is more permanent than paper anyway," I agreed with Liam. Maybe someday we'd do the social protocol. Right now I just wanted to spend time with him and learn everything there was to know about the snarky alpha werewolf I was soul bonded too.

Apa nodded. "So be it. If that is what you want. I would have liked to attend a grand ceremony." He grinned. "I remember the first time my first son got married. It was a crazy mess. Oberon's first was much more subdued. That was before he was my second. Now he says marriage is for the young."

I hadn't known Oberon had ever been married. He didn't have children. No one spoke of their partners. And *Apa*'s indication of first marriages meant there had been multiple. Had they lived human lives and their spouses died with the passage of time? Perhaps they'd been lost in some forgotten battle? How many relationships ended while lives continued eternally for the wolves. I looked at Liam and wondered how many he'd had? Just because he was mated to me, didn't mean he hadn't loved a lot of others in the past.

Liam frowned. Was he catching my thoughts? I'd have to figure out a way to filter them if possible. All he said was, "Oberon is waiting in the car for you. Perhaps it's time to head out?"

Apa sighed. He reached out and took my hand for a minute, patting it gently. "Call if you need me. I know I frighten you. I apologize for that, though I can't change it. Just know if you need me I will come. You are my son, even if we don't share the same blood."

I swallowed hard and nodded. "Thank you, *Apa*."

He let go and got up, offering a handshake to Liam, who took it while leading him out the door. I wondered briefly if this was a good thing for werewolves or a sign of coming chaos.

When Liam returned it was Korissa with him, not any of the pack. But I supposed she was pack in a way. The alpha's daughter, a protected princess, if Liam's comments about me had any weight. I bet she wouldn't have cared much to be a princess either.

She rushed across the room and threw her arms around me, squeezing tight. "Thank you so much for coming back. For saving dad and the pack."

"I didn't do much," I told her, hugging her back awkwardly. Liam just stood beside the bed with a smirk on his face.

"It's okay. Things are going to be so great now. I've got a cool and much younger second dad, who I'm sure will talk my dad into letting me do all sorts of things."

I gaped at them both, and tried to push her away. "You never told me your daughter was crazy, Liam."

"Apple, tree," Liam said.

"You know you just called yourself crazy," Korissa pointed out.

"I was thinking of your mom, but sure, Sebastian thinks we're both crazy. At least we're all on the same page."

Korissa curled up beside me, even sticking her feet under the blankets. Robin leapt off his perch and somehow landed on the bed.

"Impressive and not at all a normal cat jump," I told him. He just walked up my blanket-covered legs and sat down in my lap. I sighed as he began to purr. "Little bastard, suckering me with your cuteness and purrs."

Korissa laughed. It was a sweet sound that made me think in a few years, her dad was going to be beating the guys off by the hundreds. If she swung that way.

Liam perched on the bed beside me, kicking off his shoes and reaching over to put his hand on the back of my neck.

"No more interference?" I asked.

"Not necessary. Some of the pack just want to say hello. They won't be staying long, and I told them that the tradition of giving gifts is not necessary."

I frowned at him. "I don't need anyone's stuff. I lived for a year off of what I could fit in a backpack."

Liam took my hand and threaded his fingers through mine. "No one will be questioning your resiliency here. It's okay to be nervous. They may give you things, but I wanted it to be their choice. You walked a hard path for a while, but…" he leaned over and kissed my forehead, "Sebastian, you are not alone anymore. I don't mean just me or Korissa or even Robin. I mean the point of all this." He waved at the closed door and what I assumed was a waiting parade of pack members to see me. "Is for the pack to support you as they would me. Just like you supported them when they united to help save my life. You're a part of the conduit now."

I couldn't help but laugh a little, "In kind of a kinky way that is weird with your kid and Robin here."

"Hmm," Liam said, giving me a sideways glance. "Plenty of time for kinky later."

"Gross," Korissa said. "I mean in comics and on Supernatural we ship guys all the time, but it's just different when one of the guys being shipped is your dad."

"Shipped?" Liam wanted to know.

I sighed. "I'll explain it to you later. Bring on the masses."

Carl was the first through the door, which shouldn't have surprised me since he was Liam's second, but his distaste for people in general had me thinking he'd have skipped the party. He looked a little tired, but didn't appear to be in any pain when he moved. I vaguely remembered seeing him nearly slashed in half. The healing power of werewolves was a fierce and terrifying thing.

He nodded at Liam and actually gave Korissa a full grin before turning his attention to me. "Sebastian Volkov, *witchblood* child of the Volkov, I told Liam your presence would bring danger to this pack."

I bit my lip. Liam squeezed my hand, but didn't seem angry or on edge from Carl's comments.

"You saved my life and dammit, why did you do that?" Carl demanded.

"Because you're Liam's. His, mine, ours," I answered instantly.

Carl looked lost for words for a minute.

I sucked in a deep breath, seeing the pain on his face for what it really was without even needing to dive through Liam's link to feel Carl's emotions. "It's not your time yet," I told Carl. "We all will know when it is, I think. When it's time to join her." I glanced at Liam. "I understand the desire."

Carl nodded, his eyes going watery but he looked up at the ceiling instead of at us, blinking away his tears. "You better be worth the love he has for you."

Liam began to protest, but I stopped him. "I will be the best I can be. That's all I can offer."

Carl met my eyes and for a minute I felt like we were on the same wavelength. He nodded and turned without a word, walking out. The sound of his steps vanished down the stairs and I let out a breath I'd been holding.

"For a guy who doesn't like anyone, he seems to be pretty protective of you," I said to Liam.

"Right?" Korissa added. "I've been saying that for a while. Dylan says it's because good alpha's are so rare. Even Carl wants to keep Liam."

Someone knocked on the edge of the open door. It was Toby in human form. He looked uncomfortable, young, and worried. He kept glancing back toward the door and tugging at his clothes, but he carried a basket and slipped it onto the end of the bed once Liam had called him forward.

I wondered who was in charge right now, the wolf, or Toby? Maybe a little of both? "You okay, Toby?"

"Yes," was all he said, but waved at the basket. "From the

pack." He turned then and bolted out of the room. The reaction was so fast I thought about racing after him.

"He's changing back to wolf," Liam said. He reached down, snatched the handle of the basket and pulled it into his lap. "We're working on control. He had to stay human until he saw you today, then he could change back. Tomorrow we will set another goal." Liam began spreading the contents of the basket out on the bed. There were packets of seeds, over a dozen, some very rare from suppliers I'd had to order from online in the past. Tools, small tags to go in the garden and even a bag of clothesline clips, for hanging the herbs.

"Gifts," I grumbled.

"Gifts you like," Korissa said looking through the seeds. "Will you show me how to grow this stuff."

"Of course."

Liam's smile was wide. No one else came to the door. Korissa kissed my cheek. I hoped Dylan and Sean were okay.

"One more gift for you," Liam said, getting up from the bed and heading to the far wall which had an odd double door I assumed to be a closet. He unlocked the door and opened it. Not a closet. A huge, walkout balcony with planters built in. I gaped at him, but untangled myself from Robin and Korissa to make my way to the little oasis.

"The field is great," Liam said. "Your father's idea. He always tries to overcompensate for affection he feels but doesn't quite understand..." Liam shrugged. "This is more personal. I know you used to have an area dedicated to things you'd created, new herbs spliced together and blends that only you could imagine. This..." he waved his arms at the huge space, "is for you to grow."

Now it was my turn to blink back tears. He picked up, then held out a long plastic planter with some growing green shoots in it. "Some plants that Oberon was able to save. He wasn't sure what they all were, but he brought three of these boxes, twelve plants in each. Had someone in their pack deliver them yesterday."

I reached out to touch a leaf. The green silk of it left an impression. Almost like it was a living animal rather than a plant. The plant had energy, a trail of it if my eyes were seeing correctly. Was this part of the kitsune? Since I was a spirit of the earth I could feel it more deeply? See the lines of power that connected it all? I'd read about it in dozens of alchemy books, but never experienced it before that moment. Was it being mated to an alpha wolf? Or just something awake inside of me that had been hidden away?

It had been so long I couldn't remember what the little bud was, but there were books in my camper. Sketches made. Notations of attempts to grow some particular herb. Successes and failures. This was some kind of lavender, though it had an almost blueberry scent when I leaned in close. Some of the plants had similar energy auras. Were they the same?

The one under my fingertips sang with the touch. A ghost of loneliness arose from the plant as I tugged the little tray free from the dozen so I could look at it closer. When I put it back near the others, the loneliness eased. When I put it down beside others who seemed to have the same color energy aura, the plant perked up, almost seeming to straighten with happiness. I wondered if anyone else saw it.

Liam nudged a bucket my way with his foot. It was filled with garden gloves. Korissa set the basket of supplies at my feet. Robin rubbed up against my leg, giving me little chuff noises as he proceeded to scent-mark all the planters and edges of the balcony.

I caressed the plant and everything else faded under the need to dig my hands into the soil. All these little guys needed a new home. Just like I had when I'd arrived, they'd been yanked from everything they'd known and dropped down in a foreign land filled with a strange climate and weird soil. But I could make it work.

Liam kissed the top of my head as I arranged the trays in the order I wanted to plant them. Each new sprout telling me where it wanted to go. If Liam said something, I didn't hear him as I was too busy speaking to the plants. For the first time in years, since before I'd even met Felix, my head was filled with peace, happiness and hope.

CHAPTER 34

I hadn't really expected to sleep like the dead. Hours with the plants, with occasional food breaks prodded by Liam. And I'd worked until the sunset. All the plants had new homes. Each imbibing in my spirit in such a way that I sort of felt like a rare bottle of whiskey. The plants I touched sang and danced through my magic sensors. Using my energy to help dig their roots. By the time I'd finished and stumbled into the shower, I could barely keep my eyes open. Would Liam be mad? He didn't seem to be when he wrapped his arms around me and pulled the blanket up over us in his giant bed.

When I woke up I could tell it was early, likely early morning. Too early for most to be up yet. Liam wasn't in bed, but I could feel him in the house. Downstairs somewhere, probably some sort of pack meeting. When I'd staggered to bed Toby had been outside the bedroom door, and Liam had shooed him away, but the wolf had just collapsed into an inelegant dog puddle on the floor and refused to budge. Liam closed the door in his face. I'd been too sleepy to jump Liam's bones even though he'd looked mouthwatering in just a pair of sleep pants and slippers.

Oddly there was a lot of movement in the pack. Not close by, but a roll of sensation. Tugging. Isn't that what Liam had called it? Noise. Yet not. A radio turned to static but occasionally picking up a blip of a song. Startlingly random. Needy pack members tugging on their alpha for support. It made sense that he wasn't in bed if he was off taking care of pack stuff. But I was still sad about it.

The tugging tingled like a vibration through my spine. Too many needy wolves to make out an individual concern. How did Liam deal with all this? Nothing life threatening. No, these were little nips of need. Odd, as I didn't think of people being that needy. Though I knew I'd experienced uncertainty a time or two before. I really needed Liam to be in bed with me. Didn't his pack understand our new mating? Were they mad because I'd spent the day gardening instead of with them? I hadn't really thought about how Liam's pack would expect me to behave. Technically I was their king's consort. My word second only to his. *Apa's* mate used her power to boss people around. That wasn't really my style. Nor was I the picture of happy-go-lucky advice for disgruntled werewolves. I'd been taught to keep my mouth shut about my opinions since no one wanted to hear them anyway. So why did it feel like they were all pulling at me? Asking me for something?

I felt a bit claustrophobic in that moment. The doors to the balcony were wide open, letting in the cool evening wind, but I couldn't breathe. Maybe if I took a little walk. The camper wasn't far. I could grab a book or two and come back. A little breather wouldn't hurt, right?

Hopefully Toby had found a better place to sleep. I didn't want him following me. He needed to be nestled in the center of the pack to quiet his wolf.

There would be guards if Liam had any sense at all. The Volkov had just been in the territory and the pack had recently survived an attack from rogue wolves. I'd have put every guard I had on rotation for at least a few days. And maybe he had. Maybe that was why I could feel so much tugging from his pack. Were they worried the Volkov would come back because of me? Was there even a Volkov anymore? He was disbanding his pack and giving most of his responsibilities to Oberon. Did that make Oberon the Volkov? Or something else?

I hated the idea of the pack thinking my presence was a bad omen. It sort of had been so far. That kind of stung, since *Apa's* pack had always looked at me that way. A burden.

Distance sounded like a better idea every passing second. My sense of smell could rival most wolves, so if I just stayed downwind, I hoped to avoid them. Camper and back. Even if I lingered a moment or two, what would it hurt? Liam said my wards dulled the noise from his pack. It was not even thirty yards to blessed silence. *Big boy panties*, I told myself, *pull-them-up*.

I slipped on a clean pair of sweats, found Liam's hoodie, sniffed it a little before tugging it over my head—Liam smelled good enough to eat—and tiptoed to the door.

The unlocked door surprised me. Why I thought Liam would lock me in, I wasn't sure. But it had been my first thought. The hall was empty. Not even Toby lingered. I stepped into the hall and listened for a minute with all my senses. My nose told me how many wolves came and went regularly. It also told me the last to be by was Liam and the trail was hours old. My ears told me more than a handful of people were sleeping in the house. Some nearly imperceptible in their sleep, others a loud rattling snore that might just cover my footsteps.

My eyes adjusted slower to the dark, making out only

shadows from distant moonlight. Nothing moved. On the edges of my senses I could feel the flicker of ghosts. Not in the house, but on the land. That was normal enough for any area, more so for a land with a wolf pack. People died, and often without closure, which left a shade to linger sometimes. I wondered if they had followed the pack here after Felix's slaughter. Distance didn't mean much to ghosts. Not unless they were stuck. But everything got stuck from time to time.

All else was still. Liam was toward the front of the house, but far enough away that I could only get the barest sense of him. I crept down the stairs hoping none of them squeaked. It would be embarrassing to explain to Liam that I was running from the pack because I was too afraid to give any of them the wrong answer. I almost expected him to be waiting at the bottom of the stairs, or even lurking outside the back door. Only all was still.

The crickets and buzzing of the night's symphony spiraled around me in familiar comfort. If there were guards about, nature wasn't bothered. Still I waited, frozen with the door to my back, listening and feeling.

The property had been cleared of trees far enough to be a natural fire blockade. But in the distance the trees grew thick and dark. A little eerie as I still sensed the ghosts. The earth murmured of the creatures nearby. Nothing unusual or worrisome. Bigger predators had gone further north, steering clear of the wolf pack as was common. Nothing humanoid was in the woods. For that I was grateful.

I was tempted to make a mad dash into the tree line, go around the long way to the camper, but someone had to be out there watching. I'd never met an alpha who didn't have guards on duty, day and night. Even in the smaller packs. Liam's was a mid-sized pack, and growing, he'd stated. There was someone out there. Even if the ground didn't recognize the disruption. So I worked my way through the yard a bit like a fictional ninja might, crawling behind objects, clinging to the backs of trees, and keeping as much to the shadows as possible.

Finally, I stepped into the dark overlay of my camper door. The wards began to settle around me even before I opened the door. Inside everything was dark and quiet. Too quiet after the nightmare of recent days, so I began turning on lights. Guards be damned if there were any. I just needed a minute to breathe. At least the bugs and birds didn't stop their wild night dance.

Once the lights were on I began making a pot of tea. A smooth chamomile mix with just a bit of lemon grass. Great for easing busy minds. And my mind was swirling in that minute. I added a bit of valerian root, nature's valium, and waited for the water to heat. The flavor wouldn't be stellar, but I needed my hands to stop shaking. I hated the idea of letting the pack down. They adored Liam, and he had chosen me. I wanted so bad to be the perfect fit for him.

Fuck. Fate really was a cruel bitch sometimes. I poured the heated water into the cup over the strainer, then took the cup to the bed, deciding in that instant that I would sleep in the camper for a few more hours. When I woke I would go through the books on the plants Oberon had rescued. I had spent the last year alone. A few hours weren't going to kill me.

Of course my mind kept straying back to Liam and why he hadn't been in bed. The first thought was that I bored him already. Or he was mad because I'd spent the day with plants instead of him. Sometimes I just got lost in the art. Gardening, baking, and alchemy. It wasn't personal.

I sipped at the tea, wishing I'd thought to put a dab of honey in it before getting under the blankets. It took only a few minutes for the tea to begin quieting my jumping nerves.

Not the flavor or even the mix of herbs yet, more the simple process of sipping the warm tea and breathing in the fragrance.

The tugging faded away, then the tension, and I closed my eyes, imagining Liam's face. He had a great face, beautiful lips, and stunning eyes.

Dylan and Liam would have been a good pair. Beautiful, dominant men. Though both far too dominant to ever be a good emotional match. Dylan was just a few steps away from being an alpha himself. And while Liam was good at keeping the need for aggression beneath the surface of what he showed the world, I knew all alphas struggled with it. The wolf didn't want to be patient. Life was food, mate, shelter, and pack. Alpha's had a visceral need to protect those things.

Dylan had Sean. They seemed a good fit. A tempered balance of strength.

What if Liam had met Sean before me? Sean came across as a strong man without the aggression of wolves. He might even have been an alpha if he'd been a wolf. Though I got no sense of violence from him. Sean was good looking and successful. The thought made jealousy rise in my gut. Being an omega meant I didn't have an inclination to fight at all. Flight was more my usual path. Sean said he was trained as some sort of martial artist. He might not seek out trouble, but he could probably give back if someone came at him.

"He's also Dylan's and not my type at all," Liam said from the doorway. If I hadn't been half asleep I'd have screamed at him for startling me. "You didn't startle because you knew it was me." Liam stepped inside and closed both doors, locking them tight. "You could feel me from across the country, just as I could you. I thought the tea was supposed to quiet your mind, not let the hamsters spin in overdrive."

"Smart ass," I muttered.

He crossed the room and took the tea from my grip, then

set it on the table beside the bed. "Why didn't you call for me?"

"You weren't in bed," I told him. A million answers echoed through my head. Most much more complicated and some downright convoluted. My brain was so broken. Pulling up every negative possibility before the glimmer of a positive one had a chance of seeing the light.

"Not broken," Liam said, leaning over to kiss my lips gently. "Your perception is a little off, that's all. We'll work on that. You've been conditioned to expect the worst. It's just retraining. Stop, recognize what your brain is doing and refocus. Eventually you won't have to do all the work."

I frowned at him. It was far too early for him to be sprouting philosophy.

"Your wards are a great filter. I'd forgotten that in all the mess of the past few days. I can hear you clear as a bell right now. Felt your unrest when you woke up and left the house. I didn't mean to hurt you by not being in bed. I thought I could get back before you woke. A few of the pack members are having a hard time adjusting, so I was trying to sort that out."

"Adjusting?" I asked. "To me?"

Liam sighed. "To the idea of having the Volkov's *witchblood* child as Alpha Mate. Two have requested to leave the pack. I have been working on finding them new packs."

"I'm sorry," I began, but Liam covered my lips with his fingers.

"Nothing for you to be sorry about. It's their issue, not yours. These two have not liked having Dylan as my third either. They were very vocal tonight. So it's best to send them to a place which has the same values of intolerance they do."

"Sounds like rainbows and sunshine," I groused.

He laughed, and crawled onto the bed, straddling my hips,

then kissed me. This time a full open mouth kiss that I lingered over. He tasted like coffee and warm bread. I sighed, in that moment realizing just how much I'd missed him when I'd woken up in bed alone. How could it have happened that fast? The need to be with him. Not just physically, though that raged like an inferno every time he walked into a room, but for peace of mind. I felt safe with him. Barely knew him, yet something resonated through me. Chimes of home, happiness, and hope.

"I'm sappy after valerian root," I told Liam, when he'd stopped kissing me long enough to pull the hoodie off, and tossed it on the floor. He tugged my hair free from the rubber band, and combed his fingers through it. He was obsessed with my hair.

"Relaxed, I'd say. And that's okay. I do love your hair." He kissed my lips again before finding my collar bone and nibbling at the skin there. Who knew that could feel so nice? "Just nice?" He asked.

"You did take the hoodie away," I pointed out. "That was mean."

"Because you're cold?" He wanted to know.

"Because it smells like you," I confessed.

He grinned. "How about if I make you smell like me?"

That sounded way dirtier in my head than I think he meant it. Like his come all over me.

"No, that's about right," Liam agreed.

Heat flooded my cheeks. "I'm not good at foreplay." Had always been given the wham-bam-thank-you-sir sort of affection.

"It's fortunate for you that I am," Liam boasted.

"Hmm," I said giving him a narrow glare that I hoped conveyed my doubt. "Then why am I the only one half naked?"

"Oh, well, yes. Let me remedy that," Liam laughed as he

pushed away from me. He stood beside the bed, pulled his phone out of his pocket and a moment later a funny pop song began to play. Liam moved his hips, swaying to the music and slowly lifted his shirt.

"Really?" I asked him. Dancing was not one of his best skills. Dancing to Baby Shark was just too much. I couldn't help but laugh as he wiggled his butt, stripper like, and whipped his shirt off Magic Mike style, then unbuttoned his pants all to the little jig on his phone. He shoved the jeans down to reveal bikinis not unlike mine. I gaped at the red fabric framing his ass. "Okay that's very nice."

"Very nice?" He growled at me.

"Hey, you're working on getting naked. Keep going. Very nice is better than nice, nice."

He snorted and put the phone down on the table next to the tea, before climbing under the blanket with me.

"Hey you said you were gonna get naked," I protested.

"Mhmm. Let's play a little first." Liam straddled my hips again, but wrapped his arms around me and slid us together. I groaned at the feeling of his hard cock against my sweats. The red fabric had shocked me so much I hadn't had time to analyze the outline of his dick. I wondered briefly what it looked like. Twice in bed with him and I couldn't recall more than fleeting glimpses.

"I promise you can examine it at length later." Liam kissed me again. I closed my eyes to savor the feeling of him against me. His kiss, the sway of his hips, the press of his warmth. So very nice.

"More adjectives," he grumbled.

"Not sure what you're looking for? Good? Great?"

He sucked on one of my nipples. I sighed, sinking into the bed to just enjoy the feeling. "I'm going for speechless, stop the hamsters, mind-numb from pleasure."

I opened my eyes and looked at him. "I thought that only happened in movies and books?"

He groaned, put his hands on my hips and dragged me down the bed a foot or two until I was flat on my back and he could perch over me. Then he tugged off the sweats.

"You should probably know I'm not really a bikini man," I said. "They look awesome on you, but I always feel a little restricted. I'm a boxer-brief guy."

"Yeah?" Liam asked.

I nodded like it was the solemn truth. This whole experience was a little odd. I was used to being pushed around, shoved to my knees, or flipped over. This interaction thing confused me.

Liam shoved the blankets away and leaned over me to press his face into my stomach. I couldn't help but laugh at the tickle of his scruff. There wasn't much of it. Just enough that he'd have to shave soon, but the sensation was like soft Velcro sliding across my skin. He nipped at my hip bones while tracing my tattoos with his fingers. "Will you tell me what they mean someday?"

"It's mostly just wards. Nothing with a lot of attachment."

"Something else to work on." He cupped my ass and moved me a little until he was sitting between my spread thighs.

"Should we turn out the light?" The brightness suddenly hit me with a wave of vulnerability I didn't know I had. Liam could see all of me. Scrawny mutt that I was.

"I'd call you scrappy, not scrawny, but whatever." Liam dove back down to tease the other nipple. I closed my eyes and let the sensations run through me. Odd. Not unpleasant. Not Earth-shattering, but enjoyable. More the heat and teasing than anything else. "It's a start," Liam promised me. "Keep your eyes closed and just feel. Let your body react the way it will."

"Okay." I felt really awkward, like I should be doing something. Not that I had any idea what he meant, but I complied, letting myself be putty in his hands. He caressed my hips, a gentle glide back and forth, almost the barest of touches. Not quite enough to tickle, but close. He licked down my torso with the same slow descent. Tracing a wet line through my belly-button and then little nibbles over my hip bones.

"I think a tattoo would look nice here," he said. He used the flat of his tongue to trace a line at the top of my underwear. Then grabbed the sides with his fingers and pulled them down. I opened my eyes to watch as he stripped them off me, depositing them on the side of the bed. I was only half hard, which didn't seem to bother him.

"Underwear tattoo would not be sexy," I informed him.

"Not underwear," he insisted. He used his hands to cup my hips. "A little design on each side, framing the sweetness to come."

"Cheesy," I said.

"Hmm, a treat for only my eyes," Liam said, his mouth finding my skin again. He didn't go near my dick, just licked along the crease of my thighs and kissed the back of one knee. "You trust me, right?" He asked.

"Yeah." Funny how fast that answer was. No trace of doubt. Not right now.

"Then close your eyes and feel. I know you're uncomfortable with touch. Too long deprived of it, I think. But that's okay. We're in this together. Just lie back and feel."

I shut my eyes and tried not to let my mind wander. Liam's kisses traveled down my right leg, all the way to my toes and back up. Just little kisses, nips of his teeth and occasional licks. It was relaxing more than sexual, but Liam didn't protest my feelings. He switched to the other leg and did the same thing, lingering a little while on my inner thigh, sucking on the vein there maybe. It felt good, a warmth that traveled up my leg to harden my cock. I didn't realize he'd shifted my legs around until his lips landed on the back of my thigh, right before my butt.

"Mmm." I mumbled at him.

"Feel," Liam said against my skin. His hot breath making me hard as it slid over my balls like a warm caress. "Just like that." He kissed each butt cheek, licked along the curve and rested his head on the joint between my hip and leg for a moment. I was tempted to look, but reminded myself he wanted me to feel. Instead I relaxed again, focusing on the sensations. His hair on my thigh, his breath against my skin, dancing in tiny waves across the base of me, and even a bit of tickle over my hole. Was I that exposed? There was a brief moment of panic, but Liam ran his hand down the opposite thigh, soft, slow. A drag of texture around my knee and back up.

It focused me enough to push back the panic. Liam found a rhythm with that caress, down around, and back up, almost like he was stroking my cock instead of my thigh. I sucked in a deep breath when his lips found that vein again, nibbling, suckling, and kissing along the length.

The butterfly kiss on my dick where my balls met the shaft almost had me spurting all over him. My legs trembled a little. It was only the barest touch. He kissed the side of my sack, then the other, before sucking the whole thing into his mouth, swallowing it in warmth.

"Holy fuck!" I said, unable to keep my eyes shut. He looked good there, nestled between my legs, my balls in his mouth, my cock sticking up in his face. I had a dick like most men. Average. Though with so much of Liam's pale skin nearby, I looked very dark in contrast. He released them and gave a long swipe up the length.

"Last time we were in bed," he said, "I got the impression no one's ever done this for you." Had I said something? I didn't recall ever telling him. But he was in my head. "Nothing to be ashamed of. I like being your first for this." Another long lick left me shuddering as he rolled the head of my cock between his lips for a moment, teasing me. That felt good, beyond good. Hot. Teasing. Fire building. "Showing you how it can be."

Liam licked around my shaft, base to tip for a few seconds before taking me down the back of his throat. I almost came out of my skin. The heat and suction. The sensation of his tongue, the tightening of his throat as he swallowed around me. It was a slow wet sound. Reminiscent of porn, only so much better because it was Liam wrapped around me, cradling me, and encasing me in his wet heat. I vaguely wondered if this was what it was like to fuck someone. The heat, the pressure, the slow glide in and out.

I could have moved, thrust against him to quicken the pace, but I didn't want to miss a second or speed up my release. Would I get to experience this again soon? Or was this just a onetime thing?

Despite the trembling of my body, my mind kept rolling off on tangents of worry. Liam pulled off with one final hard suck and I whimpered. "Sorry," I said. "Sorry."

I squeezed my eyes shut waiting for a reprimand, but it never came. Instead the odd texture of Liam's nose nuzzled into my balls, followed by nibbles and teasing. He sucked my balls in and out of his mouth a few times, his hand finally wrapping around my cock. The slow glide of his fist almost painful. My body wanted release, even if my head was wandering another planet.

Liam lifted my sack, attacking the underneath with his lips and tongue, pressing his nose into the sensitive flesh. I trembled. Some of the scattering thoughts vanished. His kisses moved further south, just on the edge...

He wouldn't? Would he? The first lick around my rim

nearly sent me off the bed. Liam's arm locked around my hips. "Shh," he whispered, heat into the cooling spit he'd left covering my taint and rolling over my hole. "Doesn't hurt."

No, it didn't hurt. It was like nothing I'd ever imagined before. Who'd have thought an asshole was that sensitive? I was sure there was a funny pun I could have made there, but Liam's lips returned to my hole. Tiny licks at first. My legs shook like something I'd only seen in an exorcist movie. It was the need to come, of just being on the edge. I swallowed hard and almost choked on my own spit.

"Liam…"

"Hmm," He said into my skin. Tongue, broad and wide, lapping at my entrance like I was some new flavor of fast melting ice cream.

"Fuck."

Liam chuckled. The vibration nearly undid me. I reached down not sure where he was, afraid to open my eyes for fear it a dream, and found his hair. I set my fingers in it, taking a moment to focus on the thickness and texture. It was barely enough to keep me from exploding into a pile of come and metaphysical goo.

"Liam. Get naked so I can do you before I come."

"Hmm," was all he gave me again, seeming uninterested in his own pleasure. He flicked at my hole a few more times before gliding upward again, nibbling at my taint, a pressure I never thought so good, and taking my cock into his mouth again.

"Liam…" But I was at a loss for what to say. His heat and suction were beyond what I could imagine. He let his fingers caress my sack while he sucked and then there was a digit teasing at my entrance. Almost as decadent as the tongue, I gripped his hair and pulled, hoping to dislodge him. But he dipped that little finger inside, curled a little, hitting something already begging for touch, and my world exploded.

I couldn't even find the strength to warn him before I shot down his throat. Pumping into him like I hadn't come in a decade. Power surged between us, a roll of passion, intensity, and metaphysical fire. He gasped for a second, but kept going. He didn't stop sucking or fucking me with his finger, and I shook with the force of the orgasm. Mind-blowing was a good word for it. Nothing else existed in that moment other than Liam and the pleasure he gave me.

Just when I began to think it was all too much, and I'd become far too sensitive, he eased off. He let my cock go and gently rubbed my hole a few more times, pressing a little at my taint. If I could have come again, I would have. The magic began to ease. I trembled with the weight of it, but Liam seemed to pull it into himself rather than letting it linger between us. The release of it was almost as good as the orgasm had been.

Instead I lay there, realizing at some point I'd opened my eyes to stare at him, watching him as he had taken me into his mouth. He'd lost his underwear at some point because he was stroking himself lightly. Breathing hard, his wetness painted my thighs, mingling with his saliva. He rubbed it in as he laid his head down on my stomach.

I was boneless. So wrecked from an orgasm like I'd never experienced I couldn't move a muscle. Though I was a little sad I hadn't gotten to watch him come.

"Next time," Liam promised. "I promised you could examine my cock in detail. I'll even feed it to you if you'd like." He smiled up at me, his face smeared with some of my come, and his hair sticking up in places from where I'd pulled on it. The idea of taking his cock again, whether it be down my throat or in my ass, was enough to send me into another mini-orgasm. I struggled to breathe for a minute. The vision was so vivid. I could *feel* him between my lips. Almost taste him. Fuck!

"Good to know that works," Liam said. "It will be a fun game to play later. To get you all hot and bothered for me."

"You're putting those images in my head?"

"Just sharing and amplifying what's already there." He didn't sound chastened at all. He rubbed his hand over my stomach, smearing the mess around. "Too bad all we have here is your tiny shower. Can't fit both of us in there like we can my shower."

I sighed. "Without you, I'm a mess." I looked down at us. "Okay, well with you I'm a mess too."

"I like this kind of mess." Liam was grinning from ear to ear. His phone rang with the tune It's Raining Men by Geri Halliwel. It was the first time I realized that the song he'd danced to had ended ages ago, leaving us with random other tunes I hadn't noticed.

He groaned.

"Let it go to voicemail," I said. "Quality time with your mate is more important."

"It's Dylan's ring tone." But he made no move to pick it up. It stopped ringing and then a few seconds later started again. Liam sighed and reached across me to grab it. At least it wasn't Facetime. That would be an eyeful.

"Yeah?" Liam said by way of greeting. He didn't sound put out, but he also didn't sound like he was thrilled about the interruption either.

"Crazy little bit of power rolled through the pack a little bit ago. That wouldn't have been you by chance?" Dylan asked.

Liam looked me over. It'd been a first time for me, so if he was looking for an explanation I was just as lost.

"Perhaps you and your new mate?" Dylan prodded.

"Do you actually need something?" Liam asked. "If not, I'll be going back to enjoying some quality time with my new mate. Read a story about ass babies recently. Going to see if I can get him pregnant."

I sputtered.

Dylan laughed. "A couple of the pack called me with concerns about a power surge through the pack bonds. I'll send them to Carl. You know how he loves that stuff. *I* didn't feel any of the sex stuff through the pack bond, so I'm not sure what they are talking about. But hey, if you want to send a full recording, feel free."

Liam growled.

"Sean agrees. Oh, and since I hear Sebastian back there choking on your ass babies comment, tell him thanks for sending help to Sean's garage. The new guy has been great, keeping the shop open, and even extending the work hours. The garage is in the black. More business each day."

"I didn't send help…" I said more to Liam than to Sean.

"Oberon said he was a friend of yours," Dylan said. "I've got to say, you've got an odd choice of friends. Vampires eat you, man. They aren't friends. So I'm keeping an eye on him still. If he so much as looks at Sean the wrong way, I'll rip his heart out and use it as auto paint."

"Vampire?" Liam wanted to know, his eyes narrowing on me.

I gave him a shrug because I had no idea who he might be talking about.

"Does this vampire look like a *Nordic God from romance novels? Flowing hair and goofy clothes?*" Liam demanded, repeating my own description of Hugo.

"Uh…" Dylan began.

There was no way Hugo would have followed me here and set up shop in some auto mechanic's garage. While I wasn't alarmed, apparently Liam was because he rolled off me ready to rage out into the early morning and kill some vampires.

"It's not Hugo," I promised Liam. "Hugo would never dirty his hands with menial labor."

"Looks more like a metal head. Thin and rangy, covered in tattoos and rock band T-shirts," Dylan said. "Should I be worried?"

"No," I said.

"Yes," Liam replied.

We shared a stare.

"Sounds like Alexis," I said.

"Who?" Liam wanted to know.

"Goes by Al," Dylan interjected.

"Technically he was one of Hugo's vampires." Meaning he'd been made by Hugo. I always got the feeling that Lexi wasn't always that loyal.

"What?" Liam demanded.

Oh, this wasn't going well.

"He helped me escape though. So he's mostly a good guy," I pointed out.

"Mostly?" Liam growled. "Sebastian…"

"I think I'll call you guys back later," Dylan said, humor in his voice. "Be sure to keep the pack bonds open for the make-up sex."

I stared up at Liam wide-eyed, and wondered if I was ready for a first fight or make up sex at all after the best orgasm of my life. Not over Lexi, for sure. "Come here," I demanded of Liam.

He glared at me, his whole body a rope of coiled tension.

"Liam," I softened my tone.

He growled again and climbed back onto the bed, pulling the covers over us and kissing me fiercely. "He can't have you," he said when he released my mouth.

"He doesn't want me, and I don't want him. I want you." I assured him.

"Yeah?" He looked genuinely worried.

"Uh, you just blew my mind while you licked my ass. I think you're stuck with me. I expect a repeat performance at least a couple times a week."

"I'll put it on the schedule," Liam said. He yanked me into his arm for a tight hug. "After I meet this Alexis."

ABOUT THE AUTHOR

Lissa Kasey is more than just romance. She specializes in in-depth characters, detailed world building, and twisting plots to keep you clinging to the page. All stories have a side of romance, emotionally messed up protagonists and feature LGBTQA spectrum characters facing real world problems no matter how fictional the story.

BOOK LIST

Also, if you like Lissa Kasey's writing, check out her other works:

Inheritance Series:
 Inheritance (Dominion 1)
 Reclamation (Dominion 2)
 Conviction (Dominion 3)
 Ascendance (Dominion 4)

Hidden Gem Series:
 Hidden Gem (Hidden Gem 1)
 Cardinal Sins (Hidden Gem 2)
 Candy Land (Hidden Gem 3)

Haven Investigations Series:
 Model Citizen (Haven Investigations 1)
 Model Bodyguard (Haven Investigations 2)
 Model Investigator (Haven Investigations 3)
 Model Exposure (Haven Investigations 4)

Evolution Series:
    Evolution
    Evolution: Genesis

Under the pen name Sam Kadence

Vocal Growth Series:
    On the Right Track (Vocal Growth 1)
    Unicorns and Rainbow Poop (Vocal Growth 2)

Made in the USA
San Bernardino, CA
23 July 2019